I0763564

THE EVANGELIST

A STORY OF JOHN MARK

A NOVEL

ROBERT SIMMS

This is a work of fiction. It is based on the historical figure of John Mark, the generally recognized author of the New Testament's Gospel of Mark. Otherwise, names, places and incidents are either the product of the author's imagination or are actual persons, place and incidents used fictitiously, and any resemblance to actual persons, living or dead, or their actions, or to churches, events, or locales is entirely coincidental.

ISBN: 978-0-9995929-9-1
Published in the United States by
Robert F. Simms
Greer, South Carolina

THE EVANGELIST

1
Alexandria, Egypt, A.D. 68

Raucous rioters shouted epithets at the beaten man and called out vile encouragement to the men wrapping chains around his legs. His hands had already been bound with chafing rope and his head bled profusely into his hair and out onto the stones of the street. The angry crowd formed a wall of writhing protest but kept out of the way of the armed activists leading the mob as they turned the victim over and continued securing his legs in the iron links. The sadistic men finally fastened the chain to itself and hooked the other end to a wooden bar extended from the yoke that two horses wore. The animals were champing at the bit, eager to be given the command to charge forward. Two of the rioters' henchmen already astride the horses kept their mounts barely at bay as the animals snorted and urged their riders to go.

When the mob on the ground had finished, they backed off and one of them, in his loudest command voice, roared to the crowd, "Thus it is to the leaders of The Way!"

Then he nodded to his mounted companions, and with a barked order the riders unleashed their animals' dumb fury and began moving. At first slowly, as the crowd ahead of them divided to make way for them, and then at a trot, they dragged the bloodied man behind them up the street, his head bouncing over the stone pavement, as the mob behind him and some running alongside him cursed and jeered.

"Heretic!" some shouted. "Jewish trash!" said some. "Christian!" said others. Mixed in toward the back of the dozens who had gathered there were a silent few, hiding their sympathies behind shocked faces, barely controlling the tears they would soon release in torrents in the privacy of their homes and in the dark sanctity of their houses throughout the city.

Somewhere in the few seconds of consciousness he possessed before the impact of his body and head with the street rendered him finally unconscious, John Mark remembered the words his Lord had cried loudly from a cross nearly forty years before, "Receive my spirit!" Before all Mark's thoughts in this present world went to blackness and silence, he thought, "This is how it ends, but Master, this is how it begins!"

2
Alexandria, Egypt, A.D. 14

On the edge of the growing city, in a small house on a hillside where the sapphire Mediterranean could be seen gleaming, Miriam called to her little son playing with his dog, telling him to come in for supper. Little John Mark tumbled in the scrubby grass with Puppy, the name he had called him for a year since they acquired the nondescript dog. No one in the family had come up with a better name than that, and it had stuck. Puppy danced around Mark's rolling body and pounced on him in happy attack.

"John Mark, tell Puppy to retreat, and you come in!" Miriam called. "Your father will be home soon. I have supper ready for you both."

Mark sprang up and ran for the door, Puppy close on his heels, until Mark turned, picked up a bone near the house and tossed it back into the yard. The little dog pivoted and chased it to where it landed, retrieving it for his youthful owner, but Mark had disappeared into the house and Puppy was left to growl at the bone and gnaw it in make-believe furor.

Inside, Mark scampered into his mother's arms, who stood waiting for him with a damp cloth to wipe his grimy, four-year-old hands.

"Go take off that cloak and put on another one," she said. Daddy is probably coming in the front door." She swatted his backside affectionately and Mark ran to the next room. Miriam went back to the corner of the room where they ate and put bread and rice and a little meat stew in some saucers and placed them on the table, an old wooden thing rubbed smooth by years of use. It had come with the diminutive house, which she and her husband Tullio had moved into two years before.

Miriam thought back to the day they walked into this abode, thinking it would have been something more befitting a captain in the Roman army, but grateful to have a place of their own. At least there were no more barracks for Tullio, whose promotion had earned him the right to housing. He had been promised better lodgings, and some were being built, but housing for Roman officers was still scarce in Alexandria, and they hadn't seen it yet. There was talk of another move still, probably to Judea, where garrisons were full and the might of Rome was needed to quell, if only by their armed presence, the rebellious undercurrent that characterized that country.

Miriam knew well the feelings of her own countrymen. Her father, Jacob, and her mother, Joanna, had reared her in a substantial house in the heart of Jerusalem, in an atmosphere of growing tensions over the invasion of Judea during her grandfather's and his father's time. When she was just a girl, her homeland officially became a Roman province.

Miriam poured water and diluted wine for her husband and drew spoons from a nearby box for them to use on their stew. Outside, a few soldiers trod up the street, boisterous and happy. She remembered when she had first seen soldiers in the marketplace in Jerusalem. They sauntered casually in the crowded streets, unthreatening in manner, though little knots of Jews made way for them and avoided them. As she had come of barely marrying age, she found the soldiers handsome and rugged, and most of them not intimidating at all, if one discounted their armor and the weapons hanging from their sides. The Jewish temple guards by contrast seemed surly to her and her friends. There was something exotic about the Romans, with their accents, some of them Italian, and others, mostly the conscripted soldiers, an unidentifiable mix of Greek sounding pronunciations.

Unlike her father, who held a determined but quiet resentment of the infusion of military and political personnel into the country, Miriam had not personally experienced anything so far in her brief life that made her hostile to Romans. In fact, she was more frightened of tales of uprisings by zealots who seemed more interested in riots and murder than in peace and stability.

But when, out of the blue, she told her father one day that she wanted to marry a soldier—there was no one in particular at the moment—he barely withheld a fury within him that in later years she understood, though by then she forgave him. He was a product of his times, and she of hers. And though she was not one whit less a good Jewish girl than he was a respectable Jewish man, she believed she could embrace the world she had come into, and find in it a romance and adventure that seemed to be woven into the advancing epic of the growing Roman Empire.

That was what she had told herself and others when she married Tullio five years ago. Two years before that, at the age of fifteen she had traveled to Cyrene with Aunt Ruth and Uncle Omer, with the original plan that she would visit with them for only a few months and then return to Judea, some 750 miles away by sea. Her father agreed to the trip because his brother Omer and his wife, who had come to Jerusalem for the Passover, had described the beauty of their coastal town and convinced him that it would be good for Jacob's daughter to meet her cousins, who were somewhat older.

Miriam hadn't left her father without household help; Jacob was wealthy and had servants. In addition, Miriam had a slightly younger sister, Rachel, not yet married, who would be ample help for her father and Miriam's mother in Jerusalem. Rachel hadn't wanted to go to Cyrene. Miriam was the child with a spirit of adventure. Miriam's older sister, Tirzah, had married and lived nearby, and already had a son, Barnabas, nine years old. It hadn't been like Miriam was leaving her parents alone.

Once in Cyrene, she met Tullio, then not a captain, but still a tall, imposing soldier with dreamy eyes, sinewy arms and legs, and the demeanor of someone going somewhere. She had fallen in love with him instantly.

Tullio was a soldier with responsibilities greater than most, and one day he just "happened" by the house where Omer and Ruth lived and told Miriam he had been promoted to the position of captain. It was then he also told her he wanted to marry her. Respectfully, he informed her uncle and aunt of his desire.

Recalling those days a few years before, Miriam now stood at the door and peered down the way to see if Tullio would soon turn a corner into their street and walk the final half furlong to their house. She remembered the day she had waited for him to come to her uncle's home in Cyrene, to take her to the city clerk to be married, the rest of the family following along in procession.

It was not the normal course of things for Jewish girls to marry without the consent of their fathers, but she was a long way away from home and in the care of her uncle. Once Tullio's desire had been expressed, Omer had reasoned that since he was acting *in loco parentis* for Miriam, it was his duty to say whether she could marry, and how. And while Jewish brides were not sold, *per se,* a gift to the father and his family was in order. Tullio understood the custom, and once he presented the agreed sum, Miriam's uncle sent the gift by way of courier to Jerusalem, and the deed was done.

They had remained in Cyrene less than two years, during which time John Mark was born, before Tullio was reassigned to Alexandria. He took a contingent of soldiers with him when they moved by carriage and horseback along the coast of Africa to their new home. And here in this little home they had lived another two years, continuing to raise their son in relative peace, in a city of culture and learning, and religions of all kinds, including an enclave of faithful Jews.

Tullio had no particular religious devotion but he understood that his new wife did and he happily allowed her to be part of the Jewish community in Alexandria, and to teach her little son about the LORD, the Holy One of Israel. His theory was that as long as everyone was peaceful, no one should care what others believed or whom they worshiped.

John Mark acquired three languages as he grew. His first words were Aramaic, his mother's first language, but he learned Greek in equal measure from Tullio, who only haltingly spoke Latin. And Miriam taught Mark what Hebrew she knew, which was not as halting as Tullio's dreadful Latin but still not as fluent as she had been told her grandfather's Hebrew had been. The elders in the Alexandrian synagogue used Hebrew regularly when they read the scriptures and taught, but even they were more eloquent and comfortable using Greek, the scriptures long having been put into the language of the previous empire.

As Miriam mused, Tullio emerged from a side street and began marching up the hill toward the house. Miriam stepped outside the gate and waved at him, still impressed with his stature, his gait, his handsome, angular face, the way his crimson cloak swung about his muscular frame. She loved him as much as the day she had first seen him.

They embraced briefly in their doorway as he came in, unbuckled his sword belt, removed his breastplate, and reached for little John Mark, who was coming out of his room. Mark dashed into his father's arms and Tullio held him up and kissed him. Mark squealed in delight and Tullio put him down as they all headed to the table. The boy sat on a cushion on a stool. Tullio waited for Miriam to speak a blessing on the food, a memorized prayer she had learned from her father, and then they eagerly ate and talked of their day and all the news of their city and whatever they knew of the world beyond.

The sun set, a few candles were lit throughout the little house, and soon Mark was put to bed, where he snuggled up warmly in tousled blankets and soon drifted off into childhood dreams. Miriam and Tullio retreated to their own room, a small cubicle where she had regularly deposited new pillows acquired here and there in the market, and some of which she had made herself. They embraced and sank into a cluster of these cushions, talking like the lovers they still were. In an hour or so, they both drifted off to sleep.

Somewhere in the middle of the night a pounding came at the door, waking them both. Tullio told Miriam to stay in bed while he went to see about the commotion.

The man pounding at the door was one of Tullio's soldiers, coming to tell him urgently that his presence was required back at the garrison. Miriam overheard the soldier say there was trouble in the western quarter of the city, that one squad had already been dispatched and that Tullio's men were to be added to that force in attempt to quell the disturbance.

Tullio quickly informed his wife he would be back as soon as he could, and he strapped on his gear, grabbed his helmet, and exited with the soldier, walking at a fast pace back the way he had come a few hours ago.

Whatever the commotion was, it was far enough away that once Miriam lost the diminishing sounds of her husband's boots going down the street, the night returned to its relative silence, the only noise the hooting owls and insistent crickets.

Until just before dawn. Two soldiers arrived at the door and brought Miriam out of her light slumber with another sound of knocking, though now more respectful and polite than the earlier pounding. She opened to them and somehow knew, in the sober looks on their faces and their mutual reluctance to be the one who spoke to her, that their news was the worst it could be.

Tullio had been struck by a fist-sized stone thrown by someone in a small, rioting crowd. The projectile had caught him squarely in the left side of his forehead. Two inches one way and it would have been deflected by his nose protector, or two inches the other way and his temple strap would have taken the brunt. Either would have given him a debilitating headache but left him otherwise uninjured. But the blow had killed him instantly.

After dawn, Mark padded sleepily into the front room, finding Miriam still sitting at the table, staring at the open doorway, her cheeks lined with dried tears, her soul disconsolate. When she was able to gather her thoughts and actually form words, she told her young son that his father would not be coming home.

It took a day or two for Mark to understand what had happened. A boy of four, he couldn't conceive of his world without his father. It made no sense to him. By the third day, however, he had graduated to crying himself to sleep, refusing to eat, and lying out in his little back yard with Puppy next to him, the dog sensing that his master was sad.

In the next few days, Miriam sent word back to the west to Uncle Omer and Aunt Ruth in Cyrene of Tullio's death, and she scraped together enough coin to buy passage for her and her son to sail to Judea. Friends came and went, their sympathies warm and helpless and the same. They were all heartbroken for her.

The army would require the surrender of the little house for the use of some other officer, whomever they would transfer to take Tullio's place, most likely. So Miriam had to leave one way or another. She was going home to her father, her dream shattered, with only the hope that the Lord would redeem her circumstances and bring out of them something good.

As she looked at her son, she realized that John Mark was something good, that he was what Miriam now had left of her bold, handsome husband, and that as she returned to her own childhood home, Jerusalem, she would pray for Mark to find in it a citadel and a sanctuary, a place to find both peace and strength.

She bundled her few belongings, placed them in a friend's cart, shut the door to the house, and left for the port, where a small ship would skirt the coastline of Egypt and head for the port city of Joppa, east of Jerusalem. She prayed as the cart jostled along the city streets. She prayed the Lord would make her father's heart soft and compassionate toward her. The last word he had from her had been that she was going to marry that soldier she had dreamed of, and whom he categorically disapproved of, no matter who he was. Now, she had lost her soldier and was returning home, alone but for her boy.

She looked at him. John Mark was bouncing up and down in the carriage floor, trying to hold on to frightened Puppy. Mark was quiet and expressionless, staring off the back of the cart at the receding road. The brief years of his past were retreating from him, soon to be seen no more and remembered only in vague images. His future was unseen, unknowable, with only one certainty, that he would never see his father again.

3
Jerusalem, Judea, A.D. 15

The sparkling sea presented tribute of bedazzling diamonds to the setting sun as the Cyprian corbita heaved and sloshed toward the port of Joppa with its cargo and passengers from Salamis. Joel and his young son Barnabas stood near the prow of the rounded ship, watching the harbor come nearer and looking forward to being on solid ground. At fourteen, Barnabas was old enough to be of at least some help to his father when he sailed across to Judea on business and to see his father-in-law Jacob. On this occasion, Joel's wife Tirzah had come along, to see her sisters Rachel and Miriam. She had not been with Miriam in more than five years.

Three months ago, before the turn of the year, Joel and Tirzah received a message from Jerusalem that Miriam had moved back from Alexandria, and had brought with her John Mark, the grandson Jacob had not met until then. They were living in the home place again, as Miriam struggled to recover from the sudden and violent loss of her soldier husband to rioters in Alexandria.

"Abba," said Barnabas, "how old is John Mark?"

"About four, I think. Perhaps he has turned five," said Joel. "We heard so little from Miriam after she went to Cyrene. But I think the last time my uncle Omer sent word, Mark had just been born, and that was nearly five years ago. Do you remember? You were nine."

"I remember," said Barnabas. "Will Aunt Miriam find a new husband?"

"No idea," said Joel. "If she does, I hope she looks among our people. Your mother is afraid your grandfather wouldn't take to another Roman soldier."

The two held tightly to the rail as the ship plowed through a brief band of rough surf just out from shore, and then they backed away as the ship's crew moved into place for docking. They returned to quarters and retrieved the few belongings they required for their short stay on the mainland. Tirzah joined them topside as they waited for the planks to be put down.

Once debarked they found lodging at an inn and spent the night, waking now and then, still feeling like they were rolling on the waves. In the morning they hurriedly ate from their provisions and then left the inn in search of a carriage. Not far from the inn they paid for travel by a commercial raeda, which had some atypically comfortable seats in its bed. It would take them about four or five hours to get to Jerusalem where Jacob lived and where, as Joel believed, most of the rest of the family would be gathered.

They climbed out of the carriage late in the afternoon at the edge of the city and walked the rest of the way to Jacob's and Joanna's gracious home. Joanna, who always seemed to have had an extra sense about her to know what was happening entirely out of her sight, burst from the house when Joel's little family was a sprint away, and she lifted up her hands, thanked God for their safe passage, and invited Barnabas to hurry to her arms for a hug. She was breathing more heavily than they remembered as she embraced them, and they walked more slowly back to the house, Joanna's hand patting her heaving chest.

Inside the home, Rachel soon flitted into the front room, looking considerably more mature than the last time Joel and Tirzah had seen her, when she had been a mere wisp of a girl. Girls changed so quickly at her age. Did she have a probable husband yet? She must, they thought.

Rachel greeted Joel, her sister, and Barnabas, whom she had

seen just a few months ago. Then she excused herself to the kitchen.

Then from an inner room, Miriam appeared, her five-year-old son leading the way shyly. The front room became quiet as Tirzah looked fondly and soberly at her younger sister, who somehow had attained not only a half decade of years but also half a lifetime of sober maturity about her face and frame. Tirzah could read in an instant the transformation worked in a young bride by the catastrophic loss that had come upon her. Tirzah, older by ten years but not as old as Miriam had become almost overnight, opened her arms and began weeping as Miriam flew to her and they embraced tightly, as everyone else waited, knowing how close the sisters had been as children.

Miriam drew away slowly and then put her hand on Mark's shoulder. "This is John Mark," she said. Tirzah smiled down at him and asked if he was taking care of his mother well these days. Mark nodded enthusiastically.

"Mark, this is your cousin Barnabas," said Tirzah, putting her hand on her son's shoulder.

"Hi, Mark," said Barnabas, and the two waved their hands at each other.

Joel squatted down and offered his forearm toward Mark, who hadn't seen his father greet men in that way, but had seen Jewish men at the synagogue in Alexandria do so, and he took a step toward his uncle and grasped him as high up on his forearm as he could, once Joel had already put his hand in the crook of his elbow. They grinned at each other.

"Mark," said Joel. "That's your father's name? Your grandfather's?"

"My grandfather," said Mark. He looked at Jacob, the grandfather he had just met a few weeks ago. "My other grandfather," he said.

"And John?" said Joel. "Was that someone's name, too?"

Mark looked at his mother. She said, "That's Grandfather Mark's *father*; remember?"

"Grandfather Mark's father," said Mark.

"Well, it's a fine name," said Joel. "And I'm Uncle Joel."

Mark managed a little grin, but backed away to the safety of his mothers knees. Joel stood back up.

"Is Jacob here?" he asked Joanna.

"Yes, where's Abba?" said Tirzah.

"He's always here now," Joanna said in a low voice. "He isn't well, Tirzah. He fell ill just after you left last year. Rachel and I try to keep him comfortable. But he can't walk more than a few steps and he hardly eats."

"I'm sorry to hear that," said Joel. Tirzah put her hand to her mouth suppressing a gasp.

"He seemed so good a few months ago," she said.

Joanna's voice trembled a bit when she spoke, but she brought it under control. "The physician says it's what took his brother two years ago."

"Abba?" called out Tirzah. "Is he in the main room?" she said to Joanna, pointing down the passageway.

"Yes. Go see him. He's awake, at least."

Joel and Tirzah went down a short passage and through a doorway.

John Mark watched them leave the room and then looked up at his mother.

"Can I go play?" he said.

"Yes. I think you should," she said. "Stay in the back. And feed Puppy the scraps by the door while you're out there." Miriam looked at Barnabas. "Why don't you go with Mark and get acquainted."

Mark scampered toward the back of the house and disappeared. Barnabas trotted after him and Joanna and Miriam were left alone.

"Rachel doesn't know how bad it is," said Joanna.

"She'll guess it soon, Imma."

"Yes, but let her."

"What if Abba dies before morning?" said Miriam.

"Life will go on."

Miriam cried softly into her hands. Joanna put her arms around her and the two stood there in the atrium as the sun disappeared and the gloom of night steadily cast a pall over the streets.

Before week's end the family, their neighbors, and friends from all over the Jerusalem trod soberly through the widening streets and made their way to a family tomb outside the city, where Jacob's body was laid to rest. Joel concluded his business but stayed a few days longer to be with Joanna and the rest of the family.

But after two weeks he had to return to Cyprus, and he, Tirzah and young Barnabas said their goodbyes and walked back to the city wall, where they found carriage transportation back to Joppa, and from there, a crowded corbita back home.

Miriam busied herself helping Joanna with food and other things, mostly to be with her and not because she needed help; two servants did everything that needing doing, an older woman and her young daughter, Rhoda.

Joanna herself was not in the best of health. Winded now and then, she paused or sat until a spell would pass, sometimes looking pale and wan. Four weeks after her husband's passing Joanna took to going about the house and neighborhood only if she had the company of Rhoda or Rachel, in case she should need support or emergency aid.

One evening after the meal Joanna corralled her two daughters into her chamber, making sure that Rhoda kept an eye on Mark out in the main house.

"I wish Tirzah were here, too," said Joanna. "We have to talk about my dying."

"Mother, no," said Rachel. "No such thing!"

"Yes, dear, we must. And now."

"Imma, you're going to live a long time!" argued Rachel. Miriam was silent, looking at her younger sister with compassion newly learned by her husband's death and reinforced by her father's. She was pensive and solemn. Her gaze slowly turned to her mother, and as Joanna's eyes met hers the elder woman nodded slowly.

"Your father has left me well provided for. This house, the house near Bethlehem, and the one in Bethel. Tirzah and her family stayed in Bethlehem a few of their last trips over from Cyprus."

"What are you saying, Imma?" said Rachel, worried.

"I've had our family lawyer draw up my will now that Jacob is gone. I'm leaving the land in Bethlehem to Tirzah, and in Bethel to you, Rachel."

"Let's not talk about this now," cried Rachel.

"We must," said Joanna. "There may be no later."

At this, Rachel quieted, stunned. Miriam daubed a tear but remained composed.

Joanna continued. "Miriam, this house is to be yours. Whatever money I now have will be divided between the three of you."

Rachel spoke in a barely audible voice. "But, what will I do?"

Still looking at her mother, Miriam answered her sister. "You will stay here as long as you need to," she said, then turning to Rachel, she added, "When you marry, you may move to Bethel, or whatever you like."

Joanna nodded, grateful for Miriam's quick grasp of the task at hand and thankful for her assumption of responsibility. More tears were shed, but soon Joanna rose and went to her chamber, closing the door.

Miriam found Mark, went outside with him, breathed the fresh air, enjoyed their garden of flowers, watched her son tumble and run with his pet, and knew that very soon this childhood home of hers would be her sanctum alone.

One month to the day from Joanna's heart to heart talk with her three children, she didn't come out of her chamber at the usual morning hour. Rhoda went to ask her about the morning meal, and found her still and cool.

Jacob had provided a place beside him for his dear wife to be laid, and the day following her death she was enclosed there. Little John Mark walked alongside his mother and Rachel. People die, he thought to himself. Before you know it.

Some seemed to die for some purpose. His mother had told him Tullio died protecting them. Bad people killed him.

Others just died. Mark was just getting to know Abba and to realize he wasn't young enough to play. But he was a comforting presence and a solid knee to sit on. He taught Mark a little more Hebrew, and he told stories and winked and smiled at him, and Mark liked him. And he died.

Now Grand-imma. It was as if she followed Abba out of this world, wherever that was. She followed him to the cemetery, borne by family and friends.

Would Mark die someday, himself, he wondered? Could anything stop it? Could anything make it better?

Word about Joanna had been sent to Tirzah, but she would not receive the message for days and, of course, they could not wait to bury Joanna until Tirzah's family could get there, even if Joel would be able to get away from Cyprus again so soon.

After entombing Joanna the family returned to the spacious home and appreciated the company of dozens of friends who mourned with them and ate with them. There were children near

Mark's age, and he invited them to go out back and play with him and his dog. The crowd continued with the family through much of the day, remembering with them and rejoicing in the goodness of God who had given Joel and Joanna many years and a loving family. Then the friends gradually dispersed, a few at a time.

When everyone had gone, Rachel and Miriam sat on a bench in the back yard, Mark sedately beside his mother, no one saying anything. Puppy brought some well-chewed object to John Mark's feet and dropped it but was disappointed at getting no response, and soon he trotted off with the thing to wrestle it from an imaginary opponent. Mark swung his little legs off the edge of the bench and occasionally looked up at his mother. Miriam looked back, smiled reassuringly, and then continued gazing contemplatively at the pretty spring flowers her mother had cultivated. They were just coming to full bloom.

4
Jerusalem, c. A.D. 20

On Mark's tenth birthday, Barnabas and his family were in Jerusalem, Joel on business and the rest of them just taking a holiday. Barnabas now had a baby sister, and since his last visit his cousin Rachel had married a strapping fellow whose parents had been close friends of Joel and Joanna. Barnabas, at nineteen, was now tall and muscular, angular in face and bronzed from his time in the Cyprian sun. Miriam found herself staring at him and thinking of Tullio.

The next morning Tirzah tended to her littlest and talked with Miriam about everything from children to the state of the Empire, while Barnabas, familiar with the Jerusalem area from his many visits, took Mark with him to the market streets. They wended their way through the inner labyrinth of Jerusalem's narrow passageways filled with bins of verdant vegetables and flaming fruits and baskets of bister breads, all of which wordlessly billed themselves even without the inducements of their sellers. Mark fished out one of the coins his mother had given him and bargained with a woman bartering baguettes of varying lengths, finally agreeing on several and trading them for his bit of metal money and putting them in a bag he had brought, proud of his growing acumen learned from his mother in the markets each week.

Barnabas smiled and led him on, picking up dried fish and other things for their evening meal as he went, encouraging Mark to watch how much or how little he paid for ripe produce or their lesser green versions.

Soon they were near the Pool of Bethesda, where they watched from above as crowds milled about near the waters, some dangling their feet as the water slowly replaced itself from the upper pool and ran underground out of the city.

"What are they doing?" Mark asked.

"Waiting for the water to stir," said Barnabas.

"Why?"

"Some say an angel comes down and stirs it."

"Do they see him?" Mark said, his eyes suddenly widening with wonderment.

"I don't think so. He just makes it bubble or swirl, I think," answered Barnabas.

"Why?" said Mark.

"It's supposed to heal people."

"How?"

"I don't know. I've never seen it, myself."

"Will it happen while we're here?"

"Probably not."

With that, they turned and went farther from the city, across the Kidron Valley, trudging up the side of the Mount of Olives.

Halfway up, Barnabas stopped and turned around, looking at Jerusalem from end to end, stretched out over the hill running north to south. "I love seeing this city," he said.

"Me, too," said Mark, though he didn't often see it from here.

"See that gate?" said Barnabas, pointing at the Eastern Gate to his right.

"Mm hmm," said Mark.

"King David said the Messiah would come through Jerusalem's gates someday."

"Mm hmm," said Mark, though he didn't know that.

"He said, 'Lift up your heads, O you gates, and the King of Glory will come in.'" Barnabas's eyes gleamed as he smiled in dreamy hope.

"You know about the Messiah, don't you?" he said to Mark.

"Not much."

"He'll come to restore us, our whole country, to God's favor," said Barnabas.

"Doesn't God like us now?" said Mark.

"It's not that," said Barnabas. "Favor is more like blessing. Full blessing. The Lord loves us, but we have to go through hard times."

"Why?"

"Because of sin."

Mark didn't quite understand, which was evident. Barnabas filled in the blanks.

"Like the thieves always being caught in the market or stealing sheep outside the city. Or like bad priests who get drunk or go..." Barnabas was about to mention harlots and then thought better of it. He didn't know if at age ten Mark was fully aware of what harlots do. "They go places they shouldn't go," he said in completion of his sentence. "And like men who murder."

"Oh, and like tax collectors!" said Mark, getting the hang of it.

"Yes, like that," said Barnabas. "But like all of us, too, when we don't live as we should, or love each other enough."

"And he's punishing us?" said Mark.

"Well, yes," said Barnabas. "He punished us when he let the Babylonians take our people away. A long time ago. You know about that?"

"I learned it in synagogue," said Mark. Then, looking worried, he added, "Will that happen again?"

"I don't think so. The Lord is going to send Messiah to save us."

"What does that mean?"

"Well, some say Messiah will raise an army and kick Rome out of our country."

"Really?" said Mark.

"That's what they think."

"Do you think that?"

"No." Barnabas continued to look at the city, its fair white walls shining back in the late morning sun. The Eastern Gate was bustling with entering merchants and exiting travelers. "I think Messiah will make us all love the Lord."

"I love the Lord," said Mark.

"I know you do," said Barnabas, turning to Mark smiling, tousling his hair. "But even more!" he said. And then, he said wistfully, "And then one day, we'll all be free again." Then he broke back into the full reality of the warming day. "But after we get the olives." He turned and continued their upward walk.

They trudged uphill together, arriving in a little while at Gethsemane, where olive sellers offered baskets small and large with the green or purple fruit. They each carried away a small basket, wandered a bit in and among the trees, watching the pickers harvesting the elongated orbs, enjoying the slight shade the scrubby branches offered. After a while they headed back for the city, burdened enough with their few acquisitions, and they threaded their way back home, depositing their purchases in the kitchen.

Mark followed Barnabas out into the yard in back of the house. Puppy had died the previous year of something that had reduced him to a thin and feeble thing who would not eat and was finally found one morning relieved forever, nestled in his favorite spot under a tree. They had buried him there, and Mark had not asked to replace him, unable to believe that another dog would ever be what his little companion had been to him. Another life gone in a moment.

Barnabas sat on a bench. "Maybe next time I come," he said, "you can go back with me to Cyprus for a visit. See what Abba and I do in the business."

"Can I go this time?" said Mark, excitedly.

"I don't know. Maybe. I haven't talked with Aunt Miriam yet."

"Is it pretty? Cyprus?"

"It's beautiful," said Barnabas. "And there are pretty girls there," he added, wondering if Mark were interested in girls yet. Perhaps not, at only ten.

"That's okay, I guess," said the boy, not revealing much.

"I'll mention it tonight, and we'll see," said Barnabas. "We could stay two or three weeks. I could bring you back myself if Abba wasn't coming back that soon."

The two kicked around a leather ball stuffed with wool, a toy Puppy had bitten generously when he had occupied the yard. Mark thought of Barnabas as the older brother he didn't have. He felt, more than reasoned, that he probably would be his mother's only child; she had not married again.

When the call came from inside for everyone to gather at the table, Barnabas and Mark went in, and as they all enjoyed the variety of foods Rhoda and her mother had prepared, Joel suggested the plan of a visit by Mark to the island. Perhaps Mark might become interested in Joel's business. Even at ten, Mark was not too young to be introduced to possible careers. Tullio long out of the picture, Mark had no fatherly counsel, and Joel had tried, on his frequent visits, to fill that role just a little bit. Perhaps Mark's future lay in managing Joel's business on the mainland. Who knew?

Miriam quietly considered the proposal, perhaps too quietly for Tirzah, who sensed that her sister was thinking ahead to how she couldn't do without her son, how she would miss him, feel keenly the loss of the mirror of her husband's face, whom Mark was coming to resemble so much, and need his help from day to day.

"It would only be a few weeks," said Tirzah softly. "And we'll take good care of him. Barnabas will be by his side all the time."

Mark looked expectantly at his mother, not saying anything. He knew by now to wait for her to think things through.

"I suppose—" she said. Then she brightened, somewhat artificially Joel thought, and she added, "—I suppose it would be good for him."

"So, can I go?" Mark said in a voice younger than his ten years, for its plaintive effect, and then in a tone beyond his age, "I really want to."

Miriam smiled at him as he made his case with convincing appeal, and then she said, "Yes, of course."

5
Jerusalem, c. A.D. 27

"Too much," said the man in front of Mark. "It's too much. I can offer twenty shekels per lot."

Mark scratched his thin beard, still coming in. "I really must have twenty-two," he said. Then he added, trying to echo the way Joel had said it when Mark was assisting him, "The supplier raised the price on his last shipment from Corinth."

"The last price Joel gave me was twenty."

"Perhaps, but as I said, the supplier…"

"Yes, yes, the supplier. Perhaps I could wait a week or so for Joel to come from Cyprus," said the man.

"Do as you like, but twenty-two is fair, and I don't think Joel—"

"I've been in business a long time, my boy. I know what is fair. You've been in this office for what—a month?"

Mark bristled inside and struggled to control himself. "Six. And I'll risk my employment by taking twenty-one."

"Well, then," the older man said, and sighed as if contemplating taking a loss. His fingers combing through his long-gray whiskers, he grunted. "Twenty-one, perhaps. It will nearly break me, but twenty-one." He looked up from under his bushy eyebrows at Mark as he made the counteroffer.

"*If* you can take delivery tomorrow," said Mark. "I can't guarantee twenty-one after the Sabbath." Mark had heard Joel say that, too. What the passing of a Sabbath had to do with anything, he didn't know, but it sounded officious and it seemed to have worked well for Joel.

"Ah," said the buyer, extending his portrayal of a man against the wall. "Agreed, then. I will have my carts here by the third hour on the morrow." He sighed and turned to go, and then turned back partly and added, "I hope we can strike a better bargain in the future. I have done business with Joel for years, but these rising prices could ruin me."

"We'll do the best we can for you," said Mark. "And we're glad you always come to us."

The man exited and joined his driver outside. Mark stepped to a window and caught a glimpse of the buyer climbing into his carriage. Briefly his face turned to his driver, and though Mark could not hear them at this distance, the buyer was smiling.

Mark thought of the proverb Barnabas had taught him along the way in his training to run the business in Jerusalem on a strictly trial basis: "'No good!' the buyer cries, but when he has gone his way, he boasts." It was the time-honored, or at least time-worn, custom of haggling among their people. Among most people of the Semitic world, he assumed, though he understood that the Romans tended to fix a price and stick with it.

The truth was, the business could survive twenty-one or even as little as eighteen shekels per lot on that particular item, but not if Joel's plans for expansion were to be realized next year. And if Mark hoped to keep running the business in Jerusalem for Joel, he couldn't turn in a net loss. It always had to be a gain. Mark wasn't an expert at keeping the books: Joel had a bookkeeper in Jerusalem come by every week. Mark just wrote down in single columns what he sold and what he paid suppliers for when they came now and then. He made it legible, neat and accurate.

Arriving home in the evening he found his mother busy about various things, supervising the kitchen work, for one. Rhoda was alone nowadays as the household help. Her mother had suffered a stroke when Mark was fifteen. By then, Miriam had finally

?recovered from the several years she had spent depressed over Tullio's death. Being back in Jerusalem, renewing childhood friendships, making new friends of older and wiser people, and finding a group of women her age who had varying but equally stressful situations in their lives, finally brought Miriam into the sunlight. In fact, she was well known for her community involvement and benefaction.

Miriam's share of her father's estate, the same as her two sisters' shares, had been a significant sum, and she had invested it in several ways and was living off the income. With some of the profits she had decided to enlarge the grand old house, building a second story room above the bed chambers. It was an undivided area with numerous windows and a porch on the back with a view of hundreds of rooftops and other buildings in the south of the city, as well as of the garden below in the back yard. The space could accommodate a hundred people or more and had its own, sparing kitchen. Miriam had heard her friends say many times they wished for some place to hold wedding feasts or other gatherings, and their own homes were not large enough for all their own extended families, much less neighbors and friends from out of town.

Miriam intended "the Upper Room," as they called it, as a venue for these frequent gatherings, which she would rent at a very reasonable price. People could bring their own foods, hold a feast or a meeting completely separate from the rest of the house, even come and go by an outside stairway for the Upper Room only.

Mark went into the kitchen and greeted his mother, snatching a piece of hot bread from a pan Rhoda had just brought in. Miriam slapped playfully at his hand.

"Go take your coat off and go to the table. We're bringing in everything in a few minutes. Jude and Hannah will be here. That may be them, now," she said, listening toward the front door.

Mark had known Jude and Hannah since he was twelve. On

Mark's birthday that year, Joel and Tirzah had brought Barnabas with them and the family had made a great event of things, both at the temple and back home. Miriam had invited Joel's and Tirzah's friends Jude and his wife Hannah, whom they had met through business connections. The friendships between the adults had grown and now Jude and Hannah were nearly as frequent visitors as Mark's blood relatives.

Jude and Hannah came in, greetings were warm and happy, and presently around the table everyone was busy not only eating but talking about the latest news from around the country. Jude managed a sheep business for wool as well as meat, from Hebron all the way to Nazareth and Capernaum. Multiple dozens of flocks were his, tended by shepherds from their individual locales, where most of the meat was sold, and some of the wool. The balance of the wool was carted to Jerusalem or Bethlehem for processing, or sold for export farther north into Syria. Jude traveled often between cities, coordinating the work at all the sites.

"Miriam tells me you're managing Joel's Jerusalem office," said Hannah to Mark.

"Well, I'm the only one there, anyway. For the past six months," said Mark. "If I don't make a mess of things, he might keep me on."

"Oh," said Hannah, laughing, "You won't mess up anything at all. Joel wouldn't have trusted you if he thought you would. We know him quite well," she said, nodding sideways at her husband.

"I'm sure you'll succeed," said Jude. "Do you think this will be permanent?"

"Permanent for now," said Mark. "That sounds contradictory, but I just mean I don't have other plans right now."

"What do you like to do? Besides sell things?"

"I like to write."

"Ah," said Jude. "You could write a book. You know what Solomon wrote: 'There is no end of making books.'" A titter of laughter followed, but Mark smiled only a little.

"What do you write about?" said Hannah.

"Just things that happen," said Mark.

"He wrote about his dog, Puppy, when he was only seven," said Miriam. "Mark, I mean, not Puppy. He gave me the sheet of paper. I still have it." She looked at Mark adoringly, and Mark blushed. "He came back for the paper and added to it when the poor thing died, too. It was very touching." Miriam put her hand on Mark's arm and smiled at him.

"I wrote about some things I remember from Alexandria," added Mark.

"You remember that far back?" said Jude. "You were only, what, four when you moved away from there?"

"Almost five," said Mark. "But I remember a lot."

"Those were days both of us remember," said Miriam soberly. A moment of silence was observed spontaneously around the table.

"Well, there may be a lot more to write about soon," said Jude. "I guess you've heard about the prophet traveling around in Galilee."

"Just bits and pieces here and there," said Miriam. "We've heard more about the Baptist."

"As has everybody. He's baptized all along the river valley, from Jericho to Aenon."

"The Pharisees around here aren't too happy with him," said Miriam.

"He's upsetting the applecart," said Hannah.

"Some of them are upset over petty things, like why he's baptizing," said Jude. "But it's more than that. John is saying the Messiah is coming. He's saying it's the prophet."

"Who is the prophet?" said Mark.

"Name is Jesus. From Nazareth, I think. Came to John a few months ago. Was baptized. A lot of people were there and said it thundered in broad daylight when he was."

"Wow!" said Mark. "What happened then?"

"He disappeared for a while. Reappeared in Galilee in a month or so. My men up in Tiberias say he did a miracle on the other side of the lake."

"What kind of miracle?" asked Mark.

"Way I heard it, he was on the side of the mountain over there, teaching or preaching, and there were thousands of people from everywhere from Capernaum to Hippos. They say he fed all of them from just a couple of fish and an armful of bread." Jude took a bite of bread, himself.

"Everybody?!" said Mark.

"More than five thousand. I got that from Natan, head shepherd in Genessaret. Never known him to lie or even to embellish the facts," said Jude.

"What do you think it means?" said Miriam.

"Don't know, other than that we're probably going to hear more out of him." Jude reached for some fruit. Everyone munched thoughtfully.

"What's he saying?" said Mark. "The prophet?"

"Oh, things like John, but he goes further," said Judah.

"How do you mean?" said Miriam.

"John is telling everyone to repent; the kingdom of God is *coming*. I hear that Jesus has said, 'It's *here*.'"

"Here? Where?"

"Just telling you what I've heard. Natan said Jesus went into a synagogue in Nazareth, read from Isaiah, and said he— meaning himself—had just fulfilled the prophecy of the Messiah."

"So he's claiming it himself, then," said Mark.

"What it sounds like," said Jude. "They ran him off, but he gave them the slip somehow."

When everyone had enough food, they retreated to various parts of the house. Mark followed Jude out of the room, hoping to hear more about the prophet, if there were anything else to tell.

Jude turned to him. "Show me this Upper Room you're having built."

"It isn't quite finished," said Mark.

"Well, let's take a look at it."

They went down a hallway and to the back of the bed chambers. A new stairway had been constructed there, and they ascended into dimness.

"We're going to put a window at the top, but that isn't done yet," said Mark. They got to the top and partly felt their way to the door, which wasn't locked.

"There's an outside stairway, too," said Mark. "This door can be locked from the inside or the outside."

"So wedding guests can't come down and help themselves to the family kitchen, I guess," said Jude wryly.

"And so the family can't go to the wedding uninvited," added Mark. They went into the room, which still smelled of sawn timbers and was breezy from unshuttered windows.

"It's nice," said Jude, looking around. "Good light. You'll have shutters on the windows before it rains?"

"A day or two, I think," said Mark. "And cloth on the inside."

"Anyone reserved it yet?"

"I don't think so. Mother's in charge."

"Business will come," said Jude. "Talk it up. Word of mouth. Anything else you can do. I'll mention it to my people."

"Mother will appreciate that."

Jude walked through the room and then to the door at the back, which was the side wall of the house, between Miriam's house and the one next door. He opened the door. The space between the houses was about fifteen feet, with grass and a few flowers. A stairway, newly built, went to the bottom, and a walkway of flagstones led to the street.

"Nice," he said. Jude turned to Mark. "You can have *your* wedding here." He looked at Mark with one eye raised suggestively, as if expecting a reply.

"There's no one right now," said Mark, a little embarrassed.

Joel walked back toward him. "I know," he said. "Your mother told me when we were here a month ago. I think she'd like you to get out of the house more."

"She needs me here," said Mark. "Since Rhoda's mother's death, the girl has been her only help."

"She has all the help she needs. You wouldn't be abandoning her by finding a wife."

"I keep thinking she'll find a husband. Or at least I did. Maybe she won't, now."

"I know she depended on you a lot at first. Joel tells me that."

"She still does."

"Forgive me if I sound like an uncle, but I think she depends on you less than you depend on her." Jude made a gesture of humility and said, "Again, forgive me if I'm treading on very private ground."

"I'm not offended," said Mark, wondering if that were entirely true.

"Every man must find his way in the world and still honor his parents," said Jude. "You're entitled to be the man of your own house."

"If God shows me someone, I'm sure I will be." He thought his reply sounded respectful and mature.

"He might have an easier time showing, if you're actually looking."

Mark had already insisted he was not offended, but he didn't know exactly how to answer his quasi uncle.

"I know you care about my future, sir."

"Well, no more from me."

"Changing the subject," said Mark, "Really, what do you think of the prophet?"

"You mean do I think he's our Messiah?"

"Yes."

"Haven't seen enough, Mark. Or heard enough. Just reports. Haven't seen him for myself."

"Do you plan to?"

"It would be hard. Unlike a lot of people nowadays, I work. Can't just go traipsing off following somebody."

"I can't either. It's just me handling the business."

"I'll be sure to tell you anything I hear about him. Probably won't need to, though. Everybody is talking about him."

Mark was pensive. "Barnabas talks about Messiah some. Has for years. He thinks he'll come into Jerusalem through the Eastern Gate."

"The Psalms. 'Lift up your heads.'"

"Yes. Do you think so?" said Mark.

"I think somebody will come. Somebody great. Could this be him? Don't know. Time will tell."

"Are you staying in Jerusalem until Passover this week?" asked Mark.

"Home until the feast is over. Then going over to Emmaus."

"We'll see you again before then?"

"Probably," said Jude. "I think your mother wants us to come for dinner again the first day of the week."

On the other side of Jerusalem, thirteen men unobtrusively entered the city north of the temple mount, circled it and then went into the temple courts, amid throngs of other people, many of whom went straight to moneychangers so they could acquire the right coinage, and others to animal sellers, to buy sacrifices. The leader of the other twelve reached down and picked up bits of leather thongs, cords and ropes discarded as tethers were undone or packages were unwrapped. Patiently he braided and tied them, until he had a whip as long as a man's shadow at the ninth hour.

Before sundown, the news had spread to every part of the city that the man had driven out every last seller and moneychanger, and then had delivered a scathing rebuke. Everybody quoted him calling the temple "my Father's house."

6
Jerusalem, Spring, c. A.D. 28

Barely a sound could be heard on the Sabbath as Mark and his mother sat in the Upper Room looking at the remnants of a wedding feast that had been held the previous day. The party had gone long into the afternoon and the guests, mindful of their need to depart long enough before sundown to get to their homes—the happy couple went to their new abode—had taken the decorations and food they had brought with them and left by the private entrance at the back.

Miriam looked around. Some cleaning still needed doing, but it would have to wait until the Sabbath had ended. Mark and Miriam had simply come up to the room to survey the damage and to eat breakfast. They were sitting in the middle of the room at one of the little tables, delighted that the venue was being used regularly and bringing in some additional income.

They ate fruit and bread baked the day before while the guests were noisily celebrating upstairs. Other than their own clinking of cups and plates, the city around them was silent, no clattering carts or shuffling shoes on their street or anywhere, as people mostly rigorously observed the day of rest.

"Did Rhoda get to the market yesterday?" asked Mark.

"She'll have to finish tomorrow," said Miriam. "She didn't get enough meat."

"Are they running short?"

"No. She got distracted."

"By what?"

"She came back saying there was a hubbub about Jesus of Nazareth going on. He's back in Jerusalem."

"Where?" said Mark, sitting up.

"I don't know, right now. If he's who they say he is, he's home. Or somebody's home, anyway."

Mark finished an apple and put down the well-trimmed core. "One of my buyers told me he came through Sychar some time ago and people told him Jesus had been there."

"What was he doing in Samaria?"

"Who? The buyer?"

"No, Jesus."

"I don't know. The buyer said he and a group of men were traveling through there."

"Strange for a holy man."

"Beats going around the whole region," said Mark. "Seems to me we wouldn't have to avoid Samaria altogether just to keep from speaking to Samaritans."

"You went to Capernaum in the spring. How did you go?" said his mother.

"By the river road."

"Ah. The river road," said Miriam. Mark realized he was trapped.

"Everyone does that, and there are Jewish camps on that road."

"I see," said Miriam. "So you only go that way because everyone else does."

"Anyway, Jacob's well is there," said Mark. "In Sychar. I suppose they stopped for water. Jesus and his group."

"This buyer say anything else?"

"Only that the whole town was excited. They said they were sure he's the Messiah."

"On what basis?" said Miriam.

"Seems he met some woman at the well and told her all about

herself, when he had never met her."

"Soothsayers do that."

"It was more than that, apparently. Enough to convince her he was a lot more than a prophet."

Miriam finished her bread and wiped crumbs from their little table into her hand, folded up some napkins and got up to go back downstairs. Mark got up with her and they went down the inside stairs to the bedroom hall.

As they returned to the main house, they heard the flutter of footsteps passing in the front street at a rapid pace. In another few seconds, two or three other people passed at the same rate. They glimpsed a few men holding their robes up and trotting down the way.

"Must be a fire," said Mark, not seriously.

"I hope it isn't more than a Sabbath day's walk. Pharisees are out watching, I'm sure," said his mother with light sarcasm.

"Seriously, I wonder what's going on." His curiosity was piqued when a third group, ten or twelve men and women, hurried by. "I think I'll find out," he said.

"O Mark!" said Miriam.

"They can't be going far. I'll just see what it is and come back."

Mark grabbed a shawl and went out the front door, following the sound of the last group as they scurried through the neighborhood. He really didn't have to worry about exceeding the maximum Sabbath Day's journey, unless where all the people were going was outside the city, which was when you had to start counting steps. But at this point he didn't know. When he soon came to the Sheep Gate, he started counting, but hadn't taken many steps at all when he came to the edge of a growing crowd that had gathered around the Pool of Bethesda.

Working his way through clusters of onlookers he came to the edge of the colonnaded pool. There didn't seem to be anything in particular going on other than the excitement of the crowd. The usual smattering of sick and lame were there by the pool, waiting, he presumed, for the waters to stir, as Barnabas had told him years ago. They were there weekly, even daily, he guessed: he didn't know and hadn't paid much attention to goings on at the pool over the years. He hadn't heard any stories of healing that were credible.

Then he saw a man break away from a little crowd nearby and run—he nearly leaped like a deer—up and away from the pool area.

"There he goes," somebody said. "That's the man he healed."

Mark wedged himself between two people and touched the speaker's arm, who then turned to him.

"Who?" said Mark. "Who healed him."

"I didn't see it happen," said the man, "but everybody here is saying it was that Jesus of Nazareth."

"Here in Jerusalem again?" said Mark.

"Apparently." The man turned back to his friends. Mark threaded through the crowd and found others talking about what they had heard. One man was the center of attention.

"I was down there," he pointed over the crowd to a spot near the pool. "Right over there near him," said the man. "He was lying there on a mat. I've seen him before. He's there all the time."

"And he just got up?" said someone else.

"Like a newborn calf!" said the first man. "The other man told him to. He looked at him a second and then just tried his legs. Suddenly, they worked! Never seen anything like it."

"Who was it?" said Mark to the speaker. "The other man?"

"I'd never seen him, myself, but everybody here is saying it was Jesus, the prophet from Galilee."

Mark wandered around the other side of the pool and looked about. There was no indication that Jesus, if it had been Jesus, was still here, just the gaggles of witnesses—most of them second and third hand or more—who hoped something else would happen they could see for themselves. He caught the drift of conversations coming from some other knots of reporters and listeners, satisfied himself that he had heard all there was to be heard, and then made his way back to the edge of the crowd and walked at a normal pace back home.

He told his mother what had been going on. Miriam asked few questions. She seemed absorbed in thought, as if musing on the rising consensus, and the growing hope everywhere, that Jesus of Nazareth might well be Israel's Messiah. That was Mark's own thinking, anyway. Perhaps he just assumed that his mother was thinking the same thing.

"I'm going to my room to rest," said Miriam. She went down the hall to her chamber and closed the door behind her.

Mark went out back to the enclosed yard and sat down on a bench with a tall back. In a few minutes he drifted into a light nap.

7
Jerusalem, Summer, c. A.D. 28

Not many men of barely eighteen ran businesses by themselves, but Mark, whose father had not been in the picture since almost before he could remember, and who had no grandfathers who had a chance to influence him either, had been trusted by the uncle who was as close to a father as he possessed, and he had shown himself to have reasonable aptitude—for his age, anyway—in his business. With the encouragement of his cousin Barnabas, who knew all about the Supply House of Joel of Cyprus, Mark was handling the little Jerusalem office adequately at the very least, and in Mark's own estimation, acceptably well.

In other respects, Mark still saw himself as not quite a man, owing in part to his stature: he was a head shorter than most boys his age. His father had been of average height, but he was broad and packed with muscle, leaving no doubt as to his maturity, virility and brute power.

But Mark's self-image as a boy owed more to the casual disrespect with which some other businessmen regarded him. It chafed, but at the same time he himself couldn't manage to think of himself as an adult. He was prepossessed with embarrassment in thinking that the men he had known through the business were so much more savvy than he. He also assumed, with abashed humility, that the men at the synagogue, if they were any older than Mark, were adults, thought like adults, and acted like adults. The men in his family, including Barnabas, nine years older than he, were adults, too, in every way Mark could observe. Barnabas had been like an older brother, but Barnabas had never seemed like someone who had been a child. By the time Mark knew him, Barnabas was a teenager, and to children of five, teenagers were old.

The word “adult” just had something foreboding about it. Mark thought of it like a destination by sea from which there would never be any return. He had a few friends in his neighborhood who were approximately the same age as he, and he wondered if they thought the same way he did. Most of them worked with their fathers in their family businesses, some of which had been run by their grandfathers, great grandfathers, and beyond into the past. One of his friends, a boy named Uri (and Mark still called his friends “boys,” too) told him once that he thought he would never be as old as his father. Mark had asked him what he meant, and Uri had said he just believed he would never think in as old a way as his abba. Mark thought the same way about all adults, though he admitted he couldn’t nail down exactly what that meant. He just assumed that adults thought of themselves as old, or at least as adults, while he thought of himself as a boy. Even on the cusp of being an adult—when did that *really* happen, he wondered? —he didn’t expect to feel like an adult. Ever.

There was just something about adults that Mark believed he had not become, not acquired, not even gotten near. Yes, he could handle business—Joel had given him a few simple tasks—but he was just imitating what he had seen Joel do. He thought that at some age he would wake up one morning and think to himself, ‘I’m an adult, now.’ But it hadn’t happened, and Mark was fairly certain he didn’t want it to.

He remembered his Uncle Joel’s friend Jude telling him it was likely that he depended on his mother more than she depended on him, and it still stung him a little when he remembered Jude’s saying it, but it was probably true. He hadn’t become the man of his own house in part because he just didn’t feel he was a man. Boys were supposed to want to become men. Somewhere inside, he argued with himself, he wanted to be. Or did he?

There was something missing from his boyhood. When his father Tullio was killed back in Alexandria, Mark was suddenly "the man of the house." His mother had frequently told him that, even at the age of five. The emotion of that time had cemented his early memories of his soldier father in his little mind, and he had never forgotten him, even though his recollection was composed of little snippets, disconnected, embellished by desire, polished by exaggeration, and fixed in his brain by his mother's retelling over the years. His abba, his father, now *there* was a man.

His mother would have agreed, Mark knew, but from a different perspective, the perspective of a girl in love, a young wife proud of her soldier, and the grieving widow wishing time could turn back and change. To Mark, his father was the image of a man, but he hadn't had him as a father long enough to know anything different. And when Tullio was killed his mother had to be both parents at the same time. Mark knew she had tried, but while Mark became the man of the house at one moment, the next moment she might call him her little boy. It was confusing when he was younger. He finally came to understand that his mother was expressing her own conflict, her abiding grief at losing her husband, and her anxiety about the prospect of Mark's leaving home. But growing up as he had, he had developed a tenacious hold on his own youth and a distrust of becoming an adult. It was as simple and as complex as that.

All this explained why Mark had not married. If he had had a father as he reached his teen years, he was sure he would have been introduced to some daughter of a friend of the family, and by now, or just about now, he would be moving out of his house and beginning a new life with a wife. That would be nice, he supposed, but Miriam had never arranged it herself, never encouraged it, and

Mark had begun to realize when he was sixteen or so that it was because his mother didn't want to lose him. When she fawned on him now and then, she would say, "You look so much like your father." Later she would go off to her room and Mark would hear her snuffling. He couldn't escape the feeling that he would be burdened with guilt if he established his own home somewhere else.

Of course, if it were a reasonable option to marry but stay in the family home, he could, but he realized, even without admitting that it was a very adult thought, that his mother would have to take a backseat kind of role so that Mark would be acknowledged as the head of the household. It would have to be a reality, not just symbolism cached in his mother's oft-repeated appellation, "my little man." Even the phrase incorporated the conflict Mark felt and the oxymoron to which his mother subscribed unknowingly.

Deep in thought about his present and future this first day of the week, Mark was going over reports he would give to Joel later this week when he came to check up on things. Actually, he assumed that Joel might take the occasion of his visit to give either thumbs up or thumbs down to Mark's continuing to run the little office.

Somehow today, the matter didn't concern Mark either way. He had been preoccupied of late with reports that circulated regularly about Jesus of Nazareth, who for some time had had twelve official disciples traveling with him, and who had been stirring up things in both Galilee and Judea as well as Samaria. Questions about whether he were the long awaited Messiah were on everyone's lips, with some saying he was "the Prophet," a figure Moses had predicted would come, or someone else. Mark hadn't formulated an opinion yet, especially since he hadn't had the opportunity to see and hear Jesus for himself.

Dozens of people in addition to the twelve official disciples often followed Jesus from place to place. He assumed they were all unemployed or independently wealthy, which Mark was not, or he might have taken off and found them and joined them on the road for a while. Besides, he had made a commitment to Joel, and he couldn't just leave him hanging there.

Not that Joel couldn't find a replacement in a minute.

Two men entered the little office. One of them was a buyer he had dealt with before. He was officious and a bit condescending, but Mark had tried his best to accommodate him and show him respect. The other man was about the same age, somewhere in his fifties, and turned out to be a business partner of the first.

"Eleazar, hello," said Mark.

"Young Mark," said Eleazar. Mark had already been put in his place. "This is Tobias, my right hand man. Tobias, this is Mark, Miriam's boy, Joel's nephew." Mark was young, and he was a boy. This was now Tobias's perspective on him, too.

"Mark," said Tobias.

"Have you run out of supplies already?" said Mark.

"Almost," said Eleazar. "Can you have more of what we need in two weeks?"

"I'll have to ask Joel when he comes the day before the Sabbath."

"Of course. I can't expect you to know. Well, when he comes, tell him I need half again as much as a month ago."

"I will."

"And ask him if we can't agree on a little discount for greater volume."

Mark started to say he could decide that himself, but instead he said, "I will. Anything else?"

"No, that's all. We were just going down to the market streets and thought we'd stop by," said Eleazar. "I guess you've heard the news."

"What news?" asked Mark.

"About the Baptist."

"John," added Tobias.

"I hear bits and pieces about John now and then," said Mark. "Not so much since he baptized Jesus a while back. What now?"

"Then, you haven't heard." Eleazar looked at Tobias and then back. "He's dead."

"What?!" said Mark. "When?"

"Ten or twelve days ago," said Tobias. "I heard from somebody who had come from Tiberias last week."

"What happened?"

"Herod executed him," said Eleazar. "Took off his head."

Mark was stunned, but he had never heard John personally, any more than he had Jesus, and hadn't formed much of an opinion about him. "What did he do?"

"What we heard," said Tobias, "is that he crossed Herod one too many times about his wife. Herod had him put in jail, and then just up and executed him."

"Wow. I wonder if Herod will go after Jesus next," said Mark.

"Who knows. The way I hear it, Jesus has been talking a lot about the kingdom of God. Herod might get a little territorial," said Eleazar.

"Have you ever heard him?" said Tobias.

"No. Neither of them, in fact," said Mark.

"You should. Next time he's in Jerusalem. He's really interesting."

"Interesting?" said Mark. "Is that all?"

"Well," said Tobias, "I'm not sure I buy into everything he's saying. A lot of people do. They think he's more than just the latest self-appointed preacher. And of course, there are the miracles."

"Have you seen any of those happen?" said Mark, expecting a story.

"Not me. I heard about a blind man in Jericho. Made him see, people say."

"Really?" said Mark.

"Of course, you never know about what you hear. Women passing along gossip. By the time it gets out there very far, it's a more impressive story."

Eleazar nodded at his associate. "Well, we'll go. Perhaps we'll come back again the day before the Sabbath and speak to Joel ourselves? When do you expect him?"

"Late in the afternoon," said Mark. "He'll make the trip from Cyprus the day before, and come from Joppa the next morning."

"Ah," said Eleazar. "Just so. Peace to you," he said, and he and Tobias turned to go.

"And to you," said Mark, and the two men left.

By the end of the day Mark had taken in about the average receipts, and he closed the office and walked back through the edge of the market toward home. The air was a bit chilly now at the end of the year and fewer edibles were being sold, mostly bread, fish and dried meats. He bought some other supplies that he could carry in a satchel and then worked his way up through the neighborhood streets until he arrived at home.

His mother was scurrying around in the back of the house giving instructions to Rhoda that made it sound as if she were leaving presently. And so it was.

"Mark. I'm glad you're home. I'm going up to the colonnade. Esther from next door said Jesus is there and I want to hear him."

"Jesus? Really? I'll go with you," said Mark.

"Of course. Come along," she said, as she headed for the door.

"Let me put these things away," he said.

"Meet me there," said Miriam, and she hurried out of the house.

"Wait for me," said Mark, but she didn't.

Mark unloaded his purchases quickly, but by the time he exited the house, his mother had already disappeared up the city street. He took the route he thought she would have walked but he didn't catch up to her. When he came to Solomon's Colonnade, he encountered a glut of people shifting this way and that, all trying to position themselves to see something, anything.

Mark went around the crowd and worked his way toward the western entrance to the colonnade area. When he sensed that the people around him were somewhat hushed, he thought it likely that they were trying to hear someone speak, and they were.

"Well, don't leave us in suspense," someone called out.

"Yes. Just *tell* us!"

"Are you the Christ?" said someone else.

Mark couldn't yet see the speakers. He didn't want to be rude, but he pushed gently on several people to either side of him as he excused himself for inconveniencing them and worked his way to the inner edge of the crowd and glimpsed some men who appeared to be city elders and Pharisees standing near another group of men. One of the men was clearly the one the elders were addressing. He was surrounded and backed by a dozen or so other men. Mark instantly concluded this must be Jesus and his disciples.

"I *did* tell you," said the one Mark believed must be Jesus.

A hubbub obscured their reply, if they were making one. There was a lot of murmuring going on in front of him.

"...and you didn't believe me."

"When did you—" Mark could make out, and then, "—my Father's name."

Mark went around a knot of people in front of him and got a few feet closer, still some distance away.

"—everything I have been doing," said Jesus. "All of it witnesses to who I am."

"Why should we believe you," said someone loudly.

"You don't believe because you are not my sheep."

"So, he's a shepherd," said someone near Mark, privately to the person next to him.

"Kind of looks like one, doesn't he?" said the other.

"What I heard is that a bunch of those who follow him are just fishermen."

"Let's listen to him!" said Mark in a whisper to the men, whom he didn't know. They looked back at him, saw he was young, and screwed up their faces in dismissal.

"But my sheep listen," said the man who was Jesus. "I know them, and they know me."

The crowd hushed a little, and Mark heard Jesus' next words.

"...I give them eternal life. No one will snatch them out of my Father's hand—and I and the Father *are one!*"

The crowd, which had been relatively silent, burst instantly into agitated shouting and turmoil, from the front where the Jewish leaders were, working its way back quickly. People were angrily using the word "blasphemy" and arguing with each other. Several men around Mark began calling out, "Stone him!" and the crowd rapidly morphed into a mob, undulating and moving forward.

Mark couldn't keep from being moved along with those around him, and he could hear only a little of what was going on around Jesus himself, though he picked up the words, "not what you did, but what you said!"

A few men were picking up little rocks in the street. A man to the side of him bent over to look for a stone and then couldn't stand up again because of the press of the tightening throng. He was trampled when he tried.

Presently Mark was able to step up to his left and see above the crowd. He could see the center of the writhing mass and barely make out a man in a dusty white robe, being pushed along, and others trying to surround him protectively. In a moment, though, he had lost track of the man, and the ones surrounding him as well. Within a minute, he couldn't see them, and the crowd around them took on the look of cattle who had been herded into a pen and had nowhere to go.

In another minute no one seemed to be able to find Jesus, and they milled about angrily as someone would call out, "Where is he?" and others, "Get him!" and still others, "Don't let him get away!"

The mob lost its sense of direction and simply undulated in confusion, until after a few minutes it had quieted from lack of focus. It was like a dust devil out in the wilderness, appearing suddenly and stirring up the dirt, then dissipating in a moment and dying out in the summer sun.

When the swarm of onlookers had thinned to a less dense congregation, Mark threaded his way back through it, headed for a back street toward his home. Suddenly, he saw his mother, on a stairway to a house nearby, standing with several other women where they could have seen the entire incident. He was glad she had not been jostled or injured in the throng.

Miriam spotted him and the two met up in between, quickly taking little lanes and getting away from the scene.

"I saw you down there," she said, as they continued scurrying back to the house.

"Things were getting out of hand. Where did Jesus *go?*" he said excitedly.

"I lost sight of him all of a sudden," she said. "I don't know."

They finally came to their home and retreated into the comfort and safety of its pleasantly darkened interior.

"Who were those women you were with?" Mark wanted to know.

"Just a few other Marys," said Miriam. "There are so many of us," she said, managing a nervous laugh.

"You should know, Mark, that I'm one of several women who support Jesus." She paused and became very still and looked at him straight in the eye, as if expecting that if he were going to give a response, now would be the time.

"You've heard him before?" he said.

"Several times," she said. "I've met him."

"So, you believe him?" he said.

"Yes, Mark, I do," she said with quiet confidence. "I believe he is the one to come."

"The Messiah," Mark said.

"Yes."

Mark looked at her for a moment, and Miriam did not detect any disagreement in his face. In fact, Mark was as likely to derive his beliefs from his mother as he was from any independent thinking, and as he looked at her he saw now in her eyes an unwavering assurance. He was gently swept up in the moment and began to feel what she must be feeling.

"I've heard priests at the temple and teachers in the synagogue and nobody ever talked like Jesus," said Miriam. "Who else could he be?" She sat down in a chair in the main room.

Mark took off his shawl and laid it on a table, and sat next to her. He smoothed the fine hairs of his youthful beard and then ran his hands back through his thick, dark hair.

"If you're right, then what's next?"

"I don't know."

"When you said you 'support him,' what did you mean?" said Mark.

"There are several of us. I don't know how many. A lot of women who have heard him and met him. He has to live, have food and shelter. We give him some money."

"Money," said Mark.

"Yes, money," she said. "Some of the income from the Upper Room is going to his ministry."

"I see."

They sat there wordlessly a few minutes. Rhoda appeared at the doorway from the hall to the kitchen.

"Are you ready to eat, ma'am?" she said.

"Yes, Rhoda. Thank you." Miriam got up, and Mark with her. As they ate, they talked, and Miriam told her son some of the things she had heard Jesus say and had seen him do. Somewhere in the evening, as they ate and then warmed themselves by a fire and then retired for the night, Mark came to believe for himself.

8
Cyprus, c. A.D. 29

Barnabas stood on the main Salamis wharf watching Mark's ship approach the harbor. He thought he could identify his cousin at the rail near the prow as the vessel, burdened with cargo, plowed toward land, her crewmen laboring at trimming sails and manning the tackle as they prepared to dock.

Barnabas's father, Joel, had decided midwinter to send a new trainee to Jerusalem to handle the little office there, and to bring Mark over to Cyprus to further school him in the business. Mark wasn't certain how he felt about leaving his mother for an extended time, but Uncle Joel said it would be for only three weeks. Mark figured his mother, who was by no means elderly, could survive without him as long as she had Rhoda. Finally, Mark admitted to himself that his uncertain feelings were really about him and not his mother's well being. He reminded himself of his need to become independent of his mother, at least insofar as he could while living in her home. This awareness engendered persistent struggle with himself against his innate need of nurture.

Mark spotted Barnabas on the wharf, waved broadly, and Barnabas returned the greeting. When the gangplank was lowered and the ship debouched its fares, Mark joined the line of the dozen or so other passengers who had secured lower berths in the ship and endured the conglomerated, mostly unidentifiable, sometimes mephitic smell of various cargoes, vegetative, mineral, and human. Stepping ashore was always welcome, and he traversed the dock and gripped Barnabas by the arm in greeting.

"Did you get to meet Linus?" said Barnabas.

"Yes, he arrived three days ago. He came to the house. I took him to the office to show him around," said Mark.

"The place he's staying isn't as nice as your home, but Abba didn't want to impose on Aunt Miriam by asking if he could stay there."

"She wouldn't have minded."

"I know, but the inn is fine for three weeks." Barnabas took one of Mark's bags and the two left the wharf environs and wended their way through city streets toward Joel's home. Once they were there, Tirzah hugged Mark and pushed him toward the back of the house telling him to wash up. It was close to suppertime.

The meal verged on the sumptuous, with greens that Mark was not familiar with in Jerusalem, lamb stewed in various vegetables, and freshly baked bread. Back home, Rhoda was a good cook, but somewhat limited, and Mark's mother had never urged her to expand her culinary horizons.

"Any problems on your trip?" said Joel to Mark.

"No. None. A few crusty sailors."

"Be glad you're not learning *that* as a career," said Joel.

"How's your mother?" said Tirzah.

"She's fine."

"What a wonderfully complete report," said Tirzah, facetiously.

"Sorry," said Mark. "She's—well. Does whatever she likes. No pains, no doctors. She does the shopping with Rhoda about half the time, to make sure it's done right. And she's getting some business for the Upper Room. We had a wedding two weeks ago."

"I'm trying to convince your uncle I should go back with you in three weeks to see her," said Tirzah.

"Don't listen to her," said Joel. "It was my idea in the first place."

"I'm sure she'd love to see you," said Mark.

"If she does," said Joel, "could you return with her to Joppa and see her off back here when she's stayed two or three weeks?"

"Sure. Of course." Everyone ate. The stew was succulent, flavored with some spices Mark hadn't had back home.

"What do you hear of Jesus of Nazareth lately?" said Joel.

Mark finished a bite and sat back for a moment. Onboard ship he had thought about the fact that he would be expected to fill everyone in on what was happening in Judea and Galilee concerning Jesus, at least what they hadn't already heard. Traffic between Cyprus and Judea was regular, and he was certain that travelers coming out of Caesarea and Joppa had kept the island up with the latest news. While on the ship, Mark had rehearsed what he might say.

"I think we're about to get a speech," said Barnabas wryly.

"You probably know as much as I do in general," said Mark. "Jesus has been in Jerusalem several times. I usually don't hear about it until too late and then I miss being able to see him."

"But?" said Tirzah. "I feel a 'but' coming."

"But," said Mark, smiling, "three months ago I got home from work to find Imma leaving the house to go to the temple area to see him."

"Did she?" Tirzah said excitedly.

"We both did," Mark said, nodding, "but it was sort of cut short. He was having kind of a loud conversation with the Pharisees about who he was. They demanded he tell them straight out. And then they took offense when he told them. Because he said that he and the Father are one." Mark paused for effect.

"One," said Joel.

"One," said Mark. Joel looked serious, reflective, and thoughtful. Tirzah's face was blank, but Mark assumed she was taking it all in. Barnabas looked fascinated.

"They tried to stone him," Mark said.

"What?! Did he get hurt?" said Tirzah.

"No. In fact, he kind of disappeared into the crowd. It was like his followers swallowed him or something. In fact, they sort of disappeared themselves, like they blended into the crowd and couldn't be identified. There were so many people there, it's not surprising, I guess. The whole thing just broke up."

"That all?" said Joel.

"All I know. We went back home."

"We get a good bit of news here from the mainland," said Joel. "He's had quite a few run-ins with Pharisees, what I hear, and lawyers and rabbis and the like. There are a few Pharisees here on the island, transplants, and they mutter and gripe about everything they hear about him."

"Mother supports him," said Mark, blurting it out. He hadn't planned on saying anything about that, but it just came out.

"What do you mean?"

"She thinks he's the Messiah," Mark said, sorry he'd used the word "support" and hoping to keep from having to explain his imma's financial support of Jesus and his disciples.

"I told you, Joel," said Tirzah. "I told you she would." She drilled a finger into Joel's arm and then said to Mark, "Everybody here—well, everybody in the Jewish community—is talking about him, and of course, everybody has an opinion."

"Most don't think he's the Messiah," said Joel. "I only told your aunt I didn't think her sister would think so, either."

"What else did she say?" asked Tirzah.

"Pretty much just that. She said who else could he be, talking like he does and doing the things he does."

"I agree," said Barnabas. "From what I've heard, nobody else has even come close. Who else do you know who can make blind men see and lame men walk? He has to be telling us something by doing things like that. I agree. I think he's the Messiah."

Joel and Tirzah both looked at Barnabas, neither disapproval nor endorsement on their faces. If Barnabas had been Mark's age, certainly if he had been younger, they might have been quick to tell him to keep quiet or to correct him for jumping to conclusions. But at the moment, their faces said they were somewhere between nonplussed and outright impressed.

"I'm reserving my opinion for the moment," said Joel. Tirzah looked as if she were about to say something, but then took another bite of stew, perhaps only to stop herself from speaking.

"What do you think, Mark? You're there, closer to the action," said his uncle.

"Not close enough," said Mark. "Lots of people follow him around. I mostly hear reports." He sat back up, dipped some bread in the stew and ate a bite. "But what I hear, it's amazing."

"So, no opinion, then?" said Joel.

Mark swallowed and composed himself. He felt compelled to be honest. "I didn't say that. Matter of fact, I agree with my mother. And with Barnabas." He nodded at his cousin.

"Well," said Joel. He slung an arm over his chair back. "That would be something, wouldn't it."

"It kind of already *is* something," said Mark.

"Of course it is; I didn't mean it wasn't," said Joel. "What I meant was that *if* he's the Messiah, we're in for some major events in the very near future. History in the making. If what the militants among us believe is true. And by the way, I've never been able to figure out what the other option is. If he's not coming to set us free from Rome, I mean."

"Me, either," said Barnabas. "But I wish there were one."

"Where do you think it's all going, Mark? I mean, if you have an opinion," said Joel, and waited for Mark expectantly. This was a kind of respect Mark didn't ordinarily get from adults back home, and he found himself reveling in the moment, though he reminded himself not to let it go to his head.

"I don't know. Either something will happen and practically everybody will follow him, or—" Mark paused while looking for a word but didn't exactly find it— "something will happen, something bad."

The table fell silent for a moment. "I mean, some powerful people are against him. Some of *our* people, I mean. To say nothing of the Romans."

"From what I hear," said Joel, "that hasn't kept him quiet. Seems he speaks his mind and comes right at them."

"It's going on three years, now," said Barnabas. "How long will it take people to realize who he is?"

"Who said they would?" said Mark. Everybody looked at him. "Doesn't the scripture say he would be 'rejected by men'?"

"But not everybody rejects him," said Tirzah. "You, Barnabas, your mother. Hundreds wherever he goes."

"So you're saying he's *not* the Messiah," said Mark.

"No, I didn't say that."

"Then you don't believe the scripture was speaking about the Messiah."

"I didn't—" Tirzah paused, feeling trapped in her own words. "What I meant was, right now people are divided. But if he's the real Messiah, then soon—" and again she realized she had nowhere to go with her own logic.

Mark completed her sentence for her: "Soon they should all join him. Or soon, they will all turn against him. And that's what I was saying."

"Oh," said Tirzah quietly.

Joel relaxed in his chair and looked at Mark with a gentle smile mixed with the furrowed brows of contemplation.

"Clearly you've done a lot of thinking about this," said Joel. "You've remembered your scriptures, too. Have you talked with any of the rabbis about Jesus?"

"No. Only my mother."

"Aha. Well, I would encourage you to keep studying the matter. Keep an open mind," he said with gentle noncommital.

Mark listened to Joel and thought he sounded like a Greek academician in discussion with his students on some shaded hillside, or like a scholar trying to work out a puzzle that didn't come with any urgency to solve it. Perhaps it was the result of being over here on the island, where the news of Jesus was more like a story than an event, a distant tale rather than a present reality. Perhaps on Cyprus no one felt compelled to come to a conclusion, to arrive at a belief, to take a stand. Mark was only eighteen, but had come to believe that he had to make up his mind, for or against. To believe, or to oppose.

9
Jerusalem, Spring, c. A.D. 29

The first day of the week of Passover was like other Passover weeks for residents of Jerusalem, who redoubled their market trips and got their other shopping and household business done early in the week in expectation of fasting, feasting and other observances at home, in the synagogue and at the temple during the high, holy time. What made this particular first day different was the buzz of confirmed reports that the Nazarene would be coming in the Eastern Gate that day with his official disciples and a band of dozens if not hundreds of other followers. He would join the thousands of travelers who had crowded Jerusalem's inns, inside and outside the city, to celebrate the ancient deliverance of Israel from Egypt, through the sacrifice made for them in a lamb's blood, then applied to the doorposts of their slave quarters in that land of bondage so long ago.

Late in the morning, a band of men and women appeared in the distance on the road coming around the Mount of Olives and trod steadily toward the gate, being joined by others who had gone out of the city to see the procession. At the head of it was Jesus of Nazareth, mounted on a young donkey barely old enough to handle even the trim Nazarene's weight. In front of him, as the little foal clopped dutifully around the cemetery and made its way up the hill, many of the people who had come out through the Eastern Gate or had come from the south of the city were throwing palm fronds in front of the procession, greenery they had brought from home or snatched from trees in the area, denuding some of them mercilessly, but eager to do their part to pave the way for the celebrated rabbi and prophet.

Inside the gate, awaiting the entrance of the procession, stood two women, both named Mary, whispering to each other and nervously repositioning themselves such that they would be able to speak to Jesus when he finally reached the gate and came through. The growing crowd around them made it difficult for them to stay at the front of the press, but they elbowed and jostled with equal urgency and remained in the way.

As the parade came up the hill and into the flatter road just outside the gate, the shouting and singing became nearly overwhelming.

"Hosanna!" called out the joyful mass, finding its rhythm and chanting, "Blessed is he who comes in the name of the Lord!" and other bits of Psalms. Mary and Mary moved nearly into the way of the procession as Jesus passed under the shadow of the gate's arch and officially entered the city.

Once inside, the entire procession paused out of necessity because the crowd had all but blocked the way, the excited onlookers unable to contain themselves and clear a path. As the disciples moved up to flank their leader and to attempt to move the people aside one way or another, Jesus looked around and spotted the Marys, and one of them came quickly to his side.

Jesus leaned down and said something to her. She nodded several times, he spoke again, and then she backed a step away and smiled broadly. Jesus straightened up as the disciples had cleared the way, and he continued for a distance up the street, disappearing from the Marys' view, while they hurried up another street to the side, lacking in any crowd, and took back streets to the house of Miriam and Mark.

Once there, they knocked at the door, gained entrance as Rhoda came to see who it was, and the door was shut.

Flutists sounded what would be their final number for the bride and groom as they joyously grew weary of theirs and others' dancing in the Upper Room in the early afternoon of the fourth day of the week, just one day before the day of sacrifice. For the new groom, Jacob, it was a wonderful choice of a day to celebrate his bride, Abra, after their seven-day retreat to their huppah following their vows the week before. They stood at the head of the assembled friends in the rented chamber and clapped and laughed as couples and the odd assortment of unattached old men and women danced spontaneously, some of them awkwardly, roughly to the music, all in festive observance of the bride and groom, all of them becoming exhuberantly exhausted.

The groom's humble home had been entirely insufficient with regard to room and facilities to host such an event, and a friend of a friend had recommended Miriam's Upper Room as the venue for the wedding feast. Everyone had enjoyed the traditional foods and plenty of wine and everyone was ready to go home in the glow of a good time. The flutists' lips and cheeks were becoming fixed in their pursed positions and they began to miss their notes and make erratic sounds, bringing on additional laughter, all in good natured response.

Shortly the musicians concluded with a flourish and the dancers collapsed into chairs or on cushions. Wine cups were clinked in final toasts to the couple, and then the master of the feast declared the end of the festivities, as well wishers gave blessings to the bride and groom and one by one exited at the end of the room and carefully descended the outside stairs, going their separate ways into the city streets toward their respective homes.

When the newlyweds had also gone, the master of the feast gathered up a few last things belonging to the party and made his own exit, leaving the spacious Upper Room empty of revelers and ready for cleanup, a service included in the rental price Miriam had set and had already been paid.

Down in the main room of the house, when Miriam became aware of the silence, and the noise of exiting guests had diminished from the street outside, she called to Rhoda, who was peeling something over a basin in the kitchen, and the two went upstairs to begin to wash, gather bits of trash, and clean up.

"I want everything to be especially tidy," said Miriam.

"Yes ma'am," said Rhoda.

"I know you always do a good job, Rhoda. I'm not saying you don't."

"I know, ma'am."

"It's just that we have special guests coming tomorrow."

"I'll do my best."

Miriam took some miscellaneous trash with her in a basket and headed for the inside door to the private part of the house. "You can finish up. I'm tired."

Rhoda nodded and picked up a broom. "You rest, ma'am. I'll make it spotless."

Miriam went downstairs, disposed of the trash and then went to her chamber and lay down. Before she could drift off for a nap, she heard Mark coming into the house. At her request, he had closed the office around noon and had come home, expecting his mother would have some physical task for him to perform that she felt less and less capable of handling. She was well, but she was tired these days and Mark had begun running errands for her that a year or so ago she would have done herself, or perhaps with Rhoda.

Mark called to her down the hall and Miriam said, "Back here. I'm coming."

She came up the hall and greeted him, thanking him for taking the time off to help her.

"So where is it? This Herculean task you need me to perform," he said.

"Oh, nothing like that. I just need you to go do something for me."

"Market?" he asked.

"No." Miriam went into the main room and sat down again. Mark sat beside her.

"Are you feeling all right?" he said.

"I'm fine."

"What's the errand?"

"I need you to go up toward the Eastern Gate."

"What for?"

"You know where Simon the potter's shop is on the main road coming in?"

"Of course."

"I need you to go there."

"Did they break a pot upstairs," Mark said, a bit of irritation forming in his voice.

"No, no. I need you to buy one, though."

"We don't have enough pots?" said Mark, curious.

"Quite enough, so I don't need a big one. Just any sort of pot that might hold enough for a wash basin."

"What in the world for?"

"Put some water in it—Simon already knows you are coming."

"Okay. Why?"

"I need you to stand outside the shop and wait."

"For what?" Mark was becoming increasingly inquisitive about what sounded like a little charade.

"Someone is going to meet you there in a little bit."

"Who?"

"Someone from Jesus' followers."

"A disciple!" said Mark, excited.

"Yes," she said.

"Who?" he said. "Which one?"

"I don't know. Just one of them. Or two. Two of them."

"Obviously, you've already arranged this," said Mark, interested.

"I did," said Miriam, offering no details.

He had not been able to go to the Eastern Gate on the first day of the week, but he was aware that Jesus had come into Jerusalem to much celebration, and had been in and out of the city during the week. When he was outside the city, few people had any idea exactly where he was.

"Did you talk with them—with him—personally?"

"No, not this time. Mary did."

"Which Mary?"

"That's not important. The point is, arrangements have been made." Miriam seemed to be politely keeping the exact details of her planning to herself, and Mark knew not to probe further than he had.

"All right. I'll be outside Simon's shop. Then what?"

"Just wait there. Someone will come up to you and identify himself as one of Jesus' disciples."

"How will he—how will they—know who I am?"

"You'll be where you're supposed to be, standing there holding a water pot."

"Oh. Okay."

"Bring them back here with you. We're going to show them the Upper Room."

"Ah," said Mark. "Oh! They're going to meet here?"

"Yes. They're going to eat the Passover upstairs."

"That's wonderful!" said Mark.

"And it's a secret," said his mother, deadly serious. "Don't tell anyone. Anyone!"

Mark was taken slightly aback. "Secret" was clear enough, and one "anyone" was certainly enough. But clearly his mother was urgent to make certain that no one knew the Upper Room would be hosting Jesus and his disciples that night.

"How long will they be up there?" he said.

"I don't know. It doesn't matter. As long as they need it. We have nothing else scheduled until the week after next."

Mark waited to see if Miriam had anything else to say, and sensing that the conversation was over, he got up and headed toward the kitchen.

"You need to leave now," said his mother.

"Right now?"

"Yes. It's time."

With another blank look Mark made sure his mother wasn't about to add anything to her instructions, noted her expression of somewhat nervous anticipation, and then he turned and went out the front door.

Simon's pottery shop was on the main road in from the Eastern Gate, about a hundred steps into the city. Sellers positioned themselves there at odd times during the day, most of them coming and going as their wares were depleted. There was also a guard's station continually manned by Judean personnel, but mostly for show.

Simon was busy turning a wheel in the back of his little shop, an enclosure no more than thirty feet deep. In the front, where he maintained a small desk for customers, pottery of all sorts was stacked on the floor and displayed on wooden shelves that lined the walls. Mark rang a little bell hung in the doorway when he entered, and Simon looked up from his work long enough to see who it was. He continued turning the wheel until he had finished a small cup, but called out to Mark that he would be right there. He washed his hands off and left the wheel, drying them with an already thoroughly clay-colored towel.

Mark had met Simon before on several occasions. When they had built the Upper Room, Mark and his mother had come to Simon's shop for numerous vessels to equip the little food preparation and serving area in the venue. Simon had been a good friend of Mark's grandfather, Miriam's father, and though he was getting on in years, he still plied his trade day after day, supplying the endless need of people for pots, baking dishes, serving platters and other things.

"Mark," said Simon. "Good to see you."

"Simon," said Mark. "The Lord bless you."

"And you."

"I need a small pot. Just big enough to fill a hand washing basin."

"I know. Take your pick," said Simon, pointing to the front corner.

Mark looked in the corner and found a vessel about three hand breadths high and quite slender. "This one will do," he said.

"That didn't take long," said Simon.

"We're not particular," said Mark.

"You may not be, but your mother is. At least, she always has been."

"Not this time," said Mark. "It's not for any special use."

"Well, just so," said Simon.

Mark paid Simon what he wanted for the water pot, and thanked him.

"Oh, and I need—"

"Water. I know. Fill it from one of the jars in the back," he said, ushering Mark back into the shop where three wheels of differing sizes stood, an uncompleted project on each. Along the back were several jars of water. Mark filled his jar from one, but only halfway—there didn't appear to him to be any need of water, actually. It was the jar that was supposed to tell the disciples who were coming that Mark was the man they were to see. After telling

Simon goodbye, Mark exited the shop and went to the side of it, standing in the partial shade of a thatched awning next door. There he waited, without any clue as to how long he might have to be there.

Hundreds of people passed through this particular thoroughfare any day of the year, even more this week, the week of Passover. Mark started to count them just for something to do, but gave up after a half hour or so. He held the pot on his shoulder for half that time, in his arms another few minutes, and then put it down to rest. After another moment he picked it up and hoisted it to his shoulder again.

No sooner had he done so but two men appeared, their shawls over their heads either for maximum protection against the high sun or to keep from being recognized. They approached him casually and one of them spoke.

"Are you to lead us to a room?" he said.

"Yes," said Mark. "Come this way." He kept the pot on his shoulder, turned and went up the street, making a series of turns and finally arriving at his home. He had them wait a moment while he went in and had Rhoda go up and unlock the private, outside entrance.

Then Mark took them around to the outside stairway. Ushering them in, he showed them the food facilities and the places where bowls and utensils were kept.

"I understand you'll be coming tonight."

"Yes," one of them said. "Everything appears to be ready."

"If there's anything else you need, please let us know," said Mark.

"Thank you," said the other disciple. Neither had given him a name. They all understood it was neither required nor necessary.

"Well," said Mark, "I'll go down. You can leave by the outside stairway whenever you're ready. Here is a key to the door." He stood a little nervously to see if there were any more conversation to be had, and deciding there wasn't, he turned and went into the house, closing the inside door behind him. The two disciples presently went out the outside door, locking it, and disappeared back through Jerusalem's bustling streets.

Mark and his mother ate an early supper just before sundown. She finally divulged that she and the other Marys had been in frequent contact with the disciples through a network of other women supporters of the traveling ministry. Mark had not had any clue they had been so involved.

Miriam obviously felt the time had come to tell her little man, the man of the house, the eighteen-year-old—apparently perennially so—young man the details of her involvement. She had kept it almost entirely secret in order to protect herself and him, Mark. She had received regular reports through the other Marys and a dizzying array of connections throughout Galilee and Judea, and she knew a great deal more than Mark about where the Nazarene had been, what he had said, and what he had done. From a little more than a year ago when she had been skeptical about any prophet who would casually travel through Samaria, much less chat with a woman by a well, Miriam had come full circle to being a defacto disciple, supporting possibly in substantial amounts—she didn't tell her son how much she gave—the ministry of Jesus and his disciples.

"I still don't understand what you have been protecting me from," said Mark.

"His enemies."

"Jesus' enemies?"

"Yes. His friends will be in danger from his enemies just like he is."

"Aren't you exaggerating a bit?"

"No."

"What about his grand entrance through the Eastern Gate the first day of this week? I didn't see anybody in danger there."

"No. Not then."

"People don't seem afraid to crowd around him wherever he goes," said Mark.

"No, they don't," said Miriam. "His enemies are afraid of his supporters. But that's going to change soon. It's coming."

"What's coming?"

"I hear things. There are plots."

"Plots? To do what?"

"Stop him."

"Stop him. Like put him in jail? For what?"

"Whatever they can concoct."

"The worst I've heard is that he doesn't let the Sabbath keep him from healing somebody," said Mark. "And how many Sabbath breakers does the Sanhedrin send out temple guards to arrest? None."

"It's more than that, and you know it. The day you heard him say, 'I and the Father are one;' do you think they've forgotten that?"

"Who?"

"The Pharisees, Mark. The Saducees. The lawyers. The rabbis, the priests, everybody on the other side."

"That was more than a year ago."

"They have long memories, son. These people rehearse their grievances every day. They get up thinking about how they can stop him."

Mark thought about that for a moment. He had decided sometime before going to Cyprus that he believed Jesus must be the Messiah, and when he told Uncle Joel and his family what he believed, he had said he felt either something good or something bad would happen. But he had begun to believe that it would be a while until anything did, and in the meantime the national popularity of Jesus of Nazareth had increased—at least, he thought it had.

Admittedly, Mark didn't have a lot of friends on the inside of Jewish government that might tell him in an offhand way what was going on inside the counsel or in the chambers of the high priest. If they were furiously discussing the fate of Jesus, Mark wouldn't know about it. And while many people got their news from their ample social circles, Mark wasn't the most gregarious person in Jerusalem; he was a bit timid, to be honest. His circle of friends was very small. Miriam's network was a giant spider's web with every crisscrossed strand a friend, stretching from distant branches of different trees. Mark's was a very small web in the corner of a windowsill. He didn't hear about much that was going on unless someone coming to the business happened to feel chatty when coming to deal with "Miriam's son." And obviously, in the past three years, he hadn't learned much from his own mother, and she had known a great deal.

Suddenly he realized he had been very much in the dark and had come into the light at what could be a perilous moment.

Toward bedtime, Mark and Miriam were both sitting in the main room of the house, winding down from the day. Mark was re-stringing a stool with a length of coarse twine. Miriam was mending a tear in a linen under-tunic of Mark's. The house was silent.

They had scarcely heard any sounds from the Upper Room, but presently they heard the faint sound of the room's outside door closing. Mark got up silently and went to the atrium. He opened the narrow shutter to a small window near the front door and peeked out. One of the men gathered in the Upper Room had come down the outside stairs and was hurrying up the street in the dark. He disappeared into the maze of Jerusalem's byways. When no one else came out, Mark returned to the main room.

"One of them must have been sent on an errand," Mark said.

Miriam looked up at Mark and then generally toward the upper end of the house. She appeared to have little curiosity about the exiting disciple.

They both returned to their little chores. In another half hour or more Mark had finished the stool seat and tried it out. It creaked as it always had, but the twine was tight and neat and it held weight as it should.

Miriam tied off the ends of the thread on her project, folded it and reached for another, one of her own robes. She inspected it for a hole, and finding it, began working at patching it. Mark moved from the stool back to his chair, relaxed and watched his mother.

"Doesn't seem like the one who's running an errand is coming back," he said. "It's going on an hour."

Miriam didn't look up from her work. "He may have gone on ahead of them."

"Ahead of them where?"

"Gethsemane," she said. "They were going to eat the Passover and then go to the olive garden."

"What for?"

"That's all I know. They said they would need the room until the middle of the evening and then perhaps tomorrow and the next day for a while."

Mark sat a few minutes and watched his mother patiently stitching her robe.

"Do you think about Abba much, mother?" said Mark. He hadn't brought up his father in a long time, assuming that the subject would make Imma sad. But sometimes he longed to talk about him, and there was no one else who had known him but his mother. He paused while she stitched and then smiled gently.

"Yes. Often," she said quietly. "Why? Do you?"

"Sometimes," he said. He thought a moment. "Do you think, if Abba had not—if he had lived, that he might have been, might have become, a God-fearer?"

Miriam tied off her threads and stretched the fabric out to inspect how smooth she had made her repair.

"I don't know. Probably not. Becoming a God-fearer is a big step for a Gentile. Much less a Roman Gentile, I suspect. I was barely more than a girl then. I was content for him to be a soldier and a Roman. And for me to be a Jewish girl. And of course, your very young mother. I wasn't thinking much about years to come."

"He never went with you to synagogue, did he?"

"No. He was usually at the garrison anyway." Miriam folded the garment, laid it aside, and put her hands in her lap. "Why do you ask?"

"I just wondered. I think about him sometimes and wonder what he would be doing now."

"We probably wouldn't be here in Jerusalem, for one thing," said Miriam.

"I guess," said Mark.

They sat another few minutes in comfortable silence, when from upstairs they heard the soft strains of singing, words from a psalm, worshipfully intoned by common men, a melody learned in youth, chanted in a synagogue, echoed in quiet hours of reflection. When the singing ended, a muffled rustling ensued, then steps on the boards above, footfalls on the stairway outside, and the door closing. Then all fell calm.

After another minute Mark got up, placed the newly repaired stool in the corner and stood around as if he were wondering what to do next, although he knew what he intended to do.

"I think I'll go out for a walk. Full moon. Warm." Mark made as if to go.

"No, Mark," said Miriam, looking up at him and sounding every whit like his mother ten years ago, firm and resolved. "They should have their privacy."

"I wasn't—" he started to say, and then stopped. Because he was.

"And no one is to know where they are," his mother added.

"I wasn't going to tell anyone. I just thought—"

"I know," she said.

"It's just that I've seen so little of him. Them. And they were right here, in our house."

"Perhaps tomorrow."

"Of course."

Mark sat down again. They were both silent. Miriam sat with her head cradled on a cushion at the top of her chair back, her eyes closed in thought. Mark stared at a candle on the table. Miriam broke the revery when she opened her eyes and got up.

"I've had a long day," she said. "Going to bed."

"I suppose I will, too," said Mark.

Miriam kissed Mark's cheek and wished him a good night, then went down the hall to her chamber. Mark blew out the candles on the table in the center of the room and carried the remaining candle with him to his bed chamber, closing the door.

The house was dark and soon became quiet as Mark and Miriam both got into their beds. Miriam sought sleep. Mark lay quietly until he was certain his mother was soundly slumbering. Then he got up, put a dark robe over his light nightshirt, silently slipped on his sandals and tiptoed toward the door. On second thought, realizing that the front door often made entirely too much noise when opened and shut, even carefully, Mark went to his window. Opening the shutters, he hoisted himself up, crawled through into the back yard, leaving the shutters ajar, went around beside the

Upper Room stairs, and emerged into the street.

10
Mount of Olives, 2nd Watch

A brilliant vernal moon cast distinct shadows from the olive branches onto the pebbly surface below them and the worn paths between, bathing in silver the figures walking or reposed in clearings here and there, and hiding any who might have crouched under a tree's low limbs.

Eight of the eleven men who had hurried on foot with their leader around the Kidron Valley and up the side of Olivet were reclining sleepily in the moonlight, diligently trying to do as bidden, to remain awake and to pray. Their master was deeper into the grove in another clearing, having taken three of the eleven with him, while he went yet some distance again and knelt, then fell upon the ground, praying.

Back near the Eastern Gate of Jerusalem, just outside the wall, a lone figure clad in a brief robe over his nightshirt hurried down the hill and saw in the lustrous light of moon and stars that he was coming up behind what appeared to be a detachment of soldiers, temple guards or the high priest's men, from the look of them, going the same direction as he. Curious about their purpose in going out of the city but not wanting to approach them or even give away his presence, Mark dashed to his right and down into the Kidron, a narrow basin more like a gigantic ditch than a small valley. He dodged gravestones and other obstacles as he ran crouching through the rocky notch, then ascending on the other side toward the road the soldiers would be treading before long. Having gotten ahead of them around a curve from where they could see, he left the road and ran up the hill, soon coming to the edge of Gethsemane.

He stopped and listened, hearing only the sounds of the night. Then he disappeared between the trees and made his way into the grove. When he came near a clearing and spotted six or eight men to his left sitting on the ground, silent, he stopped at some distance and concealed himself under the nearest tree, shrouded in its deep obscurity.

To his right, Mark could hear a voice nearby, plaintive yet strong, not near enough to detect words. He remained motionless at the trunk of the tree, crouching on one knee, waiting for whatever might happen.

Momentarily a clatter of staves and trudging feet interrupted the serenity of the garden. Mark peeked through the branches and saw the soldiers and others he had avoided on the Olivet road, emerging through the trees at the entrance to the garden and coming toward the eight men in the clearing. The eight got up apprehensively and assumed a kind of loosely defensive posture, not knowing what the purpose of the detachment and its associated little mob might be.

At the same time, Mark heard the rustling of feet from his right, and saw Jesus and three other men coming out of their copse into the pathway and walking without hesitation toward the rest of the men, obviously the disciples, who were being questioned by the soldiers. The group was still too far away for Mark to hear much of anything being said, so he ventured to leave his deeply shaded niche and cross to another, closer tree.

There was movement in the cluster, confused scrambling, among the detachment as well as the disciples.

"Put away your sword!" said a strong voice, followed by a comment softer and indiscernible.

Mark attempted another silent dash to yet a closer tree, hoping to hear what was being said.

Suddenly there were raised voices, a cacophony of vocalizations;

the disciples began to scatter, while several soldiers tried to seize them as they did. Three of the disciples ran past where Mark was secreted in the shadows, and Mark stepped out behind them, suddenly realizing the soldiers intended to arrest some or all of them.

He found himself at the tail end of the disciples racing into the depths of the garden, but not far enough ahead of the soldiers pursuing them and him. No doubt the disciples knew the garden's paths and knew that they would come to its edge and be able to burst beyond onto the hillside, where they, unburdened by armor or swords, would be able to outrun their pursuers handily. Mark knew he could, as well.

Only, in his haste to get away from his house, he had not tied up his sandals securely enough. They had almost come off during his dash across the Kidron Valley, and the lacing of one of them now had come loose, a half knot soon no knot at all, the thongs unwinding to the sole.

As his sandal came loose, it came off, and Mark tripped in the pathway, scrambling to get up but feeling suddenly an iron grip on his ankle. A temple guard quickly dragged him back down to the ground and attempted to keep him on his stomach and bind his hands behind him.

Infused with the sudden strength of terror and the frantic fury of a cornered animal, Mark struggled free, clawing at the ground in front of him to rise from all fours to his feet. But the guard was upon him again, using Mark's robe against him, trying to hold him with the woolen fabric around his waist.

Mark twisted and turned, throwing his arms back toward his assailant. The robe, which had not been tied around his waist, came off one arm, freeing him to attempt to push away from the man, who was meanwhile preparing to fall on Mark headlong and hold him to the ground. When he did, Mark, at the moment very glad to be an agile, young man, rolled with lightning speed to one side, and the guard fell on his face in the dust of the path. The moment gave Mark just enough time to get up, clutching a tree branch and skittering away a few feet.

The soldier recovered and began to get to his knees, barking out some order about remaining still.

But Mark had spotted his sandal at hand's length near the guard's feet, and in an instant had grabbed it, and tried to slip between the clutching claws of the guard and the scratching branches of the tree. The guard caught Mark's robe and held on tightly, and as Mark squirmed and pivoted, the robe came off in the guard's hand. Still on his knees, the guard swiped around with his other hand and caught the light fabric of Mark's nightshirt, which ripped as Mark desperately sought purchase with his feet, one of them in a sandal and the other bare. He managed two struggling steps away from the guard, at the cost of his light garment, which tore off his shoulders and around his waist, leaving him with a band of white linen which he grasped with his free hand. Thus freed, though virtually naked, he bolted away, dodging left and right to lose the soldier and get to the garden's edge.

Running unevenly, one foot shod and the other not, he came down uncomfortably on a rock here and there, but fear enabled him to ignore or endure the pain and make it to the end of the grove, where he emerged into a small field. Mark risked a brief look over his shoulder to see how close his pursuer was, and was surprised to see no one. He risked stopping for two seconds to listen, and realized that the guard had given up the chase. Still having no feeling of security, he ran some distance further, to some cedar trees where he turned again and found himself all alone and no longer hunted.

Where he could still see the edge of Gethsemane, he sat on the ground and laced on his other sandal, tying it tightly. When he got up, he inspected the pittance of material left of his nightshirt, and he tied it about his waist the best he could, realizing he was gird in little more than a robber would be when hung on one of the Romans' ghastly crosses. In fact, some of them were not even afforded the scant dignity of a girdle of linen against the stares of the gawking crowds.

Mark's return to Jerusalem's gate, which he could see a few hundred yards away, would not be difficult to make unobserved, if he traversed the Kidron again, between scrub brush and tombstones. But entering Jerusalem at this time of night would be less anonymous, especially if he used the Eastern Gate. Besides, the soldiers in Gethsemane were probably headed back toward the city at this moment, and certainly they would return through the Eastern Gate.

Looking farther south, Mark saw that the Dung Gate seemed to be without any traffic at this hour, which had to be well into the second watch, perhaps nearing midnight. Even better, it was below the corner of the eastern wall and was cast in shadow from the moon. So Mark sprang up and headed down the hill, crossing the Olivet road and entering the valley, weaving here and there around obstacles but otherwise making a beeline to the Dung Gate above him.

A short road led up to the gate from the edge of the Kidron Valley, and he sprinted as fast as he could toward the darkened entrance to the city. The gate was not normally guarded, and wasn't tonight, and Mark raced through its narrow opening, startling a man coming out with a pack of some sort on his back, who wheeled and cursed at Mark and made some crude reference to his state of undress.

Mark knew the streets from here to his home and picked what he thought would be the least likely ones to have anyone walking in them, which was already unlikely at this hour. Still, he met the occasional resident, whom he shocked by his appearance, as he attempted to use his hands to hide his face, which he turned away as much as possible.

It took him a few minutes to reach home, which was mercifully close to Jerusalem's eastern wall to begin with, and he darted into the shaded, darkened area between his home and his neighbors' house, back alongside the Upper Room stairs, into the back yard, and up into his window, closing the shutters behind him.

Trembling hands took off his sandals and set them quietly under his bed. He stood and untied his shred of a nightshirt, realizing he would have to hide and then dispose of it so as not to give away to his mother his evening's activity. He had bought it from a seller in the market streets and could buy another in a day or two.

He lay down quietly on his bed, still heaving from his run but trying to breathe through as wide a mouth possible and to control the rate to keep from making noise. His eyes fixed on the ceiling, his thoughts went to the scenes just burned in his mind from Gethsemane. Why were the soldiers there? Obviously, they were there to arrest Jesus, but how did they know to go there? Who told them?

In his mind, Mark counted the men he had seen sitting or lounging in the clearing. A group of three, a cluster of four, and one to the side. Or was it a group of four, another cluster of four, and one other? He thought it was eight, not nine. How many came from the right with Jesus? He was certain there were only three of them. That made eleven disciples, plus Jesus. Where was the other one?

Then he remembered one disciple had left the Upper Room early in the evening, just after it got dark. He hadn't returned, that Mark knew of, before the rest of the group left together. Perhaps he had gotten caught by the temple authorities. Maybe they were on the lookout for any of the group, Jesus or the twelve, and someone recognized him, even though it was dark. Maybe they had made him tell them where Jesus was. Mark didn't have any answers for certain.

As his breathing came back to nearly normal, he found himself with a feeling of foreboding, worrying about what would happen to Jesus. And had they caught any of the disciples? The three he was following got away, but had the others?

What would the temple authorities do with Jesus? Question him? Scold him? Threaten him? Certainly they had nothing to charge him with—did they? Would they come out at midnight with swords and staves and a small mob because he healed people on a Sabbath or two? Would they even take those measures for someone who cryptically talked about himself and the Heavenly Father in the same breath?

Perhaps. But at the moment, it seemed absurd to Mark. Whatever they imagined that Jesus had done, it seemed wildly exaggerated for them to arrest him over it. But there was nothing imaginary about what had just happened to him across the Kidron Valley. Jesus was in the grasp of the temple guards, and in the morning he might face investigation and questioning at the very least. Surely they wouldn't be able to mount any charges against Jesus successfully. Surely he would be released with stern reprimands for whatever it was they objected to.

If he was the Messiah, perhaps this was the critical moment. The time of a turning tide. The recognition of his calling.

11
Streets of Jerusalem, Dawn

The disc of the imposing moon that had cast shadows as if at midday during the second watch had almost sunk below the horizon as dawn approached on the fifth day. Cooks preparing food in double portions in preparation for the Sabbath were already up and working throughout the city, kneading dough for extra bread, preparing fresh vegetables and fruits, and making certain there was sufficient drink, water and otherwise.

Miriam was also up and around, first supervising Rhoda, but now nervously standing near the outside gate. Mark had just gotten up, having been fitful in attempts at sleep since just past midnight. He emerged from his chamber to find only Rhoda in the house. She told him she thought Miriam had gone out the front door.

Mark peered through the window near the door and saw his mother with neighbors. Other people were moving hurriedly in the street, appearing to be either going to, or coming from, the same place. As he watched his mother engaged in conversation, the first light of dawn became streaks of gold over the rooftops and illuminated the sycamore trees. She was speaking in urgent tones with a couple from down the street, who were gesticulating in unsettled excitement. Miriam threw her hand to her mouth to stifle a gasp. She shook her head, but the couple nodded theirs.

Mark couldn't hear the words, but he knew the neighbors bore distressing news. He could easily guess what it was about, though his mother didn't know what he knew. When the neighbors had gone on down the street toward their home, Miriam stayed at the gate, staring up the road in the direction of Herod's palace.

Several people came by, headed that way. Miriam stopped them. Again, Mark watched, unable to hear but seeing that his mother was asking them what they knew. They spoke to her briefly and then hurried on.

Miriam turned and came back toward the front door. Mark backed away and went down the hall until he heard her come in. Then he wheeled around and came toward the entrance again, stifling a yawn.

"Mother. You're up," he said.

"Yes. But Rhoda will be fine without me for a while. I have to go somewhere."

"Where?" he said.

"There are people gathering near the Praetorium. I'm going there—"

"The Praetorium? What for?" Mark was genuinely surprised. He knew the conversation outside had to have been about what must have taken place after what happened in Gethsemane, but he had thought Jesus would have been released by now.

"Oh, Mark! They've arrested Jesus!" said Miriam, her self-control unraveling.

"What? No!"

"Yes. People in the street are saying the Sanhedrin is involved and that he has even been taken in front of Pilate." Miriam nearly broke down saying this. Jewish authorities brought cases to Pilate when they were seeking death penalties.

"That can't be!" said Mark. He almost divulged his thinking of a few hours ago, based on what he had seen, but stopped himself before doing so.

"I'm going with you," said Mark.

"No. I'll be fine."

"I'm sure you will," he said, "but I want to go, too."

"Someone needs to stay here."

"Rhoda can handle the house by herself," said Mark.

"Perhaps, but I would feel better if you were here and in charge," said Miriam.

"Mother," said Mark assertively, "I'm concerned with what may be happening to Jesus, too."

Miriam peered into Mark's eyes and realized he was right, but she pressed her case.

"It may not be as bad as people think," she told him, trying to sound convincing not only to him, but also herself. "I'm just going to go for a little while. To be there. To show my support. There probably won't be anything to see anyway. It may all be for nothing."

"I don't think you believe yourself," said Mark.

"Please, Mark," she implored him. "Stay. I'll come back with whatever news there is to tell."

"Mother—"

"Mark," she said, with newly recovered resolve. And the conversation was over.

Mark watched his mother leave and walk quickly up the street and then west toward the government buildings a mile or so distant. His heart was beating fast. He looked back at the house, and then up the street. He considered his options. If he waited five minutes or so and then took another route, he wouldn't catch up with his mother on the way, and once there, the crowd might be large enough that he would be able to get lost in it so that she wouldn't see him. Then again, it might not be that large, and he might wind up in the same place by accident. And if she returned home before he did, she would know that he had not honored her wishes. While he was not a child anymore, the commandment to honor her still applied.

In agitated displeasure Mark stayed. He stood around the

kitchen a few minutes watching Rhoda, who now and then cast an eye his direction, clearly hoping he would go about his business somewhere else. Mark finally got the message and left the kitchen, going to the main room.

Finally, it struck him that someone might have come back to the city and gone to the Upper Room. It was still theirs to occupy, and they had the key. Mark turned his ear toward the upstairs of the house and listened intently. There was no sound. And there might not be, even if someone were there.

He crept up the stairs to the room and listened at the door. Nothing. He pressed down on the latch. It was not locked. He opened it slowly, almost furtively, as if he didn't have a right to be there, and he peeked in. There was no one there.

Where did they go when they ran all directions from Gethsemane? Mark hadn't stopped to think about that since just seven hours or so ago when he frantically freed himself from his pursuer's grasp and hobbled out into the fields south of the olive garden. The three disciples in front of him had run out of sight that direction. They may have gotten to the road going around east and continued on it to Bethphage or even as far as Bethany. Perhaps the others had gone north around the mount, hiding in the hillside. Maybe everyone had avoided the city except him.

At any rate, the disciples weren't here.

Mark returned to the kitchen and took a piece of bread from a covered tray. He was hungry but too disquieted to sit down to a meal, but he thought he should eat something instead of letting a griping stomach make worse the sense of unease he felt. He sat in the main room in a chair, stuffed a pillow behind his neck, munched at the bread with closed eyes, and not intending to, he gave in to the sleep he had unwillingly dodged during the previous six hours.

When he woke, it was to the sound of his mother's return. He stirred at the noise of the front door and opened his eyes when

Miriam swept down the hall and to her chamber. He could hear her crying.

Mark got up at once and went down the hall. His mother was on her knees in front of her bed, her head in her hands on the bedside. At first he thought she was praying, but she was sobbing almost uncontrollably. He waited a moment and then spoke.

"Mother?"

Miriam brought herself under some semblance of control and then turned to Mark. She seemed to be thinking of saying something, but the look on her face was communicating with eloquent anguish. Finally, words formed.

"They're putting him to death," she said, almost quietly and with a trembling from deep in her soul.

"What?!" said Mark. He looked outside, saw a shadow from a tree in the front and deduced the time. While he was getting the sleep he had missed from the dark hours, about three hours had passed. Whatever was going on at the Praetorium had apparently proceeded in rapid order.

"What do you mean, 'putting him to death,'" he said, as if he didn't know the meaning of the words.

"On a *cross*, Mark. On a *cross!*" And she broke down again.

"Where, mother?! Where?" Mark was urgent and insistent.

"Golgotha," she managed to utter.

"I have to go," said Mark, bending over to re-tie his sandals. This time, Miriam made no attempt to stop him.

Mark ran down the street a short way and then veered to the east, navigating the lanes until he came to the Dung Gate, where the previous evening he had sneaked back into the city unobserved. He realized he would probably be able to get to the north of the city faster by taking the road around the city wall, than by trying to go through the Second Quarter district and its cluttered and narrow byways, already packed with market-goers at this hour. Once on the road, he picked up speed, soon passing the Eastern Gate, the temple mount to his left, the top of Herod's temple gleaming in the morning sun.

Once past the Sheep Gate he passed the Pool of Bethesda, and it occurred to him to wonder, even as his feet pounded the dusty road, why Jesus, who healed lame men and, at least from what he had heard, had raised a man from his tomb over in Bethany, couldn't keep himself from being crucified if it came to it. Why?

It was just another few hundred yards to Golgotha as Mark rounded the curve where the road to Samaria cut off to the north. He could see the rocky outcropping in the distance, and an unexpectedly large crowd surrounding it. Hundreds, perhaps a few thousand people had gathered, most of them obviously from inside the city. Likely, they had come out the Fish Gate. They were packed tightly around the ghoulish looking hill, that had gouges in the white rock that looked like eye sockets in a skull.

Atop the hill were several soldiers accomplishing their gruesome task. They had already pounded the long nails in their victims' wrists and ankles and had hoisted the roughhewn instruments of execution into holes in the ground, which kept the crosses erect while their occupants slowly died from exhaustion and asphyxiation. Mark could just tell Jesus from the other two of the three men on humiliating public display. The Nazarene was in the center. The other two he didn't recognize, which told him they were not disciples. Perhaps they were two men already awaiting their executions. The disciples had all gotten away without capture.

Mark had found a place on a little rise where he first stood and then sat on a rock and rested from his running. There was really no purpose in trying to get closer. The mob was thick. Near the front were Jewish authorities of one sort or another. Mark could make out the distinctive dress of Pharisees clustered around the cross area, though being kept from creating congestion around the soldiers. On the upper side of the hill were a number of women, crying on one another's shoulders and comforting each other as somehow they managed to observe what was going on.

Mark found himself wondering how people had come to this point, this state of dulled natural senses, such that they could, and would, gaze on the inhumanity of conquerors intent on using the terror of pain and agony to strike fear into subjugated peoples. Yet, he was here himself, unable to turn away, not inured to it but desensitized by having seen it before, this awful, barbarous savagery of Romans, not different in any degree from the merciless brutality of the cruel and inhuman kingdoms they had overthrown. The soldiers themselves, charged with executing an ongoing line of malefactors, whether their victims were truly deserving of death or merely hapless targets of political censure, were obligated by necessity to toughen themselves, to develop callused hearts, if they were not already soulless monsters who had signed on to the army for the very purpose of venting fiendish violence on others. And Mark, like probably many of the onlookers, was horrified, appalled, yet fascinated, even riveted, a living exemplar of the terrible contradiction that was humanity.

How long he stood there he didn't know; he lost sense of time. It was long enough to hear several cries from the dying men, at least two from Jesus, though indistinguishable in meaning from this distance.

Some soldiers marched by him, coming from the general direction of the execution site. Crowds had given them generous berth. In one of several squads of soldiers coming by where he was standing, one of the men eyed Mark with curious interest. In his mind, Mark imagined that this was one of the soldiers who came to Gethsemane, though no Romans had been in that detachment. But the danger of the moment made him doubt himself and attempt to turn away without seeming to be doing so suspiciously. The soldiers marched on.

Getting this close to the hideous event, he had been trembling, both from the unaccustomed exertion and also from the sudden sight of the execution in progress. Now recovered from the running, a sense of empty despondency had come over him, a dark and threatening cloud. Staring unblinking at the scene in the distance, he closed his eyes, and with a sudden and overwhelming shudder they poured torrents of grief.

Mark sprang up, panicked in dread and dismay, turning away from the horrific sight and hurrying back the way he had come, along the road around Jerusalem's wall. Some were retreating by the same path, still others hastening to glimpse what they had heard was happening at the place of the skull, eager to cringe for themselves at the abominable sight.

In a half hour's time he had come back inside the city and dodged the glut of the daily crowd, probably not many of whom were oblivious to what was happening a mile or so away on a hideous hill. As he looked into the faces of the people milling about he wondered how many of them had thought that Jesus of Nazareth was the long awaited Messiah.

As he dodged carts and tripped occasionally on the cobblestones John Mark held back tears as he realized the impact of his own crumbling expectations. Just as he and probably many others were coming to believe that Jesus might be the one who was to come, Mark fought against the descending disappointment that this messiah was only one of many who had risen to popularity only to be squelched by the vehement opposition of his own people and stamped out by the violent suppression of their hated rulers.

A crossbeam in a carpenter's shop along the way stood against an outside wall, an ironic reminder of the Romans' stiff penalties for murder and sedition. Perhaps the two men being tortured with Jesus today were deserving of such punishment. Doubtless the swift and awful sanctions deterred the commission of such crimes and stanched any flow of insurgency. There was, and had been since Rome had established rule in the country, an undercurrent of unrest, but any flood of rebellion had been kept at bay by the prominent and frightful sight of crosses that frequently punctuated the avenues outside Jerusalem and other major cities where the suffering souls and still corpses of criminals fearfully festooned the roadsides, a grim reminder to bow to the will of the conquerors.

But what of Jesus? As far as Mark knew, his only rebellion had been against the hypocrisy of the Pharisees and the abuses of the priests. Had he posed any threat to the unwelcome outsiders or rallied Zealots or encouraged insurrectionists? Were his sermons about the excellency of love and the shame of immorality any justification for his death?

At the gate of his home Mark hurried in, hastening to his chamber, sitting unstably on his bed and burying his head in his hands.

He had sat a few minutes when he felt a presence at the door. His mother walked in silently, sat beside him and put her arm around his shoulder. They trembled and cried together until they had no tears left. In an hour or so they both thought to themselves, though neither said so, that it was probably all over by now.

Shadows lengthened through the afternoon, a deep cloudiness that never produced rain cast the already shaded home into a singular gloom, and the time passed until the veil of night descended slowly and the house became murky as well as silent. Miriam and Mark sat speechless in their main room, having not risen to light candles, which at the moment seemed the appropriate inaction. Rhoda tiptoed about in respect, and it occurred to Mark that he didn't know whether his mother had spoken to her and she was cognizant of the day's events, though he believed she must be.

Presently Rhoda entered carrying a candle and lit the other lights in the room as she apparently had in the other rooms. Quietly she spoke to Miriam.

"Ma'am, have some bread at least."

"Thank you, Rhoda. We will in a moment," said Miriam. She sat another few minutes as Rhoda exited and went to the kitchen. Mark looked up. Miriam was looking at him with soundless despair. They read each other's grieving thoughts, and then Miriam got up and went into the kitchen. Mark soon followed, with little enthusiasm but conscious of his need to eat something. He had not consumed anything since early that morning.

In the kitchen, they nibbled at this and that, as did Rhoda, and they drank some water. No one talking, for fear that if they did, speech would emanate in torrents of distress and hopelessness.

In the midst of this pall of despondency a knocking came at the front door. Rhoda put down her food and hurried out of the room. In a minute she returned with a curious look on her face.

"Ma'am, two men are here. Two of the disciples," she said.

Instantly, Miriam got up. "Let them in!" she said.

"I did. They're in the front room," said Rhoda.

Miriam hastily left the kitchen and went toward the front, where the two men were standing. She didn't know all the disciples' names, but she greeted them with a new flow of tears, which she wiped away with her hands as she met them.

"Miriam," said one of them, "the rest of us are outside nearby. We'd like to go back to the Upper Room. We need a place to—hide. We hate to ask you, but—"

"It's yours," she said quickly. "As long as you need it." A sudden look of concern came over her face. "Are they after you?" she said.

"Probably," they said. "Perhaps. We don't know. All of us escaped the high priest's detachment last night. Except—"

"Except the Master," said the other disciple. "We assume you know everything."

"Yes. I know," she said quietly. Feeling Mark join her by her side, she said, "We know."

"We don't know how long we'll need to stay. A few days, perhaps—"

"It doesn't matter," she insisted. "Stay. No one will know."

"Thank you."

"It's Miriam."

"Miriam," the disciples said. "And we know you and the other Marys are, were, his supporters. We know this is a dark day for you as well."

"You still have your key?" she asked.

"Yes."

"Lock the outside door," she said. "You can come down into the house if you need something. Don't hesitate to do it. I will tell Rhoda to tend to your needs. And if there's any news, one of us will bring it."

"Thank you, Miriam."

The two left by the front door, went through the gate, and were joined by seven others who in the rapidly deepening gloom appeared to emerge from nowhere and joined them in scurrying up the stairs on the side of the house. Soon they were in, the door was locked, and only occasional, muffled sounds indicated to Mark or Miriam that they were there. Outside, what little light produced by the few, small candles they lit to help them see themselves was blocked from any outside view by the closed shutters and the woolen curtains on the inside.

Mid evening, an hour or so before he would even attempt sleep, Mark heard Rhoda coming down the hall from the staircase to the

Upper Room. She had checked on the disciples as Miriam had requested at the third hour. She came into the main room where Mark and Miriam were occupying themselves without enthusiasm.

"Sir," she said to Mark, "Peter wants to see you."

Mark got up immediately and went down the hall, ascending the stairs in the dark and opening the door to the large chamber. A burly, familiar man was standing nearby, waiting for him. Peter.

"John Mark," he said. "I'm Peter."

"I know," said Mark. "I've seen you before, though we haven't met."

"First, thank you for your hospitality. Uh, we're all grateful to your mother and you. For everything. And for a place to stay."

"We'll do anything for you. Anything," Mark said firmly.

"You've been helpful," repeated Peter, seeming to be at a sudden loss for words, no doubt still stunned by the events of the day, as all of them had to be. Mark looked behind Peter at the clustered disciples, whose faces combined bewilderment, fear, and dazed sadness. A few of them nodded in agreement with Peter's words.

"Now," said Peter, "our presence here has to remain a secret."

"Of course," said Mark.

"Please. No one outside this house must know."

"Of course," said Mark, insistently.

"One or two of us may leave now and then. We expect to provide our own food for as long as we're up here, and we'll need to go out for whatever we need."

"Whatever we have we will share with you," said Mark. "It's the least we can do."

"Thank you," said Peter, "We won't burden you. There are eleven of us. We can't expect you to feed us."

"We can help, at the very least."

"Thank you," said Peter again. "For now, we could use a little juice and water, perhaps a few loaves of bread. We won't be able to go to the market until tomorrow."

It was now some four hours into the Sabbath. Mark thought of Rhoda's shopping early that morning as well as the previous day and believed the household stores would be sufficient to supply them all with enough food and drink until the First Day, about twenty hours away.

"Anything we can do for you?" Mark said awkwardly.

Peter turned to see if anyone else had something to say. "No," he said, turning back. "If you will just send Rhoda back up with a little food. Most of us haven't eaten since last night, when we were here."

"I'll send her right away," said Mark.

"Again," said Peter, "uh, thank you."

Mark thought about the sounds from the Upper Room last night, the Psalm the group had sung, and their exit after dark. He thought about their gathering in Gethsemane and he started to blurt out to Peter that he had seen them there, but he thought better of it. If he ever revealed that story to anyone, how he had spied on them, had run when they did, and had nearly been caught, it would be a long, long time before he did.

Instead of speaking again, Mark turned and left the room.

12
The Upper Room, the Sabbath

A colorful, glorious sunrise, unsympathetic to the bereaved, ushered in Sabbath's morning, not countenanced by the eleven huddled here and there throughout the Upper Room, still slumbering restlessly in spite of exhaustion. Mark, awake before light, treaded softly up the stairs and tapped on the door lightly, with no response. He peeked in, and seeing no one stirring he backed out as if to go when Peter, lying on a cushion near the door, turned over abruptly.

"Is that you, John Mark?" Peter whispered.

"Yes."

Peter got up quietly so as not to disturb the others, and came to the door. "I must have looked toward the door a dozen times in the night, thinking I heard soldiers coming. A dream, perhaps."

"I'm sorry," said Mark. "I thought I should check on you. Can I get you something?"

"No. Thank you," said Peter. "We'll be fine. Nothing much to do but wait out the Sabbath."

"Rhoda will bring some food in a little while," said Mark. "I'm going to go out and see if anyone is talking about—you know, everything."

Peter looked at Mark with appreciation and an expression of heartbreaking bereavement.

"I know, son" he said, and he nodded then shook his head in acknowledgment, and then shook it slowly in continuing disbelief. "If you hear news, when you come back, come right in. Just be one of us."

"I will," said Mark, smiling, complimented by his inclusion, and he left.

Mark passed his mother's bed chamber on the way back through the house. She hadn't gotten up yet. Rhoda was in the kitchen already—when did she sleep? Mark sat down for a few bites and sips of something, thanked Rhoda, and then left.

Out in the streets the silence of the Sabbath reigned, though a few people made their way here and there, probably going to houses of other family members, or to synagogue, or even to the temple courts. Most people moving about were alone or in pairs, moving with dispatch but quietly, even reverently, attempting to keep the Sabbath with their very demeanor.

But a few knots of talkers stood here and there, and Mark slowed and tried to catch the conversation of one of them, four men beside a closed seller's shop on a corner. He was afraid to stop, to presume to join a group of strangers to listen in. Instead, he drifted slowly by, feigning indifference.

"They didn't have to," said one man.

"Why not?" said another.

"Already dead," said the first.

Mark turned the corner and then stopped, out of view.

"Took the other two a while, though," said the first man. "They broke their legs, though, and then they went pretty quick."

"I hate it," said another of the men. "There's no mercy in it. At least if a man is stoned, it's quick."

"That's the whole point," said the fourth man. "Draw it out, make people look, scare them."

The rest of the conversation devolved into a debate over Roman rule and bad governors. Mark walked on. He worked his way toward the center of the city, taking smaller streets hoping to encounter others talking about the previous day's events. He noticed that few women were about; the talk on the streets was mostly among men. Unexpectedly, he spotted one of Joel's customers strolling away from the general area of the temple. Mark waved at him as he approached, and the man stopped.

"Ezra," said Mark, hoping he had remembered the man's name correctly.

"Mark, is it?" said Ezra.

"Yes, sir," said Mark. "How is your business?"

"The Lord gives me success," said Ezra. "And yours?"

"The same, sir." Mark hadn't planned how he might bring up the subject of the moment, and it occurred to him that Ezra might be one of those glad to see Jesus gotten rid of. He would have to choose his words carefully.

"What do you hear this morning of yesterday?" he said.

"I presume you mean about the Nazarene."

"Yes, sir."

"A terrible thing, terrible thing," said Ezra, his sympathies still unclear to Mark. He might be stating his feelings about the general upset of the city, as if he were sorry that Jesus had stirred people up so.

"It is," said Mark. "Do you know anything more?" More than what, he didn't say.

"Not much," said Ezra. "They took him down—took all of them down—before sundown, of course. Nobody came for the two thieves, but several people were there to take the Nazarene's body away. That's all I know." After a pause, he repeated, "Terrible thing."

Mark nodded. He was serious and solemn. The two stood there a moment, and then Ezra made his excuses and walked on. Mark went another block or two and then doubled back, arriving at the house in another half hour or more.

He entered the front door to the sound of voices in the main room. Mary, another Mary and Sarah sat with his mother, passing along what they knew.

"Mother," Mark said.

"You were up early," said Miriam.

"I was out, trying to find out—anything."

"Mary came a while ago. She's already been up to see Peter and the others."

Mark sat down on the edge of a chair near his mother and looked at the other women. "What have you found out?" he said quietly.

"How much do you know already?" said the first Mary.

"Just that they crucified him like a common criminal," said Mark.

"Joseph, the Arimathean, took the body."

"The councilman?" said Mark, somewhat surprised. He knew the name, though not the man.

"Yes."

"I heard he strongly objected to the Sanhedrin's decision," said the other Mary. "I know others did, too, but they were too scared of the majority to say so."

"Where did he bury him," said Mark, in an even more somber tone.

"Joseph had a tomb on the north side of the city. He had it cut out for himself, but he used it for Jesus."

"Do you know where it is, exactly?"

"I do," said the first Mary.

"No use going there," said the other Mary. "They have guards there."

"What in the world for?" said Mark.

"They think the disciples are going to go steal his body," said the first Mary. "A friend of mine knows a boy who knows somebody in the Praetorium. He says our chief priests begged Pilate to post guards to keep Jesus' followers from taking his body. The priests thought his disciples would claim he was alive."

"Surely they'd at least let you see the tomb, though," Mark said.

"From a distance, maybe. Probably wouldn't let you get close."

Mark slumped back in the chair, let out a deep sigh and closed his eyes, shaking his head back and forth slowly.

"Anybody who saw it, anybody who knows anything about a crucifixion, knows he's not alive," Mark said.

"Where were you?" said Sarah.

"On a little rise east of the site. I couldn't get much closer."

"Do you know about Judas?" she said.

"Who is Judas?"

"One of the twelve," she said, a little surprised Mark didn't know.

"I didn't know many of them by name," said Mark. "I'm just getting to, now. Now that they're here, upstairs."

"Oh," said Sarah. "Well, Peter and John told me it was Judas who led the temple guards to where Jesus was, so they could arrest him." She spoke with a low voice of shame.

"One of his own disciples!?" Mark thought of the detachment in the garden. One of them must have been Judas.

"Yes," said Sarah.

"We can't understand why he would do such a thing," said the second Mary. "But the other eleven said they weren't surprised."

"Well, he'd better run fast and far while he can," said Mark.

Mary, Mary, Sarah and Miriam looked at each other quietly.

"His body was found just before dawn," said Sarah.

"His body?" whispered Mark.

"Yes. At the bottom of that little cliff on the south side of the city."

"You mean the one above Hinnom?" said Mark.

"Yes. He had a rope around his neck."

Mark's jaw dropped. "You don't think the disciples—I mean, they were here, all of them, all last night. They still are—aren't they, mother?"

"Yes, Mark, they're all up there."

"They didn't do it," said Sarah. "Judas did it himself. That's what I heard, anyway."

Mark found himself wondering where they heard all they had. Friends of friends of somebody who knew. Connections within the inner sanctums. And a speed of communication that almost defied belief.

"Why did he do it?" he added, more as a statement than a question. It didn't make sense to him.

The second Mary said, "They paid him. The chief priests."

"Paid him!?" said Mark. A look of disgust and then confusion crossed his face. "Still, to follow him all this time, see everything —what could possess him?"

Then Miriam said, "Maybe it was just that." The others looked at her. "Something possessed him."

Mark shook his head and stared into the ceiling. "I just can't believe anyone that close to him could do it. And for *money!*"

The group was silent. Finally, Mark got up. "I think I'll go talk to Peter."

"We told them everything we know."

"As mother said, yes," said Mark. "But Peter invited me to come up if I wanted to." Mark went to the door and turned back.

"I like him. Peter."

"We do, too," said one of the Marys.

Mark went down the hall and up the stairs to the Upper Room, at least for a while the hideaway of the remaining eleven disciples.

A few others had joined the eleven, familiar faces from Jesus' other visits to Jerusalem, probably close friends of Sarah and the Marys. Mark sat with them all, mostly listening, wondering what would happen now that it was all coming to an end. Would they go back to their former lives? Would they be fugitives? Or would the chief priests, who had gotten rid of Jesus, now be satisfied that they had taken the air out of the movement, and ignore Jesus' followers unless they began stirring up things themselves?

In an hour, Rhoda appeared at the door with a tray of food for the men, followed by Miriam, who had another. Mark excused himself and came back down, retreating to the solace of his bed chamber. A little table stood in a corner and a stool beside it. The light came in through a window and cast a sharp, square beam across an unlit candlestick, a small pot with a sprig of herbs, a stack of a dozen or so sheets of papyrus paper, a tiny ink pot with a cork in it, and a quill, stained from almost daily use.

Mark sat at the table, inked the quill, and began to put down tersely what he had seen and heard. As usually he did, he employed his Greek, learned from his infancy in the streets of Alexandria, from his father who spoke it as his first language, and from his mother.

There was a poignancy about Mark's use of Greek. He spoke it in the course of business when dealing with people not from Judea or Galilee, and there was nothing special about that. But he had learned its rhythm and meter, its imagery and lilt, from his father, whose image in his mind by now was beyond dim, but the sound of whose voice had never left the ear of his mind. His mother had adopted Tulio's Greek as the tongue of their Alexandrian home, the home so early and cruelly struck by the loss of her soldier husband. When Mark spoke Greek, he heard his father, deep in his heart, and it comforted him.

ЄСТАΥΡΟСΑΝ ΑΥΤΟΝ СΗΜЄΡΟΝ, he began: They crucified him on the day of sacrifice.

13
The Upper Room, the First Day

Miriam rose early on the First Day, a strange peace having enabled her to sleep soundly despite the tragedy and trial of spirit of the preceding twelve hours. She had wakened before dawn and prepared food for the eleven, taking it up to them even as the sun flooded the treetops behind the house.

Mark was still abed at that hour, having sat up late writing and then enduring mostly insomnious hours haunted with the images he'd seen and the impact of the sudden, violent end of months of rising expectations, an overwhelming wave of disillusionment and defeat. When he woke an hour or so after sunrise, he prayed the previous two days had been a nightmare, and they were, but of the sort that actually and mercilessly do exist.

Mark padded down to the kitchen and found his mother just finishing reconstituting some grape paste into juice, filling a large pitcher that would in turn fill twenty or more cups.

"You're up," she said. "Good. You can take this up to the men."

"Of course," said Mark, hoisting the clay pitcher. "They've eaten?"

"While you were still asleep." Miriam put away the skin of paste and began washing her hands.

"How are they?" he said.

"How would you be?" Miriam said, wiping her hands, and then she turned to him and looked apologetic. "Oh, Mark, I know you're grieving, too, as we all are. I'm sorry."

"That's all right, mother. Not like they are. Not even like you.

I didn't really know him." He shifted the pitcher in his arms. "I'll take this up." He went down the hall and up to the Upper Room.

Peter and the rest of the disciples were standing around a fire pot on the balcony off the back of the room, looking over Jerusalem's sun-golden housetops. He and several others, among them the youngest—John, he believed—turned to see who had come into the room, and nodded to him as he put the pitcher on a large table in the center of the area and stood as if waiting to be either invited to stay or to be ignored, which would signal him to leave. Peter smiled and lifted his head.

John came in from the balcony and spoke.

"I'm John."

"I'm John Mark—Mark," said Mark. They gripped arms in greeting.

The others came in shortly and closed the door, and those he had not met individually introduced themselves, all in subdued manner.

"Thank you for this place," said the one who had introduced himself as Andrew.

"Yes, thank you," said Thomas.

After a few moments of awkward silence, Mark somewhat falteringly said, "Where will you go from here?"

Most of the men eventually looked at Peter, who finally took his cue. "Probably back to Galilee. We've been talking about it."

"Of course," said Mark. They were principally from the northern province, and Jesus had spent much of his time there.

"Will traveling be dangerous?" Mark said. "I mean, right now?"

"We'll probably wait a few days," said Peter. "We'll pay you for the room, of course. And the food."

"We're not concerned about that," said Mark, speaking for himself and his mother, certain of her unconditional hospitality.

"We don't know if we'll be—if they're going to be looking for us," said Matthew.

"We're hoping that Mary—Mary Magdalene—and some of the other women will be able to tell us what they hear on the streets," said James.

"And I'll try to find out anything I can," said Mark, eager to be of help. The others nodded hopefully.

"You're Barnabas's cousin, aren't you," said Peter.

"Yes. My mother's brother is his father."

"I know him," said Peter. "A fine man."

The group found places to sit in the room and most of them settled in chairs, burying their hands in their robes in the slight, morning chill. Peter motioned Mark to a chair, and they both sat.

"Some of the other followers will be joining us this morning. We're going to be praying about what to do," said Peter. "You're welcome to stay."

"Thank you," said Mark, still feeling a bit like an interloper but willing to test the waters if he felt they really didn't mind his being there.

"It's not over," said Bartholomew. "It can't be, so it isn't," he said in a lower voice, more to himself than to anyone else, a sort of stubborn tone arguing his case.

"I'd love to agree," said Nathaniel, "but I'm trying to figure out just how we could continue."

"When we split up," said Jude, "with the others, seventy of us, we were by ourselves, just in pairs. We were without him *then.*" He looked around for any sense of agreement with his implication that they could go on proclaiming the kingdom of God.

"Yes," said James, "but he was waiting back in Capernaum."

"But," said Jude, "he gave us—he was *with* us somehow. We did such *things*!"

"Because he was here," said Peter. "He was still *here.*"

The response of all was unspoken but insistent in the silence that ensued. Because Jesus wasn't here anymore.

Mark got up. "I need to help my mother with some things," he said. "When the others begin coming in, I'll show them up." He left quietly and went downstairs, finding Miriam in the kitchen with the ever-present Rhoda.

Shortly a knock came at the door, and Mark went to the front room. Opening the door he saw the Mary he recognized as the Magdalene and another Mary, Joses' mother. They had a strangely urgent look about them, a conflation of excitement and worry. Mark assumed they had a report from the streets about danger to the disciples. He stood aside for them to come in.

Miriam came from the kitchen and greeted them, instantly reacting to their visage.

"You know the way up," she said, since clearly they wanted to rush up to the disciples. "Feel free to use the private entrance from the outside," she said to them. "It's for you, too." They nodded wordlessly and hurried down the darkened hall, ascending the stairs at the end. Mark heard the door open to their knock, and then close again.

Noise of upstairs gatherings was muffled, by design, but as with any group gathered there, voices could be heard sometimes, and Mark and Miriam stood together in their main, downstairs room looking at each other and trying, in spite of themselves, to catch what was being said. One of the women could be heard saying clearly, "...seen him!" followed by a confusion of voices in response.

For several minutes there were exchanges between the women and the men that seemed mildly argumentative, sometimes insistent, and then there was a lull. Then there were more exchanges, none of them decipherable through the ceiling, and then another lull.

Finally, Mark and Miriam heard the outside door to the Upper Room close, and footsteps could just be detected as at least two people exited. Mark went to the front room hurriedly and looked out the window next to the door. Mary Magdalene and Joses' mother had come from the stairs and into the street, scurrying down the road to the south and out of sight.

Returning to the main room Mark said, "I wonder what that was all about."

"Threats, I imagine," said Miriam. "I heard that while Jesus was being held somebody identified Peter in the courtyard outside the high priest's hall. No doubt they were going to arrest him, too, but he got away somehow." She paused and then added, "Apparently, it's not over."

Mark looked at her oddly. "That's what Bartholomew said, too."

"Well, he's right, I'm afraid."

"But he didn't mean it that way."

"How did he mean it?" said Miriam.

Just at that moment, they heard the door to the outside stairway close, and they both went to the front door, just in time to see Peter and young John exit between the two houses and turn up the street, going north.

"Where do you suppose they're going?" said Mark.

"Who knows. They'd better pull their shawls over their heads."

Mark and Miriam stood there a few seconds and then Miriam said, "Well, I have things to do," and she went toward the kitchen.

"And I need to go to Joel's office, I suppose," said Mark, with reluctance, realizing that business would probably need to be conducted today. Life went on, in the midst of the feeling of death they were now carrying with them in the core of their hearts.

As Mark left the house presently, he met a few of the others Peter had spoken about, showed them to the outside entrance, and then made his way down through the city lanes to the office of Joel's business.

By the time the sun was at its apex, no one had come by the Supply House for any reason, to sell or buy, and Mark left a note on the door that he would be back later. He returned home at a brisk walk, noting the usual traffic in the streets and wondering how many of these people, now rustling, shopping, and talking in the usual way, had been part of the mob shouting, "Crucify him!" just the third day before today. In spite of the fact that many thousands of people populated Jerusalem, only a few of whom by percentage were at the Praetorium during Jesus' trial, Mark found himself looking at everyone he passed suspiciously, one by one, as he made his way back home.

When he arrived at the house, he found his mother coming to the door.

"I've been waiting for you to return," she said, almost whispering, but with an urgent kind of excitement.

"What's going on?" said Mark.

"I'm not sure. Peter and John came back a little while ago. I was in the front garden. To tell the truth, I was waiting for them."

"What did they say?"

"I didn't—I didn't want them to think I was spying on them. I was just out front, that's all. I saw them go up the stairs. Then I went inside."

"But what happened? Something must have happened."

"They started talking. I could hear them up there. Some of it was loud." Miriam motioned Mark to go into the main room with her. She sat down.

"I heard Peter say, 'It's empty, just like they said,'" said Miriam. "And then just bits and pieces."

"Like what?" said Mark, eager to know.

"I think Mary Magdalene and Joses' mother told them the same thing this morning. I think they think Jesus—" Miriam stopped mid sentence, less uncertain about how to say what it was she started to say than uncertain she should even utter the incredible idea.

"Jesus what?!" said Mark.

"—that he—he came back from the dead," said Miriam, putting the period to her sentence with a profound silence and a piercing look into Mark's face.

"What do you mean?" said Mark. "That he wasn't dead to begin with? Because I know—"

"No, I mean came *back* from the dead."

"They *said* this?"

"I picked it up from what they said. From what I could hear, anyway."

Mark paced around slowly. He looked at his mother. There was both incredulity and the risk of hope written on her face.

"They were afraid—the priests were—that his followers would steal his body. Could they have?" said Mark.

"With guards all around?" said Miriam with a look of skepticism.

"Well, if the guards who were *supposed* to be there *were* there," said Mark, "how did Mary Magdalene get to look in the tomb?"

"*I* don't know. I didn't talk to her."

"Or how did anybody steal—"

"I don't *know!*"

Mark and Miriam sat across from each other on the edges of their seats and just stared at each other for a moment.

"Do you think he really—"

"I don't see how. I can't—it doesn't—"

"If he really did raise a man from the dead in Bethany," began Mark, and stopped short.

"Then why not?" asked his mother.

"I guess," said Mark.

"This is just too—"

"I'm going to go ask them what's going on."

"Oh, Mark, I don't think you should! I know they said you were welcome, but—"

"You don't think this is important?" said Mark.

"I didn't say that. It's just, well, we should let them tell us when they're ready."

Mark got up, circled the room, and wound up at the door to the hall. He looked down toward the stairway to the Upper Room.

"An hour. Then I go up. We have to know!"

Miriam nodded at the suggested time limit.

About thirty minutes later some of the other followers, whose faces by now had become familiar to Mark though he had no names to go with them, came down the street and went up the outside stairs. Mark heard the multiple footsteps and looked out the front door in time to see several people go up. This was followed by the sounds of milling around and multiple conversations. In another quarter hour, two of the new arrivals came down through the house, led by Thomas, who called for Miriam.

Mark's mother appeared out of the main room. Thomas said he was going somewhere to get provisions and would be glad to get anything she needed. Miriam first said thanks but she couldn't think of anything, but then said, "Oh, get me two fish."

Thomas nodded, not betraying anything of what had obviously been going on upstairs, and he left, followed by the other two, one of whom continued a conversation they had been having in the hall and which Mark missed but wished he had strained to hear.

"We'll do that when we get to Emmaus," said one of the men to the other.

With that, the two unnamed followers left, with a nod to Mark and Miriam.

Mark scrupulously observed his own hour's waiting time before going upstairs to the Upper Room, but when he actually did go, he crept up the stairs noiselessly and then stood at the door, just listening.

There was little to be heard, though he did pick out what he believed to be Jude saying they all just had to wait until they had some confirmation.

After a few minutes, Mark tiptoed back down the stairs and retreated to his room. He decided against returning to the business this afternoon. He probably wouldn't miss any customers there, but he would certainly miss something important *here*. The customers could come back, or—they knew where he lived.

In another two hours the sun disappeared for the night and the shadows of Jerusalem's houses and buildings became a thorough and steadily deepening gray. Nothing had happened in that time. Thomas had not returned, though the marketplace was certainly deserted by this time. No one else had left or arrived, and it had been fairly silent above Mark's and Miriam's heads. But as darkness set in, a commotion took place in the Upper Room.

It first sounded to Mark, who was in his bed chamber, as if the entire group shifted positions, with the noise of jostling feet and the sound of people getting up from chairs or from the floor. There were a few loud gasps. Then there was a silent gap. If there were conversation, it must have been deliberately subdued. Mark strained to hear anything comprehendible but couldn't. He didn't know how long he stood there stock still and listened; it could have been a half hour. But the silence from above was suddenly interrupted by another collective gasp and then a confusion of conversation that continued for a minute and then faded.

Then a few footsteps began sounding on the outside stairs. Mark went to the front window in time to see some of the unnamed disciples leaving. He thought probably their departure left just the eleven, minus Thomas, upstairs.

Miriam had been in her bedroom all this time, with the door

closed, and Mark thought it likely she had been listening to the goings on as he had. As he went back down the hall, he made no noise passing her room and going to the stairway, where he again ascended without making any noise, and positioned himself at the door.

The door to the Upper Room wasn't as sound-deadening as the ceiling. Mark could clearly pick out a few things being said that were louder than normal conversation between people hoping not to be overheard.

The first word he heard startled him. "Ghost!" It was followed by bits of conversation:

"How did he get in here and then get out?"
"...doors are locked!"
"...looked like him."
"Galilee? Why Gal—"
"Can't be. Just can't."
"...saw him die."
"...think I'm going back to fishing."
"...think we should stay right here."
"Where is Thomas?"
"...errand"
"...yeah, but he'll never— he's just that way."
"What? Nobody could fool us. Not after this long—"
"...but who looks that much like him?"
"...we'd better stay. —Miriam says as long as we need to."

Someone was coming toward the door. Mark hastily tiptoed down the stairs and ducked into the kitchen. Rhoda was standing there wide eyed. She had been listening, too, but through the ceiling, so doubtless she couldn't understand as much of it as Mark. Mark put his finger to his mouth in silence, as they both heard someone reach the bottom of the stairs and come down the hall. It was John.

"Have you seen Thomas?" said the youngest of the disciples.

"No," said Mark. "He hasn't gotten back yet?" Mark knew he hadn't, because he hadn't brought any fish to Miriam.

"No," said John. "Uh, can we have something to drink?"

Miriam appeared, having come out of her room. She reconstituted some grape paste from a skin and gave a pitcher to John, who went back upstairs.

"Did you go to see them?" Miriam asked Mark.

"I went up to the door but changed my mind when I got there. I came back down." Mark left out his listening through the door.

"They'll tell us something when the time is right, I'm sure," she said, and she went to the kitchen.

A half hour later, Thomas came in the front door with a package wrapped in cloth—the fish. He gave the fish to Miriam and went upstairs through the inside stairway.

Mark returned to his bedroom, closed the door, and listened hard.

"It's true, Thomas. We saw him."

"We all did."

"...Well, do you think we've made it up?"

"I don't know..."

"I felt the same way at first, but..."

"There's no other explanation."

"He ate. Right in front of us..."

"...I just can't—I won't believe it, until I see him for myself."

Apparently, in the softer conversation that had followed what Mark had heard earlier, the disciples had decided they all *did* believe what they had seen. Now, they were trying to convince Thomas, who had been somewhere else in the city.

All that was left for Mark to conclude was that it was Jesus the disciples had seen, right there upstairs where they were. Right there in the Upper Room of Miriam and Mark's home. If that was what was happening, then there was no doubt about it. Jesus had come back from the dead. He had risen. Somehow.

It was almost too much to take in. It was almost too much to hope for. It was almost too good to be true.

14
Jerusalem, the Second Day

Sleep was difficult for Mark that night. It was unlike what had kept him awake four nights ago, after he dashed from Gethsemane across the Kidron Valley. Then, he had been full of nervous and fearful thoughts of what might happen to Jesus, who had been arrested and marched back into Jerusalem. Nor was his struggle to sleep at all like the agonizing bereavement of the next night, when images of the killing of the Nazarene were seared painfully into his agitated consciousness.

Instead, this sleeplessness was filled with the possibility of something beyond belief, something which, if it eventuated as true, would turn everything upside down. The disciples. Mark and his mother with them, too. The whole of Jerusalem. Even more, perhaps.

Mark's thoughts swirled in his mind, as he chased rabbits of thought here and there, coming back to, and rehearsing, the central theme of the haunting and astonishing conclusion—as yet on tentative grounds—that Jesus had somehow left his grave on his own power, after being certifiably dead.

Somewhere in the night, his brain gave way ineluctably to the exhaustion of furious thought and the forces of nature, and he slipped into soothing slumber for a few hours.

He woke an hour after dawn, the anxiousness palliated. Still, he deliberated upon this mystery, the spotty news of it, the implicit secret of it, and the explosive potential of it. Disinclined to tend to the usual business of his day, he nevertheless left the house and went down through town to Joel's Jerusalem office. Mark wished Joel himself were here instead of in Cyprus, so that he would have the day to be nearby for whatever were about to happen. Certainly *something* would happen today.

Going through market streets on his way, he bought a few pieces of fruit and showed some interest in a few leather goods, as he overheard conversations by other shoppers. There were still people talking about the crucifixions of the fifth day of last week, but it wasn't the dominant topic; many people were discussing the typical and the mundane.

As Mark was looking at some writing paper he might need to purchase, he became aware of a commotion at the next corner, a stone's throw away. Two Roman soldiers were questioning multiple persons they had forced to stop and stand against a wall. Mark moved as casually as possible toward the corner, coming within listening distance.

"Do you know the men?" one of the soldiers said. "His disciples?"

"No, no" came the nervous reply, the poor man's head shaking. "I don't know them." The man was insistent as well as scared.

"But you've seen them," said the other soldier.

"No. Well, I mean, yes, but not since before."

"Before what," said the first soldier with a sly smirk, knowing exactly what the man he was questioning meant.

"Before—last week!" said the increasingly frightened man.

"If I find out you're lying—" said the soldier.

"I'm not. I'm not!"

"And you," said the first soldier, moving on to the next person against the wall. "What do you know about his disciples?"

The interrogation went on like that until each person had been questioned and everybody had denied knowing where the disciples were.

About the time the soldiers were questioning the last person they had detained, Mark realized that he was dangerously positioned in the street and might become a candidate for interrogation himself. He turned slowly, and as casually as possible he strolled back into the crowded market goers and disappeared up the street, taking another route toward the office.

He realized, as he came to the office door, that he hadn't overheard anyone saying anything that indicated there was any news abroad in Jerusalem about Jesus' being alive instead of dead. All the talk was about how sad—or glad—they were that he was gone. Obviously, the unnamed followers who had come to the Upper Room had not gone out and spread the word of what the disciples had experienced, or passed along any speculation. Mark thought it likely, too, that if Mary Magdalene and Joses' mother had accessed the women's communication chain in the city and had told what they knew, the word would be out on the street. But he had picked up nothing about it in anything he had heard. And beyond question if there were news circulating about resurrection, it would have displaced talk of crucifixion almost completely.

The note Mark had left on the door the previous day was undisturbed, and no one had sought him out on business matters at home. Going in, Mark busied himself looking over records for sales and shipments the previous two weeks, purely out of boredom. Nor did anyone come to the office throughout the entire day, though he stayed continuously without going home or a few doors down for something to eat. When he did return home late in the afternoon, everything appeared on the surface to be normal. Rhoda was preparing food for the evening meal. Miriam was sewing. She looked up as he came in. Her face communicated flustered patience, as contradictory as that seemed. There was no noise from upstairs, though Mark assumed everyone was still present up there. They were evidently waiting it out, whatever "it" was. Obviously, there was nothing new. Whatever Mark might have thought would certainly happen today hadn't. He went to his room, propped himself up on a cushion on his bed, and ate one of the pieces of fruit he had bought that morning.

Almost incredibly, the rest of the week went by in the same manner. Each day, Mark listened in the streets for news and heard none. Each day, Miriam busied herself with her home chores and with errands. Each day, Rhoda prepared food for Mark and Miriam and for the eleven disciples, which she took to the Upper Room wordlessly at the usual hours, returning with nothing to say, because the disciples didn't tell her anything.

And each day, Mark was astounded that nobody out in the city was saying anything about Jesus being anything but dead.

What Mark did hear was a rumor that some followers of Jesus, whether part of the twelve (or eleven) or not, had stolen Jesus' body. In fact, one day—the fourth day of the week, he thought—he had actually heard a soldier browbeating a merchant, telling him he was to pass the word along that Jesus' dead body had been taken from his tomb by some of his followers. He, the merchant, was to tell everybody he sold anything to that this was what had happened. The soldier emphasized the order by picking up the diminutive merchant by the collar and front of his robes and pinning him to the clay brick wall beside his little stand. The man nodded fast and furiously and promised to tell everyone exactly what the soldier said. With that, the soldier let go of him, and the poor merchant crumbled to the ground.

By dusk on the fifth day, as the Sabbath was about to begin, Mark consigned himself to what might be a new reality. If Jesus were alive instead of dead, by whatever inexplicable means, perhaps nothing would come of it. Instead of earth-shattering revolution, widespread or not, perhaps the disciples would fade into the background of their previous lives, aware of some amazing experience that took place in the wake of that awful weekend, but otherwise unshaken, left to ponder the implications for their future, either severally or together.

The Sabbath also passed uneventfully. Miriam and Mark went to synagogue a few blocks away. The reader for that morning was Levi ben Isaac, probably the oldest man in the neighborhood and a kindly sage everyone loved to hear voicing the word of God. The scheduled text in the lectionary was from the fifth book of the Tanakh. Everyone paid dutiful attention as Levi read:

> All the firstborn males that come of your herd and of your flock you shall sanctify unto the Lord your God.

The passage seemed unusually moving, but Mark couldn't exactly explain to himself why. Just a week ago, they had sacrificed the Passover lamb, so there was that; but the lectionary quite regularly and purposefully aligned with the Jewish feasts throughout the year. The moving Mark felt inside him was something else. Levi was still reading:

> You shall therefore sacrifice the passover unto the Lord your God, of the flock and the herd, in the place where the Lord shall choose to place his name.

Mark thought back to the Passovers he and his mother had celebrated with the community over the years. They had always been meaningful. Everybody looked back with the cultural memory created by the description in Shemot: their ancestors smeared the blood of a lamb on their doorposts and escaped the angel of death, which passed over their homes when he saw the blood. That was still a moving thought, yet something else stirred in Mark's mind, just beyond the range of conscious comprehension.

Levi read on:

> You may not sacrifice the passover within *any* of your gates that the Lord your God gives you: *only* at the place that the Lord your God shall choose to place his name in—*there* you shall sacrifice the passover…

Mark was living in the ultimate place of God's choosing for the Passover sacrifice. This was Jerusalem. Just a few blocks away was the temple square. A few days ago hundreds and hundreds of sacrifices were made there in addition to the one made by the high priest in the holiest of holy places, a few square feet of sacred space that virtually no one had ever seen. Perhaps it was the mystique of this whole time of year, the high expectation of people gathered in Jerusalem for the Passover Feast, the hope of worshipers for some sense of the Lord's presence and blessing. Maybe it was the culmination and intersection of all these strains of spiritual anticipation that Mark felt as ben Isaac read the word of God. Still, there was something in the words that would not let him go, that begged to be understood, recognized, realized.

Levi ben Isaac was closing up the scroll. He handed it to the attendant, and without further comment, he sat down, like the old man he was, a wrinkled, stooped, creaking body of decades of living expectation, a community's symbol of the enduring dream of the fulfillment of the nation's hope.

There was silence and prayer, and then a singer rose and put notes to a familiar psalm, joined by the rest of the congregants in their varying degrees of ability, and then the time of worship was over. Mark and Miriam shuffled out with the small crowd and returned home at a slow pace, enjoying the peace of the day.

As they walked into the house they heard the strains of soft singing from the Upper Room. Apparently, the disciples, unable to be out in public because of the danger to them, had held their own synagogue service and were just concluding. Well, more power to them, thought Mark. And if Jesus were really alive instead of dead, they probably had a sense that their leader was near them somehow. What could be better than that?

15
The First Day

The previous week had sped by and the day of rest had refreshed Mark thoroughly, he noted to himself as he got up from his bed on the First Day and rustled around dressing and then going into the front of the house to eat. His mother was carrying a plate to the table with fruit and bread and had already set out something for Mark. They greeted one another with a loving touch and the usual "shalom" and sat to begin their day.

"Joel will be here tomorrow afternoon, I think," said Miriam. Uncle Joel had been unable to come to Jerusalem for the feast, though most years Mark could remember he and his family had come for Passover and stayed with Mark and Miriam.

"Good," said Mark. "I haven't seen Barnabas in a month of Sabbaths."

They ate without rushing. There was nothing urgent to accomplish today. Mark was decreasingly interested in work. For some reason, business activity was off, but that wasn't the reason for his indifference. Over the past year in particular, Mark had been preoccupied with the ministry of Jesus, the visits of the disciples and Jesus to Jerusalem, and the topic of the whole country's conversation. Now, with the cataclysmic events of the past two weeks, Mark's distraction had almost completely displaced any thoughts of the business. He wished for conclusive relief from it.

On that count, there was little doubt in Mark's mind that his mother's resources were quite sufficient to provide for him as well as her, even without his working. But apart from some pressing practical reason for his quitting his job, Mark felt a dutiful compulsion to stick with it.

Nevertheless, he was the one in charge of the local Supply House. He was Joel's only employee in Jerusalem. And as long as customers didn't come, if shipments were taken care of there was no reason Mark couldn't take significant amounts of time off from work—not simply to loaf, but to be here, where the disciples were still in hiding, and where something, *surely something*, would happen soon.

When they were finished eating, Rhoda cleaned the dishes and cups while Miriam and Mark went into the main room.

"What will you do today?" asked Miriam.

"Go to the office, I suppose," said Mark.

"Much to do?"

"No."

"Are you expecting anyone?"

"No. Not this morning, anyway."

"Will you come back at noon to eat?"

"I'll probably go a street over and get something to munch on from the market."

"I could bring you something."

"You should be here. Something might happen." Mark looked at his mother and thought he saw in her face that she had been thinking the same thing as he, that they were on the cusp of momentous events.

"I haven't heard anything out of them in days," she said. "Other than requests for a little food and drink."

"I would have thought—your being a supporter and all—they might have told you something," Mark said.

"I guess there's nothing to tell."

Mark looked at his mother inquisitively. He had listened at the door to the Upper Room, alone. He had listened from his room, alone, for what he could make out through the ceiling. He didn't know what his mother knew on her own. They stared at each other a moment, each wondering what the other was thinking.

Finally, Miriam spoke. "I've heard things. From upstairs."

"Me, too," said Mark.

"So you did go see them," she said.

"No. I—I listened through the door. And the ceiling isn't that thick, either." Mark looked only a little embarrassed as he said it.

"No, it isn't."

"What did you hear?" Mark asked.

"Enough to think—" and she paused, trying to put words to the incredible.

"Think what?"

She whispered her reply. "I think he's been up there with them." And in an even lower whisper, "Jesus." She wore her amazement in her whitened cheeks and slightly gaping mouth. "At least once," she said. "Somehow."

It was clear to Miriam that Mark had reached the same conclusion, and they stood there looking at each other, disadvantaged by being outside the circle of confidence, eager to have confirmation of what they thought they knew, and hoping soon to be included in some revelation that would revolutionize the awful and depressing events of Passover week. Mark finally spoke.

"Oh, mother, if it's true—! If it's not just their imagination—what's going to happen?"

"I don't know—I don't think there's any way to know." Miriam fumbled for thought. "I suppose that would be up to—him. To Jesus himself."

"I can't go. To work. I just can't," said Mark.

"I understand. But it could be hours or days."

"I know, but—"

At that moment there was a detectable commotion upstairs,

some movement of feet and then a murmur of voices. The suggestion of surprise. Then silence. Someone was speaking. They couldn't understand what was being said or identify who was saying it.

Mark and Miriam stood in the main room, listening keenly to the sounds, but to no avail. The men upstairs were clearly keeping their voices low.

Mark and his mother stood that way for ten minutes or more, rapt but without gathering anything useful. Finally there was a bit more shuffling of feet, and then a few words they could understand.

"...have to go—now."

At least eleven sets of feet moved about the floor of the Upper Room. Chairs were moved. Objects were shifted around. Then the footsteps moved collectively toward the outside entrance, and Mark and Miriam could hear the men descending the stairs. At the same time, a single person came down the inside stairway and came up the hall.

Miriam and Mark went to the hall entrance and met him. It was Peter.

"Miriam. Good. I'm glad you're here," said Peter.

"What's happening?" asked Miriam.

"We're leaving," said Peter. He looked as if he would say more but stopped short.

"Where are you going?" said Mark.

"We've been here too long," said Peter. "I can't thank you enough for your hospitality. And your patience. I know you're wondering what we're going to do."

"You should know by now that you can stay as long as you need to," said Miriam. "Please, please! Don't worry about that."

"But we need to go," said Peter.

"But where?" said Miriam. "We know—" and she cut herself off, but continued before Peter could speak, "we know something is happening! Tell us!"

"I—I can't. Not just yet. I know you want to know. But we're not sure what is going to happen ourselves. When we know— when we know, you'll know," said Peter.

"But where are you going?!" repeated Mark, hoping his insistence didn't translate as rudeness.

Peter looked into Mark's eyes and Mark could tell he was reading the probable knowledge, or suspicion, of what had been happening in the Upper Room.

"To Galilee, Mark" said Peter, in a way that indicated he was not going to give further details. To punctuate his implication, he added, "That's all I can tell you for now."

Miriam looked at him for a beat and then nodded as if understanding she and Mark were on a need-to-know basis. And they didn't need to know. At least for now.

"And I need you to keep everything secret. For now. Don't tell anyone where we're going. Don't say anything until you hear from us. I assume at some point you will hear at least *something* from us. But for now, please," said Peter.

"Everything is secret," said Miriam. "We understand." She looked at Mark.

"You can trust us," said Mark, somewhat reluctantly but suppressing any facial expression that would communicate it.

"Good. So, goodbye for now," said Peter, and he handed Miriam the key to the Upper Room. Then he turned and went toward the front door.

The men outside had gathered at the bottom of the stairway and had waited for Peter. Peter approached them and spoke quietly. In a moment, he, John and James departed, going down the street south, to the right. A minute later three others went left together, up the street to the north, then turning east. Still another minute later two of them went south, and finally the remaining three went the way the second group had gone. All had their shawls on their heads and walked as if looking for coins dropped in the street. Finally, all of them were gone.

16
Jerusalem, c. A.D. 29

To everyone in Jerusalem life resumed its normal pace and substance as travelers who had glutted the city filtered out, as the inns emptied or resumed their usual patronage, as people went home to the reaches of Judea and beyond, and as ships in Joppa and Caesarea sat lower in port with seasonal passengers. By the middle of the week Mark went back to regular hours at the business office in the little building in the central district of the city. Miriam returned to household projects and spent the usual amount of time with friends conducting and underwriting benevolent work here and there, and of course, talking about whatever was going on in Jerusalem and beyond.

Miriam and Mark, in their respective places of business and social discourse, found it difficult to remain mum about the likely events that had transpired above their heads in the Upper Room, but they kept their word to Peter and said nothing about where the disciples had gone or about the astounding conclusion they had reached about the reappearance of Jesus just days after he had been pronounced dead by the soldiers in charge of his execution. Mary Magdalene, whom they both saw now and then, had obviously been sworn to secrecy as well, and she never hinted that she knew anything other than that Jesus was buried, his body possibly moved, or that in fact he was alive. Joses' mother kept to herself and resumed her usual business, whatever that was.

The weeks passed, counting down fifty days from Passover until the Feast of Harvest, when a smaller but devoted crowd would again overpopulate Jerusalem and the surrounding area, John Mark tried to concentrate on keeping the shop full of product and keeping customers happy.

Uncle Joel had come to Jerusalem as expected three days after the Sabbath following Passover. He, Tirzah and Barnabas stayed with Miriam and Mark, occupying the remaining two bedrooms available, the one that had been Mark's grandparents' and the guest room. Meals were wonderful and joyous, and there was lots of talk, though not about anything speculative and not a hint of the possibility that Jesus had come back from the dead. All that Joel's family knew was that Jesus' ministry had come to an abrupt and horrifying end when he was betrayed, arrested and crucified.

Joel and Tirzah didn't know how involved Miriam had been in her support of Jesus' itinerant ministry. Miriam, who had sometimes been lumped together with the other "Marys" who had been anonymously—other than their first names—referred to in local gossip about Jesus, had somehow escaped being personally identified as a follower. So, when Joel and Tirzah returned to Cyprus during the third week after Passover, they were none the wiser.

Barnabas stayed on in Jerusalem when they left, though he spent the remainder of his time there with a friend instead of imposing on Miriam's hospitality. She was family, of course, but that was no reason to presume. He had friends his age in Jerusalem who had routinely invited him to stay with them when he was in town.

It was Joel's plan that Barnabas should work with Mark and make forays north into Galilee to drum up new business. Mark was glad to have the help. In fact, he was glad to be able to turn over the office to Barnabas when he was in town. The feeling had not left Mark that he was not going to make a lifelong profession out of Joel's trade, and he hoped that Barnabas would simply take over the local office himself before long.

Not that Mark had any idea what he was going to do for a living when and if he gave his notice. He had not trained for any other trade or profession. But something gnawed at him. He had a wanderlust not uncommon to all young men. Travel for its own sake was of great interest to him, and he could have considered himself capable of traveling at a whim as long as his mother did not mind his dependence on the family wealth to make it possible. But something about his future was framed with a glow of possibility that he couldn't precisely identify, an anticipation that was just around the corner.

As the Feast of Harvest approached, Mark found his mind wandering to Galilee. Where were Peter and the others? Capernaum, possibly. Peter and Andrew had probably gone back to fishing. Jesus had spent a lot of time in Capernaum. The disciples probably all had connections there. Every implication of what little Peter had told Mark and Miriam when the disciples went back to Galilee a few weeks before was that the eleven were going to stay together, or certainly in close communication. Mark could make a trip there and just "happen" to run into them.

It was better if he didn't, Mark thought, though he couldn't say exactly why. He remembered that Peter had said that when they knew something, Mark and Miriam would know it. No, Mark thought, he should sit tight and wait.

Three days before the Feast, Mark and Miriam were sitting at supper when a knock came at the door. They heard Rhoda go up front and momentarily Peter appeared. Mark and Miriam immediately sprang up from their seats as Peter came into the room. Mark reached out with his hand and Peter clasped him in greeting. Mark and Miriam both called his name but then said nothing, waiting for Peter to speak.

"I was hoping we could come back to the Upper Room for a few days," said Peter. "Is it being used?"

"No, no!" said Miriam, controlling her excitement. "It's yours." She looked toward the door. "Are they with you? Is everyone here?"

"Not yet," said Peter. "They'll be coming."

"It's all tidy," said Mark. "We've kept it ready for—well, for whoever."

"We will take care of you, of course," said Peter.

"I don't need—you don't need to," said Miriam.

"No, we'll pay our way," said Peter.

"It's my gift," said Miriam.

"Well, we'll talk about it," said Peter. "We'll probably need it a few days. Maybe a week."

Miriam went to a table in the corner of the large room and got the key to the Upper Room. She gave it to him.

"Come and go as you like." Her face turned somewhat more serious. "Do you think it's safe now?"

"You would know, better than I would," said Peter. "Is it?"

"I think so," interjected Mark. "Things calmed down within a week after—after you left."

"Good," said Peter. "Well, I'll go up and wait on the others."

"Is there, uh, anything to tell?" said Mark, tentatively.

"No. Not really."

"What's the talk in Galilee?" Mark pressed him, carefully.

"Probably like it is here," said Peter. "News from here reached there in a week. Died down in another week."

"Has anything happened? Anything at all?" Miriam said.

Peter paused a moment before answering. "I'll tell you more when we're ready. I will." With that, he went back out the front door and around to the side and up the stairs.

Mark and Miriam sat back down and just looked at each other, anxious but in a hopeful way. In a few minutes they took their plates and cups to the kitchen.

"Ma'am?" said Rhoda.

"Yes, Rhoda?" said Miriam.

"What did he say?"

"Just that they're coming back."

"Nothing more?"

"No. Sorry. When we know, you'll know. Who knows? You know may know before we do!" said Miriam, laughing softly. "Be sure to tell us if you do!"

Rhoda smiled and began cleaning up.

"We'll need more food for a few days," said Miriam.

"Of course," said Rhoda. "I'll go down into the market in the morning."

"I'll go with you."

"I will, too," said Mark. "We'll need more for the Sabbath the day after tomorrow, too."

"Let's be sure to get several skins of paste," said Miriam. "Those men go through grape juice like horses through water."

Miriam went back to the main room. Mark went to his bedroom and sat at his writing table. During the previous weeks, he had thought better of recording anything that had gone on upstairs or anything Peter or any of the others had said to him, what little there was. Even now, he didn't write what he was not permitted to say to anyone. Still, he jotted down a few thoughts, aborted the process, set pen and paper aside and lay back on his bed, pondering it all. In a short time, in the gloom of descending night, he dozed off.

The noise of feet above him told him he had missed the arrival of at least a few of the disciples. He got up and went to the front room to find his mother standing near the window by the door. There were no candles burning in the dark entrance area, and Miriam had opened the inside shutters slightly, enough to see yet another group coming up the street and going to the stairway between the houses. While they both stood there, two more groups arrived, which made all eleven, they supposed.

Inside, the noise from above indicated that the group had bedded down in various parts of the room, and soon there was no sound at all. It was everyone's bedtime, including Mark's and Miriam's, and they soon retreated to their rooms and slept.

The next day, Mark, Miriam and Rhoda bought as much as they could carry back home in the way of foodstuffs and grape paste and found extra space for it in the kitchen. There was little going on upstairs that they could tell. Rhoda had taken breakfast upstairs from what they already had in the house, but by noon they had replenished their supplies and she fixed more food and took an overloaded tray to the men.

Mark went to the office late in the morning and spent the balance of the day in total distraction. At noon he ate bread and fruit from a stand a few doors away, returned to the office, and sat pretending to study the books or browsed through the inventory in the storeroom until the descending sun cast shadows on the shop across the street that told Mark it was time to close up and go home. He and Barnabas clapped each other on the back and prepared to go their separate ways.

"Something's up," said Barnabas.

"What?" said Mark.

"You tell me."

"Nothing."

"Not nothing. You've been as nervous as a bird all day."

"Well," said Mark, searching for an excuse, "it's nothing."

"You've got a girl!" said Barnabas.

"What? No! I don't," said Mark, flushing. "I wish I *did.*"

"My friend Benjamin—the guy I'm staying with—he knows plenty of eligible young ladies. He'd be glad to—"

"No, that's not—not necessary," said Mark. Then he laughed somewhat artificially and said, "I'm fully capable of—"

"Oh, I know you are," said Barnabas. "But what's a cousin for?"

"Well, if you know all these people, why don't you have a girl yourself by now?" said Mark, realizing that what he said didn't come out the way he meant for it to.

"How do you know I don't have a dozen good possibilities in Cyprus?" said Barnabas. "Abba wanted me to get married several years ago, to the daughter of a good friend of his. I mean, she's nice and all, but I guess I have some of the same blood as your mother: I want to make my own choice. Hey, but I was talking about you!"

"Same here," said Mark. "I'm waiting for 'the one' to come along."

"Yeah."

"You know," said Mark, "if my father had been here, I guess he would have arranged something." Then a thought occurred to him. "Do Romans even do that?"

"What? Arrange marriages for their children?"

"Yes."

"Sure. As much as anybody does."

"Oh. I hadn't really paid much attention." Mark closed the office door and the two walked out into the street.

"Will I see you tomorrow at synagogue?" Mark said.

"Maybe. Can I come eat with you?"

"Sure. I'll tell Imma to have Rhoda make extra."

Mark and Barnabas parted ways and Mark wove through the lanes going home, arriving just as direct sunlight abandoned the streets, the air began to cool, and a little breeze stirred the trees around the house.

As he came into the house he realized that he had invited Barnabas to eat with them tomorrow when his cousin didn't know there was anyone inhabiting the venue space on the second floor. When he came, he would certainly figure out that a group was there, and he would ask about it—innocently, but he would still ask.

Mark found his mother first thing to figure out what to do.

"Imma, I need to ask you something."

"What is it?" said his mother.

"I may have made a mistake. I asked Barnabas to come eat with us tomorrow."

"He's always welcome, you know that. Why—" she said, and then it occurred to her what the problem might be. "Oh."

"It would probably raise more suspicion if I went to his friend Benjamin's house and retracted the invitation, than if we just let him come."

"Oh, no, you can't do that," she said. "I have a better idea."

"What?"

"Go talk to Peter."

"Ask him to let us tell Barnabas?" said Mark.

"Yes. He knows Barnabas. He will know he can trust him."

"Okay. I should go now," he said, and headed down the hall to the stairs. In ten minutes he was back, nodding with relief at his mother, confirming that they could tell Barnabas that the eleven—the twelve—were upstairs clandestinely.

When sunset gave way to the Sabbath, Mark, Miriam and Rhoda gathered in the main room over some fish, figs, apples, unleavened bread, olive oil with various herbs to dip it in, and some almonds to crunch on and finish up with. Rhoda had taken the same foods up to the eleven an hour before.

Miriam regularly invited Rhoda to eat with her since she was like family—she had her own little room in the back hall, even though she stayed with her mother some weekends. Before Miriam had moved back to Jerusalem when Mark was a small boy, Rhoda's mother had been Jacob and Joanna's servant, in their employ for years. She had brought Rhoda along even as a girl, and had trained her in how to manage a household.

The three of them ate casually, sat around quietly and enjoyed the rest the day afforded. Rhoda got up mid evening and checked on the eleven, replenishing their drink.

Taking the opportunity of Rhoda's momentary absence, Mark broached the subject ever on their minds in the previous weeks.

"Why do you suppose they came back?"

"Why do you?"

"They may have been told to," said Mark.

"By?"

"You know who."

"I wish they'd say something."

"They will. Like Peter said, when they're ready."

Miriam leaned forward and put her hands together as if praying. "I think something is about to happen," she said quietly and with studied import.

"What?" Mark said, leaning forward himself and peering into her eyes. He had always thought that his mother had a kind of prescience about things. At least since she had left the impetuousness of her girlhood behind.

Miriam didn't answer at first. She gathered a few things and took them to the kitchen, leaving Mark sitting there. When she returned, she sat down again and resumed her posture of prayerful contemplation.

"We'll just have to wait," she said.

Rhoda came back down at that moment, and reentered the main room.

"Ma'am," she said.

"What, Rhoda?" said Miriam.

"The eleven," she said. "There are twelve of them."

"Not—" Miriam began, with uplifted eyebrows.

"No, ma'am. Not him. It's one of the ones who were with them before they left. The other disciples."

On the brilliant Sabbath morning that dawned after solid sleep in the fragrant air of a superb spring, Barnabas knocked at the door of Miriam's house. Mark opened to him.

"I thought I'd just come by and walk with you to Synagogue," Barnabas said.

"Glad you did," said Mark. Barnabas stepped in "Let's go, mother," he called down the hall.

Miriam spoke from the door of her room. "Go on into the main room, Barnabas. I'll be ready in a minute."

As they went into the room, Mark decided to divulge their secret to Barnabas.

"I need to tell you something," he said.

"So there *is* a girl."

"No!" he said, humorously irritated. "Quit it, will you? This is something else."

Barnabas dropped the humor. "Okay, what?"

"The disciples of Jesus. They stayed here, in the Upper Room, after Jesus—you know."

"Wow. Didn't know that."

"Really, mother knew them more than me."

"I knew Peter, from before," said Barnabas.

"I know. He told me."

"You spend time with them up there?"

"No, I've just had a few short conversations, mostly with Peter or John."

"You said, they 'stayed.' So they're gone."

"They left after a few days."

"Okay. Is that a secret? That they *were* here?"

"No, but they're back."

"Upstairs? Now?"

"Yes," said Mark. "That's the secret."

Barnabas still looked surprised. He didn't know much detail about Passover week, since he hadn't been here. "Okay," he said. I can keep it."

"You probably won't hear anything out of them. Just sounds of walking around."

"What are they doing?"

"I don't know, really, and what I do know I can't tell you."

"Wow. You really are full of secrets, aren't you?" Barnabas said, ribbing his younger cousin.

"When we know, mother and me, you'll know."

Miriam came out of her chamber and joined them. The three of them walked down the street and made their way to the synagogue house. Three dozen or more people were already there, any conversations being whispered and then shushed by older congregants.

The singer for the day rose at the front and motioned gently with his hands for the gathered worshipers to be perfectly still. He closed his eyes and everyone followed suit. Then he began to sing the words of the first Psalm, and the group recognized the tune he usually applied to the scripture and they hummed along, though they allowed him alone to say the words. After he had finished reciting it once through, he began again, and everyone joined in reverently.

Barnabas sang more loudly than Mark or anyone else—Mark figured it must be the custom on Cyprus. When they had all recited in song the admonitions and promises of the Psalm, the singer sat, and the scripture reader for the day rose and took a scroll from the attendant, who pointed to the place where the reading was to begin. In a strong, mellifluous voice the reader began from the prophet Jeremiah:

> But this shall be the covenant that I will make with the house of Israel; After those days, says the LORD, I will put my law in their inward parts, and write it in their hearts; and will be their God, and they shall be my people.

The reader went on to another passage from a second scroll, part of the Tanakh. Everyone listened reverently. The reader, who was also a rabbi, then made a few remarks in the way of teaching.

Mark's mind was elsewhere. It was in the Upper Room. The eleven—now, mysteriously, the twelve again—were probably holding their own synagogue time. Mark wondered if they had any scripture scrolls to read; he presumed not. Why would they? Probably several of them contributed from passages they knew by heart from childhood.

The rabbi was finished, and Mark was privately embarrassed that though he had been staring toward the front of the room, he didn't know the first thing the teacher had said. The singer rose again and led the little congregation in two songs everyone knew and that usually concluded their synagogue time each week. Then, everyone shuffled out quietly, holding their conversation in abeyance until they had gotten into the street, where little knots of friends got together and caught up with the week's goings on in their respective lives.

In a little while, everyone had dispersed, walking back to their homes and to their upcoming midday meal. Mark, Miriam and Barnabas arrived just as Rhoda was coming down the street. She had gone to her mother's house to attend Synagogue with her. Miriam went to the main room while Mark and Barnabas went through it and out into the yard and garden in the back of the house. Rhoda went to the kitchen to gather the food already prepared for Sabbath.

"You looked preoccupied at Synagogue," said Barnabas.

"What do you mean?" said Mark, knowing very well what he meant.

"Same thing as yesterday at work. Something's going on. If it's not a girl—" said Barnabas.

"It isn't," said Mark.

"You changed the subject yesterday. Very deftly, too. Nicely done. But I still want to know."

Mark had prepared himself for Barnabas to inquire again. His cousin wasn't stupid. "I'm not going to lie," he said to Barnabas. "But I can't talk about it. Not now."

"Oh. A mystery. Now you really have me interested."

"Barnabas—"

"Not to worry, cousin," said Barnabas. "If you can't, you can't."

"I'm sorry."

"I just hope it isn't something terrible. You know I'm here for you, don't you?"

"Yes. I do. And no, it's nothing terrible."

"Okay. I'll sit tight." They were both quiet for a moment, and then Barnabas tacked on a new thought.

"It wouldn't have anything to do with your wanting to quit the job, would it?"

"I didn't tell you that I—" Mark said with surprise.

"You didn't have to. Whatever else is going on, I can tell you'd rather be somewhere else."

"I'm sorry. It's not that I'm not grateful to your father for the job. It's just—well, *things.*"

"Hey, don't misunderstand me. This isn't exactly my dream vocation, either," said Barnabas. "Sometimes I feel there's something else waiting around the corner."

"Me, too."

"At least, I hope there is."

"Your father loves his work, I guess," said Mark. "He seems to.

Happy all the time."

"You've been to Cyprus. Great place. Beautiful scenery, nice people, and Father makes good money. Travels here and there when he needs to or just wants to. What's not to love?"

"But it's not the same just running the office here, day after day," said Mark. "But that's not it, or not all of it. I just have the same feeling as you: something's around the corner."

"Well, if I turn that corner, I'll let you know. Maybe it's your corner, too."

Mark saw Rhoda bringing a tray into the main room. He headed back for the door, and Barnabas joined him. Meanwhile, Rhoda had set down the tray, gone back for another, and she returned and set it on the large table in the center of the room. She joined them for the meal.

Mid afternoon, Mark and Barnabas decided to walk north toward the temple area, just to get out of the house. Miriam was taking an afternoon nap and neither of the men wanted to tiptoe around to avoid disturbing her.

As they wound through the residential lanes and then into the environs of Solomon's Colonnade, they noted how foot traffic in the streets had become substantially heavier. Nobody was working, of course, but people were coming and going from the temple area and it was clear that the usual travelers from out of town were here, populating the inns, crowding their relatives' houses, and enjoying the welcome good weather for the Feast of Harvest tomorrow.

Up around the Colonnade, Barnabas and Mark became part of a virtual throng. People weren't doing anything in particular, just inhabiting the public place. Groups small and large engaged in conversation, family reunions, and the like. As with Passover, there were Jews from all over the nearby world, and some from even farther away. Barnabas pointed almost imperceptibly to a couple of brightly clad men with unusual headgear near them.

"Egyptian?" he said clandestinely.

"Or Ethiopian," said Mark. "How about those?" Mark nodded in another direction at a group of four.

"That's a Roman style," said Barnabas. "I've seen them in Cyprus."

As they strolled closer to the Roman group, Barnabas and Mark could hear their conversation, but neither of them understood it. They passed them and went out of earshot.

"That was Latin," said Barnabas. "Not all Romans speak it all the time, but they do if they want to be respected."

"What's this," Mark almost whispered, cutting his eyes to one side and then back to Barnabas.

Barnabas listened in and then offered, "I don't know exactly, but I'd guess some dialect from Mesopotamia. They look like they're from there, too. Look at their sandals."

The two strolled around in the grand courtyard, took in more of the sights and sounds, and then headed back home.

"There will be twice this many here tomorrow," said Barnabas. "Pentecost has gotten to be almost as popular as Passover."

"You use the Greek term," said Mark.

"What, Pentecost?"

"For the Feast of Harvest."

"Outside Judea, most people do," said Barnabas. "Means the same as 'Feast of Weeks,' the older term. Besides, the first harvest isn't much to celebrate, lots of other places."

As they neared the house, Barnabas was going to peel off and go back to his friend's house. His plan was to stay the rest of the upcoming week and then return home to Cyprus. But Mark convinced him to stay an hour or so more, just for some company.

When they passed the neighbors' house and came to the front of the gap between the houses, there were half a dozen or more men and a few women going up the stairs to the Upper Room. Mark and

Barnabas stopped in the street and watched them.

"That's some of a larger group that was with them before," said Mark. "I recognize them." As he said that, another group of about twenty turned into the street a block down and began approaching the house. Mark recognized them, too. As they drew closer, one of them whose face he knew put up a hand slightly in a furtive wave.

"What's going on?" said Barnabas.

"I don't know. I wasn't aware that anyone had left since they got here three days ago, but obviously they have. Somebody must have gotten out word there would be a gathering."

Mark and Barnabas went into the house and settled in the main room. Miriam was no longer napping. She was standing at the front door as if logging the arrivals.

After about a half hour with no more influx of people to the upstairs venue, Barnabas hazarded a guess that there were an extra twenty people with the twelve. With the day wearing on, he finally decided he would head back to his friend Benjamin's home for the night.

"When you go to the office tomorrow," said Mark, "come by here, and we'll walk together."

"Will do," said Barnabas, and he left.

After Barnabas was gone, it was just Mark, Miriam and Rhoda. Rhoda had secluded herself in her bedroom. Mark and Miriam sat comfortably and quietly in the main room, sometimes talking, sometimes not. The day was well spent. With sundown, it had become the first day of the week.

"Mother," said Mark.

"Yes?"

"Did you have something to do with the people who've gathered upstairs?"

"Yesterday, Peter asked me to get word out to the Circle to come today near sunset."

"The Circle?" said Mark.

"That's what we call them. Close followers. Other than the twelve."

"I didn't know there was a name for them. Are you in the Circle?"

"No. I'm a Friend."

"Is that a name, too?" said Mark.

"Yes. Friends are like the Circle, but we never left our own towns—our homes—to follow Jesus somewhere. Most of us are supporters—we give money, food, things like that."

"That's important, too. I don't see why—"

"We're *all* followers. Not everybody can be the twelve. And everybody didn't need to follow Jesus from town to town. Somebody needed to stay home and make things work."

"How *do* things work?" asked Mark.

"There's a list. I don't keep it. One of the other Marys does."

"So you told Mary—"

"And she told three others, who each had a group to tell, yes," said Miriam. "We're well organized."

"Obviously," said Mark. "So you know what's going on."

"No. Just that the twelve wanted the Circle to join them tonight. Nothing more than that."

"Are they just going to celebrate Pentecost, is that all?"

"I don't know. The Feast of Weeks is big these days. It could be." Miriam retreated from the atrium and went back to her bed chamber. Mark watched her go and then went to the kitchen to see what was in preparation for supper.

Just before the post-sunset light was completely gone, footsteps could be heard on the outside stairs to the Upper Room. Mark went to the dark front room and peeked out the window. As many as fifty additional people went upstairs, maybe more.

Back in the main room they could tell there were more people, but evidently the crowd was trying to be quiet. What was most surprising about the arrivals was the timing. Did they intend to spend the night? It was certainly possible. There was plenty of room. But it probably wouldn't be very comfortable. And certainly not private. And what had they come for?

After perhaps a half hour, things got quiet above them, and Mark and Miriam decided to go to bed instead of keeping a vigil for some unknown event that might not happen anyway.

As Mark and Miriam slept, upstairs the twelve disciples—the original eleven plus a strapping young man named Matthias—were in various parts of the room, each with ten or twelve of the larger group that had come to the Upper Room over the past few hours. There was a soft murmur coming from each smaller group as the disciples prayed with them, and as whispered Amens came from various ones.

Toward midnight, Peter said, barely above a whisper, "Brothers." Everyone stopped and the group turned toward the front of the room.

"We should sleep. The Master wants us here together, but we will continue in the morning. First, let me pray."

Everyone became still. Some bowed. Some looked up toward heaven, gazing through the ceiling. Some looked at Peter, their hands clasped together. Some kneeled; some stood. Peter spoke very softly.

"Jesus, Master, you said to wait here. Here we are."

17
Pentecost, c. A.D. 29

In the brilliant first hour of light Mark slowly rose from deep slumber and wiped his watering eyes, finally getting up and putting on his clothes, adjudging the hour and telling himself he would eat a late breakfast before getting started for the day. Birds chirped energetically outside. Mark peered out his window at the back yard in the windless morning. The slight chill would soon burn off and the day would likely be pleasantly warm.

In the kitchen Rhoda was just putting fruit, a little fish, and some bread on plates, and as Mark came in she put one of them on the little table to the side and smiled at him.

"I heard you getting up," she said. "Is your mother coming?"

"I haven't heard her stirring yet," said Mark. "She'll probably be up soon."

"The people upstairs are awake," said Rhoda. "They have been for a while. Not making much noise. But I think they're praying. I hear one of them now and then. Talking to the others. Or to God. I can't understand what they're saying."

"I think they're trying to keep things quiet," said Mark.

Mark ate slowly, and before he finished Miriam came down the hall. She came into the kitchen and Rhoda handed her a plate, made one for herself, and the three of them sat at the table and ate together.

"I'm going to the Colonnade in a while," said Miriam. "Are you going to work?"

Mark ate without hurry. "Not sure. I should, but nothing is

supposed to happen today. Everybody should be celebrating."

Just then, the wind made an unusual roaring noise, not gusty but swirling, as if before a spring rain. The shutters to the kitchen were not whistling, but the whole upper level of the house seemed to reverberate with the sound. It continued for a few moments, as Miriam, Mark and Rhoda looked up from their breakfast, curious about the whirring. Mark could see the sycamore tree just outside the kitchen window and two sparrows taking turns descending a few feet to the ground for seeds or bugs. Not a leaf on the tree was moving. Not the slightest breeze moved its branches. Odd.

The meeting upstairs began to break up. The occasional, single voice was replaced by numerous voices, louder but still unintelligible, a mild cacophony, crowd noise, almost like singing. Then footfalls on the outside stairs, the movement of the group toward the exit.

The threesome eating paused and looked at each other, and soon a head passed the window, going toward the front door. In seconds there was a knock. Miriam and Mark immediately got up together and went toward the front room.

At the door was Peter. Others who had left the Upper Room had paused as a group between the houses, and dozens were coming down the stairs after them, stopping at the bottom and waiting for Peter to return, apparently to lead them.

"Mark," said Peter, a brilliant smile on his face. "I want you to come with us."

"Where?" said Mark.

"The temple," said Peter. "The colonnade area. Miriam, you come, too."

"What's going on?" asked Mark.

"You'll find out soon enough," said Peter, and took a step away. "Come just as you are."

Mark and Miriam looked at each other and then back at Peter, and they nodded in assent, picking up some of his obvious excitement. Rhoda had appeared behind them, and Miriam reached back for her hand, bringing her out of the house with them. The three joined Peter and the rest of the group, which was larger than they had estimated hours before, and the twelve, the Circle, and their hosts moved en masse up the street.

A look, an unusual but compulsively inviting look, was on the radiant faces of everyone in the group. Few spoke at all; their faces were set on their destination, as if they were on a mission soon to be undertaken there. And the sound Mark and Miriam had heard while still in the kitchen, the indefinable wind, a gentle but strong whirring, seemed to follow them, up the streets, above all their heads, a deep but unthreatening turbulence, like a powerful force in which they were moving, but which moved not a leaf of bush or tree, or the slightest dust at their feet.

When they began to enter the area of the Colonnade, the glut of feast celebrants was evident. Instead of mingling around the edges, the entire group, which by now Mark had estimated to be more than a hundred, politely worked their way forward into the porch and aimed for the center and the front of the area. Oddly enough, the milling crowd gave way to them, many of the assembled people quieted somewhat by the entering group and perhaps fascinated by the look on their faces.

John, Andrew and James had moved into position at the front of the mass with Peter, and in a few minutes, they had arrived at the place where the portico joined the eastern side of the outer temple court. There they stopped, and Peter and the others turned to face the crowd of thousands that filled the Colonnade and spilled out into the streets beyond.

What happened then could almost not be described. The sound of wind that had enveloped them as the Upper Room group walked briskly from Mark's house increased to a protracted, powerful zephyr that seemed to swirl around the twelve and out among the hundred or so others, who one and all reveled in it, lifting their faces toward the sky and beaming with delight. Around them, the other people fell nearly silent, at first distracted by the sudden wind which they heard but curiously did not feel, and then drawn to the brilliant expressions of joy and elation on the faces of the newest arrivals to the Colonnade.

Presently, first among the twelve, then throughout the Circle, the voices of men and women were raised in words of praise. Single voices, sounding out their own songs, songs without discernable notes, rose up together, yet oddly in harmony with one another, and even more strangely, in words that seemed familiar, but that, as shortly became evident, were in other languages, many of which Mark and Barnabas had heard the day before. There were people here from many countries, but the Circle and the disciples were all from Judea or Galilee. While most of them spoke Greek as well as Aramaic, surely not many of them spoke the tongues of people beyond Syria, or from Africa. Yet the disciples were speaking in some of these languages, and everyone Mark saw who had been in the Upper Room was voicing praise to God in something other than Aramaic. And on the faces of the enthralled crowd, many of them from distant places, could be read the recognition of their native languages.

Mark, Miriam and Rhoda stood together, entranced by this phenomenon, picking up words here and there that they recognized as the name of God, or expressions of praise, spoken by people from Syria, Asia, Arabia and elsewhere. They looked at each other with wonderment and delight, realizing that whatever was going on had started in their own home, in the room over their heads, as the followers of Jesus had assembled in silence for days.

Before long, observers throughout the crowd were appealing to the speakers for an explanation. What was going on? A few of them who had moved aside for Peter as he led the disciples with him to ascend the steps at the front of the area now stepped up beside him and presumptuously began to demand the crowd's attention. One of them, apparently in the habit of being a spokesman for the rowdy, called out toward the entire assembly. The crowd, which except for the Upper Room group had largely become quiet, gave him their attention.

"I can tell you what's going on!" he said. "It's feast day! They've had too much wine!"

A titter spread throughout the mass, as people eager for an explanation accepted, if somewhat uncomfortably, the insulting comment of this self-appointed mouthpiece of the celebrants. But Peter, with a polite wave at the boisterous spokesman, never losing his captivating smile went up a step and called out, his voice never so strong before, and never so winsome.

"They aren't drunk—why, it's only the third hour of the day!" The entire crowd laughed, more eager to believe the burly fisherman with the charismatic look about him than the cynic who was quick to condemn. As the laughter died down, Peter continued.

"No, no. I'll tell you what this is. It's what the prophet Joel told us would happen: 'God said, I will pour out my Spirit on all flesh. My servants and handmaidens will prophesy!'"

Such an irresistible power carried Peter's words to all parts of the Colonnade, that not only could the thousands gathered there hear what he said, but they also stood rapt and hushed for minutes as he quoted the words of the prophet and then began to describe what had happened in Jerusalem seven weeks before.

In a whirlwind of words fraught with conviction, filled with divine energy, and then charged with persuasive appeal, Peter coursed through the story of Jesus' riveting ministry, the violent opposition of authorities, and the immense crime of the crucifixion. Then, in a sudden turn of dramatic intensity, Peter stunned the entire mass of people fixed on his words.

"But God raised him from the dead!" Peter said.

The throng of people let out a collective gasp. Not one in a hundred failed to be startled by the shocking announcement.

Mark and Miriam looked at each other with unexpected surprise mitigated by their confirmed suspicions. Peter was not saying Jesus had not really died. He was not saying he had swooned and revived in the cool of the tomb. He was not even saying Jesus had appeared as a ghost of some kind to the disciples in the Upper Room. He was saying Jesus, who really died and was buried with finality, simply rose from the dead.

That changed everything.

Peter was quoting King David, and Mark's attention flew back to Peter's voice and hung on every word: "God has made this same Jesus, whom you crucified, both Lord and Christ!"

Jesus, the itinerant preacher, the healer and miracle worker, the man run out of towns by mobs and sought devotedly by thousands in every city, the one who came into Jerusalem to praise and was marched to Golgotha to jeers, the stripped figure on a blood-soaked cross and the lifeless corpse carried to a cold grave—this Jesus had risen from the dead and had been proclaimed by God to be the Lord and the Christ. One with the Father, as he himself had said, to the fury of a mob. The Messiah—*mashiach*—Christ, as people had debated, and many denied. Peter was saying God had raised Jesus from the dead to be the King of the Kingdom of God and the Lord of every person.

The stir that had begun immediately with this declaration and swept over the entire Colonnade died down as the pronouncement sank into the hearts of the crowd as into one man. Everyone was waiting for Peter to continue. Instead, it was another man, the same cynic who had accused the disciples of being drunk. He now wore a frightened look of grief and near panic on his face, which had become almost white with alarm.

"Men," he began tentatively. "Brethren!" he continued as if pleading for their forgiveness for the previous slight but more urgently begging the disciples to rescue him and the whole assembly from the unfathomable peril in which they suddenly found themselves, having killed their Christ. "What shall we do?!"

And Peter, turning to him with the warmest acceptance, then turning to the mass before him, gave them all the answer.

"Repent and be baptized, every one of you, in the name of Jesus Christ, for the forgiveness of your sins, and you will receive the gift of the Holy Spirit!"

The glowing, urgent, celebratory, dynamic, joyful aftermath of the phenomenon that took place on the grand porch of Solomon's Colonnade on the day of Pentecost swept more than three thousand of Jerusalem's inhabitants that week into a suddenly attentive body of worshipers, eager for instruction, encouragement and assurance from the disciples of Jesus.

Among them were Mark, Miriam and Rhoda who, upon hearing as the entire crowd did the shocking but to them the not unexpected news that Jesus was alive, were instantly moved to tears, drawn like everyone else in that great mass of people into a sudden sense of their sin and their need of God's forgiveness.

Never mind that they knew vastly more about Jesus than anyone in that crowd who wasn't part of the Circle or the Friends. Never mind that they had, in the past two years or more, already come to a mental conclusion and a hope of heart that Jesus was the Messiah. Never mind that the twelve had roosted over their heads when Jesus had obviously been visiting them, as they now knew for certain. No, it had come down to the necessity of a personal response from everyone who heard Peter preach, and they were no exceptions.

Upon hearing the command to repent and be baptized, Mark

had stepped forward instantly, having been only feet away from Peter, and had kneeled in front of him. Peter had grasped his hand and pulled him up. Miriam and Rhoda followed suit, as did dozens around them. Throughout the porch area thousands kneeled or stood with their hands raised to heaven, tears flowing down their cheeks. Members of the Circle along with some of the twelve moved about in the throng and put their hands on shoulders and heads, clasped the arms of some, embraced others, either wordlessly or with a simple word of encouragement confirming the urgent decisions and compelling desires of person after person.

Mark looked around at the vast crowd and suddenly saw Barnabas, face lifted toward heaven, the light of glory on it, his eyes afire with belief and worship.

Later that day, and for several days thereafter, Peter and the rest of the twelve gathered various places throughout Jerusalem, both inside the city walls and outside at places such as the Pool of Bethesda, to immerse the new converts to the Lordship of Jesus Christ. Peter later told Mark that Jesus had commissioned them to baptize people who believed their preaching. However, the disciples had not realized they would be handling the logistics of arranging places of baptism in such numbers, and they made use of the suggestions eagerly offered for sites where pools of water could be employed and candidates fully immersed. At any town from Capernaum to the Dead Sea they could have baptized in the Jordan River. But in the middle of Jerusalem they used whatever they could find.

Toward the end of the week, the twelve were lining up places throughout the city where the newly baptized could meet with others and worship, and experience the presence of the living Lord. Many of the Circle had room enough for a few dozen to gather in their homes, and some of them decided to meet in common areas, or in copses on the Mount of Olives, or around prominent rocks in the Kidron Valley, or even near Golgotha itself.

In the weeks to come, the disciples and a goodly number of the Circle—many of whom were now assisting the twelve in organizing and leading smaller gatherings of the new believers—refined the organization of the Jerusalem followers such that to a great degree the places of weekly worship were becoming regular and well known.

Almost no sooner than the Feast of Weeks had come to an end, Peter and John held another crowd speechless when Peter healed a lame man through the power of Jesus and then told the startled and amazed onlookers, and the crowd that instantly formed around them, that it wasn't his power or his and John's holiness that was responsible, but Jesus himself. They had only called on the power of Jesus' name. In the wake of Peter's preaching on that day, another three thousand or more people became declared followers of Jesus, further packing the houses of Circle members and the other impromptu places of worship already established with more people needing teaching and exhortation. And the converts were keeping the robes of the disciples drenched in the glorious waters of makeshift baptismal pools all over the city.

Mark was among the first to be baptized. Peter himself lowered him under the surface of the Pool of Bethesda, speaking the name of the Father, the Son, and the Holy Spirit.

18
Jerusalem, c. A.D. 41

Jonathan and Asher closed up books, cleaned pens, straightened up things in the storeroom and generally made the Supply House of Joel of Cyprus look tidy, ready for the next day's business. It would then fall into mild disorder again as customers came and went, placing orders or loading their carts with orders received, and as importers' goods arrived several times a week. Joel had just returned to Cyprus after a brief visit, not really spending much time at the Supply House, only cursory hours catching up with what was going on at this location of his business, one of four now operating in Judea and Galilee.

Jonathan carried a report on a small sheet of paper to John Mark, who had a little office at the back of the front room. About five years previous, just after the business acquired the bakery next door when it closed, the dividing wall was knocked down to expand storage and provide for an office. Two years after the Great Pentecost Event—it was interesting how many things followers of The Way dated from that day—the business had grown sufficiently to justify hiring another man, and three years after that, yet another. As manager of the branch by that time, Mark rated an office. His employees, Jonathan and Asher, scurried around up front, moved products into and out of the storerooms, unloaded delivery carts, and did anything else Mark required.

Back during the days of Jesus' ministry, Mark had seriously considered quitting his job but had wisely held off. Once the Great Pentecost Event set things in motion for The Way, Mark focused his life-attention on his discipleship and, as it turned out, his increasing role in ministry and leadership in the Jerusalem church. A major congregation met in the Upper Room, which at first Miriam had continued to rent during the week for banquets and the like, but which was rarely available nowadays because of the frequent meetings and activities of the branch of the church that met there. Mark invested himself in the growth and life of the church, and as he did, the lack of fulfilment he had been experiencing concerning his job had faded. Once his priority had become the kingdom of God, his job—which was important—fell into its proper perspective.

Mark nodded to Jonathan and put the report in a stack. Asher appeared momentarily, the two gave a verbal list of their accomplishments for the day, and then both of them waited for any final instructions, the business day having drawn to a close. Mark told the two they could go home, and they wished him a good evening as they went out the front door. In a few minutes, after ascertaining that nothing was yet undone that couldn't wait until the morrow, Mark went to the front door himself, locking it as he left for home. Rhoda was cooking for a few extra people tonight, Miriam was helping as much as overseeing, and Mark couldn't wait to taste what was in the offing.

Going his way through the stone-paved lanes, Mark waved frequently and spoke often to numerous people he had met over the years since he moved into acknowledged manhood. Only a few of those people frequented the Supply House. Most of them were followers of The Way. He passed Caleb and Devorah, a couple in the church, waved and then stopped briefly to speak before moving on. Micah, a deacon, paused to pass on a bit of news. When Mark finally arrived home, he could smell what he thought was one of his favorite stews wafting out of the kitchen window.

Miriam was in the kitchen sitting down, as she was most of the time, suffering as she was with spells of ailing health. She was peeling and paring things. She lifted her cheek for Mark's kiss as he came in, and pushed some vegetables toward the other side of the table, placing a spare knife there as well.

"Might as well help with what you're going to eat," she said.

"Glad to," said Mark, sitting down and taking up the knife.

"I have a surprise," said Miriam.

"What?" said Mark.

"Your great Uncle Omer is coming back to Jerusalem."

"Really?! I suppose I knew he was still alive, but I haven't heard anything about him in years."

"I don't even think I've heard anything from him since he was here for Passover when you were twelve or thirteen. Anyway, I had a message through friends who traveled this way. He's moving back here. For his last days, I guess." Miriam was momentarily wistful.

"He has to be, what—eighty, eighty-five?" Mark said, sounding incredulous.

"No, not quite that old." Miriam looked into the ether and did some mental calculations. "He was five years younger than Imma. She died when I came back to Jerusalem. She was fifty-five. You were five then. Mother died soon after we moved. You're thirty-one, now. That would make him—" she paused and seemed dizzied by her own numbers— "seventy-seven. I think."

"Still, that's a bit old to be traveling," said Mark. "You didn't mention Aunt Ruth."

"I'm sorry. The message said Ruth died two years ago. That's why he's coming, I suppose. He wants to be back home. Where he grew up."

"When is he coming?"

"Soon. In fact, he was leaving shortly after he sent the message. He may be here by tomorrow. If his estimates of travel time are accurate. The road between here and Alexandria is wonderful, they say. One of the benefits of the Romans, I'm afraid to admit." Miriam put down her knife, finished with her bowl of fruits and vegetables.

"A lot has changed in that time," said Mark. "Not the least of which is The Way."

"And that may be something we'll have to explain to him carefully," said Miriam. "I think your Uncle Omer is not a believer. In fact, I'm not sure how he could be."

"Well, how much could he know?" said Mark.

"I don't know. I'm not aware that any of the Apostles has gone toward Alexandria, yet. Some of the people who became believers at Pentecost were from North Africa, but how much they've been able to do to tell people about Jesus of Nazareth I don't know."

"Should we urge him to join us in the Upper Room for First Days?" Mark asked.

Miriam thought the matter through a moment. "I don't know. I don't know how regularly he goes to Synagogue on the Seventh. When I was in Cyrene with him and Ruth, they weren't very faithful about worship days. That may have changed as he got older. If he's become more faithful with age, he may be hard to persuade."

"But you're special to him, aren't you?" said Mark. "Maybe he'll listen to you."

"I was thinking the same thing about you, son."

"Why would he listen to me more than you?"

"Uncles sometimes dote on nephews."

"Grand nephew. And he hardly knows me."

"He remembers a boy of about two, and a teen with the face of his father. He and Ruth didn't have children. I think he always thought of you as the son he would have liked to have."

"That might be why he wouldn't listen to me," said Mark. "He might not be able to see me as anything but a little boy."

"Perhaps. But you understand things so well, and you explain them well, too. I've listened to you teach on First Days. You have a way with words. More than I do."

Mark didn't say anything self-effacing. He had cultivated his communication skills by listening to others and studying the best speakers, including the prophets in the church as well as the rabbis in the synagogues. He often wondered if his future held a teaching role.

"We'll see," he said. Miriam nodded and smiled, then parceled out her fruit to three plates. Rhoda was ladling out stew, which she then placed at the table in front of each of their places. The three ate happily and then shared in clean-up of the kitchen.

After supper Mark went upstairs to the Upper Room. The task of straightening up and preparing the room for First Days was now his, as his mother experienced increasing trouble ascending stairs and doing physical work.

A small banquet had been held the previous day and there were remnants of their celebration in the room. The fire pot on the balcony reminded Mark of the disciples, hiding out during the week after Jesus was crucified. Mark went out on the balcony and stood with his back against the railing, looking back into the Upper Room. Images of the past twelve years flooded his memory.

He recalled, as if it were yesterday, hearing the sound of wind from this room as he stood downstairs, and joining the disciples hurrying up through the streets of Jerusalem to Solomon's Colonnade. Peter had later described what the Holy Spirit had done among them as they stood in this room. Though Mark had not been here, upstairs, his mind created an image of what happened as if he had been inside those closed doors.

He remembered the first day a hundred or more new believers met here after the Great Pentecost Event, to worship God and exalt Jesus, the Christ. It seemed natural, in light of what had happened—the crucifixion and resurrection of Jesus, and then Pentecost—but it was so dramatically new, so startlingly different, from worship on weekly Sabbaths. Synagogue meetings were like calmly memorializing the past, with little exuberance over the prospect of the future. But First Days were like excited celebration of the present, of what God was doing now.

Maybe that was part of the reason opposition to The Way had grown over the last ten or twelve years. Too much change to the old ways. Initially, scores of priests had become believers at Pentecost and in the weeks that followed. Mark remembered having thought that the movement was going to sweep the priesthood and the council and that soon the whole nation was going to sign on to the messiahship of Jesus. That initial revolution lasted a while, but it changed. The number of priests who had come to believe Jesus was the Christ was so great to begin with that the resistance of the others was virtually squelched. But a great many of the priests who believed were old; in the successive decade most of them had died. Priests who didn't believe, and vowed never to believe that Jesus had been the Christ, came back into the majority, and the tide turned against The Way.

A robe hung over a chair just inside the door. Someone with the banquet party had left it. Mark would have to contact the organizer and tell him to come for the garment. As he looked at the robe, Mark remembered the robes doffed and dropped at the feet of a Pharisee named Saul. It was nine or ten years ago since that day. Mark had not been present, but his mother had, and she told him how Stephen, a dear friend by then and a believer who worshiped with them regularly in the Upper Room, had been hauled before the council on charges of blasphemy. Miriam told Mark she watched as the gathered mob, given silent leave by a complicit council, threw Stephen to the dirt and stoned him. Some of the men took off their cloaks so they could throw harder and deadlier, and Saul, by then the de facto leader of the growing opposition to The Way, had placidly guarded them, a vague, self-righteous smirk on his hard, thin lips.

Mark grimaced, and then smiled and shook his head slowly. How ironic. How perfect. How wonderful. That within a few months, Christ himself had put Saul in the dirt and converted him. Mark had not yet met Saul personally. He had glimpsed him once, before his conversion. He was in the temple area. Someone had pointed him out and Mark just did catch sight of him, a tall, lean man with black hair under a formal turban, and a sharp, severe look about him. Mark wondered what he looked like now.

Saul shortly disappeared for a time after he was converted. When he reappeared, Mark's own cousin, Barnabas, had been instrumental in convincing the followers that Saul was no wolf in sheep's clothing, that he was just as surely a believer in Jesus as any of them.

Barnabas had moved permanently to the mainland after Pentecost. He had become a regular part of the movement, at first in Jerusalem. Somewhere in that first year or so, Barnabas stopped working for his father. He held some position in the church that occupied him full time and he was supported by the growing gifts of the people, as were the Apostles and a number of others.

Cousin Barnabas moved to Antioch—the church had sent him there, Mark believed. When Saul had come out of hiding—wherever he had been—Barnabas had taken him in front of the leaders of the congregation in Antioch and staked his own life on the genuineness of Saul's conversion. He had always been that way, Barnabas had. Believing in others. Taking their case. Standing up for them.

Mark looked at the chairs in disarray in the room. He remembered bringing many of them up here when it became apparent that older members of the growing congregation would not be able to stand for long periods of time during their meetings. When Saul was still militating against The Way, the Upper Room had been packed for First Days, as had every meeting place of followers throughout Jerusalem. They were as secretive as they could be, but they weren't entirely successful. Remarkably, however, the Upper Room was not immediately identified by authorities as a place where believers gathered.

Over in the corner of the Upper Room a stool stood, its usual place when not in use. Mark remembered the First Day gathering when the first Gentiles had come to meet with them. It was a young couple, barely in their twenties, among the first Gentiles to respond to Peter's preaching on the north side of Jerusalem. Peter had brought them to the Upper Room. They first positioned themselves in that corner, she on the stool and he standing beside her, out of the way, trying to be unnoticed, though everyone in the room knew they were newcomers, and knew who they were. Peter had introduced them to the group. Mark remembered the slight tension in the air. A good bit of uncertainty lurked in the secret places of Jewish hearts that day—the inevitable tinge of prejudice that takes time, effort and grace to change, even in the hearts of the genuinely redeemed.

But everyone knew by that time what had happened to Peter, his vision in which the Lord told him nobody was unclean and everybody was deserving of the gospel. Peter himself had launched the gospel movement among Gentiles in Caesarea four or five years ago, and The Way spread like wildfire along the coastal cities and into Syria.

A tall stand, like the one used in the nearby synagogue, stood in its usual place at the front of the Upper Room. Mark remembered how Peter had stood there late one night about two years ago and hastily told gathered followers how he had just been rescued from prison by an angel. The group was engaged in an emergency prayer meeting, called because Peter had been dragged to prison—Herod clearly intended to have him summarily executed as he had James, a short time before. Mark had joined the group that night and everyone was fervently praying, when Rhoda raced upstairs and excitedly interrupted the group, telling them Peter was at the front door.

Mark couldn't help but laugh as he remembered how nobody believed her, in spite of the fact that they were praying for God to intervene for Peter. When some of them finally went down, because they heard knocking, they saw Peter, not much the worse for wear, standing there in the chill, wondering if he had to have a password these days to get in. Once upstairs, he had stood before them, leaning on that tall stand, resting from his ordeal and his hasty travel through midnight streets, his ribs still sore from where an angel had struck him in the side to waken him, his wrists bruised from the shackles that had simply fallen off when the angel told him to get up and walk out. Stunned silence had fallen over the room as Peter told what had just happened, and then he left, under cover of darkness, with one of the brothers going along for safety, as he headed for some undisclosed location.

Hanging on the wall of the Upper Room were three wooden bowls. Normally they were for fruit or bread during banquets. Mark remembered taking them down and employing them creatively the first time the Jerusalem congregations across the city decided to gather gifts for things the believers wanted to do as a body. Among these things was a monetary gift to the poorest of their members. The church in Jerusalem had struggled with poverty among its members ever since the Great Pentecost Event. Hoards of people who had come to Jerusalem for Pentecost, and were then converted when Peter preached, didn't want to go back home and had sought to stay with relatives and find jobs. Many were unsuccessful. Other reasons existed for economic distress: some followers found themselves out of work when their employers caught wind of their new religious sentiments, and others lost breadwinners in a wave of persecution.

There were a few people in the Upper Room congregation who were nearly destitute, and various people who worshiped with them each week had privately been helping as they could. Miriam had long ago stopped taking any money from the congregation's leaders for rental of the venue for meetings of The Way, insisting that whatever they would have paid her should be divided among the neediest members. Miriam was not as well off as she was when she first inherited the house from her mother. Investments had done only so much to bring in a living. Mark had contributed what he could out of what he was paid, which was more now than it had been, but the economy of the city and the whole of Judea was creating problems for everyone. And as poor as they were becoming, the Upper Room congregation was better off than some of the other congregations meeting throughout Jerusalem and in the villages immediately around it. They were rich in the Lord but they were becoming poor in every other respect.

The air was becoming chilly and Mark went back in and closed the balcony doors. He straightened up the chairs, gathered odd pieces of trash and went back downstairs.

Two arrivals memorably marked the events of the next day. Miriam was right in her prediction that Uncle Omer would get to Jerusalem. A carter brought him to the house about noon, just before Mark came home for a brief lunch. Omer had gotten as far as Bethlehem the previous day but the carriage he had taken from Bethuel ran out of light before they could reach Jerusalem and the driver absolutely refused to continue in the dark. The passengers had spent the night in an inn and had continued the next morning.

Omer looked his age, and moved with commensurate slowness. When Mark came in the house, Omer greeted him with the glimmering eyes of an old man happy to have relatives who remembered him. And he acted as if he were the grandfather that Mark had lost as a child. After the usual remarks about how much shorter and younger Mark had been the last time he had seen him, Omer peppered him with questions about what he was doing now, how the business was going, and what was the latest from Tirzah, who was Omer's niece.

When the initial flurry of conversation died down, Omer settled into a chair in the main room and took an impromptu nap. Mark left him alone and retreated to the kitchen to eat. Miriam sat with him and munched on a piece of fruit, which was about all she did at midday these days. They kept their conversation down, though it was not likely that Omer, down the hall in the other room, would hear them and wake.

"Where is Omer going to live?" asked Mark.

"He is renting two rooms with an old, old friend," said Miriam.

"You offered him a room here, I suppose," said Mark.

"Of course, son. When he sent that message to me telling me he was coming, he didn't say anything about where he was going to live, so I presumed he had made arrangements, but yes, I offered him a place here. He wouldn't hear of it."

"Who's the friend?"

"Somebody he knew here before he moved to Cyrene. I think the man had visited him once there, back years ago."

"We'll have him over for meals often, I guess."

"Now, Mark, you don't have to tell me how to be a good hostess. Much less a good niece. We're the only relatives he has left here. In fact, I've already made him promise he would come this Sabbath for dinner."

Mark went back to work after the brief lunch, leaving Omer snoozing and his mother heading slowly to her bedroom for a nap herself. It worried Mark that his imma was declining. She wasn't yet fifty years old. He didn't want to lose her anytime soon. If she was consulting a doctor he didn't know about it, and he guessed that she wasn't.

The second arrival, unlike Omer's, was quite a surprise. Mark had come back home at the end of the day's work and was waiting for supper when a knock came at the door. Mark called to his mother to stay wherever she was; he would see who it was. Six people stood at the door. Four of them were complete strangers, wearing warm smiles. One of them was his cousin, Barnabas. And the last one, standing near the back of the group, was a tall and lean man with black hair now tinged with a little bit of gray. Saul.

Barnabas threw open his arms and embraced his cousin. He went around the group with him, introducing the four Mark didn't know and finally Saul. When Barnabas introduced Saul, he couldn't completely mask the significance he attached to the man. As Barnabas would later say to Mark in private, it wasn't that Saul thought anything more of himself than he ought to; he didn't. But everyone else knew that Saul was an unlikely believer in the first place, that he had come to faith in Christ in a profoundly different way than almost anyone else, and that he was probably going to have a more significant impact on the growing church than almost anyone else, precisely because of the import of his conversion.

At the moment, Mark was impressed with how Saul was unlike the man he had glimpsed in a temple crowd several years before. There was no hard look of over-zealousness, no demeanor of self-righteousness, no aura of outrage. And the turban had been replaced with a simple shawl, indistinguishable from that of any Jew around him.

Saul thrust his arm out toward Mark. Mark took him at the elbow as they greeted each other. The smile Saul wore was glowing, genuine, and instantly contagious. Mark liked him immediately.

Mark opened the door wide and invited the group in. Barnabas led the way, followed by Saul and then the others. Miriam appeared at the door of the main room and joined the group as well.

Two of the four Mark hadn't previously met brought in a small wooden chest. Inside the main room, Barnabas explained the purpose of their visit. The latest news of the growing economic hardship of the Jerusalem congregations had reached the church in Antioch, and they had mounted a drive to collect gifts for their Judean brothers. They had timed their trip so they would arrive today, the sixth day of the week, have tomorrow's Sabbath to rest, and then be with the Upper Room congregation for the worship meeting on First Day. They wanted to present the church with the monetary gifts at that time. The chest was packed with money and messages from the Syrian believers.

There weren't enough extra rooms in the house for each of the men, and Mark was trying to figure out how to approach the matter when Barnabas sensed what he was thinking.

"Don't worry about putting us up, cousin," he said. "I have friends who are making a place for us. Same one I usually stay with. Benjamin."

"Still," said Miriam, "if you need—"

"Nothing. We need nothing at all," said Barnabas.

"We came to give, not receive," said Saul.

"What were your plans for the morrow," said Mark.

"Ah. The Sabbath. It's gotten to be one of the questions of the day, hasn't it," said Barnabas.

"We'll do what you think is wise, Mark," said Saul. "Do most of your people still go?"

"Some do, some don't," said Mark. "It's hard for some of us not to go, simply because we always have. But having followers of The Way in attendance has caused dissension in quite a few synagogues. Some of our rabbis here are avowed enemies."

"I think it's the same most places here in Judea," said Saul. "Not quite the same in Syria, or even Galilee."

Barnabas said, "I think in a few years, we'll realize that Jesus himself set the precedent. He rose on a First Day. He appeared to the twelve on a First Day—"

"Twice," said Mark. "I was downstairs the whole time, as it turned out. We had no idea." The group laughed with Mark and Miriam.

"The twelve said he commissioned them on a First Day. In Galilee," said one of the four new acquaintances.

"And Pentecost," said Barnabas. "The day you and I were born again, Mark." Barnabas beamed. "First day of the week. It's right there in front of us, I think."

"Do you agree, Saul?" said Mark.

"I do," he said. "Everything has become new."

"But you said, or I think you implied anyway, that in Antioch it doesn't create much of a stir for believers to go to synagogue on the Sabbath," said Mark.

"Not like here," said Paul. "Most of us still go. I go. I haven't broken with any traditions. Yet, anyway. I'm trying to keep good company with my countrymen. It's useful."

"What about Gentiles?"

"You mean, do they go to synagogue on the Sabbath?"

"Yes."

"No. Not by and large, anyway. It's not their history."

"So, you're saying you will or won't attend synagogue tomorrow?" said Mark.

"We'll do what Benjamin and his family do," said Barnabas, "I think they worship on the south side of the city."

"Yes, in Tovah's house, I think," said Mark. After a silent pause, Mark continued, changing the subject. "So, how do you want to do this, on First Day?" He motioned toward the chest.

"You tell us," said Barnabas.

"Well, the elders should decide. I'll go see Thaddeus right away."

With only this minor detail undecided, the group transitioned to other conversation and soon Barnabas noted that the light outside was steadily dimming and that they should hurry to their place for the night. Mark and Miriam saw them all to the door.

Barnabas said, "I assume it's secure enough for us to leave the chest here until First Day?"

"We have a locked cabinet here that can hold it," said Mark. "I assume no one else knows about your chest. And we've never had anyone break in."

"It would probably be safer here than at our accommodations," said Barnabas. Mark led the two bearing the chest back into the main room where, in the corner, was a large, heavy cabinet that looked unimposing and unimportant, but that actually had a barely noticeable lock on its wide doors. It was empty when Mark opened it and the two men put the chest inside on its bottom shelf.

"I'll lock it right away," said Mark.

The group left after another round of embracing. Saul gave Mark another firm greeting, with a look of promise about him. Barnabas was the last to get back on his animal after saying goodbye.

"We have to talk, cousin," he said. "I may not go to synagogue tomorrow whatever the rest do. Are you going nearby—your usual place?"

"Probably not," said Mark. "Like I said, things have become tense there. I'd rather not see that happen."

"Then I'll come over in the morning."

"That's fine. What is it you want to—"

"I'll tell you tomorrow," said Barnabas. "Save me some fresh bread."

"Just come for breakfast," said Mark. "Rhoda always has enough prepared and then some, laid out and covered up before we go to bed the night before."

"I'll do that," said Barnabas, and he went to his animal, a sizeable donkey also laden with his travel provisions. The group clopped south from Miriam's and Mark's house and disappeared from sight. Within the hour, the sun's last glow had gone from the horizon and it was fully dark. In another hour, candles were blown out throughout the house and Mark was asleep.

First thing in the morning, while others were preparing to go to synagogue, Mark walked a few blocks to the home of Thaddeus, one of the elders of the Upper Room congregation, and he informed him of the visit of the delegation from Antioch's thriving church. Thaddeus thanked him and said he would inform the other elders of the special guests and their mission. Mark returned home, passing many worshipers going to synagogue.

Barnabas arrived in time to join Mark and Miriam for a pleasant breakfast. When she had first gotten up, Rhoda had placed a crock full of already baked bread on top of the outside oven, which had held some of its previous evening's warmth overnight. The bread was now delightfully warm and soft, and the four of them sat at the table in the kitchen enjoying it, along with fruit, raisins, dates, and some dried, seasoned fish dipped in a vegetable sauce.

Afterwards, Mark and Barnabas retreated to the back yard. Barnabas walked around the small garden and looked at some of the blooms Miriam tended when she felt like getting outside.

"I sense you didn't come over to look at roses," Mark said.

"No," said Barnabas, turning back to Mark. "I didn't." He exhaled in thought.

"Out with it, then," said Mark. "I've never known you to be this reluctant to talk."

"Well, this isn't shop talk or anything trivial. This is pretty important."

Mark didn't respond. He waited Barnabas out, now completely

still with curiosity.

"Saul and I want you to come to Antioch with us," said Barnabas simply, and stopped, waiting for some reaction.

"I can do that," said Mark, without hesitation. "Jonathan and Asher can handle things while I'm gone, and I'm sure Imma will be all right a few days without me."

"No. Not a few days," said Barnabas. "We want you to move to Antioch."

"What?"

"We want you in the Antioch church. It's that simple. We want you—I want you—to help us lead. And teach. And grow."

"Move? But what about the bus—"

"Abba and I discussed the business last month when he visited me. Jonathan will take over there and we'll hire another young man to replace him."

"But—" Mark said, and couldn't piece together his thoughts immediately. "This is, this *has been*, my home almost all my life. I mean, I don't know anyone in Antioch. Well, except you. It's just that—" He stopped again, groping for words. "Imma. You know she's not well. What will she do? I'm her—"

"I know about Aunt Miriam. I don't know what to say other than that she'll be all right. The Lord will take care of her. She has Rhoda and—"

"And *me*," said Mark. "She has me. I'm her only family." Mark grew insistent.

"I know, Mark. I know you think she can't do without you. I don't have anything to say to that except—"

"The Lord?" said Mark. "I mean, I know the Lord will take care of her. But I'm the one who—"

"What do you do, Mark? You're not a doctor."

"No, but I do what I can."

"We've talked about that," said Barnabas. "The church there

will send some help. The church here will, too, I'm sure. Mark, I can't answer all the questions. I only know we've prayed and prayed about it and I believe, I believe to the bottom of my heart, that God wants you in Antioch." Barnabas stared at Mark hoping to communicate the strong sense of conviction he had that whatever the difficulties and uncertainty Mark had would be overwhelmed by the sense that his cousin—and Saul—were right, that the Lord wanted Mark to move to Antioch.

Mark sat down on the little garden bench and put his head in his hands, rubbing his temples and then combing back through his curly hair. He stared at the grass, looked up and stared at Barnabas, looked away and studied the flowers.

"Why me?" said Mark.

"Ask God," said Barnabas. "Saul and I have prayed about this for weeks. It's just what we think the Holy Spirit is telling us."

"Then why hasn't he told me?" said Mark.

"Yet," said Barnabas. "Even if he didn't speak to you *yet,* he may now." Barnabas went to the bench and sat by Mark. "It was my idea first. I couldn't shake the feeling that God wanted you with us. That's what I told Saul. He hadn't even met you but he thought immediately that I was hearing from the Lord."

"Saul did?" said Mark.

"Instantly," said Barnabas. "We went to the elders and all of us prayed about it. They all agreed."

"But none of them knows me, either," said Mark.

"No. But they know me."

Mark got up and went to the other side of the yard, then turned back toward Barnabas. "What would Imma say? You haven't—you haven't talked about this with her, have you?"

"No, of course not. That's yours to do."

Mark breathed deeply. Barnabas waited him out.

"I would have to be able to come back. Now and then, I mean.

I can't just go and never see her again."

"Of course. And we'll pay your expenses. We've already talked about that with the church."

Barnabas got up and went to Mark. "Let's do this. Let's pray about it, you and Saul and me. And the others who came. They know what we were going to say to you."

"When?" said Mark.

"Today. Come to where we're staying. If you aren't sure then, we can probably wait, but this is important. If it weren't, we wouldn't have asked you now, on this trip."

Mark put his hands on Barnabas's shoulders and looked into his eyes. "You're sure about this?" he said.

"I haven't been able to think of any reason I would have had the idea in the first place if the Spirit hadn't put it in my heart. I like you; I always have. I've always enjoyed being with you. You know that. But that wasn't any reason for me to think you should be in Antioch instead of here. God just put it in my heart to think it. It's as simple as that."

That made sense to Mark. He thought of times in the past dozen years when he had felt the Spirit moving him. He thought of his interactions with Peter in the first few years of the congregation's gathering in the Upper Room, when Peter revealed some urgent feeling he assigned to the Holy Spirit. Mark believed in the Spirit's leading, and he had experienced it himself. Here was his cousin telling him the Spirit was imparting the genesis of an important decision through him.

His mother had been feeling the effects of her age, it was true. She didn't flit around as she had when Mark was young. She didn't walk a mile or more down into the market regularly as she had a few years ago. But she didn't complain of anything serious. Maybe he had worried too much about her, even though he sometimes thought guiltily he didn't worry enough. And there was her endless network of friends and neighbors. They already took care of her while Mark worked and went here and there.

If Barnabas was right, if Saul was right, then the Lord had a plan for Miriam and he would provide for her.

"You want to go now? To your Benjamin's house?" said Mark.

"Time is short. Yes."

"Let me tell Imma," said Mark. "Just that I'm going with you for a while."

"Good," said Barnabas, clapping Mark gently on his shoulder. "I walked from his house. We'll walk back there together."

The two of them went back inside and Barnabas waited in the atrium while Mark went down the hall, stepped inside the open door of his mother's room and told her he would be back in a while. Then he joined Barnabas up front and they left.

Saul and the other four men were waiting when Barnabas and Mark arrived, and the seven of them went into the house, retreating to a bedroom. They sat or kneeled around the room. After a few minutes of silence, Barnabas began praying. Interspersed with periods when they were mute while they listened to the Infinite in the silence, each of them spoke from his heart, including Mark. An hour passed, then two. Eventually, there was a calm stillness, a lull that became an unquestioning cessation. Their heads rose almost together, and on each face there was a peaceful assurance. It turned into a gentle smile on one and all, including Mark. The Holy Spirit had spoken in his still, small voice to every one of them, and they knew.

19
Antioch, c. A.D. 45

Mark rode a horse back into Antioch on a radiant, glorious afternoon, a pack horse and two friends from the Antioch church with him, as they returned from Jerusalem, where he had found his mother doing well. She had been delighted to see him on this, his third trip to his former home within the year. As his traveling party came back in the southern side of the city, between two of the four little mountains where Antioch was situated, they enjoyed the wide, beautiful streets laid out during the time of Seleucus, generations ago, and beautified perennially by the Romans who now thought of Antioch as their eastern capital. The road had not suffered much damage in the earthquake that collapsed numerous buildings a decade or more ago during Caligula's time, except for a crack between paving stones here and there that didn't much affect travel and had been left unrepaired.

Mark led the group off the main thoroughfare and into the quarter at the foot of Mount Silpius, behind the theater and in the shadow of the citadel of the city, into a residential complex where the growing church of Antioch met in a building that had been formed out of six houses renovated and connected to form a spacious area for hundreds of Christians to gather. The citizens of Antioch had concocted the name "Christians" for believers in Jesus with a mild level of contempt, but it had been seized upon by the followers of The Way as the perfect designation for what they were: "little Christs." Besides, there was nothing so satisfying as turning your critics' attempts at dismissal into a banner of celebration.

The travelers dismounted and unpacked their things, bidding one another a good day and walking toward their respective homes. Friends waiting for them at the church took their horses and returned them to their owners.

Mark went into the church house and said hello to a few members who had come by to pray in the afternoon and were just leaving. Justus, a caretaker, was straightening things for an evening meeting in the main hall. Mark waved at him as he went back into the building and into a small room that once had been a bedroom but was now a library. He returned a parchment scroll to its place on a shelf and went back out of the church, leaving it to Justus's care.

Mark had a little house a few blocks away, which he purchased with some of his own money and a little help from the church when he moved, which was coming up on being four years ago exactly. He remembered the tinge of anxiety he had felt riding away from Jerusalem. Once Mark had explained the plea of the church at Antioch, the certainty of Barnabas and Saul, and his own confident acquiescence, his mother had assured him she would be fine, while exacting from him the promise that he would come to visit every few months.

After his first trip back to Jerusalem six months later Mark had lost almost all anxiety and worry. Miriam was feeling well, Rhoda was doubly helpful, and his mother had even hired another girl to help, someone who was the age Rhoda's daughter might have been had she married, and who was even older than Rhoda herself was when she first began helping her mother in Jacob and Joanna's house, long before Mark and Miriam moved from Alexandria. In fact, Miriam was doing so well, judging by appearances, that Mark began to think she had actually improved since he had left for Antioch. He hoped that didn't say anything about his effect on her when he had lived there.

His house had not been disturbed while he was in Jerusalem for a week. He had as good locks on his home as the average person did, for what use they were. His uncle Joel had a way of saying that locks were for honest people. The ones who really wanted to break into your home or business would not let a lock stop them. But burglary wasn't much of a problem. Most people didn't have expensive things and most people kept their money elsewhere.

Mark deposited his travel packs in his little bedroom and went into the next room to find a bite to eat. There was really nothing there. He had intentionally eaten all the bread and fruit in the house in the days leading up to his Jerusalem trip. All that was left was a closed box with some raisin and date cakes, and a nearly flat skin of *oinos* paste. He went outside to a covered jar and ladled some water into a small pot, then returned to the small kitchen and reconstituted some grape juice. Then he sat and consumed two dried fruit cakes and drank a cup of the tepid wine, happy to be home.

At first, his accommodations had been a stark reminder of what he had left in Jerusalem. Having been raised in a large house with a servant and plenty of room to entertain and have guests stay over, and then having the Upper Room as part of his family's domain, Mark had become accustomed to space, more than a modicum of convenience, financial security, and a moderate amount of discreet beauty. Here, while he might well have been able to afford a larger house, he deliberately chose to downsize his life, sensing that his future lay not in the acquisition of property and money, but in the significance of the service to which he had committed himself. And he had the perceptible impression that more important, and possibly more personally costly, service was yet ahead.

With still an hour left of afternoon light, Mark realized he would need food supplies, and he left for the nearest market street.

The evening's meeting was a brief gathering for prayer and

fellowship. Mark joined a few dozen others who came into the smaller of two meeting rooms and laid out a spread of various foods. Everyone had forgone supper in the prospect of enjoying other people's favorite dishes, and the first order of business was to eat. Afterwards everyone wrapped up what was left of his or her contribution to the little meal and then rearranged their stools and chairs for a short meeting.

Barnabas and Saul were present for the gathering, as they usually were on this particular weeknight, and Mark sat with them near the center of the group. Everyone sang a few songs the musicians among them started spontaneously, and then several of them told interesting accounts of what had happened to them during the week so far, a few of them confident that someone they had spoken to about Jesus the Christ would come to worship with them on First Day.

When they had first gone to Antioch with the gospel, the disciples referred to the days of the week in the way Greeks and Romans did—*die Solis, dies Lunai,* etc. They were quickly corrected by their indignant Jewish brethren of the diaspora, who insisted that they weren't about to call weekdays by the names of pagan gods.

When the stories of their recent influence in and about the city ran out, one of the elders, Shimon, stood and gave some reflections from his study of the scriptures, which almost always ended with his exhortation to the entire group to pray for some specific challenge facing the church.

This night's devotional reflection seemed particularly moving. Mark thought it wasn't just his imagination that the leader frequently made a thoughtful point and looked his direction, or more exactly toward Barnabas and Saul next to him, as if they were the objects of his remarks. Shimon began to quote loosely from the prophet Hosea, saying, "Where the people were not God's people, they will be called God's people." And then he skipped to the prophet Isaiah, as Mark thought he recalled, and said something like, "With language foreign to them, I will speak to those people."

Beside Mark, Barnabas and Saul, who had been respectfully quiet anyway, seemed profoundly still and unblinking. Mark looked at Saul's face and saw a deep comprehension reflected in his eyes. Barnabas wore the same look.

Then the speaker paused, finished with his generic thoughts, and became almost unprecedentedly personal.

"Brothers, I believe I have a message from the Lord."

Another elder, seated beside where Shimon was standing, said, "Speak."

Shimon said, "The Spirit is saying we are to set apart Barnabas and Saul for a special work. What it is, God himself will make plain." With that, he stopped speaking and just looked at Saul and Barnabas.

In that moment more than any time before, Mark saw Barnabas not as his cousin but as a man of God. Barnabas stood, almost in unison with Saul, and the two remained there, motionless, ready to be the subjects and objects of prayer, as if they had previously intuited the import of this hour and moment, and had implicitly volunteered for whatever they might be thrust into by the hand of God and hands of their fellow Christians.

Mark later didn't remember who had first called out to the Lord and begun to pray, but whoever did had launched an hour's petition and soul searching, ending with cries of surrender and agreement with the word given to Shimon's heart. Barnabas and Saul would go. The mission was to evangelize new places and begin fellowships of Christians—nascent churches. The Antioch church would send them. Where and when would be questions decided within days by Barnabas and Saul along with several others who would meet with them continually.

It took less than three days for the group to map out the

direction and the places Saul and Barnabas would go. Mark wasn't part of the group making those decisions. He declined to join it when asked by Shimon. He explained that he was not being reticent. He was simply deferring to those who already had a vision for the mission, for the shape it should take. Other than recognizing the obvious fact that the mission should be to preach the gospel and begin churches where possible, Mark had no sense that he was to be part of the decision making process.

Three days after the fellowship-prayer-meeting where the revelation of the Spirit's message was confirmed, Mark was home for the evening when a knock came at his little house's door. Mark had frequent visitors, usually members who either wanted a word of counsel or had just come by to contribute in some way to his support by the church.

It was neither this particular evening. Barnabas stood at the door. Inside, Mark offered something to drink and they sat in a little room that acted as a place to read, talk, write, eat, or just sit.

"I'm going to assume you came to tell me where you're going," said Mark. "As Solomon wrote, 'A little bird told me' that you've decided."

"Now, see," said Barnabas, "that's why you're so good here in Antioch. You remember every scripture your rabbis read when you were growing up."

"I wish," said Mark. "But lots of them, yes. Anyway, I heard you've decided. And the bird, by the way, was Lucius, just after your group broke up mid afternoon. He came by the meeting place to tell me."

"Oh. So you know already."

"No, just that it's decided. Lucius said you'd tell me where."

"I told the group I wanted to. I had something else to tell you at the same time." Barnabas stopped, wondering if Mark would guess what it was.

Mark had a quizzical look about him, laced with good humor. "Where do you want me to move this time?"

Barnabas laughed, remembering the day four years ago when he had rattled Mark's world telling him he wanted him to move to Antioch.

"Well—?" Barnabas said, hemming and hawing slightly.

"Oh, no, you really *are* going to—"

"Now, don't get ahead of me," said Barnabas. "This time it *isn't* for keeps. Just for a while."

"To move? Really?!" Mark said.

"I said don't get ahead of me. Saul and I want you to come with us. On the mission. To help us."

"Where are you going? How far? For how long?" Mark said. He was sure Barnabas could read an entirely different attitude than four years ago when he had to be persuaded by argument as well as prayer that coming to Antioch was God's will.

"To Cyprus first. Across the island, then over to Asia, to the other Antioch, down toward Iconium, a few other places in between, then back here. It's pretty much all laid out. How long is another question. Not sure. It depends on success or lack of it. Could be two years. Maybe a little more."

"That long?"

"As you well know, it takes time to establish a church. Won't be like Jerusalem. It sort of just came together instantly there."

"I know."

"We want you to help in lots of ways. You're so good at planning and organizing, and there's some of that. But you're good at teaching, too. So if we get something started, we'll need all three of us to teach. And, well, there's just something about three people."

"When?"

"To leave? Not next week, for certain. We need to put things together. Organize resources. Get the entire church behind it. The elders want the whole congregation to commit to backing us. All the way."

"You know there won't be any problem with that."

"No, I'm sure you're right," said Barnabas. "So, you'll come?"

"Unless you think we have to pray about it, I'm ready to go. With one provision."

"Uh oh."

"No, nothing big. No bigger than before. Somebody has to go to Jerusalem to check on my mother."

"Already talked about it. Every six months or more. I promise. I have somebody already picked out. Subject to your approval, of course."

"Then it's done."

"Well, this was a lot easier than getting you to move to Antioch."

The two laughed. But they still prayed. They grasped each other's arms and appealed to heaven to bless the mission, and each of them, and to make each step of the way plain.

Barnabas left. Mark sat in the little reading, writing, talking, eating, sitting room until the daylight faded away and he was in the dark. By then his head was against the back of his chair, his eyes were closed, and he was deep in sleep, dreaming of what might be.

It was early the next year, in the fifth year of Emperor Claudius, when all the planning came together and Paul, Barnabas and Mark were ready to sail for Cyprus.

During the last few months everyone had begun to call Saul Paul, the Roman version of his name. It seemed fitting for someone who had become an entirely different person upon his conversion to have a different name. Simon had become Peter. Mark knew a few not-so-famous believers in Antioch and elsewhere who had changed their names—at least they had nicknamed themselves—because their birth names had meanings that they didn't want attached to themselves after they came to be believers in Jesus. One fellow named Aurav, which means "god of dawn," renamed himself Theophilus, meaning "lover of God." His mother was appalled, until she subsequently became a believer and realized why he felt the way he did.

In great part, Paul himself was behind the change in his name. In conversation between the three of them one day, Paul told Barnabas and Mark that he wanted to be known as Paul on the mission venture. After all, he was a Roman citizen, the places they were going were cities in the Empire, and they would be appealing to Gentiles as well as Jews everywhere they went. Barnabas said he hoped he could get used to it, and they all agreed that Saul would be Paul from that moment. Mark slipped only a few times.

Among other things they had to plan ahead for was communication and transmission of some resources: money. They wanted to be able to get messages to and from Antioch, at least every few months if possible. And they didn't want to count on being funded locally by the few people who might be brought to believe in Jesus Christ. With no way to know how many people that might be, or whether those people would instantly take to the idea of supporting itinerant evangelists, Paul thought it prudent to arrange for some funds to be transported or transferred from back home. Several members in the Antioch congregation were well connected with reliable messenger services, a few of them were in the banking business, and between them they promised to make it happen. With an itinerary fairly fixed except for the times involved, everyone believed courier transport could be made to work. Mark would be the one to work out the details on the fly as they traveled.

The day before they were to go to the coast to sail to Cyprus, Mark wrote a letter to his mother, telling her of his upcoming venture with Paul and Barnabas. He found himself expressing his excitement to his imma in terms he had not even admitted to himself so far. Always one to minimize his own emotions, Mark had not exhibited an intensity of anticipation about the journey, not even as much as some of the members of the congregation who weren't even going. Yet as he wrote, his words told on him. Deep inside, Mark knew he was excited about going, but annoyingly nervous as well. In spite of the instant readiness to go he had communicated to Barnabas, there was a little streak of hesitancy in him, the source of which he couldn't pinpoint. He didn't tell his mother about the negatives, however; he wrote only of the positives. She shouldn't get the idea that he was in any way afraid or unsettled about the venture.

His letter went by Malach, a friend in the church who traveled every few months to Jerusalem on business. When he handed the missive to Malach, Mark felt a finality about leaving on a journey of unknowns that until that moment had not pervaded his mind.

The next morning was not the dry, warm, sunny day all had hoped would provide the backdrop for the departure of the mission team. It was rainy and chilly. Fog enveloped the valley between the four mountains surrounding Antioch. Around a hundred believers gathered at the church house just after dawn to send off Barnabas, Paul and Mark. After clustering together warmly around the three, members spontaneously took turns praying and laying their hands on the heads of their missionaries, symbolizing the church's commission and the Holy Spirit's empowerment.

Not waiting for the fog to lift, the team headed out on donkeys, accompanied by two other church men who would return to Antioch the next day with the animals. One of the two was Lucius, a fellow teacher. The provisions, clothes and other things they took were really quite minimal. They remembered the Apostles' story of the time Jesus' sent them and fifty-eight others out on a mission to the surrounding country to proclaim the kingdom of God. Jesus had specifically told them not to take anything with them, just the clothes on their backs. Mark, Paul and Barnabas had brought a little more than that, but they liked the idea of traveling light, trusting God to provide for them, and having the ability to pick up and go at a moment's notice.

In a dismal lack of visibility the five of them made as rapid progress as feasible for both man and animal, directly toward Seleucia, about seventeen Roman miles away. It would take them three hours or more to get there. Mid morning the fog was gone and they came out of the light rain that had swept over Antioch's valley. Skies to the west over the Great Sea were clear as far as they could see. Perhaps their voyage to Cyprus would be smooth and pleasant. By late morning they came into the outskirts of the port city and worked their way toward the waterfront.

Mark had personally made arrangements for the ship they would take to Cyprus. Once at sea they would be headed for the port city of Salamis. Mark knew the city fairly well from his visits during his youth to see Uncle Joel, but of course, these were Barnabas's stomping grounds; he would be able to guide the team where they needed to go, which meant principally the synagogue and the marketplace.

On his trip to Jerusalem to see his mother just a few weeks before, he had inquired about Joel and Tirzah—had they become believers, to her knowledge? She was fairly certain they hadn't, unless something had changed in the previous year. The last visit Joel had made, he clearly had not joined The Way. All the Jews in Cyprus knew about the Christian movement on the mainland. Miriam had spoken at length with her sister about it and Tirzah, who also had not become a Christian, represented their position as being neutral, intellectually interested, friendly, or tolerant.

As they neared the wharves, Mark thought philosophically

about the crowds of people everywhere in the streets, coming and going. How many of them were Christians? Obviously, one couldn't look at people in a crowd and know which ones were Christians and which ones not. When you got to know people, the question could be easily answered, but just to look at them in the street, anonymously, in a bustling city, there were no spiritually discernable flames atop their heads, or not, for Christians to see and be able to identify them. But the difference between otherwise indistinguishable people was monumental, gargantuan, eternally significant. Some were going to heaven. Many were not. That was the bottom line, and that's what this journey was all about.

Mark reminded himself to keep the gospel message at the heart of his new relationships made on the road, and at the center of whatever he might teach as they went from place to place. The weight of the responsibility sobered him, but the challenge invigorated and innervated him.

Finally, they came in sight of the port complex. The fat corbita they were to board was nestled calmly in a slip toward the northern end of the wharf. Cargo was still being hoisted onto it, mostly small crates and some pottery. A few paying passengers were already aboard and watching the dockhands and sailors from safe positions at the bow. The team came to a stop where travelers were gathered and paying their passage before going up the gangplank. Dismounting, the five men tethered their donkeys for the moment and huddled to the side of the area.

They put their arms around each other's shoulders and Lucius voiced their common prayer, a petition for safety in sailing and success in preaching, wherever they went. Then they clapped each other on shoulders, embraced, and the team went aboard. They trusted God. Without wavering and without conditions. Even so, they didn't know his inscrutable will. They didn't know if they would succeed or would live to venture abroad with the gospel again. They didn't know if they would become martyrs. They didn't know if they would ever return home.

But they did know that right now they were supposed to go. And so they went.

20
Cyprus, c. A.D. 46

The harbor of Salamis, Cyprus's leading city and de facto capital, greeted the mission team's ship at one of its busy and well equipped docks along a wide swath of waterfront stretching almost a mile from the northern edge of the city to the south. Inland the municipality went back nearly another mile before thinning out in the foothills of the mountain ridge that formed a natural defense on Cyprus's northern seacoast.

As the commercial corbita gently glided into the calm harbor, the three missionaries stood at the rail and readied themselves for the beginning of their work. They would get a decent meal, to begin with, for all of them were famished and had not wished to have full stomachs at sea. Then Mark and Barnabas would lead the way to the main synagogue, which was up the hill from the water, up the main road past the theater and the baths, south into dense streets of houses, and to the edge of a market area.

It was not the hour for a regular synagogue gathering, but Barnabas would certainly want to meet the local Jewish synagogue authority, who would probably be there. Barnabas had been gone from Cypress long enough that he knew the people in charge of the synagogue had changed, probably several times, but he still knew the ins and outs of relating to the Jewish community, his having grown up a Jew in this city.

Laden with their individual packs, the three went down the gangplank and worked their way through the chaotic harbor buildings and up to the main road. Within the hour they were at the synagogue, a surprisingly impressive edifice for this town, Paul thought, and said to the other two. Barnabas hadn't thought about it, but then, he had grown up with practical disorder and found it not only familiar but refreshing.

Barnabas had been enjoying his re-acquaintance with the city, homes he remembered, businesses he knew. More than once he thought he saw someone he recognized, though perhaps not. Before they went into the synagogue, he thought it well for them to talk about what they were going to say. They went off to the side of the street and in the shade between two buildings to finalize their strategy.

"I think we should probably introduce ourselves but very little more," said Barnabas. "In my mind, we should simply say we're Jews from Antioch, part of the main synagogue there."

"You don't think we should say why we're here?" Mark said.

"I think if we mentioned The Way, that by itself would probably tip him off," said Barnabas.

"I see your point," said Mark, "but—"

"Without question, we must not try to deceive anyone," said Paul. "We don't have to lay out our entire plan. But if we fail to say we're Christians, we may be accused of deception anyway when we announce our purpose in the synagogue."

"That could be," said Barnabas. "But if we come right out and tell the synagogue ruler our plan to preach the gospel and he's already an opponent of The Way, then forewarned, forearmed."

"As I said, we don't have to lay out our whole plan," said Paul.

"That may not matter," said Mark. "My uncle—Barnabas's father—isn't a Christian, but he knows we are and he knows that many other Jews in Antioch are Christians. I imagine that the synagogue ruler knows that, too. Just saying we're from Antioch may be enough."

"So you're saying he's going to know, one way or another," said

Paul.

"I think so," said Mark.

"Well, then, it doesn't matter what we say, beyond introducing ourselves. Do you agree, Barnabas?"

"I think that's a reasonable conclusion," said Barnabas. "Do you want to do the talking, Paul?"

"No. No, this is your hometown. I think you can mention that fact and probably make friends more quickly. Why don't you take the lead?"

Barnabas nodded humbly. "Fine. Everybody ready?"

Paul looked heavenward and said, "Lord, this is your mission. You came to seek and save people who are lost. Go in front of us and prepare the way. Holy Spirit, fill us."

They all looked at one another, smiling in agreement, confident that the one who sent them would lead them. Then Barnabas led the way into the synagogue. They found the local synagogue ruler, Asher, studying in the main gathering space.

The ruler welcomed them with courtesy. Among other things, he told them the time of the assembly the next day. Officially, he assured them they were most welcome.

When they left the synagogue about ten minutes later and were talking about their impressions, they all agreed they had detected a little flinching in the ruler's face, just a slight movement of his eyes, when they told him they were from Syrian Antioch. They concluded he knew very well why they were here. No one doubted that when they joined the assembly on the morrow, everyone by then would know three strangers had come to Cyprus to try to make Christians of them.

The clear weather that had blessed their voyage continued the next day, and in a quickly warming morning the three missionaries left what they hoped would be temporary accommodations at a nearby inn and walked down the street toward the synagogue, stopping briefly at a Gentile seller's booth open early with bread and other food for sale. When they neared the synagogue, little groups of people were filing in. Barnabas saw some people he recognized as near neighbors of his father and mother. He briefly introduced Paul and Mark to them and then all of them went in, finding places on the right side near the front, not far from the stand where the reader for the day would unroll a scroll.

After they had sung for a while, the assigned reader took a scroll from the attendant and read from the prophet Micah. Barnabas found it odd, though perhaps revelatory, that the man read how the Jews scolded the prophets for prophesying, claiming that God was not impatient with them and would not judge them. But he went on to read Micah's prediction that God would gather all Jacob, the remnant of Judah, "like sheep into a pen," and finally, that "he will teach us his ways so we may walk in his paths." Barnabas looked at Paul and could tell he was noticing the irony. But then, Paul had shown, through his teaching in Antioch, that he was well versed in how the messages of the prophets all pointed to the coming of *mashiach*, the Christ.

When the attendant took the scroll and returned it to its place in a decorative shelf, the synagogue ruler spoke for a few minutes. He waxed eloquent in his anticipation of the day when God would reassert his sovereignty among the nations, though there was a tone in the elder's voice and choice of words that implied he believed the time was still far off, or at least beyond his lifetime. When he was finished, it was appropriate for any man of age in the little congregation to speak.

For a moment, the group was silent, willing to let the elder's words be the final ones. Then Paul rose and asked for permission to address the assembly.

Mark had heard Paul teach numerous times, but never with quite the immediacy and quiet force of that day. A new sense of Paul's anointing swept over Mark's heart as he followed the logic of his presentation, the passion of his conviction, and the persuasion of his argument. He remembered Paul's remarks later with detailed recall. He had begun with the reader's own citations of Micah, moved to the predictions of Isaiah, and used the clear imagery of the prophets to show that Jesus of Nazareth, with the report of whom all the worshipers were familiar, was the Messiah, the anointed one of God, the promised Savior.

The shifting noise of the assembled worshipers betrayed their general uneasiness, the uncertainty of some and the disagreement of others, with Paul's assuredness, and one of them—respectfully, it must be said—questioned quietly and simply if the passage of more than a decade since the Nazarene's death had not demonstrated that he might not be the Christ. With equal respect, Paul answered that Micah's own words pointed to a time of gathering of the sheep, an era in which God would bring together his people, a remnant of faith, before the final day when the Kingdom of God fully came.

Instead of calling for decision, Paul wisely concluded his remarks by saying that he, Barnabas and Mark, visitors who loved Israel, firmly believed that Jesus had risen and was making himself known among those who believed in him. Then he said he welcomed the opportunity to speak further about the matter to anyone who was interested. He thanked the synagogue ruler for the privilege of speaking, and he sat down.

Brief silence punctuated Paul's speech, and then the elder in charge tenuously thanked him for his words, intoned a prayer out of the Psalms, and dismissed the assembly. Exiting worshipers mostly smiled politely and went their way quickly, though a few avoided contact with Barnabas, Mark and Paul, and some simply wandered away without interest. Barnabas suggested that the three should go to his father's house, and they did, hoping perhaps that Joel would invite them to stay. The inn was convenient, but uncomfortable, noisy and not conducive to privacy in any way.

Barnabas led the way and they came to Joel and Tirzah's home in a short time. Having had no advance news of Barnabas's coming, Tirzah was overcome with happiness at seeing him, and she embraced him with excitement then hugged Mark as well. She and Joel both greeted Paul enthusiastically when Barnabas introduced him. In fact, they had heard about Paul from Miriam on their last visit and from other Jews coming and going from Cyprus. Few Jews who kept up with the news of their home country had not heard of the man who went from being the staunch enemy of The Way to being one of its leading advocates.

It was clear, however, that Joel, in particular, didn't know exactly how to relate to Paul. He called him "Saul" a few times before getting used to "Paul." Without precisely explaining the reason for the change, Paul simply said, "I go by Paul, now," and the matter was settled.

Paul was in no rush to take charge of conversation, this being Barnabas's home, but eventually he did summarize their purpose in being in Cyprus as one to persuade Jews throughout the island country that Jesus wanted the people of Israel to believe he was the Christ and to become his followers. Initially, at least, Joel and Tirzah were polite but passive.

They did, however, instantly offer the three a place to stay. Joel's home was gracious, like his hospitality, and Tirzah immediately said the three could have Barnabas's old room and the guest room for their accommodations. That evening, she prepared a spread of wonderful foods, some of them new to Paul but familiar to Barnabas and Mark, dishes common on the island but not the mainland. They ate outside in a fenced yard, surrounded by hissing oil lamps and attended by little dogs who pestered them for scraps.

At first, Paul mostly listened to the rest of them, who heartily recounted their history and caught up with each other's goings-on since last they had been together. When an opening provided opportunity, however, Paul told Joel and Tirzah how he had come to be one of the people he had hounded and hunted. They listened at first with caution and then with deepening attention as Paul told about his experience on a dusty road to Damascas. They found themselves accepting at face value his description of inexplicable blindness; the visit of Ananias; Paul's sudden recovery of sight; and the conspicuous and authentic difference there was in the man before them who had formerly been a vicious zealot.

Joel, in particular, had always ascribed to a philosophy to live and let live, and he had never felt himself particularly opposed to the movement of the followers of The Way, or especially drawn to it, either. His son, after all, who was sitting there with them, had declared himself to believe that Jesus was the Messiah, even before news came from Judea that the Teacher had been crucified.

Somewhere in the evening, however, as darkness deepened and the five of them munched on dried cakes of almond paste and relaxed in the flicker of candlelight on their faces, Joel fell into deep thought and felt a long-repressed hunger that had attended him as a boy, long before he met Tirzah and fell in love with her. It was a hunger for the words of the rabbis to come alive, for the God they taught to be a present reality for him, and—as he admitted to himself during that hour—for the neediness of his soul to feel right with that same God.

As he hung on Paul's words, Joel began to slough off the exterior of casual apathy he had long cultivated about the faith of his countrymen, and the calculated indifference he had displayed to both ardent Jews and its cool critics, and he found himself listening with a building anticipation of some momentous decision.

Barnabas had sat quietly while Paul talked, soon watching his father's face as much as Paul's, realizing what was happening. Silently, Barnabas was calling on the Spirit to work in both his father's and his mother's hearts.

Mark saw Joel's response, too. He read it in his body, his hands, his eyes. And he saw his aunt following it all, with a look of growing emotion. She seemed to be waiting something out, as if hopeful while tentative.

As he spoke at length, Paul was not self-absorbed, but rather measured his words constantly, sensitive to what was taking place in his listeners. Finally, he paused, peered into the eyes of first Joel and then Tirzah, and invited them to believe in Jesus Christ.

Barnabas had never seen his father look so teachable, so like a child confronted with mystery, so willing to be led. Oblivious to the others, he asked Paul what he had to do. Paul told him to pray. Joel spontaneously sank to his knees in front of his seat, and in words Paul suggested to him, Joel poured out quickly his confession of sin, his need of a Savior, and his belief that Jesus was the risen Lord.

The moment seemed as if no one existed but Paul and Joel. Barnabas froze at the edge of the lamplight. Mark was motionless, his head against clasped hands, his eyes tight in prayer. Tirzah was awestruck, face tilted up, her eyes gently closed. Momentarily, there was silence, and then Paul reached over to Joel's shoulders, an affirmation of Joel's decision and, somehow, an impartation of the Spirit's own blessing. Joel shuddered, at first with surprise, and then in forceful joy, opening his eyes, which now gleamed with both tears and wonder.

Then, before anybody else could say anything, Tirzah fell to her knees beside her husband and spoke to Paul.

"Jesus is the Lord!" she blurted out.

And in the cool of the moonlit night, a family was united in spirit and in its eternal destination, and the first church in Cyprus had its genesis.

21
Cyprus, c. A.D. 47

Through the rest of the year following Joel's and Tirzah's becoming Christians, Paul, Barnabas and Mark worked their way around systematically to the three other synagogues in Cyprus, smaller places where forty or more people could comfortably gather on Sabbaths and other days. They found themselves being students of people's sensitivities, of their differing levels of passion about their Jewishness—which wasn't altogether predictable—and of their receptiveness or lack of same to this new message, the news about Jesus Christ.

For everyone who was amenable, there was one who was averse, it seemed. Those who were receptive obviously evoked excitement in the missionaries; those who were reluctant even to listen prompted both caution and prayer for boldness; and those in between who were indifferent merited patient consistency of life and testimony.

Mark watched Paul closely in his life and work, observed him carefully in his teaching and preaching, and listened to him thoughtfully in his prayer and private conversation. Looking at Paul, it was difficult for Mark to imagine the Saul who had marched from place to place with cruel austerity, dragging off people who believed in what the scriptures promised and believed that God had provided it in the present time. *That* Saul seemed impossibly removed from this man, a reflective, calm, self-controlled person who rarely seemed perturbed.

Rarely. Not never. There were moments. But it took great

provocation.

The hopeful beginning of the work in Salamis led to a small group of worshipers out of three of the four synagogues, who enthusiastically expressed their belief in Jesus, mostly women and a few of their husbands. Barnabas wound up being the designated one of the three missionaries to baptize converts. When wondering where to baptize his own father and mother, he first thought—somewhat facetiously—of going to the baths near the theater. The team scrapped what was even remotely serious about that idea when they admitted to each other that the atmosphere of the baths was not really conducive to a worshipful event, in spite of the element of witness to non-believers that it might provide. Instead, one of the new converts had property on the north side of the city through which a stream ran, and he had dug a pool in it, to beautify his garden. It was deep enough to stand in waist high. This man and his wife were the first two to be immersed in the name of Christ, followed by Joel and Tirzah, and then more than a dozen others.

At first, the new Christians continued to go to Sabbath worship and tried to find inroads of conversation before or after the meetings, but the new converts ran out of substantial things to say and most of them lacked scriptural knowledge to debate or persuade. They communicated this difficulty to Mark one day.

"Don't try to debate them," Mark said. "Just tell them your story. What happened when you believed. If you can't do more than that, don't worry: tell them to talk to one of us." That satisfied most of the new converts, except for one or two who seemed eager to be able to hold their own in conversation. For them, the newly formed teaching session Barnabas started mid year was perfectly suited.

Barnabas dug into the scriptures in preparation, Mark helping him. At first, the main synagogue ruler was not opposed to their using the synagogue's repository of Tanakh scrolls. Eventually,

Barnabas sensed, they would have to try to acquire some of their own scriptures. The team had already experienced resistance from Jewish authorities on the mainland—Paul himself had once embodied that resistance. So far on Cyprus the synagogues hadn't formally opposed the gospel, but it didn't take much imagination to think that at some point, it was predictable that they would take a hard line against The Way and begin cutting themselves off from Jews involved with the church.

At the very least, in the future they were going to have to continue to have access to the scriptures. As they continued using the synagogues' copies, they were impressed by the quality of these documents. The Greek words—the Greek translation of the Tanakh had almost completely replaced the use of the ancient Hebrew for more than two centuries—were in crisp, uniform uncials, row after row as straight and parallel as a mason's bricklaying.

On a glorious island morning Barnabas and Mark were preparing for the week's teaching and had just left the synagogue after making notes from their study in the prophet Micah.

"Is it entirely crazy for me to think of having our own copy of the prophet's writings?" said Mark. "In fact, of *all* the prophets."

"Why not the entire scriptures?" said Barnabas.

"Are you suggesting I'm being ridiculous?" Mark said, unsure.

"No, not at all. I was being serious," said Barnabas. "I've wondered the same thing many times."

"Then you don't think it's crazy."

"No. Why would it be crazy?"

"The priests and rabbis probably would oppose it," said Mark.

"Probably. They like to be in control. But who did the prophets write for? Just priests, or everybody?"

"Well, the answer is obvious. But I admit I was thinking practically. Having the books so we wouldn't have to depend on the good graces of the local rabbis."

"Which is tenuous, at best," said Barnabas. "Nobody I know of has ever had his own little library of scriptures. But I'm with you all the way."

"How could we do it?"

"Get the scriptures?"

"Yes. Could we just copy them ourselves?"

Barnabas thought about this for a moment. While it seemed easy enough to do, the idea was based on the assumption that the synagogue ruler would allow it, which was unlikely. On the other hand, the local rabbi had been surprisingly accommodating, a fact that had not been lost on Barnabas and Mark, or on Paul, and had led them to believe that in spite of himself the rabbi might be gravitating toward belief in Jesus. He didn't impose himself and sit with Barnabas and Mark as they were reading and studying the scrolls. He largely left them alone and gave them time enough to pore over the scriptures. They reciprocated by not staying over-long. So far, the arrangement was working.

"We could try," said Barnabas. "I mean, the rabbi would have to be looking over our shoulders to tell what we were doing."

"I'm for trying it," said Mark. In addition to making notes for teaching—the rabbi knew they were doing this—he and Barnabas could use part of their weekly or semiweekly study sessions to begin copying some scrolls. Starting with the shorter prophets, or some of the Psalms. Mark was a fast and neat writer. He could envision being able to copy Micah, for instance, in about two sessions, and several Psalms in any one session. He could begin with the most messianic of the Psalms, and the prophets who were most often used in Christian proclamation. He could start on the writings of Moses at some point. It could work.

"What about *dies Veneris?*" said Barnabas.

"You did that just to get a rise out of me," said Mark. "The sixth day. The *sixth day*, Barnabas."

"You might as well get used to it," said Barnabas. "The world isn't going to adopt Jewish names—just numbers—for weekdays. It will be the other way around."

"But," said Mark, "the point of what we're doing is to get people stop believing in Roman gods, or any other ones, and get them to believe in Jesus."

"Preaching to the Levites, brother," said Barnabas. "But back to the subject. What if we start *the sixth day?* This week?

"No problem here. I'll just bring a little extra paper," said Mark.

"We might be starting something, here," said Barnabas.

"I hope we are. Fitting, don't you think?"

"I do," said Barnabas. "I do indeed."

They were walking back through the city, headed for Joel's house. Mark was pensive. Little boys at the edge of the marketplace darted out selling their handfuls of trinkets or snack-sized amounts of nuts or dates, tugging at the robes and sashes of those passing by. Mentally absorbed, Mark didn't seem to notice.

"A drachma for your thoughts," said Barnabas.

"You might be overpaying," said Mark.

"Okay, an obol, then," said his cousin.

"Well, worth more than that."

"What is it?"

Mark tossed around his idea another moment, then spoke. "Cousin, how long do you think it will be until Jesus comes to restore the kingdom?"

"Wow. That's a deep subject for a lazy afternoon."

"I'm serious, "said Mark. "I don't mean to start a debate. Just the short answer. Next week, or after our lifetimes?"

It was Barnabas's turn to ponder, and he did it for the next half a block. "I honestly don't think we have any way to know," he said. "Paul has said he hopes it's very soon, but he's also said he thinks it may not be."

"What if we don't live to see it?" said Mark.

"Then it'll be like David said about Bathsheba's first son, who died."

"Uh, here's where having our own scrolls would help. I forget. What did he say?"

"You? Forget? Be ashamed, cousin!" said Barnabas, with a grin. "He said, 'I will go to him, but he will not come to us.'"

"Oh yeah," said Mark, recalling the passage. "So we'll go to Jesus, before he comes back to restore the kingdom."

"Quite simply, yes," said Barnabas. "If he doesn't come, that is. Which, again, I have no way of knowing. You have me curious, now. Where's all this leading?"

"I was just thinking. About scriptures. We're teaching out of the scriptures, every week. But we also have a new story. I mean, the prophets predicted Jesus, but they never knew his name. They foresaw the future, but we've seen the real thing. Names and places and things Jesus did."

"Which is what we preach and teach, yes," said Barnabas. "What's your point?"

"When you and I die, if the Lord hasn't come back, what are the next teachers going to say?"

"Same thing we've been saying."

"With what, as their authority?"

"The Tanakh," said Barnabas.

"But what about the gospel? The story of Jesus?"

Barnabas stopped in the street. One of the little boys hawking caught his attention and he shelled out a little coin for a handful of raisins in a small cloth.

"You're talking about writing it all down, aren't you?" he said.

"Well," said Mark, "I don't know, maybe not me, but somebody. Think about it. At some point, teachers—here in Cyprus, back in

Antioch, Jerusalem, everywhere—we have to be telling the same story."

"So we need a book that tells the story."

"Exactly."

"Why not you?" said Barnabas.

"Well, like I said, I'm not—I mean, I wasn't—"

"Now, don't be too humble, cousin. You don't wear it believably," said Barnabas.

"Excuse me?" said Mark.

"I'm kidding," said Barnabas. "But I'm not kidding about writing. Why not you? Your Greek is great—and you couldn't write it in Aramaic. I mean, that would do for Judea, but nowhere else. You'd have to write in Greek, so the rest of the world could use it."

"Your Greek is better."

"But your *experience* is better. You know the story, at least as well as anybody except the Apostles themselves."

"Well, maybe, but I'm nobody. I mean, I'm like a nondescript bystander, not like somebody who was part of the action."

"What are you talking about?! You saw him."

"Which is a far cry from knowing him," said Mark. "I saw him from a distance. Twice. The rest of what I know comes from my mother, or from the disciples. Peter, mostly."

"Sounds pretty authoritative to me," said Barnabas.

"Okay, but what about Paul?" said Mark. "He's far more educated. And he saw Jesus. And *talked* with him!"

"Not in the flesh," said Barnabas. "And even if he did write something, why not you, too?"

Barnabas started walking again and Mark caught up. They were minutes away from the house.

"Cousin?" said Mark.

"What?"

"Did I ever tell you about the Garden of Gethsemane?"

"What about it?" said Barnabas.

And Mark told his cousin what he had never told anyone in the some eighteen years since it happened, and probably never would again, unless it were anonymously. How he sneaked out of his bedroom, ran across the Kidron Valley, hid behind olive trees, and saw the Savior arrested that fateful night.

22
To Paphos, Cyprus, c. A.D. 47

The mission team of Barnabas, Saul and Mark had been in Salamis more than six months, over the last of one year and the beginning of another, and it seemed to the team that the fledgling church there was probably stable enough to carry on without the missionaries, at least for a little while.

The team had accomplished much in this relatively short time. Forty-nine people had become Christians. They were meeting separately on First Days in one of the homes of a prosperous Jewish family. They had organized and trained for attempting gospel communication with interested persons before and after attending synagogue meetings. The little church had two elders and one deacon. And Barnabas and Mark had managed to make copies of four scriptures they would take with them on the rest of their mission venture.

Still, the depth of the congregation's knowledge and maturity was key to the team's traveling to their next destination. As they discussed the strength of the little group of believers, they assessed its collective knowledge of the gospel and the salient facts of Jesus' life and ministry. If they didn't have a good grasp on this knowledge, Paul was reluctant to move on to another place to continue the mission.

Barnabas's assessment was that the leaders they had selected, the elders of the new work, had been fairly knowledgeable about Jesus before the mission team's arrival. Even before the crucifixion-resurrection events, when Barnabas was still living in Cyprus, regional news was fairly comprehensive on both the mainland and the island. What the missionaries had done was to proclaim the connection between the prophetic picture of the scriptures and what was happening under their very noses.

Paul agreed that the indigenous elders were stable, knowledgeable men, that they understood the gospel well, and that they could sustain what had been started and carry on the work of spreading the good news in Salamis. Mark concurred, though officially he was only a helper on this mission—his vote didn't count. So he didn't offer it. The decision of whether to move on west and carry the gospel to the rest of the island was up to Paul and Barnabas.

Agreed that they should move on, with the proviso that at some point they, or someone else from Antioch or perhaps Jerusalem, would be well advised to check up on the new church in Salamis, Paul and Barnabas fixed a day in the following week that they would leave the port city and travel towards Paphos.

They told the church the following Lord's Day—what they had begun calling First Days—they would be leaving in two more days. Understandably, everyone was emotional about the impending departure, but they also realized that this was what the mission of Paul and Barnabas had been all about. On the evening of the second day of the week they gathered at their meeting place and brought baskets and pots of food for a virtual feast. It might be days before the mission team ate properly—or at least, that's what the women in the church thought. And they were all good cooks.

Early in the morning on the third day the elders of the Salamis church came to Joel and Tirzah's house at dawn to see the mission team from Antioch off on their trek across Cyprus. They realized they might never see them again. The group prayed together and then Paul, Barnabas and Mark put their little packs on their shoulders and backs and walked south through the city and down the road that would lead them eventually to the other end of the little island country. A new church had begun, the first they had begun together. It was on to another place, to begin all over again.

Between Salamis, on the eastern end of the island, and Paphos, on the western end, lay a mountain range that travelers circumvented by taking the southern coastal road. The journey was a little more than a hundred Roman miles, going through many little towns along the way. It would take them a week and a half to travel by foot, provided they didn't stay any longer than overnight anywhere along the way. No one was expecting them in Paphos, so they couldn't actually be late when they got there, but once they started out, Paul said, he would be urgent about keeping the pace up.

The trio occasionally overtook slower travelers, a little family going only three miles from one coastal town to the next, a couple attending a wedding at a community only two miles away, an old man going to see his family a half-day's hike down the road. They generally slowed to the pace of others for a few minutes, introduced themselves, and made conversation.

Paul gave a brief message about Jesus to everyone they walked alongside for a short time. They stayed the first night in a copse of cedar trees, not having found a town by the time their legs begged for a rest. They found an inn at Larnaka and three days later at Kition, where they allowed themselves a slight delay in getting back on the road, for the purpose of preaching in a public area, which resulted in the making of three converts. Paul was conflicted over leaving new Christians without any nearby fellowship of other believers, but the entire team realized they would never cover much ground if they stopped to found a church everywhere they preached. They encouraged the new believers to study the scriptures and told them they hoped the churches in Salamis and, hopefully soon, in Paphos would be spreading all over the island.

In eleven days they came within sight of Paphos, lying in the afternoon sunset at the foot of the rugged western side of the mountains. Stopping at a carter's business as they came to the edge of the city, they got directions to an inn, which turned out to be within a few stones' throws on the same road. Weary from almost eight hours of walking, they bedded down soon and slept more than ten hours. They woke at dawn and went out to a hillside overlooking the beach about half a mile away, where they sat down for reflection and prayer.

"The beauty of God's creation gives me hope," said Barnabas, gazing out at the blue sea with slender foam edges on the narrow beaches fronting Paphos. The white buildings of the city gleamed in morning sun coming over the mountains behind them.

"Like the dawning of God's new day," said Paul. "Let's pray that the gospel brings light into their lives."

"Amen," said Mark.

The work in Paphos was quite different. Jewish residents were far fewer, though a synagogue in the north of the city did provide a starting place for gospel teaching. Paphos was the capital city, and a Roman proconsul had long been stationed there. The mission would face a staunch challenge in the face of active and devoted worship of Venus, the Roman goddess of love which the conquerors had syncretized with the Grecian goddess Aphrodite. The residents of Cyprus, steeped in Grecian heritage, wistfully referred to her by her older name, but without much resistance to the newer persona, so long as they could indulge themselves in her worship, which they did with enthusiasm, since temple activities involved sensual and sexual elements that distracted them from more academic issues.

The mission team acquainted themselves with the layout of the city, the bustling business, the markets, the government buildings, and the port district, before finding lodging mid afternoon and plotting their strategy for introducing the city to the gospel message.

They began at the synagogue, introducing themselves to the local Jewish leaders and trying, in an uncertain atmosphere of some underlying suspicion, to present themselves as friends of Israel and friends of anyone and everyone in principle.

The first opportunity they had on a Sabbath, they engaged worshipers in conversation about the vision of the prophets, a unified vision in their view, of the coming of someone from God who would herald a new age of God's rule in men's hearts. In smaller settings, conversations with agreeable people, they openly spoke of their belief that Jesus of Nazareth was the Christ.

Within the first month they found a pleasant grassy park near the synagogue where they managed to attract a small group to whom they formally presented the gospel, with no immediate results in the way of conversions. The work was slow, but at least so far they hadn't encountered hostility, only curiosity.

By two months into their stay, however, a few Jews associated with the synagogue had professed to believe Jesus was the Messiah, and in another week or two the number had grown to ten. They decided to meet in the grassy park daily with their little band of followers, and soon the open-air meeting grew.

When Paul and Barnabas spoke to the gathering they often took turns, as if handing off a baton in a race. Mark stood nearby, usually not doing anything but observing both his friends and the daily enlarging crowd. During the third week of their open-air meetings, Mark noticed an odd looking fellow on the periphery of the group, dressed somewhat differently from the rest and seeming to be investigating the goings on rather than really being personally interested in them. And he would never stay in the area until Paul and Barnabas ended their presentation. He would always skit away, almost furtively, as if making an escape.

One morning in their second month in Paphos, as Barnabas had finished speaking and he and Paul were moving off to the side to converse with a small group of interested persons, an official looking party of two men in fine togas and matching sashes strode toward the front and asked to talk with the two speakers. Mark joined his companions, wondering what the men wanted.

"Sirs," one of the men said.

"Yes?" said Barnabas.

"I am Tully," said the man, "deputy to the proconsul, Sergius Paulus."

"Friend, I'm Barnabas. This is Paul."

"The proconsul would like to speak to you," said the deputy.

Barnabas looked at Paul as if wondering if this were the beginning of official opposition. Paul was less suspicious, and just smiled back at Barnabas, and then at the deputy.

"When would it be convenient for the proconsul to see us," said Paul.

It was immediately evident that the deputy hadn't come to escort Paul and Barnabas to him under guard. Neither of the men was armed. They appeared to be friendly emissaries. It also appeared that the deputy might have expected to be met with suspicion, and his facial expression went from blank to pleased.

"Now, if you are willing," said the deputy. "The proconsul is in his chambers."

"We'll go with you gladly," said Paul, looking at Barnabas, who made an agreeable face. Mark was expected to do whatever the other two decided.

The five men left the park and navigated the streets around it until they came into a larger lane that led down to the civic center where the proconsul had his governing chambers. On the way, the deputy briefed Paul and Barnabas on the procedure to be followed when they met the proconsul. It was not overly-officious, but it was important to follow protocol when speaking with a representative of Rome. When they arrived at the government complex, guards nodded to the three officials and allowed the group to pass through several doorways and halls without concern.

The proconsul was seated behind a marble topped desk with legs carved like a lion's limbs and covered with hammered gold. His entire chamber was appropriately ornate for the office. When the group entered, the deputy stopped, and Paul, Barnabas and Mark stopped beside him.

"Proconsul Sergius Paulus," said the deputy. The proconsul stood and came around the side of his desk. Mark thought the proconsul's move may have startled the deputy slightly, because he appeared not to have expected his superior to demonstrate such friendliness or acceptance to these strangers. Whatever the case, the deputy recovered instantly.

"Proconsul, these are the men you sent for. This is Paul," he said, motioning to him, "and Barnabas. Barnabas, I learned on the way, is from Salamis. Paul is from Syrian Antioch, formerly from Tarsus."

Paul nodded his head deeply toward the proconsul, as did Barnabas and Mark.

"Men," said the proconsul, smiling, "you are welcome."

"Proconsul," said Paul. "We are honored to be asked to come."

The proconsul nodded at his deputy and he and the other man, who had never spoken, retreated from the chamber, leaving the proconsul with the mission team.

"This, proconsul, is John Mark. He is our assistant, and also a teacher."

"Mark," said the proconsul. Mark nodded again, acknowledging the proconsul's speaking to him.

The proconsul stepped away from his desk and closer to the group. "I hear that you have come to our city with a message about what has been happening in Judea for several years. I sent for you because I wish to hear what you're saying. I take my responsibility here in the capital of Cyprus very personally. I like to know what goes on first hand."

Barnabas took the lead. "Proconsul, again we are honored to be asked to speak."

The proconsul continued. "I will tell you first that I am not entirely ignorant of the matter. News of the Empire is prompt and regular here. In addition, as you may know, there are quite a few of your people living on this end of Cyprus as well as in Salamis. I know the synagogue ruler, Noam, personally. In fact, one of my attendants, Elymas, is Jewish."

"We met rabbi Noam when we first arrived," said Barnabas.

"Fine man," said the proconsul. "And, I might add, I visited for some days with the governor of Judea some years ago. I'm acquainted with the beliefs and customs of the Jewish people, and I'm familiar with a number of their prophets in recent years. While I was there, one of them named John was quite well known. They called him the Baptist, I believe?"

"Yes, proconsul," said Barnabas, and then after a short beat, "the Baptist was beheaded by Herod."

"So I heard. Did you know him?"

"No, proconsul," said Barnabas. Paul shook his head, as did Mark.

"I understand your message is about the other prophet. The next one who came along."

"Yes, proconsul," said Barnabas. "The Baptist spoke about him. His name is Jesus."

The proconsul turned and took two paces to one side, smiling and appearing to be formulating a remark, pivoted slowly and came back, centered before the team, who were side by side. "Men, my deputy is fastidious about the courtesies due me. He probably versed you in titles and addresses for me."

"Yes, proconsul," said Paul.

"I keep Tully around because he is good at what he does," said the proconsul. "But since he isn't here at the moment to protect my honor, you may dispense with the 'proconsul' title."

Barnabas and Paul looked at each other, smiled, and appreciated the proconsul's dry humor.

The proconsul continued. "You probably would not be comfortable addressing me by my name," he said, as Paul and Barnabas, shook their heads slightly in agreement, still smiling at him. "But if you will simply throw in a 'sir' now and then, that will suffice. Are we agreed?"

Paul chuckled mirthfully, the first time Mark had seen him do so, and said, "Thank you—sir!" And Barnabas nodded enthusiastically. Mark stifled a laugh, and nodded as well.

"Back to our subject, then," said Sergius Paulus. "I should also tell you I know that Governor Pilate had Jesus executed."

There was silence for a few seconds. "Yes—" said Barnabas, "sir."

"Yet I listened carefully to you a moment ago. You said, 'his name *is* Jesus.'"

"Yes, sir," said Paul. "Because he rose from the dead."

And with that, Paul sought the proconsul's leave to extend his remarks, and there followed one of what Mark thought was Paul's more impassioned, personally persuasive presentations of the gospel, yet delivered with a conversational intimacy that Mark frankly believed Paul had picked up from Barnabas, who had always been more casual and less formal.

The proconsul never interrupted as Paul moved from the crucifixion to the resurrection to Pentecost to the first believers to his persecution of them, and on to his own conversion, winding up his one-sided discussion by saying that he, Barnabas and Mark were here in Cyprus hoping to find people interested in knowing the God of Heaven through his Son, Jesus Christ.

They had stood all this time, about a half hour, in the center of the proconsul's formal chamber, as with crossed arms he listened intently to the Apostle speak. When it became obvious to him that Paul had stopped and was waiting for any response he might make, the proconsul unfolded his arms.

"I want to hear more," he said. "But it is noon, and I am hungry." He raised his voice and called toward the door. "Helvius!"

A man obviously stationed right outside the door opened it and looked in.

"Proconsul?" he said.

"Food. For four." He looked at the team, who looked at each other quickly and nodded.

A spread of fruits, vegetables and bread was brought within minutes as the proconsul invited the team to join him at a nearby table that seated six or eight. The food was of noticeably higher quality than the three had been eating from the nearby market each day, and they accepted the proconsul's invitation to having their fill.

When the food, plates, trays and other things had been removed by servants, the group continued sitting at the table for a short time while Paul and Barnabas followed up what Paul had said before lunch. However, the proconsul was aware of appointment pressing before him, and he indicated at one point that he must tend to duties. They agreed that the proconsul would send for them again soon, perhaps in the next week. Tully would come again, or another of the proconsul's assistants. The team should keep the proconsul advised as to where they were staying.

Then Paul, Barnabas and Mark were escorted back down through the hallways and outer rooms and toward the main entrance.

As they came to the atrium, they saw a number of people there gathered around a desk. A figure sat there whom Mark instantly recognized as the odd little man from the grassy lot. He was writing on some kind of log or record as the men standing before him gave him information. The man looked up at the entering group, appeared not to be surprised, but rather irritated, and his stare followed them as they crossed the room and exited.

When they were gone, the little man got up, excused himself from those at the desk, and walked with determination out of the atrium into the hall from which the mission team had just come.

After descending the granite steps, the mission team was in the main road, where they retraced their steps back through the surrounding city and to the inn.

Their accommodations at the inn had not really been adequate, though it shamed inns in small towns in Judea and Galilee with which the three of them were all-too-well acquainted. Here, they had an actual room—almost bare, but at least not a stall like so many in their homeland. But it was uncomfortable, and the space itself was the extent of the inn's service. No food.

An older couple who had been attending the gathering in the grassy lot had made some ambiguous statements to Mark that seemed to suggest they were amenable to the idea of housing the team for a short time—perhaps for some consideration. Back at the inn, Mark told Barnabas and Paul about his conversation and the two urged him to follow up the next day, if the couple was there. They were, and by the next evening Mark had worked out the arrangements for their new place. Surprisingly, even to Mark, the couple asked for no rent. Evidently they were becoming quite interested in what Paul and Barnabas had been preaching.

Mark remembered they had promised to advise the proconsul of where they were living, and the second day they were in the home he took an hour in the morning to walk to the government center and carry a message for the proconsul. He wasn't certain why he was nervous about seeing the odd little man at the center, but he was.

There was something about the man's visage that seemed off, strange, even eerie. Fortunately, when Mark arrived and gave his written message with the name and location of their present hosts, the odd little man was not manning the desk. Another official was, and he took the message and disappeared without comment.

Within the week, in the course of a few meals and evening conversation in the home, the mission team's host and hostess both professed faith in Jesus and became the first two converts in Paphos. They were followed by nearly two dozen others who apparently had great respect for the old couple and had been awaiting their response to the newcomers' message of eternal salvation through this Jesus they preached.

Four days from their first meeting with Proconsul Sergius Paulus, Tully appeared at the home of the team's hosts and invited them to return with him to the civic complex for another meeting with the proconsul. They informed him they were just preparing to meet with the group that had been gathering regularly in the park, and asked him if the proconsul could wait for an hour. Tully knew the proconsul was flexible that day, and he said yes.

Tully himself was obviously absorbed in what Paul and Barnabas said at the open-air meeting, and Barnabas in particular tried to sense what Tully was thinking and to aim his remarks at the concerns of a man in his position. It couldn't hurt to have one of the proconsul's assistants sympathetic to his boss's interests.

When the better part of an hour had passed, Paul dismissed the group saying they had an audience with someone in government, and they went with Tully.

When they entered the proconsul's chambers, Mark was surprised to see the odd little man there, consulting with the proconsul about something. When Tully exited, the little man started, though haltingly, to follow him—it was evident he wished to remain in the room. Noticing this, Proconsul Sergius Paulus motioned to him to stop.

"Stay, Elymas," he said. The odd little man—whose name Mark assumed to be a nickname, since it meant, "sorceror"— stopped immediately and turned around expectantly.

"You may be interested in what they have to say. Besides, we aren't finished. We'll continue afterward."

Elymas nodded and said, "Of course, proconsul," and he backed off to one side.

"Men," said the proconsul. "I trust you are well. You are staying with some of the leading Jewish citizens in the city. You probably know that."

"We do, sir," said Paul. "They have been good hosts. And they speak well of you."

"By the way," said the proconsul, "Elymas here is a Jew as well. At least, his father was." The proconsul looked at Elymas. "The way he tells it, his mother was a native of Cyprus. She wanted to name him Julius, but his father wouldn't go along with it. They compromised on 'Bar Jesus.' He goes by 'Elymas' because that's what he is: a mystic. He advises me from time to time."

Paul looked impassive, Mark could see, but Mark was certain he was trying to discern from the Holy Spirit if he should engage the proconsul in a discussion of mystics—sorcerers—and do battle here and now with the enemy in the room. That would be what Mark himself would be thinking, at any rate. He watched Paul to see what he would say.

"Sir," Paul said, "where would you like to begin our conversation today?"

The proconsul indicated that the team and he would sit at the table to the side, where they had eaten before and where presumably the proconsul had meetings of other kinds. Not being bidden specifically and overtly to do so as well, Elymas continued to stand off to the side.

The proconsul asked a question about Jesus' teaching on the subject of the Kingdom of God, and for several minutes Barnabas gave an answer, stressing the tremendous distinction between Jesus' Kingdom, which was invisible and spiritual, and any kingdom or empire of human beings, which was political and visible. He laid stress on the fact that people who were included in the Kingdom of God were ideal citizens in the way of abiding by laws of moral and ethical conduct.

Mark casually observed Elymas now and then and saw nothing to indicate that the little man took issue with what Barnabas was saying.

The discussion turned to the resurrection, and it was evident that the proconsul had been thinking about the subject since their last meeting. He specifically wanted to know how such a thing could actually happen, and what it was that made the three evangelists so certain that it had taken place.

Here, Paul shone. He launched into a quiet but fervent presentation, in succinct points, of the evidence that Jesus had really died but had also really risen from the grave. Though Paul had not witnessed the events surrounding Jesus' resurrection personally—he only encountered Jesus himself a few years later—he told the story as if he had been with the women at the tomb and later with the disciples as they saw Jesus in the Upper Room and in Galilee, very much alive.

Proconsul Paulus listened rapt, carried along by Paul's words. Before he finished, Paul briefly repeated the account of his own experience of the risen Jesus, which he had told the proconsul in their previous meeting. Then he concluded by saying that everywhere the disciples of Jesus went, the Spirit of the risen Jesus made himself quite evident in the lives of people who put their trust in him and named him Lord.

A brief lull followed Paul's speech. It was not immediately

evident the proconsul would respond or debate anything Paul had said, but off to the side Elymas suddenly took one step forward and spoke up.

"Proconsul, if I may?" he said.

"Something to add, Elymas?" said Sergius Paulus.

"Yes, your eminence," said Elymas. "These men are obviously steeped in The Way, the religion of Jesus, and it is clear they are knowledgeable about it," he said, nodding their direction with what Mark took to be feigned respect for the mission team. "But your eminence should know that their beliefs are by no means accepted by the recognized experts in the faith of their fathers—and of mine. Not only the Roman authorities but also their own high priests and temple rulers in Jerusalem disavow Jesus. They have been quite clear over the years since Jesus' death that his disciples—not *you* gentlemen, of course—but his original disciples or some of their friends, must have stolen Jesus' body. The story of his resurrection came about to explain that his tomb was empty."

Elymas nodded "respectfully" toward Paul and Barnabas, and paused for the proconsul to respond.

"I do know," the proconsul said to Paul, "that the matter is disputed."

"As is nearly everything in the world, sir," said Paul. "We have presented the evidence we know to be true. We believe it proves our case."

"If I may, again, proconsul?" said Elymas, having not stepped back into his previous position. Obviously, he wanted to engage the missionaries and keep the proconsul from becoming any more convinced of what they were saying.

"Speak," said the proconsul.

"Your eminence," said Elymas, "I have studied the matter with priests both here and in Judea. As you know, I traveled there a few years ago. The issues at Jesus' trial were blasphemy and sedition.

The first concerned my people, the Jews, because it is an *inviolable* truth of our religion that the Lord our God is ONE." And with that quotation from the books of Moses, Bar Jesus looked at Paul with a stern face, and then quickly continued. "This Jesus claimed to be one *with* God. This cannot be." He took a breath but protected his opportunity to speak by pressing on quickly.

"Further, proconsul, the charge of sedition was of great concern to his majesty the Emperor, and to every governor and proconsul in every province of the Empire. His eminence Pilate consented to Jesus' condemnation for that reason. These men seem honest enough in their belief that their religion is harmless to your eminence and the peace of this city, but consider the precedent set by Governor Pilate. He did not agree."

Elymas had spoken emphatically but with quiet restraint, which probably by itself kept the proconsul from interrupting or stifling him. But instead of looking to Paul or Barnabas to see if either of them had a response, the proconsul turned in his chair and engaged Elymas himself.

"On the matter of God," said the proconsul, "even our Roman beliefs hold that the gods have at times appeared in human form. We do not, however, conclude that there are two of them, one visible, the other not."

"No, eminence," answered Elymas, "but with respect, the Empire names sixty-seven gods and goddesses to begin with. My father's faith names but one." On that statement he turned his head toward Paul and Barnabas and glared.

"And as to sedition," continued the proconsul, "I don't know of —can *you* name one instance since The Way began, where its followers have rebelled against Caesar?"

"Your eminence, it is inevitable. I advised you, as you will remember last week, that I have foreseen trouble from these men and from those who might follow them here." Elymas waxed mystical, raising his hand slightly as if beginning some prophetic pronouncement, and letting his eyelids begin to close, as if on the verge of entering a trance. "I have seen and heard this—"

At that moment, Paul, who had gradually turned in his chair to face Elymas, rose slowly, his face like Moses confronting the faction of Dathan in the desert, when the earth opened up and swallowed him. When Paul had fully stood, Elymas had become quiet, instantly intimidated by the holy presence in which Paul was invisibly but powerfully enveloped.

"You are full of deceit and fraud," said Paul, in a low and even voice, which Mark thought would have sounded menacing had he not been simply speaking truth with calm clarity.

"You are a child of the devil," Paul continued, his volume increasing, as he stepped around from the front of his chair and faced Elymas squarely.

"You are the enemy of true righteousness," Paul said, now strongly and forcefully. "Quit trying to turn the Lord's truth into lies!"

The room became dead. Sergius Paulus, hands gripping the arms of his gilded chair, leaned forward slightly, staring in startled awe at Paul. He looked left toward Elymas. Barnabas had been watching Paul and now also looked to see what Elymas would say. Mark, near the end of the table, did the same.

Elymas was frozen in place. But a dark look began to creep across his brow and into his squinting eyes. Before he could respond, however, Paul spoke again. He had returned to the low, controlled, intense tone that seemed to come from another, invisible realm.

"The Lord's hand is against you. From this moment, you are going to be blind for a time. Not even the light of the sun will come through!"

The proconsul stared at Paul with astonishment. Elymas suddenly looked shocked and became unstable on his feet. He took a step back merely to catch himself from falling. Instantly, he threw out his arms as if maintaining balance on a ledge. His eyes grew wide. But it was profoundly obvious that he could see nothing with them.

Paul looked to Mark and motioned to him silently to go to Elymas and stand ready to help him. Mark left his seat and hurried the few feet to where Elymas was. Elymas, his arms still out to each side, was breathing hard and had begun to shudder.

"Take my arm, sir," said Mark. He took hold of Elymas's hand and placed it on his elbow. Elymas became still, though clearly stunned and aghast. Mark looked toward the proconsul, who was still frozen in place, his mouth hanging open.

Paul's stance relaxed as he turned to the seated proconsul. "I suggest, sir, that you have another attendant help him. He will need guiding for a day or more." Paul then sat. He was perfectly serene.

The proconsul called to Helvius, who again was obviously just outside the closed chamber doors. Helvius appeared immediately.

The proconsul instructed him to get another assistant from down the hall, which he did, returning with him. Sergius Paulus explained somewhat enigmatically that Elymas had suffered a temporary spell and couldn't see, and that the assistant was to help him to his quarters and attend him as long as he needed. The assistant, with a mystified look, obediently took over from Mark and led Elymas out the door, which Helvius then closed.

The room was quiet for a few seconds while the proconsul slowly sat back in his chair, looked at his clenched fists on the knobs of his chair arms, as if they were alien appendages, relaxed them slowly, and then raised his eyes to Paul, who was looking at him steadily and calmly.

"I believe," he said slowly and in a sober tone, "the evidence for what you preach is clear."

"Sir," said Paul, "do you believe that Jesus is the Christ, the Son of God?"

"I do," said the proconsul. And Mark heard in it what Barnabas had heard in his father's voice when he became a believer: the echo of a child, confronted with mystery, but ready to be led into truth.

Mark sat in the spacious guest room of their host's and hostess's house that evening, alone with his thoughts and with a letter he had begun to his mother, which he hoped would be taken by messenger service in Pamphylia once they arrived there in a month or so. It was the plan for them to commit the work here in Paphos to the Lord's keeping after four months and to sail across to the mainland in Asia. There the first courier from Syrian Antioch would arrive at a previously agreed day and the team would meet his ship.

As to the letter he was composing, however, Mark had become stalled after a single line. He had plenty to say to his mother, of course—descriptions of their travels, reports of the work in Salamis and here, in Paphos. But he hadn't been able to get the events of that afternoon off his mind.

It was difficult for Mark to find much negative about the conversion of the proconsul, obviously. In an instant the man had turned to faith in Jesus, apparently wholly and genuinely so. When he said yes to Paul's question, Paul had confirmed that decision by following up with a few others, notably about the resurrection of Jesus, which the proconsul said was obvious to him because it was clear that Paul was "inhabited" —that was his word—with the spirit of the miracle worker that Jesus was known to be. Paul had gone on to discuss briefly how he, Barnabas and the proconsul would work out questions of his inclusion in the growing fellowship of Christians there in Paphos, a matter not as simple as one might think.

But Mark found himself wondering if conversion primarily

because of witnessing a miracle was going to be a staple of Paul's strategy. He remembered something Jesus had said to people who traipsed after him following his feeding thousands from a handful of bread loaves and some dried fish. Peter told Mark that Jesus told those crowds they were following him only because they had seen him do a miracle and wanted him to do more, to feed them, or just impress them. As Mark thought at the time, miracle-induced conversions are easily suspect.

It was a bit troubling to Mark, as well, that Elymas was likely to develop great resentment because of Paul's causing his blindness. So far, he didn't seem to have responded to blindness the way Saul had when the same thing happened to him. Elymas might do a great deal of harm by poisoning the minds of fellow Jews in Paphos. It wasn't that Mark was sympathetic with Elymas; he wasn't. But he found himself wondering if he had been charged with deciding what to do about Elymas, would he have called down blindness on him, or merely rebuked him sharply?

As he thought about it now, even Paul's frequent, if not unexceptional, use of his own testimony of a supernatural event—seeing Jesus Christ in a vision—constituted the use of a miracle, of sorts, to prompt a decision for Christ. Maybe Mark was being hypersensitive to the issue of the miraculous, and he admitted the possibility, but it still bothered him. Then again, he had to admit that his own conversion had taken place in the context of a supernatural happening at the Great Pentecost Event. When he realized he had been ignoring his own history, he argued with himself to stop thinking critically of Paul.

After all, he highly respected Paul and admired his unexceptional commitment to The Way, to the calling that he had accepted in Christ, and to the immediate mission he was on with Barnabas and Mark. Paul was a bit humorless—that was what made his laughter during their first meeting with the proconsul so surprising—but Mark could forgive him for that, he supposed.

As Mark pondered it all, it seemed the bottom line was that whether supernatural events, minor or major, were involved in convincing people to come to faith in Jesus, was mostly an academic question at the moment. Mark had to admit he didn't actually think the proconsul had made a shallow decision to believe in Christ, just because the deciding factor seemed to have been a demonstration of the supernatural in Elymas's going blind. Time would tell, of course, but he had no overwhelming reason to doubt the proconsul had genuinely opened his heart to the Lord. Still, Mark wanted the gospel to convince people on its own merits.

Mentally dizzy from debating himself, Mark shook off the thought, put the barely-begun letter to his mother into a sheath, wiped his pen dry, capped the clay ink pot, and went to bed.

In a few weeks, after meeting with the newly formed church on a Lord's Day, the team had a frank discussion about moving on to the next planned destination. Their itinerary called for them to sail to Perga, in Pamphylia, north from Cyprus about two days aboard ship. Their preliminary dates for meeting a messenger from Antioch were now four weeks distant, so if they were to arrive in Perga in, say, two weeks, they would have another two weeks to begin some kind of work in Perga, and could continue there another month or so before traveling north toward Pisidian Antioch.

Mark and Barnabas thought the plan was workable. Barnabas especially noted how stable and promising the little Paphos church seemed to be. Having already had previous conversations about how they were going to have to entrust the future of all their mission churches to the Spirit of Jesus, they agreed they would tell the church the following Lord's Day, and leave the next week.

The next day, the proconsul summoned them again. The by-now friendly Tully came for them and seemed unusually chatty with them on their walk back south into the city's government complex to see Sergius Paulus. As they came near the buildings, Tully stopped them and moved to the side of the street.

"Gentlemen. Uh, Paul," he said. "I should have told you this first thing. I admit I was nervous."

"About what," Paul said.

"It's just that—" he was searching for words. "I believe. I believe what Proconsul Paulus believes. What you believe."

"Are you saying you believe in Jesus?" said Barnabas.

"I do. I do!" he said. "The proconsul told me everything you told him. He said I should believe, myself. And, of course, I know what happened to Elymas."

Paul had a serious smile, a look of happiness framed in a brow of concern, written on his sun-crinkled face. Mark thought he was debating whether to challenge Tully's assertion or just wholeheartedly welcome him to the brotherhood of believers. Instead, he simply asked him to come to the church the following Lord's Day. Tully said he would, and being otherwise speechless, he continued quickly to lead the way back to the proconsul's chamber.

Proconsul Paulus told the team he had prepared letters for regional deputies on the mainland where the mission team might visit. He proffered several rolled parchments, and Mark took the initiative to accept them. He was the official caretaker of all the other records as well as scriptures the team had. Paul thanked the proconsul for his thoughtfulness and said he was confident that such a recommendation would be quite helpful when they moved on. Then he told him that they were going to leave in just under two weeks.

"Two weeks?" said Sergius Paulus. "Well. I suppose I had assumed that you would be here much longer."

"Our mission plans were to work our way into Asia," said Barnabas. "We have prearranged contacts in several places on fixed dates, so it's necessary for us to move on."

"I have begun to think of you as friends," said the proconsul.

"And we are," said Paul. "And there is one matter, my friend, that we must take care of right away, as we discussed earlier. You must be baptized."

The proconsul, who had been standing behind his marble desk, smiled, sat down, laid his palms flat on the desk surface in front of him, studied the pattern in the marble distractedly, then looked up.

"Make it official," he said.

"It makes it public," said Paul.

"It does," said the proconsul. "There's no going back."

"No," said Paul. "I trust that you have no desire to go back."

"No," said the proconsul, shaking his head slowly and with deliberateness. "I've simply given much thought in the past few days to a Roman proconsul's having become a Christian. I suspect some of my superiors will disapprove." His tone was calm, measured, and reflective. Mark thought he didn't seem particularly frightened by the prospect, but more like he was trying to look ahead and plan for the inevitable in a deliberate way. It seemed to fit with the kind of man they had found him to be in their meetings with him.

"Proconsul," said Paul. "Brother. The Spirit of Jesus will give you courage and wisdom. Don't be afraid. You have come to his kingdom for a purpose."

The proconsul nodded. "So—baptism."

"This coming Lord's Day, proconsul—*die Solis?*" said Paul. "Barnabas will perform the ordinance."

"I will be there."

"And your first attendant knows the way," said Barnabas. "Perhaps he will be ready to be baptized as well?"

Paul said, "He told us of your conversations."

"I hope that was—" The proconsul fumbled for words, uncharacteristically. "Appropriate?"

"Sir," said Paul, "you don't realize how perfectly appropriate it was."

The team shortly left the government center and walked back to the house. Paul and Barnabas settled into some chairs in their hosts' main room to rest while talking. Mark took the opportunity of their ensuing conversation to go to the guest room and read the letters the proconsul wrote.

There was nothing remarkable about them outside the fact that they were so—so Gentile. Something about the proconsul's having assumed the posture of an evangelist to his attendant, Tully, suddenly seemed emblematic of a shift in the very core of the short history of the gospel. So far, the epicenter of the gospel was Jerusalem, or more generally Judea and Galilee. Antioch, of course, was a very strong center of the growing church, but it was because there had been so many Jews in Antioch. The Jews, the historical people of God. The people to whom the promises of a deliverer had been made. And although Peter, whom Mark deeply respected, had been the one to officially recognize that Gentiles were equally deserving recipients of the gospel with the Jews, still the church seemed, to Mark anyway, to rightfully have its center in the community of God's people of history.

You could draw a line from Jerusalem out to Galilee, a line into Syria, a line from Jerusalem across to Cyprus, like gospel lifelines, tossed to the world. That was the gospel, coming out of God's chosen people to the world. Why, even the mission team itself, Barnabas and Paul, had gone straight to the synagogue when they arrived in Salamis, and straight to the synagogue when they came to Paphos. They were doing what they sensed was the appropriate thing to do with the gospel message: take it to the Jews first. So far, in Mark's experience, it had been from *there*, from the centers of Jewish worship and history, that the gospel had gone out to the Gentiles.

Mark found himself struggling with the notion that the gospel could be, well, "turned loose" among Gentiles to spread among themselves. The struggle was between his natural affinity for what he knew, what he had always known, what had been his upbringing and experience, on the one hand, and on the other hand, the new and tradition-shattering experience of the gospel, which had long been prophesied to bring other nations into the fold of God. Again, Mark reminded himself of Peter's vision. Nobody was unclean.

It was not merely an academic struggle. Mark found himself arguing not so much with his mind as with his heart. And his prejudice was becoming defensive, in spite of himself.

But there was an academic or a practical issue, as well. Did the Gentiles know enough to carry on without the guidance of Jews who believed in Jesus? After all, the Jews had the scriptures. They had been steeped in them. Mark had been steeped in them. Paul. Barnabas. They understood the gospel because they knew the word of God from a lifetime of instruction in the Tanakh, God's word.

Mark looked at the letters. He found himself wondering if Paul were going to continue to go to the synagogues and insist on planting the church there with those who were drawn to the message of Jesus, and count on the church's expanding from a Jewish heart. Or would he bypass them, go to a town square, stand up and start cold, preach to people who had no background in the history of God's people at all?

It was something to ponder. But probably not to discuss just now with Paul. Or even Barnabas, for that matter. Paul and Barnabas seemed to be agreed on their strategy, independent of anything Mark thought. They had frequently discussed things without including Mark. He was aware he was not quite an equal part of the team. He knew that going in, of course.

And in spite of the furious analysis he was conducting with himself about these little misgivings of his, he felt the impress of the Holy Spirit in him to be humble, deferential to both his teammates and their spiritual maturity, even though he had become a Christian the same time as Barnabas and, in fact, before Paul. Still, Paul exhibited a depth that was remarkable, and Mark recognized it and honored it. His apprehensions were probably easily explicable by the Apostle out of his superior understanding.

Tears moistened many faces in the little church that Lord's Day when Barnabas announced that the team would be leaving for Asia the following week. The women hurriedly got together and planned a going away supper on the fourth day of the week. The team's ship departed the next morning.

Unexpectedly to Paul and Barnabas, the church presented the team with a monetary gift after the supper, a sizeable amount for such a small group. They knew there were expenses to traveling and they wanted to be part of the future of Paul and Barnabas's work. Mark had known about the gift beforehand but the church leader who told him asked him not to tell the two principal evangelists before the supper meeting.

Paul took the occasion to preach for about a half hour, which evoked still more tears from both women and men, and then the meeting broke up and everyone filtered out and went home after more well-wishing and pledges of prayers. Back at their accommodations the team packed up their things and prepared to leave at the break of dawn for the short walk to the harbor.

Winds were blustery for the launch of their ship; the sailors feared a nor'easter was about to blow in, but the day progressed without any negative trend. By evening, winds were steady though mild. The disadvantage to the gusty start was that the winds were nearly in their face, but the captain began a tacking maneuver that enabled them to make forward progress in spite of it. By evening, however, the direction of the wind had changed and at full sail they were able to make about average speed through the night.

Below deck the team had a berth that was the most basic of transportation, but they were thankful for it. It was only for one night, and each of them made himself as comfortable as possible on a low bench with his pack as a pillow. A calm sea except for regular and gentle swells let them drift off to sleep for most of the deep night hours. Sometime in the daylight on the morrow they would be in Asia.

The mission impelled them onward. God had given them success so far. He had paved their way, and lighted it as well. He had provided for them adequately and more. Each of them continued silently the prayer they had voiced together before they turned in for the night, that the Lord would continue to go before them and glorify Jesus in what they did.

23
Perga, Asia, c. A.D. 47

The second day of travel was faster owing to increased wind speed, and by almost sundown they sighted land. There was little to see on the coast as they approached. Perga was about seven miles up the Cestrus river from the coast. The captain headed for the mouth of the river, which could accommodate smaller ships, such as the one they had taken from Paphos. It would take them another hour to sail upstream to the little port at Perga. Slowly crawling through the gentle river with the barely moderate breeze astern, everyone onboard was swatting at the mosquitos that wafted in from shore. They arrived at the docks just as the light was becoming an issue to navigating inland waterways.

Dockhands helped secure the ship and the passengers were soon off, leaving behind any unloading of cargo, which was minimal. The little ship mostly ferried passengers and a few foodstuffs back and forth from Asia to Paphos, along with the occasional dignitary.

Two inns near the waterfront gave the travelers a choice of arrangements for the evening, and the mission team settled into one of them and bedded down after a brief foray for something to eat. In the morning, they would find the local synagogue and start their mission venture all over again.

Mark rose early and had already talked with the innkeeper and others about finding the synagogue, before Barnabas and Paul had even gotten up. By the time Mark returned to the inn the other two were off in corners praying, and Mark did the same, though outside, sitting on a low wall across the street, the port in view a half furlong away.

On the street was a growing number of people walking to work or market, and curiously, not just one but three teams of two men each, transporting bodies—covered in preliminary shrouds. Apparently these were people who had not died at home in their beds, but somewhere else, and they had to be taken home for their families to see to their burial. Mark guessed at all this, but it seemed reasonable. While he was watching the processions, Mark waved off mosquitos as they all had the previous evening, finally retreating to their room inside the inn to get away from them.

The synagogue in Perga, a respectable building in size and style, commanded a fine view of the harbor to one side, and an unfortunately wonderful view of the temple to Artemis confronting everyone leaving Sabbath day worship. The team found the synagogue easily and found the current elder in charge puttering around inside. Yakov was a doddering old man, affable and probably well beloved in the community.

"Welcome, welcome, welcome! We have lots of visitors here from Paphos," he said, after Barnabas had taken the lead and introduced the team. "Not many of our people, of course. You know elder Natan over there, I suppose."

"Of course," said Paul. "A fine leader."

"That he is, that he is," said Yakov.

"We missed being able to worship with you yesterday, being aboard ship," said Barnabas, "but we'll be here next Sabbath."

"Wonderful!" said the old man, "Just wonderful. Where are you staying?"

"We don't know," said Paul. "Last night at one of the inns near the dock."

"Oh! Terrible place. Just terrible," said Yakov. "All those mosquitos, and who knows what other crawling things. Terrible. Did you sleep at all?"

"Some. Not well," said Barnabas. "Uh, do you—can you recommend someplace better?"

"Oh, let me see," said Yakov. "Let me see." He ran a crooked finger through the beard on his chin, his eyes fixed on nothing in front of him. "Oh! Yes." His face brightened as he looked up at Barnabas, but he didn't immediately say anything more.

"Uh, an inn of better quality, perhaps?" said Barnabas.

"Oh, no, no, no. Better than that," said Yakov. "I know a man, a man in our synagogue. Nice man. Has a nice house. Wife died more than ten years ago. Nice man. Old man, but nice." He smiled and again didn't continue.

"Does he have a name?" said Mark.

"Oh, yes. Has a name, yes. It's Yakov." Yakov grinned.

"Like you?" said Paul.

"Oh, yes. Like me! Because he *is* me." Yakov grinned, showing a gap where a tooth or two were missing.

Everybody laughed. Paul said, "You're offering us the generosity of your home?"

"Yes, of course!" said Yakov. "Seem like good men, you do. And the scriptures teach us to be hospitable to strangers."

"Rabbi Yakov," said Mark, "we may be in the city for two or three months. We're not sure."

"Oh, fine. That's just fine. We'll all get to know each other, yes?" he said, cackling genially again.

Paul, Barnabas and Mark all looked at each other and immediately agreed.

"We'll make certain you are well taken care of," said Barnabas.

"Oh, no need, no need," said Yakov. "Oh, you can help with food if you eat there, but it's a big house. Well, more than I need alone. Echos in the walls. Empty. No grandchildren, you see. My wife was barren. House was my father's. I was one of seven children. Plenty of room for seven children. They all moved away. Just me, now. Just me. You're welcome to come. Bring noise!" He laughed, an old man's raspy cackle. "Today?"

"Today would be perfect," said Barnabas. "When will you be leaving here for your house?"

"Oh, in an hour or so. To eat."

"Then we'll just go back to the inn, get our things, and return here," said Paul. "Thank you, rabbi."

"I'll be here," said Yakov. "Yes, yes. Nowhere else to go!" He chuckled again and turned back toward his puttering as the team went back out the front door.

The team was back in an hour, and Yakov closed up the house of worship and led them east in the city to his home, which was as he had represented it, large. Instantly, the team members looked at each other, thinking the same thing. If Yakov could be won to the faith, he would have a lot of people, and a lot of noise, in his home every Lord's Day.

Yakov led them to three separate rooms, offering his guests individual places to sleep, study, and pray. They willingly accepted the arrangement and deposited their packs in the rooms, rejoining him up front in the house where he was just sitting in the atrium, drumming his fingers on a little side table. He seemed winded from the walk.

"You like?" he said, grinning.

"Very nice," said Mark. "Thank you again for your hospitality."

"How long will you stay?"

"As we said, maybe two months or more," said Mark.

"Good, good," said Yakov. "Are you in business?"

The team had had only a few minutes when retrieving their belongings from the inn to discuss how they would introduce the subject of their visit. It was agreed that Paul would explain their purpose in Perga.

"No, not really," said Paul. He glanced at Barnabas and almost imperceptibly shook his head. He wasn't going to begin a presentation of the gospel at this very moment. The time and circumstances weren't optimal.

"We are traveling. We came from the mainland to Salamis about five months ago. Made a lot of friends, and then we traveled the south island road to come here. This is a very beautiful island."

"Oh yes, yes. It is. As a young man, I went into the mountains, up there," he said, pointing generally to the east from the house. "Lived off the land. With friends. Hunted. Cold at night, though," he said, feigning a shiver. "Couldn't do that now. Too old. I get cold when it's hot!" He laughed, as the rest of them did, courteously.

Yakov seemed to have forgotten his original question about what they were doing in the area, or he accepted the idea of "traveling" as meaning "sightseeing," and he dropped the subject.

"Are we keeping you from what you may need to be doing?" said Paul.

"No, no. Am I?" said Yakov.

"No. But we could just walk around the city," said Paul. "Find out where things are."

"Oh yes. I could help you if you like."

"Thank you for the offer, but perhaps we'll just stroll here and there and figure it out. We'll be back in a couple of hours."

"Well. Well. I'll be here! Not going anywhere."

"Are you ready," Paul said to Barnabas and Mark.

"Sure," said Barnabas.

"I think perhaps I'll stay," said Mark.

Paul and Barnabas went out the front door and soon disappeared down the residential lane that had led up a small hill to Yakov's house. Mark watched as they left, and then turned to Yakov.

"Would you show me the house?" he said to Yakov.

"Oh, of course. Of course," said Yakov. He got up and took short steps at first as he stabilized himself. Then he took Mark on a tour of the home, showing him the rooms and the garden out back.

The enclosed garden reminded Mark somewhat of his home in Jerusalem. It was walled with light brick with a decorative crown, and it had flowerbeds surrounding a grassy area, a flat cobblestone walk, and several benches. Mark sat down on a long bench.

"This reminds me of home," he said. "My mother's home in Jerusalem."

Yakov sat down himself. "Where you grew up?"

"Yes," said Mark. "She still lives there. I moved to Antioch—the one in Syria—a few years ago."

"This house was my father's. And my mother's," said Yakov, forgetting that he had told them that earlier. "I still have the same bedroom. Different bed, though."

"Do you have most of the scriptures at the synagogue?" asked Mark. He assumed they did, but it was a lead-in to his subject.

"Oh, yes. Yes. All of them. The Greek ones, of course. Nobody reads Hebrew anymore."

"No, I suppose not."

"My father did. Yes. My father learned it from his father," said Yakov, rambling. "But he spoke Greek, like all my family here. My great grandfather was the last of our family to live in Judea. He came over here when he was just a boy. Spoke Aramaic like everyone there does now. Learned Greek here. Read Hebrew. Nobody does, now."

"Do you read the prophets much in Synagogue?" said Mark.

"Oh, yes, yes. Work our way through. Takes a long time, but we work our way through."

"I love the prophets," said Mark.

"Yes, wonderful words. Frightening, sometimes," said Yakov. "Our great forefathers must have been even more sinful than we are," he said, and then turned to Mark, raising a finger and lowering one eye. "Not that we are righteous. No. Not that we are righteous."

Mark thought this was a good sign that Yakov might be ready for the introduction of the subject of the gospel.

"What if," said Mark, "what if all the wonderful predictions of the prophets about *mashiach* came true in our own day?"

Yakov looked wistful, contemplative. "They thought they did a few times before," he said, sounding more serious, more stable, less doddering, than he had until now, and Mark wondered if he had been prepared for the subject.

"That's true," said Mark. "But not for long."

"No, not for long."

"And no one who gathered a following was a perfect man," said Mark. "The way I read the prophets, the Messiah will be a man from God."

Yakov had become quite still. He had lost all sense of the fumbling, repetitive, eccentric man he had seemed to be.

"News of the homeland is quite good here in Asia," said Yakov. Then he turned squarely to Mark. "I know about Jesus of Nazareth," said Yakov. He said it without any hint of argument or controversy, though again, it was without the chatty, conversational pace and lilt that had become familiar.

"Then you know of the church," said Mark, "in Jerusalem, Galilee, and beyond."

"Yes," said Yakov, pausing. "You are not just traveling, are you?"

"No, not *just* traveling," said Mark. "We are going here and there telling people that we believe Jesus of Nazareth is the Messiah."

"I thought it," said Yakov. He seemed perfectly agreeable about their being on a mission. "Tell me." He paused.

"Tell you—"

"Why you believe this."

This was the open door Mark had been looking for. Trying not to take too long or to drag things out, he began a whirlwind verbal tour of the events of some eighteen years ago. He told how the Baptist had announced that the Messiah had come. Then he told about the ministry of Jesus, his miracles, his teachings. He told Yakov about the crucifixion. He told him the remarkable story of Jesus' resurrection, emphasizing how many witnesses there had been that Jesus was very much alive. Then he told him about the Great Pentecost Event, how he and thousands of others had repented, confessed their belief in Jesus, and been baptized. From there, he simply summarized how believers had spread throughout Judea, into Galilee and beyond, and how Jews everywhere were turning to Jesus as the Christ, the Son of God.

Yakov listened intently, occasionally nodding his head. He never appeared to be surprised—apparently he had heard reports of it all. But Mark had the sense that he had never heard it from someone who was a believer, a Christian. Now, he had.

When he was finished, Mark was momentarily uncertain where to go with the conversation. Silently, he pled for direction. The door was opened with a tear.

A single drop descended from the pools in Yakov's crinkled eyes, getting lost in the upper edge of his gray beard. Others then followed, leaving traces as they descended. Yakov continued to look at Mark directly, not hiding his emotion.

"Rabbi," said Mark, respectfully, "will you repent and receive Jesus as Lord?"

Yakov smiled through moistened eyes. "I have hoped all my life he would come. All my life. I have repented every day, hoping he would come that day. Yes. Yes. I believe."

In the pleasant scent of Yakov's little garden yard on a windless day, the passing clouds hid the heat of the sun from the two men as they sat on the old bench. The aging rabbi put his hands together as he had every Sabbath in front of his faithful congregation to pray the prayers of the Psalmist, and he prayed with Mark for the Spirit of the living Jesus to come to him. As he did, the clouds passed, and brilliance flooded the little yard, whose colors were richer than they had ever been.

Barnabas and Paul returned in about two hours as they had said, went to their rooms to put down a few things they had bought in the market, and then searched the house looking for Mark or Yakov, finally finding them in the garden out back.

Mark and Yakov had been talking about the church in Antioch, the latter asking about their worship, their teaching, the scriptures they used, and anything else that occurred to him. Upon Barnabas's and Paul's arrival they fell into a slightly awkward silence.

"What?" said Barnabas. "Do we have grape stains on our faces or what?"

"No, nothing," said Mark, laughing. "It's just—"

"What?" said Paul.

"While you were gone, Yakov has become a Christian."

Mark briefly told what had taken place there in the garden. Yakov interrupted now and then with almost youthful excitement. Barnabas beamed.

Paul smiled. Mark noted what he took to be a bit of reserve in Paul's reaction. When the account was done, Paul asked a question or two, as if wanting to confirm for himself that what the two were saying was, in fact, the first genuine conversion in Perga.

Mark didn't miss the implication that his witness had to pass Paul's inspection. The fact lingered in the back of his consciousness at least momentarily, perhaps longer, until he suppressed it in the continuing delight of the last hour. Yakov was a believer. And Mark thought that he was probably beloved enough in the hearts of his congregation that many if not most of them would become believers because of him. The church in Perga might well begin with a sudden influx of converts.

The next day the four men went early to the market. Yakov, it seemed, usually didn't eat at home. He had a number of places in the market he liked to go that prepared food, and many of them had a stool or chair behind their fruit stands and under their meat tables that they pulled out when they saw him coming. Yakov introduced his new friends to everyone, everywhere he went, and when they had all finally had enough breakfast to last them until the next day, they wound up at the synagogue.

Yakov happily let the team use one of the back rooms to study and to plan. Barnabas had tried to memorize where things were in the city, especially the other synagogue, a smaller building and congregation on the western edge of town. They agreed to concentrate on the synagogues for now. If civic authorities got wind of something happening and the team got an invitation such as they had in Paphos, so much the better.

Before they left for the day, Mark asked Yakov, with not hint of presumption, if he and Barnabas might make some "working copies" of some scriptures while they were there. Yakov assented with no reservation, which was a bit surprising, but while the iron was hot, evidently it was very pliable.

"Thank you, rabbi. Everywhere we go, we need the scriptures, and perhaps we will not always have access to them," said Mark. He let the implication sit there at his sentence's end.

"Rabbi," said Paul, "we bought some food. For all of us, this evening, if you like."

"Oh, wonderful," said Yakov. "You must be careful where you buy, of course."

"Careful?" said Barnabas.

"Oh, well, you haven't been here. I don't know if it comes from the market or not."

"Where what comes from?" said Paul.

"The sickness," said Yakov. "The sickness. Fever. Exhaustion. Vomiting. Quite a few die of it."

The team looked at one another with concern.

"You were all over the city, yes?" said Yakov. "You saw funeral processions, no?"

"We did, yes," said Barnabas."We thought it seemed like an unusually busy day for burials."

"Nobody knows," said Yakov. "Nobody knows where it came from. It could be a spirit, I suppose. Most people think it's in the market. You should be careful, I think."

Nobody had any other guesses, though silently Mark thought it was not any sort of evil spirit.

The eve of their first Sabbath in Perga came swiftly amid their becoming oriented to the city, settling in with their host, and beginning to teach Yakov the fundamentals of Christian faith and the church. They met neighbors of Yakov's who were faithful Jews and planned to be in synagogue, and they made friends of them as well as a great many Gentile acquaintances of the old rabbi.

Long after supper, when everyone was getting sleepy, Mark retreated briefly to his room. When he returned, the other three were not in the main room. He hunted a bit and then saw them outside in the garden. They had gone out and shut the door, and they appeared to be having some sort of discussion. Mark felt strangely dis-invited, and he didn't presume to intrude upon the meeting. They weren't talking loud enough to be overheard, so he went back to his room and shortly went to bed.

The morning of the Sabbath they gathered in the spacious synagogue and waited quietly for the rabbi, the singer and the reader's attendant to begin. Presently, they did, and before long it was time for the rabbi to speak. As he began, he first introduced his house guests, saying they were from Antioch of Syria and they were part of the Christian church there. They were followers of The Way.

Then Yakov said summarily, "This week, I became a follower of Jesus. He is the Messiah the Lord promised to send us." Every eye fixed on him and the room was profoundly still.

Yakov briefly read from several prophets and said that Jesus fulfilled the predictions they made. When he had finished, he asked Paul to speak.

Paul briefly thanked Yakov and told the assembled worshipers his conversion story. Then he turned back to Yakov, who asked the singer to lead the group in a hymn, which he did, and the worship time was concluded.

At first, however, no one moved. Then a fidgety looking young man near the middle of the congregation got up, making as if to leave. The woman next to him, who appeared to be his mother, grabbed hold of his sleeve and jerked him back into his seat. All eyes were forward.

Presently, a man near the front said to Yakov, "Rabbi, You've told us you believe Jesus, the man we have heard about, is the Christ." Wide-eyed and looking helpless, he said, "Well, tell us what we are supposed to do."

The church in Perga began with thirty-seven converts out of the forty-five people present on that first Sabbath that Paul, Barnabas and Mark were in the city. The other eight people were children too young to decide such a matter for themselves, and one old man who hadn't heard a word that was said and hadn't been hearing synagogue services for several years. It took a few weeks for him to be instructed by writing, and after he caught up first with the news from Judea about Jesus, which he hadn't heard in the first place, and then the newest news about Yakov's becoming a Christian, he gladly joined the others.

The mission team spent three months in Perga. The synagogue building, instead of Yakov's house, as Paul and Barnabas had previously supposed, became the locus of the newly planted church, shifting smoothly into that identity. There were a few Jews who had not been present for that first Sabbath when the gospel was explained and proclaimed—they were mostly people who routinely absented themselves. A few of these caught wind of what was going on and visited later. A few of those few were won to faith in Christ. Most of the ones who continued to be uninterested also weren't interested in contesting the change since they had been raised as secular and uninvolved in the faith of their history.

One or two codgers, however, who had no record of faithfulness in worship with other Jews, tried to stir up opposition to the Christian movement but with little success. Jews who knew the critics were not respectable Jews in the first place were disinclined to listen to their castigation of Christians.

The ship the team had known since they left Antioch would be arriving in Perga while they were there came just three weeks into their stay. The messenger who met them at the dock in the late afternoon of the pre-arranged day was a new member of the Antioch church they hadn't met, Gidon, a man in the banking business with the members who were arranging the team's support and communication. Gidon gave Barnabas an inconspicuous looking leather satchel that contained a substantial amount of money. Then he gave each team member letters. One of them was for Mark. It was from his mother.

Yakov insisted that Gidon stay with the team at his house, which he did overnight, his little ship sailing out mid morning the next day. Over supper, Gidon caught the team up with goings on in Antioch, whatever might not be in the letters they had received from home. In the evening, they eventually retreated to their rooms and retired. Mark had not yet read his letter, and when he was nestled in his bed propped up against the wall, he opened it.

Miriam had given the letter to the couple from the Antioch

church who had dutifully visited her on Mark's behalf three months ago. She was grateful for their attentiveness. She missed Mark and his visits. She described how things were in Jerusalem and told Mark about Rhoda's having been sick briefly.

Miriam's writing seemed to be shaky. There were letters that almost couldn't be made out. The lines, which normally Miriam would have penned tight and straight, were erratically spaced and progressively slanted. And she repeated herself several times, not remembering she had written the same thing before. As he read her words, Mark became progressively worried that his mother was in some kind of rapid decline. Near the end of the letter, Miriam wrote that Mark should not worry about her. Though she hadn't admitted to ailing in any way, she never stated she was fine. Just that he shouldn't worry. As if she suspected he already had reason to worry.

The letter remained open on a bedside table while Mark slept fitfully that evening. At dawn he got up, having been awake for an hour already, and in the first streams of light in his room he read the letter again.

Mark wanted to see his mother.

The church continued to strengthen in the next three months the mission team remained in Perga. The year was coming to a close and Paul had begun to talk frequently about going on to their next planned destination. The team agreed that the congregation in Perga was capable of continuing on its own at the present. Since their plan from the first was to backtrack after their final destination and return to many of their previous stops, they felt confident in leaving very soon.

Departing might be wise for other reasons. Two people in the church had come down with "the sickness," whatever it was that so many people in Perga and throughout the coastal region of

Pamphylia had gotten. The two, a couple who lived down near the wharf, had come near to dying, though with constant attendance by friends who took them in and cared for them, they had survived. But Barnabas and Mark had frequently shared their common concern that one of the team might be stricken with the mysterious illness.

Leaving soon was also necessary because of their more-or-less fixed plans. Before Gidon had left, Barnabas had given him a projected date for him, or the next messenger whoever it was, to come to Derbe. It was about a year distant. Barnabas thought certain they could move through Pisidian Antioch, east to Iconium and Lystra, and get to Derbe by that date. If they couldn't, the messenger was to arrange with a service there to hold any letters or other material until they arrived and claimed them.

Mark shared Paul's and Barnabas's enthusiasm about the strength of the little church. He did his job faithfully, too, organizing events, helping with anything and everything the other two needed, and teaching some, especially the older children who had become a part of the church as believers.

But he hadn't told the other two, even his cousin, what Miriam had said in her letter, or what she had not said but which had become evident to her son. Mark had concluded and was certain that Miriam was in some kind of progressive and ultimately perilous decline, perhaps imminently so. And the thought was weighing on him mightily.

Finally, a week before they were to leave Perga for Pisidian Antioch, Mark went to Barnabas's room in the evening for a talk. At first they just stood in the center of the room.

"You look serious, cousin," said Barnabas.

"That obvious?" said Mark.

"Remember, I know you," said Barnabas. "I've thought something was up since Gidon came. Didn't say anything about it because I thought you would, eventually. Something in your mother's letter, isn't it?"

"Not just that, but yes, that."

"She's my aunt. I care, too," said Barnabas. "I've assumed since you got it that she didn't say anything terrible, right? Because you would have told me if she did."

"No, nothing terrible. She says not to worry about her."

"But you think?"

"She's going down, Barnabas. I know it. I can feel it." Mark's face fell into a look of grief.

"Maybe you're wrong. Maybe it's nothing," said Barnabas.

"No. I'm not wrong."

"Everybody goes down as they get older. She's probably just feeling the effects of, what, fifty or so?"

"It's more than that. I know it," insisted Mark.

"When we get back, you can go to Jerusalem right away," said Barnabas. "Until then, our Antioch members who were supposed to check on her will take care of things. I'm sure it's okay."

"By the time we get back, it may be too late," said Mark, looking at Barnabas grimly.

"You're thinking of leaving," said Barnabas. "Aren't you."

Mark turned away and stared out the window into the darkness. "It isn't just that," he said.

"What else did she tell you?"

"No, nothing in her letter. I just feel—" Mark stopped there, not finishing the thought.

"Feel what?" Barnabas realized Mark was struggling with his thoughts. "If it's something you don't think you can tell Paul—"

"That's partly it," said Mark. "But I don't want you to be offended, either."

"I promise not to be."

Mark sat down on a stool. Barnabas sat on the edge of his bed.

Mark worked himself up to speaking, and then said it as simply as he knew how. "I feel like Paul doesn't respect me."

"What?!" said Barnabas softly, so his voice wouldn't carry outside the room. "Of course he does! You're an important part—"

"As a witness. As a leader, I mean."

"What are you talking about?"

"You were there after Yakov became a believer. Paul didn't accept it until he questioned him himself. It wasn't enough that I told him what had happened. He questioned it."

"I think you're making too much of things," said Barnabas. "Paul just wants to make sure conversions are genuine."

"Do you?" said Mark, pointedly.

"Well, of course."

"But *you* didn't question Yakov's conversion. You said, 'That's great!' and seemed overjoyed."

"Well, I was," said Barnabas.

"But Paul's first thought—*his first thought*—was to question whether my witness to Yakov was good enough. To question whether *I* was good enough."

Barnabas started to object but then stopped. Mark watched his face and intuited what was in his mind.

"You've seen it, too," Mark said. "That stern suspicion."

"Well, a little," said Barnabas, "But—"

"He's questioned *you*, hasn't he?!"

"Well, once or twice, but—"

"So it isn't just me."

"No, but I let it roll off my back, cousin. He's Paul!"

"What's that supposed to mean? He can't be wrong? Wrong about me? About you?"

"No, I mean—all he's gone through. What he did before. I think he's just doubly committed to making sure that it isn't too easy for people to claim to be Christians."

"Why? Because it wasn't easy for him?" Mark said. He obviously made his point, because Barnabas froze for a moment.

"It isn't about a comparison with him. It's about—he wants it to be real. For *everybody*. We're starting churches after all. And we're leaving them to make out on their own. It has to be real. You know that!"

"Okay, I get that," Mark said. "I do. But by now he should realize that I know what I'm doing. The Holy Spirit is with me, too."

"Oh, Mark, he doesn't think otherwise. Believe me."

"I'm just saying I feel like it."

"And you're thinking of leaving," said Barnabas.

"Mostly because of my mother, but that doesn't help, either," said Mark. "And it doesn't help that we all may get 'the sickness' and die before we finish the journey." Mark seemed suddenly gloomy, as if he had been worrying about this issue as well.

"Well," said Barnabas, "there's little we can do about that, I suppose."

"Leave Pamphylia," said Mark. "Jews visiting us a month ago from Antioch, up in the mountains, said nobody up there was getting sick. Not like this."

"Well, that's where we're going. So that won't be an issue anymore," said Barnabas. "Is there anything else?"

"Nothing I can put into words."

Mark thought about trying to summarize the concern he had begun to feel in Paphos, the question of whether the church would be Jewish-centered or Gentile-centered. But perhaps he had been mistaken about Paul's sentiments before. The church here in Perga had begun in the synagogue and so far the only Gentiles who had become interested had been on track to become God-fearers anyway: they were quasi Jews in the first place. He decided not to bring up the subject.

Nor did he want to hint at any theological questions that had been prompted by their experiences so far. There were too many inconsistencies in his own thinking. He didn't want to subject himself to a debate over it.

Barnabas seemed subdued over the matter. "Well," he said, "when are you going to decide? We leave in six days."

"Give me three."

"Three days," agreed Barnabas.

"Don't say anything to Paul about it. If I don't leave, he won't know I was considering it."

"I won't."

"I don't suppose there's anyone here who could, or would, replace me," said Mark.

"I'm certain there isn't," said Barnabas. "We'll just go on by ourselves."

"I'd hate for you to be—I mean, I was supposed to help, after all."

"And you have. If you have to leave, you have to. We'll manage."

"I just keep thinking about Imma," said Mark. "If I don't go, and she dies, I'll never forgive myself."

"I'll pray that she'll get well," said Barnabas. "Whatever it is. And Paul will, too."

"Thank you," said Mark.

"*If* you leave. And if you do," said Barnabas, "I'm going to expect *you* to tell Paul." Then he added, "Yourself."

"Of course."

In three days Mark hadn't changed his mind, which was really about 99% made up when he talked with Barnabas. He was becoming quite nervous about all the people dying in Perga, and he understood "the sickness"—they didn't have a name for it other than that—was common up and down the muggy coast and throughout the low country of Pamphylia.

There was little Mark had done so far that couldn't be handled by Barnabas, who, though he had been considered the lead evangelist when the team left Syrian Antioch, had deferred to Paul more and more along the way, such that Paul was really the primary preacher and teacher now. The relative positions of the three had shifted around. Mark felt himself to be in a decidedly insignificant role now, little more than a keeper of papers and a children's teacher, and there were few pupils. Barnabas's role had been diminished, and he had time for nearly everything Mark was doing. Perhaps that's why he hadn't reacted frantically at the prospect of Mark's going back home and to Judea.

The fourth day before they were to leave, they were all basically taking the day off, having done a lot of work in the community and in study the first days of the week. Mark took the opportunity to go up the hill into a woodsy area, where he had previously found a pleasant glen, a place to sit and snack, or muse, or pray. That day, he prayed. He wrangled with God about the decision he had to make. He made his case, listened for any response, and prayed what Peter said Jesus had given his disciples as a model: "your kingdom come; your will be done."

What was God's will? If he didn't have a dream, if no angel told him, if he didn't have a vision like Paul had, then he had to use his own head and heart to figure it out. If God didn't block his way somehow, he just had to go forward with what he thought God wanted him to do. Right now, that was to go home.

But what was God's kingdom? What decision helped or hindered that kingdom? Mark could assume that the very fact that he was considering leaving a mission venture suggested that he would be acting counter to the kingdom cause. But would he? Did the whole kingdom of God rest on his being a mere helper on a mission? And did he know there wasn't some purpose in his being back home, seeing to his mother's needs? Wasn't that biblical, too? 'Honor your father and your mother?' Mark laid it out before God. God didn't speak up.

But Mark became progressively certain about his direction. Maybe that was how God was speaking. Maybe that was God's still, small voice.

By the third day before they were to go to Pisidian Antioch, Mark was settled on leaving. Except for the regret any courteous person should have about this kind of decision, he didn't have any sense of guilt. His reasons were substantial. He needed to go. At the end of the day, after they had eaten with Yakov, Mark found Paul in his room and asked to speak with him.

"Of course," said Paul. "What's on your mind?"

"I have to leave the team," said Mark. He got to the heart of the matter first, rather than dragging it out.

The reading Mark did on Paul's face was first that he seemed almost unaffected, and only secondarily did he seem vaguely nonplussed. Overall and initially, he was stolid, unmoved. When he did speak, it was in measured tones.

"I assume you've thought this out," he said.

"For some time, yes," said Mark. "In great measure it has to do with my mother, who I believe to be going down rapidly."

"The letter you got," said Paul.

"Yes." Mark decided not to go into any of the other reasons. They had mostly to do with Paul, and now was not the time to bring up any differences of opinion they had about the work they were doing. Paul was in charge. Or he and Barnabas were. Certainly, Mark wasn't. Management made the decisions. And Mark's concerns about getting "the sickness" might well be unfounded; mentioning that reason might suggest childish apprehension. He didn't want to come across as afraid.

"This is inconvenient," Paul said. He turned around and went to a chair in his room, where he sat, gathering his robe at the sides, as if a judge sitting to listen to someone plead his case. As he settled into the seat, he swatted a mosquito that had gotten in somehow. Mark remained standing until Paul's attention was focused on him.

"I'm sorry. It can't be helped," Mark said. Again, he resisted the impulse to offer another reason to justify his decision. He held it in, letting the bottom line be the only line.

Mark watched Paul's face, thinking he could detect Paul's dispassion turn slowly to a bare semblance of irritation, not quite anger, but trending toward it.

"Is there something we can work out?" said Paul, in almost requisite formality.

"I don't think so," said Mark. And then, weakening in his resolve not to justify himself, he added, "It's not you; it's me. I need to do this."

Paul looked out his window, through which nothing could be seen now in the mid evening gloom, and then turned his head back to Mark. "Have you prayed about this?"

The question struck Mark as implying that Paul assumed he hadn't. Indeed, the look on Paul's face carried exactly this meaning. One eyebrow raised. Bottom lip protruding slightly. Unmoving.

Controlling any defensiveness he felt, which was substantial, and coming across as evenly and calmly as he could, Mark said, "Of course, I have."

Paul nodded. Nodded again. Cleared his facial expressions. Stood up. "We'll be headed out the day after tomorrow. Instead of the day after that. You'll be sailing?"

"Yes," said Mark. "Tomorrow, if there's a ship in port tonight leaving in the morning."

"Mm hmm," said Paul. "I imagine there is. There's one that comes and one that goes nearly every day." He said it without feeling.

"Things will go well from here for you," offered Mark weakly. "I know they will. I'll—I'll pray they will," he said, and when Paul didn't respond other than to nod as a courtesy, Mark turned around and went out of the room. He noted as he went that Paul hadn't expressed any appreciation for the job Mark had done in the past year. None.

In the morning, Mark didn't join Barnabas and Paul for a bite of breakfast. He had hurried into the kitchen at dawn and had eaten a piece of bread and had pocketed another as well as a piece of fruit. He had told Yakov the night before that he would be leaving, to see about his mother. Yakov told him to help himself to some food for the voyage.

The others had finished when Mark was ready to go, and Paul had already left the house. Evidently, he didn't care to see Mark as he left for the wharf. Barnabas embraced him though, and wished him well, as did Yakov. Mark left the house and disappeared into the little lanes that zigzagged down toward the waterfront.

The same size ship that had brought the team to Perga was leaving mid morning. Mark bought passage on it. The boat was going back to Paphos. From there Mark would find a larger, corbita style boat for the voyage around the south of Cyprus and to the coast of Judea. He hoped, in fact, to find a ship going to Caesarea. He had scrapped the previous thought of returning to Syrian Antioch and then going down to Jerusalem. He was going to see his imma first.

In Paphos Mark paid more than he really wanted to for passage to Caesarea, but it was worth it. The rightness of his decision to leave the team at Perga was reinforced in the fresh and pleasant winds that cooled his face on deck, where he was to be found much of the four days it took to round the southern coast of Cyprus and make a beeline for the mainland. Evenings, Mark nestled into a little bunk bench below and tried to write a few lines about his experiences in the past months, frustrated with the occasional illegibility of his characters due to the waves.

When the port at Caesarea came into view, Mark found himself surprised at the relief and joy he felt at nearly being home. He had a delayed reaction to the loneliness that had been growing in him since the mission venture had begun. In an inn near the waterfront in Caesarea, he slept fitfully and rose before dawn hoping to catch one of the first raedas leaving the area toward Jerusalem. By late morning, the cart he found going that way had come in sight of the City of David, and Mark was almost overwhelmed with his emotions and the homesickness he had suppressed.

Miriam was in her little back courtyard when Mark arrived. Rhoda saw him coming in from the street and ran to the front door to meet him. He put his finger to his lips and made her be quiet as he walked through the house and to the back yard.

Miriam was sitting on a bench, a few blossoms in her hands, a clay vase beside her, apparently the flowers' destination. But she was staring out into space with a wistful look.

"Imma," said Mark softly.

Miriam turned to him. Her blank face gradually illuminated. She got up slowly and spread her arms. Mark went to her and hugged her, and they both cried wordlessly.

24
Antioch, Syria c. Late A.D. 48

Mark stayed with his mother two weeks before going to Antioch. He watched her closely for signs of something terribly wrong, hoping he wouldn't find any but worried that if he didn't he would feel foolish for having left Barnabas and Paul. His mother moved more slowly; that much was evident. She forgot a great many things.

The extra serving girl Miriam had hired a couple of years ago hadn't worked out and Miriam had hired another, someone recommended by Rhoda. The two of them did everything around the house; Miriam didn't even help in the kitchen much, except to peel pomegranates distractedly now and then. She seemed in a daze much of the time. It was wistful, as her appearance in the courtyard had been when Mark first arrived from Caesarea, but it was a more vacant stare than that. She snapped out of it when needed or when addressed, however, and seemed only to be generally feeling the effects of the coming of age—though at fifty-two, she wasn't really old.

Miriam and Mark walked to the market together one day and Mark thought she didn't really seem in the least bit frail or feeble or anything else. Her steps were shorter and she didn't walk as fast as she had five years ago, or before he moved to Antioch. But throughout the two weeks he was in Jerusalem he finally convinced himself she would be all right if he went back to Antioch and resumed his position with the church. He told her of his plans on a Sabbath morning.

On the First Day, Mark put his things together and set out for the northern edge of the city, where he found a raeda leaving for Tyre, which he reached in two days. From there he worked his way up the coast by foot or cart until he finally got to Seleucia, where he walked the final few miles east to Antioch, arriving bedraggled but relieved to enter his little house and flop on his bed.

Everything was as he had left it, both at home and at church, although the latter was a bit enlarged in its membership since he and the two evangelists had left there going on two years ago. The elders wanted to know about the mission, how it was going and so on, and they were naturally curious about his coming back while Barnabas and Paul were still in Asia.

Mark explained what he had derived from his mother's letter, emphasizing his prayer about what to do, and his feeling that the Spirit had not led him otherwise. He gave them a brief update on his mother and told them no one else needed to go to Jerusalem in his stead to look in on her. They accepted his reasons at face value. He gave them no hint of Paul's disapproval or reaction.

The year turned amid seasonally cool weather, and in the ninth year of Emperor Claudius the church in Antioch enjoyed relative accord in the community, or at least the absence of hostility. Springtime approached. The gray, winter skies became memories. And news came that Miriam had died.

Mark was at home when the message came by courier. Rhoda had written it. She said she and Miriam were eating lunch when Miriam looked at her oddly, opened her mouth, looked as if she wanted to speak but didn't, and then laid her head back against the wall behind her and closed her eyes. That was it.

Mark held the paper in his hands and sat for an hour in the same place, motionless, before getting up and walking to one of the elder's houses a quarter mile away.

He borrowed a horse and rode to Jerusalem over three days time. Rhoda was at the house. They both stood in the front doorway and cried a minute before talking. Rhoda had seen to the arrangements for his mother, who had been laid in a tomb she had purchased years before. Rhoda had sent a message to Rachel and her husband in Bethel and Tirzah and hers in Cyprus and she anticipated that they would visit soon, though she had no idea when. Other than that, she didn't know what further to do, since she was not family. Even though she was.

Rachel arrived the day after Mark, with her husband, Jonathan. Tirzah and Joel came three days after that, and the reunited family spent the following week talking about the distant past and their different lives in the present. The probability of their seeing each other with decreasing incidence in the future remained an unspoken awareness for them all.

Mark consulted with the family friend who had helped them now and then through the years with legal matters, and by the end of two week's time he had mostly concluded his mother's affairs, including arrangements for the sale of the house. Rachel left for her home in Bethel after a week in Jerusalem, and Joel and Tirzah a day later. Mark sat down with Rhoda and discussed the obvious, that her nearly-lifetime service to the family was at an end.

Rhoda had already made plans, ever the resourceful woman she was, and she thanked Mark for all the years of friendship and acceptance she had felt, living and working in the home.

When Rhoda left, Mark sat in the main room of the house as the sun went down. He found himself there at first light, having slept, exhausted, in a comfortable chair without stirring all night. Having left final instructions with the family's lawyer, Mark closed up the house, mounted his borrowed transportation, and left.

Months after Miriam's death, Mark was enjoying his work with the Antioch church, which was making inroads into Gentile communities in the city and growing in numbers about equal between Jew and non-Jews. Mark was studying up on how best to explain the background of the gospel in the history of the Jews for the benefit of Gentile converts. In his regular, small group teaching, he emphasized the consistent, divine revelation that the Messiah would come to build the kingdom of God, the same kingdom that had begun in the Hebrew scriptures, back in the beginning.

Settling Miriam's estate resulted in an enlargement of Mark's resources that frankly surprised him. Miriam left some things to her sisters, but her home and the bulk of her invested money was for Mark alone. It would make possible his living more easily on the minimal income provided by the church. The thought crossed his mind to get a little larger house, but he quickly dismissed the idea. He really didn't need anything more. He might eat a little better. He had gradually lost weight in Antioch, and during the months he was with Barnabas and Paul in Cyprus and then Pamphylia, he lost even more, in spite of church suppers. Paul ate minimally and Barnabas tried to follow his lead, leaving Mark either to do the same or feel self-conscious. With all the walking they did, Mark had become sinewy but nearly gaunt. He began buying more food.

Paul and Barnabas returned from their journey through Cyprus and parts of Asia to great celebration by the Antioch congregation. Naturally, everyone wanted to hear all about their preaching, amazing stories of conversions, encouraging accounts about the founding of churches, and tales of the interesting people and experiences they had along the way. The cooks in the church prepared dozens and dozens of dishes of savory food and the church gathered one evening during the week of the missionaries' arrival, first to eat and then to listen.

Among the many details they gave was the distressing fact that as they left Perga and headed north for Pisidian Antioch, Paul fell terribly ill. Apparently whatever was striking great numbers of people in the low country of Pamphylia managed to get to Paul just as they were leaving. When they came into the southern regions of Galatia, he was wracked with fever, couldn't keep food down, and was naturally listless. Barnabas had become greatly concerned that Paul was going to die in the midst of this significant evangelistic mission, but he related how the two of them had agreed that while Paul's illness certainly constituted a trial, they believed God was going to bring him through it and reward their plowing on to preach and found churches.

Mark was in the back of the room listening, and a wave of concern mixed with regret passed through him. If he had stayed, he might have been able to help. Then again, he was no doctor. Of course, he might have borne a little more of the load of the team's overall work. On the other hand, Paul was just fine when Mark left. Mark couldn't have afforded to think, at the time, 'What if Paul gets sick?' "What if" was never a productive game to play. If God, in his providence, makes the path clear, take it. That was Mark's belief. And that's what he had done.

Mark went to Barnabas's home the morning after he and Paul came in from Seleucia by foot. He was resting up from the trip, and he sat barefooted, soaking his feet in a shallow bowl while alternately massaging them. He and Mark just talked. Barnabas had tales to tell, but as usual he was interested in others first, and he wanted Mark to tell him about Miriam.

Mark recounted everything as it had happened, and he summed up his conviction that he had arrived just in time. He and his mother had enjoyed a few days together while she was functioning well, but she continued to decline rapidly and then, of course, died suddenly. He had been here to see her, tend to her needs, and take care of final responsibilities when she died.

Barnabas nodded, and it appeared that he agreed. He knew, of course, that people's family members died frequently when loved ones were not nearby and that word of their deaths was received long after. It was common for some children to journey home weeks or months after a parent's death. But Barnabas also knew that Mark had been privileged to have gotten news from his mother that alerted him to her growing condition, whatever that had been. And he understood that Mark believed he was supposed to leave the team in Pamphylia. As he listened to Mark, Barnabas couldn't hold it against him, not really, for making the decision he did. And he agreed with Mark that there had been no way to know that Paul was going to get deathly ill right afterwards, and there was no reason Mark should have based his decision on such unknowns.

Cousin Barnabas was also aware that Mark had also had reasons that were unrelated to Miriam, at least one of which he had explained. Barnabas had thought about that now and again since Mark had left them at Perga. He also believed there was something else on Mark's mind at the time, but Mark hadn't divulged it and Barnabas was going to respect him and not press him about it. The need to see his mother one last time seemed to be sufficient cause, and who was he, Barnabas, to say it hadn't been the Holy Spirit's plan?

Barnabas told Mark a few stories that neither he nor Paul had related in their whirlwind account of the nearly three year venture. Mark listened with excitement, able to envision the way things must have been, because of his now-expanded visual vocabulary of the kinds of places they had preached the gospel and planted churches.

As Barnabas talked, Mark kept waiting for him to volunteer anything about Paul's conversation after he left that might indicate that he was either still angry or that he had let the matter go. Mark didn't want to bring it up, and Barnabas never discussed it, so Mark assumed it was a non issue by now.

Back in church the following Lord's Day, however, Mark realized such was not the case.

That day during the worship time, Barnabas and Paul gave another report, going into detail about some of the things that had happened to them. They especially contrasted the way that while some of the Jews in Galatia were eager to understand the gospel, increasingly many of them were not and were making it abundantly clear that the future of Paul's ministry was going to be Gentile audiences.

When the worship time was over, few people left right away. Some began talking with friends around them, while a number of people made their way toward the front of the room, where Paul and Barnabas were standing on a large podium. Mark was along the back wall, where he had stood during worship and as Paul spoke. Actually, he was weighing whether he would go speak to Paul; he hadn't done so yet. When their gazes met, Paul gave a perfunctory and superficial kind of nod, subtle, almost invisible. But evanescent, and completely without any facial expression. There was no frown, no anger, and no smile.

When the moment passed, Paul turned to a couple beside him who were calling his name, smiling and speaking to them with interest. Perhaps his expressionless manner was due to the distance between Mark and Paul, over the mass of noisy people. And, he knew, Paul had become somewhat reserved in crowds, at least when he wasn't preaching or teaching. Perhaps things were just fine, now.

Still, Mark would leave it to Paul if he wanted to reach out to him. They weren't on the church leadership group together at this point, so one of them would have to manufacture an opportunity to talk, if they were going to.

Mark finally decided he was over-thinking the entire matter. He and Paul hadn't been very close associates before the mission venture. And since he was considered only an aide on the mission, they really hadn't gotten close then, either. Things had only returned to where they were before. Let it go, he said to himself.

Peter arrived in Antioch some weeks later at midday on the fifth day of the week, prompting excitement and celebration. The church put together an impromptu banquet within hours and feted the Apostle that night, to his slight embarrassment. Even before the food had all been brought in and laid out, some of the crowd already gathered insisted that he speak, and he obliged with genuine hesitation.

Peter talked about how he had spent much of his time in Jerusalem but had lately begun to make extended visits to other cities in the region. He was seen as the church's overall leader—he didn't mention this but everyone knew it. Though he hadn't sought the accorded honor he accepted the fact. Peter told about going to the coast and spending some time in Joppa, until the vision that opened the gospel to the Gentiles and the subsequent visit by Cornelius. Everyone knew this story, too, by now, but they let Peter tell it again because his first person account was so dramatic.

Peter said he had returned to Jerusalem after the encounter with Cornelius but had made a sort of circuit to other cities. What he didn't say, but was easily gathered even from his humble accounting, was that he had felt compelled to travel around because of his concept of roving oversight. It was that feeling of necessity that had brought him to Antioch.

The food was finally ready and Peter conveniently found a stopping point in his speech. Everyone milled around and collected bits of this and that in one of the hodgepodge of dishes the church had collected from various members. As they did, they gravitated to tables here and there spread throughout the room and in adjoining rooms. Mark found his way through the people to Peter and greeted him. It was the first he had seen him in several years. Peter's hands were full and he was looking for a place where the two of them could sit. There was a table near them with two Greek families already seated, and two places on the end vacant.

Mark watched as Peter saw the empty chairs and then peered around the room nearby to see if there were other options. Then he looked back at the first table, lifted his eyes in an "Oh well, why not," look, and suggested to Mark they could sit there. They did.

Barnabas was there for the meal—he always was—but Mark noticed that Paul had stepped into the back of the meeting room and had soon left again, even without eating. He thought it odd, but he was quickly distracted by conversation at his table and thought no more of it.

Mark and Peter enjoyed a reunion later. It was doubly gratifying to Mark because of his more or less undefined desire to have a connection with one of the Apostles. Since his brief encounters with Peter during Jesus' last days he had not exactly had a casual relationship, but not a close one either.

When the meal and more remarks were over, Peter and Mark agreed to attend local synagogue worship on the Sabbath, the next day. They strolled down the street toward Mark's house, which was just two streets away.

"It will be nice to attend synagogue here," Peter said. "The climate in Jerusalem synagogues is getting a bit too warm."

"The climate?" said Mark.

"The welcome," said Peter. "Less and less friendly."

"Oh."

"It's a difficult thing, trying to walk the line."

"What line?" said Mark.

"Believing in Jesus."

"I know I'm being dense, but explain," said Mark.

Peter smiled. "We're Jews," he said. "We will always be Jews. We ought to be welcome with our own people. But we who believe in our Messiah have been trying for several years now to convince those who don't. It's hard trying to be on both sides of that line."

"And in Jerusalem they're making you feel unwelcome to continue being Jews?"

"Yes."

"Welcome to Antioch," said Mark, spreading his hands dramatically to encompass the city, "where Jews mostly live and let live. After all, about a fourth of the congregation is Gentile."

Peter didn't answer.

"Is that a problem?" said Mark.

"What? Oh, no. No, not a problem," said Peter. "It's just—well, that's the other line."

"We have another line?"

"Same line: believing. Only this time it's a question of whether we're Jews or Christians. Your church was the first to lay claim to that name, you know."

"I'm well aware. I like it."

"Yes," said Peter, "I do, too. But it makes the line brighter, doesn't it."

"Jews or Christians, you mean?" said Mark.

"Yes. It's a little confusing: the Jews don't want us to be Christians, and if we are, they don't want anything to do with us. In Jerusalem, anyway. But some Jewish Christians want us to be Christian Jews, not just Christians. I think the Gentiles would just like us to get on with being Christians."

"Wait," said Mark, "Jewish Christians, Christian Jews?"

"That's the way I put it. Quite a few believers in Jerusalem insist that while we certainly *should* believe in Jesus—otherwise how would we be saved?—we should still be Jewish in every way."

"Like Sabbath rules and feasts and so on?"

"Well, pretty much everything else, too."

"Like hand washing and fasting?"

"And sacrifices, and—" Peter said, and paused, then continued, "and eating with Gentiles."

Mark realized what Peter had been struggling with at supper with the church. "Surely not," he said.

"Surely yes," said Peter.

"Well," said Mark, gathering his thoughts, "I can understand that we—we Jews—want the church to have a Jewish core."

"That's well put," said Peter.

"I did a lot of thinking about that when I was in Cyprus. I mean, how will Gentiles understand the gospel if they don't know the scriptures? *Our* scriptures."

"Exactly," said Peter.

"I have to admit, though, that a lot of what I used to do, like every other good Jew did, I don't do anymore. I don't take sacrifices to the temple."

"Oh, no, and neither do I," said Peter. "After a little while we all realized that Jesus had done that himself for the last time."

"True," said Mark.

"But the Jewish Christians notice other things we do and don't do, and they're starting to make an issue of it in Jerusalem. Like circumcision," said Peter, pointedly.

"Circumcision?" said Mark. "They're looking to see who has their babies circumcised?"

"Taking names," said Peter. "About other things, too; public things."

Mark was quiet for a moment. He realized he was somewhere in the spectrum of conflicted thinking, too. He hadn't completely settled questions of association or disassociation with Jewish life. Peter was right about one thing: it was hard. Being Jewish was what Mark grew up with, but it was decreasingly what he lived like in the present. Was he supposed to somehow craft a lifestyle that genuinely melded the two things, being Jewish and being Christian? And would anyone on either side really accept what he came up with? Even more honestly, would the life he managed to live be only for show?

"You see the problem," said Peter.

"I do," said Mark.

"Is Paul gone off somewhere preaching?" Peter said, changing the subject.

"Uh, no. You didn't see him tonight?"

"No. Did you?"

"Briefly. He must have had something to do, because he left after a few minutes." Mark now wondered what was going on with Paul.

"I'm sure I'll see him this week sometime," said Peter. "Well, I should be going."

"You're staying with Reuben and Yaffa, I hear."

"Yes."

"I thought Damianus and Agathe would offer you their rooms—they usually host guests. They practically have another house they added on one end of their home a few years ago. Lots and lots of room."

"Well, they actually did offer, I think. I went another direction."

"Ah," said Mark, wondering what that meant. "Reuben and Yaffa were some of the first people in the synagogue here to believe in Jesus. So I understand."

"That's what they told me."

Peter left soon and went to his accommodations. Mark would have loved for him to stay with him, but there was literally no room in the "hovel," as Mark called it, for a guest. Reuben was a gracious host, and his wife Yaffa was a marvelous cook. Peter would get fat if he ate there every meal. The fare at Damianus's house would have been quite different, and nothing Jewish about it. Mark wondered if that had anything to do with Peter's choice, and in light of Peter's candid admissions, he thought it did. In fact, one of the elders had no doubt arranged accommodations for Peter quickly, and it would have been unlikely that whichever elder did it would have offered Peter a choice in where to stay. How did he go "another direction," as he put it? Curious.

Peter sat with his hosts and with Mark at synagogue. Mark didn't feel compelled to attend synagogue worship anymore. Most Christians were moving that direction. But Peter had wanted to go, for no more reason than to worship with fellow Jews in Antioch. It was a beautiful Sabbath day. Afterwards, they walked from the synagogue to Mark's hovel, got some fruit from the tight little space that served as a kitchen, and sat down to eat and converse.

"I was sorry to learn about your mother," Peter said.

"Thank you. I wish you could have been there when I went back from here. But I didn't know when she was going to pass away, myself."

"No," said Peter. "That's often so. My mother died years ago quite suddenly."

"Did she live in Capernaum?"

"No. Cana," said Peter. "My mother-in-law lived in Capernaum. I met my wife there when I began fishing the Sea of Galilee. Moved there."

"Did you get the news in time to go to Cana before—before they laid her to rest?" said Mark.

"Just barely. My father had died a year before that, so there was no family left there in Cana. I stayed in Capernaum. No lakes in Cana anyway."

"What made you want to become a fisherman?" asked Mark.

"It's a good trade. My father had fished for a living earlier. Andrew and I worked at this and that when we were young, but he suggested we go to Capernaum and see if we could learn from the fellows there. And that was that."

"Did you meet John there?"

"Yes. And his brother."

"I'm still appalled about James," said Mark.

"I miss him every day," said Peter. "What possessed Agrippa to do what he did, I don't—well, I do know. He was just possessed, that's all."

"Obviously, the Lord had other plans for you," said Mark. He chuckled as he recalled the night Peter rapped on his door and Rhoda had been so nervous she left him standing outside while she went wide-eyed to tell the others in the Upper Room.

"Do you remember—" said Mark.

"Little Rhoda at the door?" said Peter, laughing heartily.

"I never saw eyes as wide as hers!" said Mark.

"A night to remember," said Peter. "Sometimes it all seems like a dream. And it seemed like a dream at the time."

"What lies ahead, do you think?" said Mark.

"I don't know. We can't know, son," said Peter.

Mark was pensive for a moment, thinking not only of Peter's future but also his own.

"Tell me about your trip," said Peter.

"You mean with Barnabas and Paul?" said Mark.

"Well, what do you think I mean?" said Peter, laughing. "Have you made any other grand journeys recently?"

"No, I just—I haven't made a big deal out of it."

"Because you had to leave?" said Peter.

"That's part of it, I'm sure. So you heard."

"Barnabas told me. In private. Yesterday."

"I hate that it happened that way. It seemed like a great opportunity."

"Perhaps the first of others," said Peter.

"Maybe so. I don't know. There's nothing in the works that I know of."

"Maybe at some point you and I—" Peter said, leaving the idea up in the air.

Mark smiled. "That would be wonderful."

"So, tell me," said Peter. And Mark gave Peter somewhat more than a thumbnail sketch of the voyage to Cyprus, the work in Salamis, the journey to the other end of the island country, the conversion of the proconsul in Paphos, and the trip to Perga. He gave special detail to the privilege he had of winning Rabbi Yakov to Christ.

"It's a precious moment, isn't it?" said Peter, when Mark was finished. "Seeing someone's heart opened to the Lord Jesus, right in front of you."

"Unlike any other," said Mark.

After their conversation Peter left to join his hosts for the Sabbath day meal. Mark munched on what was at hand, rested on a little couch and revisited Peter's curious remark about going "another way" with arrangements for his stay.

His curiosity was satisfied within a week.

Peter had been gone from Jerusalem several weeks before he actually made it to Antioch, having stopped at a few towns in between. But brothers in Jerusalem knew when he planned to get to Antioch, and a contingent of six men from the Jerusalem church, where James, Jesus' brother, was the leading elder, planned to visit Antioch while Peter was there—unbeknownst to Peter. They arrived three days after Peter had. The church welcomed these visitors, though the meal they put together was not quite the feast they put on for Peter.

The gathering was planned for noonday the fourth day of the week. A hundred or so people showed up, about the usual congregation, about a fourth Gentile believers, who often could be distinguished by their clothing or even hair styles. But the fellowship in Antioch was all but oblivious to their ethnic mix by now.

Peter went by Mark's little house and walked with him to the church's conjoined houses a few blocks away. By chance they arrived just when the contingent of the men from the Jerusalem church did, and they gathered outside the doors to chat. Everyone seemed courteous, despite what felt to Mark like a vaguely defined distance between Peter and the six. As the others were talking about how things were at home in Jerusalem, Mark noted that the group of six were all dressed traditionally and somewhat on the formal side, as if they were preparing to go to, or had just come from, a synagogue ritual. Strange, especially for an informal gathering to eat.

One of the six broke off and went over to the window on the left side of the door, peering in at the assembled crowd, who were all getting food and finding tables. After a moment, he came back over to the group and whispered something to one of them. Mark had looked at Peter while he was talking and saw that Peter's eyes had cut away now and then; he had followed what was going on.

"Well," said Peter, responding to someone in the group, "I'm sure James and the other elders are aware of it."

"Of course," said the one he was speaking with. Mark hadn't heard his name yet. "It's just that we differ on what to do."

"I understand, Baruch," said Peter. "And I'm certain he wouldn't mind your putting in your two mina's worth."

"Let's go get something to eat," suggested Mark. "We can talk in there."

The man who had received the whispered communication spoke up. "Baruch, it's my understanding that the Gentiles are simply mixed in with the Jews in the room."

"Ah," said Baruch, and turned back to Peter. "We'll have to eat somewhere else, of course."

Mark quickly studied Peter's face, and was startled to find his expression revealing uncertainty. By the time he spoke, he had decided, for good or ill.

"Of course, of course," said Peter.

Mark was certain his countenance had dropped, and he wondered if anyone were looking at him and had seen it. He took command of his facial expression and wiped it of any sign of surprise.

"Is there another room we might occupy?" said Baruch.

"There is one just beyond this room, off the hall."

"Can it be gotten to from the other end of the building?"

"Of course," said Peter. "You can—" and he appeared to be thinking through some matter, and then continued. "We can go around to the back and come in that way." Peter had decided to join them in avoiding the Gentiles in the meeting room.

"And perhaps," said Baruch, with an artificial sort of congeniality, "you can bring us some food there."

"If you like," said Peter. "Of course."

Peter started around the building and the others followed him. He looked back to see if Mark were coming, but Mark hadn't moved an inch and didn't plan to. While he didn't know what to make of Peter's going along with the Jerusalem group, he was simply going to go in where he usually did. These were Peter's friends, not his.

As the group left him standing there alone, Mark turned toward the door and noticed Paul standing inside near the window on the right side of the door. The group wouldn't have seen him from where they had been standing, and Peter's back was to him. Mark wondered if Paul had heard the conversation, and he concluded that he had.

In the main room Mark joined others in partaking of the hastily contrived meal and sat with friends to enjoy his food. He kept an eye on Paul, who was seated nearby and who peered at the hall doorway. Presently he saw Peter, who had come into the main room and then carried two dishes back out with him into the hall, repeating the effort twice and then once more, getting a single shallow bowl with some stew and bread, going back out and not returning. Paul watched it all, with a blank look on his face. Mark turned back to his food, friends and conversation, finishing in a while and looking back toward Paul, who had solemnly gotten done with his own eating and was making light talk but soon got up, made his excuses and went towards the outside door and left. Mark followed him at a distance.

Paul walked around the building the direction Peter had previously gone with his friends, with Mark a number of steps behind. There were other people in the street and Mark tried to blend in with them. As he came around the other side of the conjoined houses he stopped, seeing Paul at the corner, facing the opposite direction, watching the back of the building. Mark backed up and ducked out of sight, retreating to the front and then walking away. Paul had gone around to see Peter and the six men leaving the church.

Mark didn't see Paul again until the Lord's Day, or Peter or Barnabas, either. He didn't go to the Sabbath gathering at the synagogue, choosing to go only to the Lord's Day meeting with the church.

At church, he didn't see Peter or Barnabas, only Paul. The six men from Jerusalem were also absent. When the worship time was concluded he left and went home. In the middle of the afternoon he walked up the street and made his way out of the neighborhood and toward the community where Reuben and Yaffa lived. Peter might be sick, he thought, though in the back of his mind he thought otherwise.

He found Peter outside in the shade of a sycamore tree in Reuben's spacious yard, sitting with Barnabas, Reuben and Yaffa. As he approached, they all waved him over. He took a seat on one of several stone benches.

"I missed seeing you today," said Mark to the entire group.

"Yes," said Peter, hesitating slightly. "We went to the synagogue yesterday instead."

"Oh," said Mark. Peter looked ill at ease. Barnabas's look was inscrutable.

"We did, too," said Reuben, indicating that his wife had as well.

"Oh," said Mark.

The conversation had reached an early lull, as if no one could think of anything else to say.

"The elders taught from the prophet Zephaniah," Mark said.

"Oh?" said Barnabas.

"I can't quote it exactly—not one of those passages I memorized, cousin," said Mark, "but something like, 'The Lord will be awesome, and will reduce the gods of the earth to nothing, and people will worship him—all the islands of the Gentiles.'"

There was no direct response.

"Have you eaten?" said Yaffa.

"Yes," said Mark. "I ate at home afterward. "Have you been fattening up the Apostle?" He managed a chuckle.

There was a titter from the group. "I've tried," she said, "but he's eating like a bird."

"Have you ever watched birds eat?" said Peter, glad to have the subject changed. "They eat all the time!"

"You know what I mean," said Yaffa. "You'll dry up and blow away."

"Cousin," said Mark to Barnabas, "can I speak with you?"

"Of course," said Barnabas.

"I don't mean to be rude, but it's a family matter," said Mark to the others as he got up. "For just a minute," he said to Barnabas.

The two stepped away and to the street, just out of sight as well as earshot.

"What is it?" Barnabas said.

"I don't mean to pry," said Mark, "and if I'm out of place, just tell me."

"No, go ahead," said Barnabas, not having made any assumption about what Mark might want. 'Family matter' might have meant something about his father or mother, and his attention was riveted.

Mark interpreted his look properly. "It's nothing about your family. It's about us: *we're* family. I just wanted to talk with you, not everyone."

"Well, go on," said Barnabas.

"What's going on?" said Mark.

"Ah," said Barnabas, a little self-consciously. "You mean about synagogue, and today."

"Yes!" said Mark. His piercing look told Barnabas that he was concerned.

"We went with the men from Jerusalem. Baruch suggested we should attend synagogue with them. So, we went."

"*Should?*" said Mark. "Not just go, but *should* go?"

"That may not have been the way he put it, but—"

"But that's the way you heard it?" said Mark.

"He had a point, cousin," said Barnabas. He was becoming defensive.

"Which was?"

"Look," said Barnabas, piecing together his response. "They think it's best for us—us Jews—to stay, well, *Jews.* And they have a point."

"And this is what Peter thinks, too?"

"He—this was his idea."

"I think it was *their* idea, cousin," said Mark.

"Now, look—" said Barnabas, getting a little irritated.

"What happened to Peter's vision? What happened to, 'nobody is unclean'?"

"That's still true!" said Barnabas. "It's just that—" and he ran out of words.

"If they're not unclean, why not worship with them?" said Mark.

"It's just a formality," said Barnabas, not sounding certain himself. "And what does it hurt?"

"Is this what you told the converts on Cyprus?" said Mark, knowing it wasn't.

"I just think that—"

"Are you going to tell the next converts they have to have their own churches?" said Mark. "Or eat in separate houses?"

"Okay, you told me to tell you if you were out of your place," said Barnabas. "I think you're—"

"I'll stop, then," said Mark. "You decide for yourself." The two stared at each other, more awkwardly than angrily. Little had ever brought the cousins to acrimony. But Mark, the younger of the two by nine years, had suddenly been acting like 'the older brother' instead. He felt nervous about doing it, but even as he trembled a little while confronting Barnabas, he felt somehow that it was principle that motivated him, a principle he could not ignore, in spite of his own mixed feelings, feelings he had expressed to Peter himself when he talked about the "Jewish core" of the church.

"I'll think about it," Barnabas said. "I will," he insisted, as if he felt he needed to. Mark nodded at him, and they wordlessly agreed to return to the group. When they did, they had adopted pleasant smiles.

With a little plying Mark agreed to a snack from what was left over of the noon meal, and everyone ate a little more before Mark excused himself and went back home.

Two days later, when the church met as usual for a brief time of fellowship, Mark was in the meeting room waiting for things to begin. People were still coming in. Things would start when they started—it was all very informal.

Paul had not arrived; Mark only assumed he would come, because he usually did. Peter might or might not: Mark hadn't spoken to him since the Lord's Day and didn't know whether the Jerusalem contingent, Baruch's group, was even still in town. He assumed they were. But they weren't likely to come, even if they were. The question occurred to him, Why had they even come to Antioch, if they wouldn't meet with the church if Gentiles were present?

Then Mark saw Paul near the door. He was standing off to the side, looking out the window, as he had before. Presently, he walked rather quickly to the door and exited. Mark went to the door and saw Paul some fifty feet away, approaching Peter, who had rounded the corner coming to the church house.

As he went out the door, Mark stepped to the side and positioned himself behind a column of the porch. Even from this distance, he could hear Paul's strong voice.

"Peter," said Paul.

"My friend," said Peter.

"Let's go over here," said Paul, motioning toward a little grove of trees behind a house.

Mark followed at a distance, not letting himself be seen. He stopped when he ran out of cover, but he could still hear.

"What are you doing?" said Paul.

"What do you mean?" said Peter. "Going in with the church—I suppose just the same as you." Mark thought Peter sounded nervous.

"Where are your friends?" said Paul.

"They're leaving Antioch tomorrow."

"So they won't join us tonight?" said Paul.

"I suppose not," said Peter. "What is this about?"

"They don't seem to like us," said Paul.

"I'm sure they—"

"I noticed at the meal we had when they arrived, you left early," said Paul. "By the back door."

"Yes, uh, the direction I was headed."

"Without your friends."

"They were, uh, not quite finished."

"But when you left, you weren't there to get their food for them," said Paul.

"Uh, I'm sure if they—" Peter began.

"They won't *eat* with us," said Paul. It wasn't a question.

"I'm sure they would—"

"Because we're eating with Gentiles."

"Well, I—they are—I'm—"

"They won't *eat* with Gentiles," said Paul.

"I'm not certain you—"

"They won't *meet* with Gentiles," said Paul.

"You don't quite understand," said Peter.

"I understand very well, 'my friend,' —all too well."

"Look, brother Paul, they're—they just—"

"And then *you* wouldn't eat with Gentiles, because they're watching you."

"It's not—" Peter began, and revised himself. "They don't feel the same way we do, and—"

"You don't want to offend them."

"Well, it's not—I'm just helping them," said Peter, avoiding agreement.

"You're afraid of them," said Paul.

"No, I'm not afraid of them," said Peter, defensively, "They felt they needed to observe—"

"Cephas!" said Paul. Peter fell silent. Mark heard him clearly and was startled at Paul's reversion to Peter's Jewish name.

"They're part of a circumcision group," said Paul. "You ate with Gentiles last week. What's changed? Nothing about the gospel, I can assure you! Did you get a new vision? With a different message?" The question was rhetorical. Mark couldn't see Peter, but he imagined the look on his face.

"You weren't here with the church on the Lord's Day," said Paul.

"No," said Peter.

"You went to the synagogue."

"Yes, with Baruch and his friends."

"And your hosts," said Paul.

"Yes, with them. There was nothing wrong with that," said Peter, grasping at straws. "That was where they wanted to go."

"Who? Baruch's group?"

"Yes," said Peter, and somewhat meekly, thought Mark, from the sound of his voice.

"And Barnabas."

"And Barnabas, yes."

"So you've persuaded him to go along with it, too," said Paul.

Peter was silent. Mark noticed that a dozen or so people who had come down the street headed for the church's meeting place had noticed Paul and Peter in the grove to the side of the road and had approached them, thinking they might witness some kind of lofty, apostolic conversation. Mark stepped out in the open and joined the group.

Peter saw he and Paul were no longer alone. Paul's back was to the gathering group, but he saw Peter look behind him, and he turned briefly. Instead of letting the little crowd deter him, he turned back to Peter.

Paul said, "Barnabas went with me to Cyprus and throughout

Asia preaching the gospel. Hundreds of Gentiles believed in Jesus: *our* Jesus. *Our* Messiah. The same Jesus. The same Christ. We formed churches in all those places. Not one church for Jews and another for Gentiles, Cephas. One church. Just one."

The crowd had frozen, stilled by the holy seriousness of Paul's voice, and awed by the growing look of contrition coming over Peter's weathered visage.

"You're a Jew," said Paul, "but you've been living like everyone else here. Why? Because Jesus made us one."

"Yes, I know—" said Peter in a low voice.

"But as soon as these men come, you suddenly want Gentiles to live like Jews?"

"I know, I know," said Peter.

Then, something of a transformation took place in Peter. Mark could see it in his face and his frame, and he could sense it in the very air. In the silence that followed Paul's rebuke, Peter slowly stood up to his full height.

"I was wrong," he said evenly and with resolution. Then he looked at the little group gathered, some of them with mouths agape.

"I was wrong," he said to them. "Paul is right." He looked back at Paul, and in a lower voice, but one that could still be heard, he said, "You are right, brother Paul."

25
Antioch, Syria

In the weeks that followed the striking confrontation between Paul and Peter, things got back to normal in Antioch. Evangelism took place in the marketplaces, in house-to-house visits where people had shown themselves receptive, and now and then in or around the synagogue. The low level tension between the most evangelistic Christians and the most devoted worshipers of Hecate, Apollo and Daphne continued unabated but mostly without eruption into hostility. The circumcision group from Jerusalem left after a total visit of two weeks, apparently discouraged that they hadn't caused any more stir than they did. Peter had a heart-to-heart talk with Reuben and Yaffa to apologize for his drawing them into a wrongly conceived segregation from Gentiles. And he was profuse in his admission of wrongdoing to Barnabas, who after his little confrontation with Mark had already realized he had been sucked into error simply because it was Peter, after all, who was doing it.

And Mark settled back into his routine of ministry in the church. He was neither a ruling elder nor a deacon, but he was still being supported in a minor way by the church for being a teacher.

Paul and Peter quickly mended the brief rift that had possessed the potential of troubling the church. The elders had learned of the Apostles' confrontation but when they went to the two men to see what they could do to help heal the breach, Paul and Peter had already addressed it themselves and the matter was settled and over.

The most visible part of that matter involved the two apostles, of course, but within the two weeks that Baruch's group from Jerusalem was in Antioch, they had succeeded in sowing trouble that didn't blossom until after they left, in spite of the healing of the rift between Peter and Paul. The idea that Christians came in two varieties, Jews and Gentiles, touched the whole church in a tangential way, and not everyone was certain the question had been resolved simply because two apostles had made up. Mark caught wind of the growing controversy through his daily and weekly contacts with members, some of whom were quite bold in bringing up the subject in conversation.

At the source, the conflict was brewing full strength in the Jerusalem church and threatened to spread from there to congregations everywhere. In fact, in Mark's view the short conflict between Peter and Paul was providentially a preparation for what would soon take place, which would require a unified front between the two leading apostles in the church.

About six months after the Baruch contingent had gone home, another group of men from Jerusalem appeared one day in Antioch, introducing themselves to various elders and indicating they would stay a short time and simply observe, "on behalf of the mother church," as they put it at one point.

Something unsettling presented itself in the manner of these men, not the least of which was a presumptuousness borne in their description of their mission. And soon, in spite of their expressed purpose of observing, they had begun inserting into conversations with multiple church groups and persons the firm belief that while anyone could, of course, believe the gospel, new Christian men must be circumcised to be fully part of the church, and to qualify their wives for inclusion as well. Before long, the seeds that had been sown by Baruch and company were springing up in little pockets of contention and debate. Did Gentiles have to be circumcised?

On a hot, late summer meeting after supper, the elders met in the church house, inviting Mark and another principal teacher as well as Paul and Peter to join them. None of the elders agreed with some members of the church who held to the idea that Gentiles had to be circumcised, but they were all aware that the members were divided over it. To be most accurate, as Mark knew, it was the Jewish Christians who were divided over it: he didn't know a single Gentile Christian in the fellowship who thought he ought to have to undergo circumcision.

To Mark the issue was not difficult. Circumcision had been required of males by the covenant with Abraham. It was meant for Jews. Somewhere along the way in their history, Jews had decided to created a category they called "God-fearers," who were non-Jews who wanted to join the Jewish community as fully as possible. Their men were ultimately required to be circumcised, but that's because they were basically becoming Jews. Christians, on the other hand, weren't becoming Jews. The issue was as simple as that, to Mark anyway. Perhaps he didn't understand some hidden fact that the Jews in Jerusalem had uncovered, some interpretation of scripture that he had never been taught. But he didn't think so.

The meeting was called entirely for the purpose of the elders' deciding what to do about the burgeoning conflict. When they got underway, Shimon, who was now the head elder, made a short statement reviewing what had taken place so far in the church. He summarized the visit of the group led by Baruch and the ideas they had held about associating with Gentiles. He ended his summary by saying that some members had noticed that Baruch and the other men had eaten in a separate room at the dinner planned to welcome them. Before he went further, however, Shimon turned to Peter and nodded. Mark realized that Shimon and Peter had planned beforehand that Peter would tell his own story.

"Shimon told you our guests ate in another room," said Peter. "I am ashamed to say now that I ate with them. They were very forceful in their views, and I didn't contradict them. I went along with them. My influence led Reuben and Barnabas down the same path. I was wrong." Peter looked at Paul directly. "Brother Paul pointed this out to me. His was the voice of the Holy Spirit."

Paul took over. "We are in complete agreement about the issue of circumcision. As are all of us at this table, I'm sure."

Shimon nodded. "We are. In our meeting two weeks ago everyone spoke up. None of us thinks Gentiles need to be circumcised."

"But," said another elder, "we realize that some of our members aren't entirely certain about whether Gentiles—or even Jews, for that matter—need to follow Jewish traditions or laws."

"We're not talking about the Commandments," said another.

"No," said the first, "we're talking about the other laws. Except for the Sabbath. Jesus himself showed us that the Sabbath has given way to the Lord's Day."

"There have been some of our number," said Shimon, mostly for the benefit of Mark and the others present who weren't officially elders, "who thought we ought to be quite public in abandoning dietary laws—essentially they thought we ought to make a show of it, no matter what non-believing Jews here in Antioch think about it."

"And others," said another elder, "who think the opposite, that we have to make a point of obeying all the Pharisee's rules—with apologies to you, Paul—"

"No apology necessary," said Paul.

"—so that Jews who *might* believe will think that it wouldn't be such a radical thing to believe in Jesus. They might be more likely to believe, in other words, because they might think their fellow Jews wouldn't be so likely to criticize them."

"It's a complex controversy," said Shimon.

Mark repeated his thought to himself: It still seems simple to me.

"In a way," continued Shimon. "In another way, it seems simple. All but one of us elders," he said, then nodding toward the youngest of them, "except Ioannis, is a Jew. We all agree that Jesus freed us from the ceremonial law. Apparently, this is the source of the conflict: not all the Jewish believers here understand this freedom."

"I think," said Paul, "until the church at Jerusalem weighs in on the matter, it's going to continue to be unsettled everywhere."

"I agree," said Peter. "It's not that the Jerusalem church controls the other churches. It's just that they have led the way from the beginning, and if they lead a particular direction in this matter, it will make a great difference."

"If my opinion counts," said Mark, "I agree completely. I grew up in Jerusalem. I was a part of the main synagogue there. People looked to them for their example. They still do. When I was in Cyprus, the synagogues there would often speak of what the rabbis in Jerusalem said. It was understood that their leadership was important." Mark looked around as he spoke, and most of those present were nodding at what he said. Paul was looking at him too, but with detachment.

Conversation around the room continued for a few minutes until no new perspectives were being offered, just repetition. Finally, Shimon proposed action.

"We should send some men to Jerusalem to speak with James and the other elders. If no one has already done so, our emissaries should ask the Jerusalem church to advise us all—churches everywhere—on a wise way to approach the entire matter."

"I agree," said the three other elders, nearly in unison.

"Good," said Shimon. "Let me propose five persons to go." The others nodded. "Paul and Barnabas," said Shimon, and the other elders nodded. "You two," said Shimon, pointing at Ioannis and

Pinchas, two of the other elders. They looked at each other and then back at Shimon, and they nodded, agreeing to go if sent. "And Oren," said Shimon, looking at Mark's fellow teacher. Oren nodded his assent.

Secretly, Mark was glad he had not been suggested. Things were still uncomfortable with Paul.

"Is there any discussion or other suggestions?" said Shimon. No one disagreed or demurred. Everyone was in agreement.

"Then when can you go?" asked Shimon.

No one had a problem leaving within the week. They decided on leaving in two days.

"If that concludes your business," Paul said to the elders, "Peter and I would like to make you aware of another, related decision we've reached."

"Go ahead," said Shimon.

Paul looked at Peter, who gestured back at him, deferring to him to speak first.

"After the first contingent from Jerusalem left—Baruch's men—Peter and I talked at length about where our ministries have been headed since the first. Both of us are as Jewish as they come. You well know that I'm a Pharisee. You know my schooling, my training, my history. But God has led me more and more to preach to Gentiles. I am convinced that he wants me to go to them—not that I won't preach in synagogues or try to win Jews: I will. But the future of my calling lies beyond." Paul stopped and looked at Peter.

"I'm not a Pharisee. I'm a fisherman," Peter said, and there was soft laughter. "But more of us Jews are fishermen and bakers and millers and market sellers and potters and such, than they are rabbis and other leaders. We're the Jews who became believers first. And I can never forget the Lord told me, 'Feed my lambs.' That's what I'm supposed to do. He wants me to reach as much of our Jewish flock as I can. That's where *my* heart is."

The whole room nodded. Mark smiled, inside and outside. This was the Apostle Peter he knew. A simple man with a profound commitment to the mission Jesus had started and then had given him and the other disciples.

After the delegation to Jerusalem had set off, the elders of the Antioch church urged the congregation to put a hold on their contest over the circumcision question and all related debate about whether the entire law of Moses was binding upon Gentile believers. Except for a very few people who had been the most insistent about their viewpoints, the church followed the elders' exhortations and held the matter in abeyance, waiting to hear what the Jerusalem church, led by the widely respected James, the Lord's brother, had to say.

Several breathless weeks later the delegation came back. They all went to the church meeting place except one, who went to fetch Shimon. Shimon sent a runner to get Mark and the others who had been at the elders' meeting where the delegation had been appointed. On hand were also Judas and Silas, prophets in the Jerusalem church, and a few other members from the Jerusalem congregation. Barnabas and Paul had been officially appointed to deliver the letter and speak for James with any necessary application of what the letter said.

The delegation presented a letter to Shimon, who read it aloud. The letter began by disavowing any authority of the self-appointed members of the Jerusalem church who had come to Antioch preaching a gospel laced with Jewish requirements. There was no missing the tone of this disavowal. Those people had spoken without any authority.

The letter went on to say that the Holy Spirit had spoken clearly to the Jerusalem leaders' hearts that they were to place no Jewish burdens on anyone, which obviously meant that circumcision was not required of Christians. However, because of the strong cultural

Judaism in Antioch and other places where Jews had long had influential communities outside Judea, the Jerusalem elders listed four things the church should require of their members.

Particularly Gentile believers who had never followed Jewish practices, but *had* participated in worshiping Greek (and now Roman) gods, must consider the effect their behavior would have on non-believing Jews. So, in their letter, the Jerusalem church directed them to: abstain from foods sacrificed to idols; not consume blood; not eat strangled animals; and not commit sexual immorality.

When Shimon finished reading, before any questions could arise, Barnabas spoke up.

"All these things are part of idol worship, as you know. That's what is meant. The letter could have been much longer, of course, and some wanted to go into great detail. They finally selected four things that go on in idol worship."

"Most of us don't go to those temples," said Shimon, broadly to the entire group.

Paul said, "James's concern—indeed, that of all the Jerusalem elders—is to avoid needlessly offending Jews so much that they'll never believe the gospel."

"And on what the gospel requires," said Barnabas, "there's absolutely no question. Repentance and faith in Christ. Nothing more."

The assembled elders and others were elated. When the meeting broke up, Mark went to Barnabas.

"Good to have you back," said Mark.

"Good to be back," said Barnabas. "That's a long trip for an old man."

"Ha!" said Mark. "How long did it take for you to hammer things out?"

"Surprisingly not long. We met twice, once for about three hours and the second time for about two. Once we agreed on everything, the letter was done in minutes."

"This 'Judaiz-ing' is making its way out into most of the churches, I believe," said Mark.

"Which is why they made more copies of the letters," said Barnabas. "To get the word out to everyone."

"When's the last time you ate?" said Mark.

"Feels like last week. Why"

"Let's go get something."

It was beautiful in Antioch that day, the azure of the cloudless afternoon turning aureate and copper as the sun retired. Mark and Barnabas picked up some baked treats from a merchant packing up his things for the day, and they sat in a nearby plot of green to eat them.

"Does that letter settle things, do you think" asked Barnabas.

"What do you mean?"

"I think some of us—us Jewish believers, I mean—have had, let's just say, some questions about the direction of the gospel. I don't mean me, by the way."

"But some Jewish Christians," said Mark. "And by 'direction' you mean what?"

"Just turning the gospel loose in the Gentile world," said Barnabas.

"Odd that you would put it that way. 'Turn the gospel loose,' I mean. I've thought of it in just those words."

"I thought you had."

Mark turned to Barnabas and searched his eyes. "What made you think that?" he said.

"Don't forget I know you, cuz. I can read you like a scroll. Usually, anyway."

"It doesn't exactly worry me," said Mark. "I *do* think it's important for people to understand the gospel against its Jewish background."

"I know."

"And how do you know *that?*"

"Peter told me. Said you two talked about it."

"Well, we did. I told him that so far the church has had a Jewish core—he liked the term, by the way. And he agreed with me that Gentiles ought to—need to—know where the gospel comes from."

"But without having to be Jews."

"So says the letter."

"You *do* agree, don't you?"

"Absolutely."

"But is it time to 'turn the gospel loose' to the Gentiles?"

"I don't know."

"Why?"

"I'm not sure that's something we can just 'decide' to do," said Mark. "It will happen, obviously. But I don't think a council at Jerusalem would be able to make it happen. Or *keep it* from happening."

"No. Things are too far along for that."

"Still," said Mark, "we're pretty much steering the ship—Jews are. The prophets still basically all come out of our number."

"Eventually, it can't stay that way, though," said Barnabas. "For all we know, it already isn't."

"Asia?" said Mark.

"Yes. I have the feeling that a particularly fiery convert in Pisidian Antioch has the gift."

"The question is, Does he have the knowledge? I don't imagine you and Paul were there long enough to teach every scripture about the Messiah."

"No."

"Or tell everything you know about Jesus' life," said Mark.

"We tried."

"It's not enough," said Mark. "Oh, I don't mean your efforts."

"Then what?" said Barnabas.

"You saw some things, heard some things during Jesus' life here," said Mark. "Paul saw some, heard some. Peter saw it all. John did, too. The other apostles. And a lot of other people. But Peter can't be everywhere, go everywhere. The rest of us know bits and pieces."

"And Gentile prophets would know even less," said Barnabas.

"Not just them. Even Jews around the world. Why *would* they know what happened? Other than the sketchy news that went around at the time. It's not like they have a book about him."

"But they could."

"That's what I've been thinking," said Mark.

In the following year or so the Antioch church continued to grow in number and spiritual strength. The makeup of the church increased from a fourth to almost half Gentile. Two elders were added to the leadership team, both Gentile. Peter moved his wife and few possessions to the city and was accorded the position of head elder in Antioch, though it was more honorific than practical: Shimon continued to lead the elders on a regular basis.

Barnabas and Mark spent a lot of time together. After Barnabas's last visit to his now aging parents, he had decided to start another location of the Supply House of Joel of Cyprus, and with Mark's help had trained two young men in Antioch to handle it. He and Mark sometimes superintended the work, and sometimes actually helped load and unload shipments just for the exercise.

And, Mark spent time with Peter when he was in town. Using Antioch as his base, Peter had gone back south into Galilee once, further north into Cappadocia, and to parts east, visiting churches and filling in some of the gaps in their specific knowledge of Jesus' teachings and deeds. During one of his extended times back in

Antioch, he and Mark led a group of disciples in learning some of the parables Jesus told and the miracles he had performed. Peter's memory served the role of scripture during those sessions. Mark found himself thinking that while Peter could still tell the stories, they ought to be written down.

They ate lunch one day in Mark's little hovel, which Peter had come to like very much.

"It's comfy," he said to Mark.

"It's crowded," said Mark.

"It's just me and you, son."

"It would hardly hold more."

"Then we'll limit the guest list to *me!*" said Peter, laughing.

They ate pocket bread stuffed with spoonfuls of lamb and herbs. They finished and sat back, letting it all settle.

"It's been a long time since I heard anything about Andrew—about *all* the others," said Mark. "Do you get regular news?"

"If I had, you would've, too," said Peter. "But I usually hear things when I'm making my circuit. We *sort of* try to keep in touch. Through the grapevine."

"What did the grapes tell you last?"

"Well, of course, my brother Andrew went north. Far, far north. Best I know, he's still there. Thomas went east. Bartholomew went with him. I don't know how far. Maybe as far as the silk routes go."

"What about Philip? Did he stay in Africa?"

"Went along the coast for a while. I don't know now."

"Matthew?"

"Persia, according to the elders in Damascus. And of course, you know John is in Ephesus."

"Yes," said Mark. "What became of Matthias?"

"Ah, Matthias. He went with my brother."

"So, the four corners, so to speak," said Mark.

"That was the plan."

"Peter," said Mark. He looked at Peter with his mouth still open, while he put together what he was about to say.

"What is it, son?" the elder Peter said.

"You and the others—you can all preach and teach out of what you remember. I can't do that, not exactly. Even Paul can't do it like you can."

"That's true. What's your point?"

"Do you think the Master is coming back before you—and Paul and the other apostles—die?"

Peter shifted in his seat. He rested his head back in one of the two chairs that took up a lot of the space in the room. He stared at the ceiling. "It's beginning to look doubtful, isn't it."

"Then what are we going to teach when you're gone?" said Mark. "Not that I expect you to be gone tomorrow."

"I hope not, too," chuckled Peter. "But I've learned not to be too sure."

"Maybe we should begin writing it down. What you know. What you teach," said Mark.

"Maybe *you* should," said Peter. "My Greek is good in conversation. No doubt you write better than I would."

"We would just need to take some time to sit down where you could remember and I could write," said Mark.

"We could do that, yes," said Peter.

"And maybe when you preach here in the church, I'll sit at the back and make notes."

"Make me sound good," said Peter, smiling.

"I promise," said Mark.

In the fall of Emperor Claudius's tenth year, about two years after Paul and Barnabas had returned from the great mission venture they had taken, talk was going around the church that the consensus of the elders was that the church should fund another mission. They were particularly concerned about the growth and maturity of the churches already begun throughout Asia. Whether this idea had been planted in the elders' minds by Paul, Mark didn't know, but he thought it likely. When Paul had preached in the church recently, he had recalled incidents from the mission venture several times. Clearly, the mission lived vividly in his mind.

After one of those Lord's Days when Paul had brought the main message to the worshipers, Barnabas dropped by Mark's home in mid afternoon.

"Offer me something to drink, cousin—it's hot out there," said Barnabas.

"There's *oinos* paste in the kitchen," said Mark. "Water's in the red jar."

Barnabas disappeared around the corner into the little kitchen and reappeared in the front room with two cups of freshly reconstituted grape paste.

"Mmm," said Barnabas, licking his lips. "Almost like the real thing."

"I don't boil down my own," said Mark. "A lady in the church—you know Talia—does that for me. Makes enough for her family and for me."

"Wonder if I could get her to take pity on me, too."

"Of course, we could just get married, to good cooks."

"At this point, I suspect it's not going to happen, cousin."

"Probably not," said Mark. "For my part, I haven't tried to make it happen. I think I decided a few years ago that it's not *supposed* to happen."

"Me, too," said Barnabas, growing thoughtful. "It kind of goes along with the nature of the mission."

"Speaking of—" said Mark.

"Speaking of mission," said Barnabas, "I want to ask you something. You know what the talk has been. About another mission."

"I've heard it, yes," said Mark. "Anything in the works?"

"A specific proposal, yes."

"What is it?"

"Paul wants to go back around to where we traveled before. See how the churches are doing."

"Great! The elders would support that, I assume," said Mark.

"They've already said so, yes," said Barnabas. "That's where my question comes in."

"Well, spit it out."

"What if you go with us?"

Mark studied Barnabas's face for a moment. "Get the gang back together," he said.

"If you want to put it that way."

"What does Paul think about the idea?" said Mark.

"I haven't mentioned it to him yet," said Barnabas.

"Don't you think that would have been a good idea first?"

"Look, cousin," said Barnabas. "Okay, the thing in Perga was unfortunate. I know Paul was, uh, disappointed—"

"Angry," corrected Mark.

"Well, all right, a bit angry, when you left. But he knows as well as I do that it was for a very good reason. And Aunt Miriam didn't last, what, a month, after you went to Jerusalem?"

"Something like that."

"He found that out when we got back. I found myself thinking, What if it had been *his* mother?"

"Well, let's not be too hard on him, Barnabas. I understand why he was upset."

"But he should feel better about it, now."

"Wait, what? You don't know if he does?" said Mark.

"Not exactly. I just gather that he does. I haven't asked him in so many words."

"Words would help," said Mark. "I don't know that I have the same read on the situation. I don't really know what to think. We haven't been together by ourselves since you got back. We weren't really close before we went on the trip."

"But you haven't had any kind of clash," said Barnabas.

"No, not at all."

"Don't you think if he were going to confront you he would have done it by now?"

"I suppose so."

"I think so, too."

"So, you think he's okay about it. Now."

"He certainly should be," said Barnabas. He let the idea sit for a minute. "You know how we are. Men sometimes get over things by just letting sleeping dogs lie."

"So, just because he hasn't growled—" said Mark.

"May mean he's let bygones be bygones," said Barnabas. "And I'd like to ask him tomorrow about bringing you along. We have a meeting at my house in the morning."

Mark got up and ambled slowly out the front door. Barnabas followed him. Mark stood looking generally east, toward the sea. Sometimes he imagined he could see the coast from his house, smell the salt air, hear the waves. He remembered the excitement of the preaching encounters in Salamis, the adventure of the road, the great promise of the conversion of the proconsul in Paphos, and his thrilling chance to win Rabbi Yakov in Perga. He had often wondered what the other places looked like, the other Antioch, the Galatian cities. If Paul was willing to give him another go, Mark would like to do it.

"I can hear the wheels going around in your head," said Barnabas, behind him.

"If," said Mark, turning to him, "if Paul doesn't hesitate when you bring it up, I'll go."

"Understood," said Barnabas.

"That means you have to watch his face when you tell him. You know that thing he does with his right eyebrow."

"With the bottom lip coming out, yeah. Got it."

The two men grinned and clapped each other on the shoulder. Barnabas left and Mark went back inside.

On the morrow, Mark spent some time in the church meeting house, dropped by the Supply House and chatted with the young men running it, went to the market for food for the week, and returned home in the early afternoon. He found Barnabas standing by the front door. Mark couldn't quite read his cousin's face. He opened the door and the two went in. Mark put his purchases down in the kitchen and then went to the front room and took a seat.

"Okay, how did it go?"

Barnabas shook his head a couple of times and looked frustrated. "Not as well as I had planned," he said.

"Which means?"

"Which means, No!" said Barnabas. "I'm sorry, Mark. I really am. I thought for sure he would be open to the idea at the very least."

"I was afraid of this," said Mark. "I told you I didn't think he was over it. I told you—"

"I know, I know," said Barnabas. "And I'm sorry. I tried. I really did."

"Well, you know *I* didn't ask *you;* you asked me."

"I know. But I asked you because I really want you to go. And I think you really want to go, too," said Barnabas, fixing his eyes on Mark. "You do, don't you."

"I would love to go back, yes," said Mark.

"Well, that's good, because it's a little more than just that Paul doesn't want you to go. He doesn't want me to go, either."

"What?!"

"It was a pretty nasty scene, if you want to know."

"You want to tell me?" said Mark.

"I won't give an account of every blow—we argued probably a half hour over the whole thing."

"Just the thumbnail sketch, then," said Mark.

"I suggested we take you with us. I told him I had already asked you and you had agreed. And I watched his face like I said I would. He positively glowered."

Mark sighed. "And how did that turn into your not going, either?"

"We argued about it for a while. I made my case about you. It didn't seem to faze him. I thought about asking him What if it had been your mother who was dying? But I didn't. Nothing mattered. He said you had deserted us and didn't belong on another team because people couldn't count on you."

"You can stop, now," said Mark. "I don't need any more 'encouraging' words about me. I have enough confidence issues already."

"Okay, no more about that part of it. But I said I felt you ought to be going, and he said, 'Not with me. And maybe you and I shouldn't team up this time, either.'"

"So now, neither of us is going." Mark exhaled symbolically.

"Not quite," said Barnabas.

"What?" said Mark.

"What if we go? You and me? I think I can sell the elders on two mission teams. If I can't, then between the two of us I think we can fund it, can't we?"

"What? Yes, I suppose, but—"

"I know this is sudden, but you were ready to go with me and Paul, right?"

"Right," said Mark, "but where would we go? When we talked about this, it was with the assumption that we'd retrace our steps from two years ago."

"What if we start out going to Cyprus," said Barnabas.

"And run into Paul there?" said Mark, incredulously. "Wonderful idea!"

"No, of course not. He's going the other way. We had already mapped it out. He's going by land, up to Cilicia, over to Galatia. We can start out in Cyprus, go over to Attalia, maybe Laodicea, Colossae, over that way."

"Try not to cross paths with the other team."

"Exactly," said Barnabas. "But think of it in positive terms. We're two teams, covering twice the territory, making twice the impact for the gospel."

"Speaking of which, who else is on his team?" said Mark.

"He had already asked Silas to be the third man," said Barnabas. "Now, he'll be number two."

Mark sat silent for a minute, letting it all sink in. It was truly troubling to him that things between him and Paul had actually been fermenting in the past two years, more than he realized. It was upsetting to him now that these two missionaries, Paul and Barnabas, had a falling out over it, that they might never be friends again. Maybe they would, because Barnabas was not the sort of man to let things fester. He would try to set things right at the first opportunity. But for now, they were tense.

Mark could encourage himself only by reminding himself that instead of one mission venture, there were going to be two. It was kind of like the observation a friend of his had made about cats: when you think they're fighting, they're just multiplying.

26
A Year Later, Antioch, Syria

Mark and Barnabas sailed for Cyprus within two weeks of Barnabas's and Paul's standoff. As for the disagreement, Mark and Barnabas agreed never to make it public. They would probably say something to the believers in Salamis about the probability that Paul would be coming around later, in a year or so, but they wouldn't mention the reason for his not being with Barnabas and Mark. It wasn't relevant, after all. If Paul wanted to tell somebody that he and Barnabas had argued, that was his call. Maybe he would write about it in his memoirs. For now, Mark figured the Antioch church didn't need to see two of its leading men bickering.

Cyprus was the same richly green coast that Mark knew from visits in past years, and Salamis the same gleaming white city shining in the noonday sun.

Barnabas and Mark stayed with Barnabas's parents for the three weeks they remained in Salamis. Then they took the southern coastal road as before, only by cart this time, and spent another three weeks in Paphos, reuniting with friends in the church there, which had increased more than five times in size since they left it nearly four years before.

When they looked back later on the rest of the year after they had sailed away from Paphos, it seemed like a dream. They had gone north and west after getting to Attalia, had found themselves in and among pockets of believers everywhere, most of them tracing their Christian beliefs to the steady, loving work of the Apostle John. After a whirlwind tour they had been gone from Antioch for a little more than a year when they looked at one another one afternoon and agreed it was time to go back home.

Paul and Silas were still away when Mark and Barnabas returned. As before, a messenger was scheduled to meet up with Paul's team in at least one destination city, and he had come back from Pisidian Antioch nearly six months ago, where he had delivered funds and they had sent back word of their success so far. They were making good time to have gotten to Pisidian Antioch by that time, because they had already been to, and left, Tarsus, Lystra, Derbe, and Iconium. When the messenger left them, Paul and Silas were packing to go far west to Troas. Mark's understanding was that they planned to go north from there into Mysia and back east into Bithynia. They could be well into Pontus along the northern sea by now.

Barnabas took a few days' breather from the long journey home, but Mark was restive. The two of them gave a report to the elders of their accomplishments, thanking them for the partial support the church had offered. Barnabas's money had run dry and Mark didn't have as much money as he needed, either, which was what mostly prompted them to draw their trip to a close at the end of a year.

It didn't quite rankle Mark that the church didn't agree to fund Barnabas and him fully as they had Paul and Silas. It disappointed him, however. He assumed they must have had some idea that Paul and Barnabas had experienced some kind of falling out, and that they simply made a choice as to which team they would back to the hilt.

Never mind, thought Mark; on to the next thing. It was like "daily bread" in the model prayer Jesus' gave his disciples. "May your kingdom come" and "may your will be done" were constant requests for the day's marching orders. Mark focused on what was next *for him* in God's will. He assumed, at this point, that it would be something that didn't involve Paul anymore.

That Paul and Mark were in their own orbits now was a fading issue and no real disappointment. What would have been disappointing was if Mark didn't have the promise of friendship with Peter, who had become, in a way, a replacement for the father that Mark had known ever so briefly until he was five, and nowadays had trouble remembering at all.

The most significant news greeting Barnabas and Mark upon their return was that Peter's wife had died. She had been ailing for some time—ever since coming to Antioch, really. Her heart acted up frequently and it wore her out. One of those episodes had finally taken her to be with the Lord, about six months ago. By all accounts Peter had been steady and stalwart, subdued by his loss but soothed by the grace of God, sure in his hope, and supported by everyone in the church. People watched him and learned how Christians should respond in time of death.

Peter preached to the assembled church the first Lord's Day Mark and Barnabas were back in Antioch. At some length, Peter told the story of Jesus' calling of Matthew. Before becoming a disciple, Matthew had been one of those hated tax collectors, men who for sordid wages had squeezed their own people for Rome's due, keeping whatever else they could convince people they owed, whether they did or not. Everyone in the room listened rapt, as did Mark. Peter was a fisherman; he could tell tales with the best of them. Peter well remembered, he said, the banquet Matthew held once he had become a follower. Mark thought it possible that it wasn't quite as lavish as Peter described it, but who was to tell?

Anyway, the moral to the story was contained in the scene that took place when Jewish teachers wanted to know how come Jesus was spending his time with tax collectors, as well as other people they summarily dismissed as sinners. By 'sinner,' said Peter, they meant anything from the most rank prostitute, thief or murderer to a perpetrator of whatever the moment's target violation of petty

Pharisaic regulations might be. Jesus put them all in their place when he said, "The healthy don't need a doctor: the sick do." Then Peter went on to tell everyone in the room, "That includes you and me."

As Peter preached on, Mark's mind wandered to his distant past. He tried to piece together detached memories from his childhood. Some, a very few, were images from Cyrene, he thought, though he was very, very young when he was there; he reasoned he may have placed these events in Cyrene when they were really from Alexandria. He did remember Alexandria. He had distinct mental pictures of the neighborhood where his family lived, and he had an impression about the look of the city. He definitely remembered his little house there, and the synagogue where he and his mother went without his father, and playing with his dog, Puppy.

Mark began wondering about how much of the news of Jesus had reached and influenced Alexandria. He was much more aware of how the gospel had taken hold in Syria and Asia. But there were "sinners" in Alexandria, as well.

While Mark was perusing his distant memories for no reason he could lay his hand on, which was odd, Peter was waxing nostalgic, too. "I remember it like yesterday," he said. "We had met him before—Andrew first, and then he introduced me to him. But when he came to the lake that day as we were casting nets near shore, it was time for decision. He said to both of us, 'Follow me. I'll make you fishers of *men!*'"

Mark tried to picture the scene, and as he did he thought of Peter in Solomon's Colonnade on the day of the Great Pentecost Event, casting his net and hauling in thousands of people to the fellowship of the first church. Mark thought of the thousands here and there in Galilee who then heard the news of Jesus' resurrection, and the thousands in Antioch who heard, and the thousands in other cities. And he wondered about the thousands in Alexandria.

Mark found himself thinking about the interesting fact that people reach what they imagine might be the middle of their lives and start thinking about going back home in some way. If they've never left home, they just begin treasuring again the people and things that made home, home. But if home was somewhere else, they sometimes want to go there again, to try to resurrect the feelings they had, to reassure themselves that their memories aren't fictional imaginings. Mark was more than halfway through an average lifetime. He wondered if Alexandria was just a treasured memory or if there were something else prompting him to cherish the places of his beginnings.

Peter was saying, "Matthew was at his tax table. Andrew and I were in our boat. Where you are isn't the point. Where you're going *is*, when Jesus says follow me."

Mark realized there was little, if anything, about his deepest thoughts, his imaginings, his dreams, that was random. God was always moving, deep in his heart, to call him onward in his will.

When the worship time wound to a close, Peter and Mark chatted.

"Come to the house and have dinner," said Peter. "I'm not a bad cook. But just in case, I have a helper who's better."

"I surrender," Mark said.

After dinner Mark and Peter walked down the street to a grassy plot in the middle of a neighborhood. Two houses had been purchased by a man who planned to construct a new home on conjoined lots. Unfortunately for him, he had died suddenly, leaving no will, and the property was still in contest. It was likely to go to the city, but in the meantime grass had grown and neighbors kept it clean and made benches and other things for people to enjoy a green space in the middle of the bustling town. In what had been the back yards of the two former houses were several trees. Mark and Peter sat on a bench in the shade of one of them, with a delightful view down the hill into the center of the city of Antioch.

"What's next, my boy?" said Peter.

"I have an idea I've begun mulling over," said Mark. "I'm waiting for direction. I suppose it will be where some of those 'sick' people live whom Jesus came to save."

"So, not far away, then," said Peter.

Mark smiled in general assent.

"Jerusalem, Judea, Samaria, and the uttermost."

"Jesus' commission," said Mark.

"Where you are, where you'll go tomorrow, and as far as you can ever go," said Peter. "Sinners like us are everywhere."

"I just don't want to make the mistake of making my plans entirely out of my own imagination," said Mark.

"No," said Peter, "you don't want to do that. On the other hand, the Spirit doesn't always speak in dreams."

"You've had dreams," said Mark.

"I've had a few, but most days I just stay close to the Spirit and then go here or there, do this or that, and let the Spirit close doors. Or give me a powerful feeling that says, no, not that."

"Like the proverb. Or proverbs—several of them," said Mark. "'In their hearts, people plan their course, but the Lord directs their steps.' I think that's right."

"Close enough," said Peter. "And that gives me great relief. From the burden of figuring it all out ahead of time."

Mark mused on that thought for a minute as they both enjoyed the afternoon breeze. The wind was coming in off the coast. Clouds in the distant western sky suggested rain would probably come ashore by evening.

"I think the Lord wants me to cast the net in Alexandria," Mark said, surprising himself. As he said it boldly, peace came over him.

Peter turned to him and started to speak but then just peered into Mark's eyes. Mark believed he could see Peter's mind at work, and he was certain that Peter could see more deeply inside him, to his very soul.

"I believe you've heard the Spirit," said Peter quietly, still focusing on him steadily. He waited while Mark caught his breath.

"I hadn't planned to say that," said Mark. "It just came out."

"Ah," said Peter. "I did that once—well, I've done it much more than once!" He laughed, and Mark joined him. "Jesus asked us who we thought he was. I just piped up out of the blue, 'You're the Christ, the Son of the Living God.'"

"I've heard you tell that story," said Mark.

"I hadn't planned on saying it," said Peter. "But I had been thinking it. I had thought who else could he be? But when I said it, that was it. There was no going back."

"I guess there isn't for me, either," said Mark.

"So, what are you going to do?"

"I guess I'm going to Alexandria."

27
Going to Alexandria, c. A.D. 52

There was more to going on a mission of his own that Mark had considered initially. His first thought, that he might seek a companion, he dismissed. Something just told him this was his calling alone. His next thought, to seek the support of the church there in Antioch, he also dismissed. Unless one of the elders or prophets there came up with a word from the Lord that implied the involvement of the church, Mark would just announce that he was going, and he would go.

His final thought was whether he was going for a year, or two, or simply to stay. This decision, too, he made quickly. His mission would be open ended. With no plans to return after any set length of time, he would leave nothing behind that ultimately needed tending to. That meant selling his house and closing up his affairs in Antioch.

Mark didn't think the church would be interested in his house; it was too little for activities. And selling it would make available funds to help underwrite his journey.

He had a buyer within a week, a young widow with a child who thought the 'hovel' was perfect for her. Mark sold the house furniture and all. When it was deeded over to her, Mark met her son, who was just about the age he had been when he and his mother had moved from Alexandria to Jerusalem, to be taken in by his grandmother. Mark wondered if the boy would be able to picture his father in twenty years, or thirty. He hoped so.

It took Mark about a month to make all the other preparations.

In the middle of this time he told the church about his calling by the spirit to Alexandria. Whether he implied in any way that he didn't want them to feel obligated to commission him or support him, he didn't remember, when he thought back on it later. In any event, the church didn't assume any ownership of Mark's mission, and they understood that he wasn't thinking of his plans as temporary.

Three days before his departure Mark met up with Barnabas for lunch and conversation.

"Really, cousin, you don't have a projected date to come back? For anything?" said Barnabas.

"That's the way it looks right now," said Mark.

"So, I shouldn't ask *when* I'll see you again," said Barnabas. "You're just leaving me here to wonder *if* I'll see you again."

"Now, don't go trying to make me feel guilty," said Mark.

"Wouldn't dream of it." Barnabas sighed. "What am I going to do without you?" Mark knew he was only half serious. But the half that was serious was full of affection for his younger cousin.

"Go on another mission," said Mark. "Take one of the young men in the church. Train him right."

"I don't know," said Barnabas. "I'm feeling like concentrating on things at home. Maybe writing something."

"You, cousin?"

"You aren't the only writer, you know," said Barnabas. "I had good schooling in Salamis. I could have become a scribe if I'd wanted to, but I needed money; so I got into Abba's work with the Supply House. That gave me some traveling, too, which was fun. While I was young."

"What are you going to write about?"

"You know how you talk about the next generation of preachers and teachers needing something in writing about Jesus' life?" said Barnabas. Mark nodded. "Well, Jews are going to need something, too. Maybe something else."

"What are you thinking?" said Mark.

"When you were knee-high to a locust, I was in little schools with rabbis learning about the Torah. After I became a believer, I realized that our Jesus is really all through the Torah. In the story of Abraham. In the law. In the imagery of the temple. He's *there.*"

"Have you started writing about it yet?"

"Not yet," said Barnabas, staring off at the mountains to the east. "I'm still thinking about it. I'll let you know." He looked back at Mark. "Or maybe not."

"There you go, again, trying to make me feel guilty," Mark said, teasing his cousin. Keeping things lighthearted was their way, both of them, of preventing their descent into sentimentality.

"Maybe a little," said Barnabas. "Hey, you're talking about never seeing each other again."

They had finished their snack lunch a long time ago. Mark had tossed the last few crumbs of his bread away from the table. A sparrow that had waited patiently descended and made even those few remnants disappear.

The morning Mark left he thanked the neighbor who had given him a room for a few days after he no longer had his house. He hoisted two packs into a cart headed for Seleucia, and the cart rumbled down the road and away. Late in the day they arrived at the coast. The next morning Mark found passage on a ship going to Joppa. From there he boarded a ship going to Alexandria. On his fifth day of travel, he walked into the city he had left thirty-four years ago.

The city streets were laid out almost completely in due east-west and due north-south fashion. A recognized Jewish quarter was on the eastern side, and Mark seemed to remember some of the buildings as he headed that direction, though much was certainly new.

He intended to stop for some directions and information before wasting time just wandering around. He found it fortuitous that he soon saw a cobbler's shop, since one of the legging straps had come loose from his sandal just after he got off the ship. He could have the sandal repaired and possibly find out what he needed to know.

The cobbler was at his bench working a piece of leather when Mark entered his little shop. The man looked up and greeted Mark in accented Greek, and Mark returned the greeting in the nearly universal language—no one thinks he speaks with an accent himself. The cobbler introduced himself as Anianus. They chatted just a few seconds before Anianus looked over the problem and said he could get Mark on his way in just a few minutes. Mark took off the sandal and sat on a chair watching Anianus begin his work. The legging strap had broken at the sole and would need to be replaced.

The remark by Anianus reminded Mark of something he had heard one of the teachers in Antioch—perhaps it was Peter—say Jesus had said. It was about putting new patches on old garments: you don't. Mark thought of a way to make that principle an introduction to the news about Jesus. He also thought there was no reason he should wait for some auspicious event to inaugurate his missionary purpose in Alexandria. No time like the present.

"Have you heard much about Jesus of Nazareth here in Alexandria?" Mark said.

Anianus looked up from his work. "A little. Why?"

"I'm looking for anyone who might be a follower of his teachings," said Mark. "Perhaps some Jews who believe he is their Messiah."

"The Jewish quarter is just a little farther east of here," said Anianus, without revealing sentiments of any kind.

"This way?" said Mark, pointing down the road he had already been walking.

"Yes, and then south a ways."

"Thank you," said Mark. "Are you a Jew?" Upon entering the shop he had thought the man looked like a brother Israelite.

Anianus looked up again and sized up Mark. "I am," he said. "And I believe you are, too."

"Yes," Mark said forthrightly. "And a follower of The Way. We believe that Jesus is the Christ."

"Why?" said Anianus.

Mark heard no defensiveness, combativeness, or invitation to argument in Anianus's voice. His question sounded completely innocent. It sounded even as if something had readied Anianus for a serious conversation about the Messiah.

"Since you've asked," said Mark, "let me tell you." He began with the sandal lace. He told Anianus how Jews were always looking for a way to inherit eternal life, but that Jesus said there were no good works they could add to their lives to earn God's forgiveness and a place in heaven. He said that Jesus said not to patch the old, but begin with something new. That something new was a new heart.

And Mark told Anianus the good news of the crucified and risen Son of God, Jesus.

While Mark could have been on his way in a few minutes, as Anianus had said, it took more than two hours. Only the last five minutes were taken in fixing the sandal. The remainder was spent in an explanation of the gospel, a few questions, a solemn moment of decision, and a tearful then joyous period of prayer during which Anianus became a believer in his Messiah, Jesus Christ.

Mark was as thrilled as the day he had been blessed to be alone with Yakov in Perga and to lead him to faith in Jesus. And he was equally and as profoundly convinced that what was happening was a divine event, almost out of his hands entirely. His brain was working, his heart was yearning, and his mouth was moving, but it was the Holy Spirit who was working.

Not only was there a Jewish quarter in the city but there were also a few followers of The Way in Alexandria, though there wasn't any identifiable congregation. It was odd, Mark thought, that by some estimations at least a hundred Christians—the term "Christians" was fairly new to them—were living here and there in the city, but they hadn't established any meeting place.

The matter became clearer in the first few days Mark was there. Worshipers of the Greek pantheon alternated between indifference and smoldering enmity toward Jews, but between smoldering enmity and open hostility toward The Way, which they saw as ramped-up Judaism. The Romans, whose empire and deities had now superceded those of the Greeks, were decidedly un-welcoming of religious competition, and consequently they were even more predisposed to be intolerant of The Way. And of course, the Jews who didn't believe in Jesus were averse to those who did. The result for Christians was an atmosphere of contempt that erratically erupted into occasional persecution, whether verbal, social, political, economic, or physical. There had been violent events.

Anianus knew who a few Christians were and he introduced Mark to them. Anianus also told them excitedly that he had joined their faithful number. In a few weeks, Mark had met all of the Christians known to each other in the city, most of whom were in the Jewish quarter but a few scattered to the west.

Believers moved from place to place every week for worship. For the most part, the Jewish-Christians continued to go to their synagogue on the Sabbath and then met unobtrusively at one of several places the next day, but only for an hour or two. All the groups had individual leaders who met regularly by themselves, mostly to decide week by week on the next week's meeting places. They had functioned like this for a number of years, trying to stay low and avoid trouble.

Mark met with understandable suspicion from the first

Christians he met after winning Anianus to the Lord. But by the time the first few believers were convinced he had really come from the church in Antioch, that he knew Peter, and that he was really and truly in Alexandria to join them, they in turn spread the word to the other small groups. As Mark worked his way around to them all, he was warmly received. And, as he thought he sensed, though no one at first said so, they looked at him as the leader they had all thought would eventually come.

Several Christians helped Mark find a place to stay temporarily, which turned into a nearly two year stint with Joseph, one of the covert believers who lived near the Canopic Gate, on the far western edge of the city. It was a fairly spacious place, formerly a home for a family of ten, now occupied by just one. One of the worship groups currently met in Joseph's house about every fourth Lord's Day.

About two months into his time in Alexandria Mark asked the group leaders to meet with him at Joseph's house, which they did one evening. Mark proposed three things: that they begin to meet publically in a single place; that they find a place they could purchase instead of using anybody's home; and that they not attempt to concentrate their influence on the neighborhood where their meeting place would be, but instead all over the city, wherever they lived and worked.

Mark explained his strategy. He believed that ultimately the church would need to go public to be authentic, and he believed the time was now. To keep any negative focus off an individual believer, he believed a common building was necessary. And to keep the neighborhood of people pre-disposed against The Way from feeling threatened and becoming hostile, he believed that opting against concentrating the church's efforts on that neighborhood would be most helpful.

The group leaders, who Mark thought were really the elders of the Alexandrian believers, had a lively discussion about the three-pronged proposal. Some of them were leery of changing what had been working well for years. They were afraid of a more dangerous kind of persecution. Most believers had adapted to low level resistance, criticism, ostracism, or bigotry they faced, first as Jews and then, if they were identified, as Christians.

Mark engaged them in earnest conversation based on a saying of Jesus, that whoever would save his life will lose it, but whoever loses his life for Jesus' sake and the gospel's will save it. The group leaders, and apparently all of the Alexandrian believers, were unaware of this teaching. Mark tucked that fact back into his mind as more reason for someone to write a book about the life and teachings of Jesus.

Praying inwardly as he continued to talk and they talked with each other, Mark listened as one by one they conceded that they had hidden too long and that perhaps it was time they hold their heads up and own Jesus as Lord without apology. The Spirit was moving.

Finally, one of them said, "I say we go forward with Mark's plan." He looked at each of them, and then at Mark. "If," he said, "Mark will be our pastor."

All eyes fell on Mark. He had expected this. In the Lord, he had hoped for this. It was why he had come to Alexandria. Then and there, Mark became the leader of the Alexandrian church.

Finding a building to call their own was not difficult. An acceptable location was found just outside of the Jewish quarter in the central city area. No signs or banners were put up. No campaign was carried out to inform the city of the new home of the Alexandrian church. Believers from each of the groups simply came to the new, unified location one Lord's Day, met for two hours, and then filed back out and went to their homes and businesses.

The crowd the first day was not quite the total of all the separate groups. A few believers were worried that Zeus extremists or Jupiter extremists or even Jewish opponents might have caught wind of the meeting and decided to make trouble. But none of that happened. After a few weeks with no repercussions, attendance increased and confidence grew.

As well as proclaiming the basic gospel continually, Mark concentrated on teaching what he knew of Jesus' words and deeds, aiming to deepen the level of the Alexandrian believers' discipleship. And he assumed a personal interest in the spiritual development of Anianus. Something in Mark said Anianus was shortly to be very important to the church.

Within a year, the church had doubled in number. Well into Mark's second year, it appeared the number would grow by another hundred or more. As pastor of the church, Mark realized early on that he would need to conduct the Supper Jesus instituted at Passover on the night of his arrest. He felt a bit awkward in doing it —it was the first time he had led this ordinance—but he simply imitated what the elders in Jerusalem and Antioch had done, and no one objected. He also conducted baptisms, which they first tried performing in a nearby canal but then later moved to the waterfront near the port.

The initial, unexpected lack of resistance to the church's going public did not last. Perennial tension existed in the city over its multiplicity of religions. Oldest was Egyptian religion consisting of numerous gods and goddesses under the great god Ra. Then came the Greeks with their pantheon to be worshiped. Then came the Roman gods and a religious war that hadn't been resolved in the more than eighty years since the Empire overtook Alexandria. Jews had coexisted with various degrees of success for several hundred years, but they tended to get swept into conflict during recurring periods of heated religious intolerance. And now, Christians were there. They weren't just somewhere, lurking in the shadows but not doing anything; they were there, in the sunshine, making converts and pointing to a supreme God who laid claim to all nations everywhere.

Mark was caught up in the increasing climate of hostility, in great part because, as pastor of the Alexandrian church, he had grown into his role of chief evangelist. He had begun preaching occasionally in public places. This, along with the general spiritual growth taking place in the church, had further emboldened Christians, whose lives and verbal witness had attracted attention, some of it unwanted.

The community began to protest the worship of the church by gathering outside and chanting hymns to gods and goddesses. They attempted to persuade the city governor to ban or at least restrict the church. They vandalized the meeting place. They interrupted baptism services at the edge of the Great Sea. Some merchants who knew they were dealing with Christians or with church leaders in particular would refuse to sell to them. There were incidents of assaults in broad daylight on Christians, with little knots of conspirators helping the perpetrators get away.

It wasn't the first persecution Mark had experienced, but it was the most intense to date. Curiously, little of it came from the Jews. Perhaps they were satisfied simply seeing the pagan groups fanning the flames. Most of the persecution was from citizens, but gradually, the city government and Roman authorities began to clamp down, claiming that some church activities incited riots.

What was preventing the wholesale outlawing of Christian worship, at least temporarily, was the growing number of believers in the city, along with the fact that those believers were not shy about their faith. Reticent believers were fairly easy to suppress, sometimes even to recognize. Bold witnesses were harder to intimidate.

Nevertheless, the church realized that there was value in

moving targets. In fact, the elders of the congregation relocated frequently. In part, this strategy led to Mark's decision to turn leadership over to someone else. Down the road a few years, that leader might do the same. The thinking was that if by plan the leadership shifted with some frequency, one person wouldn't become a lightning rod for the entire church, or wouldn't stay one very long. With more leaders representing multiple fronts, perhaps the church would be considered a formidable influence that government would prefer to tolerate rather than target.

Mark met individually with each of the elders about his moving-target strategy and found them all agreeable. As he spoke with them, however, he sensed that none of them was eager to be the next head elder. Mark inferred that each of them would have been glad to nominate someone else. All but Anianus.

Anianus frankly told Mark, "I'll do whatever you want me to do."

Anianus had deepened in faith as well as scriptural and gospel knowledge over the years Mark had personally shepherded and discipled him. He had become an elder and all the other elders respected him completely and trusted him implicitly. So, when Mark brought before them his intention to appoint Anianus as pastor of the church, no one gave a hint of reservation.

Anianus was installed as the pastor of Alexandria's church on a bright summer Lord's Day as the church met an hour after sunrise. The other elders laid hands on him. The church sang songs of praise to God. Anianus spoke briefly with words of encouragement.

And Mark announced he would be leaving Alexandria for Antioch the next day.

Technically, Mark's plan was to take an extended vacation while the new head elder, Anianus, took charge. Mark was the church's first true pastor and he didn't want his presence to be a source of conflicting leadership, even if he weren't its instigator. People have a way of holding on to past leaders, he thought, which made it hard for new leaders to truly take charge and be followed. If Mark were not in Alexandria for a while, it wouldn't be possible for him to be consulted about Anianus's decisions and directions.

In truth, Mark didn't know when he would return. Just as he had come to realize while in Antioch that the Lord was leading him to go to Alexandria, now he realized the Lord was leading him back to Antioch. He simply didn't know why.

A week before consulting the other elders about changing leadership, Mark had awakened in the middle of the night, sat up in bed, and had a clear image in his mind's eye of the church in Antioch, worshiping on the first day of the week. In a kind of waking dream Mark saw Peter standing before the crowded room, preaching with a passion that could have been rivaled only by the Master, himself. At the height of his message, Peter extended his hands toward the people, and it seemed that his eyes were on Mark himself.

"Come!" Peter said.

And with that, the waking dream, or the vision, or whatever images left over from sleep might have been, dissipated into the dark of the room. Mark lay back down slowly and drifted back into deep slumber. When he woke, he had become certain he would leave the Alexandrian church to another's leadership and would return to Antioch.

Now, with Anianus's installation as pastor, there was little to do but pack his things and leave. While in Alexandria he had scrupulously avoided acquiring anything that he couldn't carry on his back. The moving-target strategy further required being able to pick up and move frequently. Leaving was remarkably easy in one way. It was monumentally more difficult in another. This was his first place of solo leadership. Indeed, while he had not planted the work in absolute terms, he had established Alexandria's first bonafide church out of roving groups of cautious individual followers of Christ. It was difficult leaving them, even though he had described the move as possibly temporary.

That was odd, he thought. When he had left Antioch for Alexandria, he had told the church there he mission was open ended. Now he was returning there and he was telling his friends in Alexandria his journey to Antioch was open ended. On the one hand, it troubled Mark that his moves might be thought of as the result of caprice, deeply rooted indecision or lack of commitment. On the other, he had been profoundly influenced in his discipleship by people who understood the Christian's pilgrimage as dependent on the wind of the Holy Spirit, whose moving was unpredictable.

As he tied up his packs and said goodbye to the hosts of his current living quarters, Mark let his confidence in the inscrutable sovereignty of God reassure him about his decision to leave the church in other hands. If he were coming back, whether in a year, or two, or ten, he would know that when the right time came. If he weren't, then God's will be done.

28
Antioch, c. A.D. 55

Everyone was delighted to see Mark come into the Antioch church's house of worship on the Lord's Day two weeks later. Mark's travel had landed him in Seleucia midday on a Sabbath. He had taken a cart to Antioch through the afternoon. He found a place to stay overnight. No one in the church had seen him until he strolled into their meeting place the next day. Everyone was surprised.

Except Peter.

They found each other amid the hubbub of the happy congregation after the worship time concluded. Peter was accosted, as usual, by many people wanting to speak to him and have him speak to them. Mark pretty much stood in place off to one side and let Peter navigate the crowd to get to him. They went outside and strolled slowly down a side street, talking and catching up.

"Come with me," said Peter.

"Glad to," said Mark. They headed up the street in the general direction of Peter's home.

"What finally convinced you to come back," said Peter.

"A convergence of things. Circumstances," said Mark.

"What finally convinced you to come back," said Peter again.

Mark stopped. "A dream. I had a dream."

"Ah," said Peter with a knowing smile. "Who was in it?"

"You."

Peter didn't seem amazed or even slightly surprised. He began walking again. Mark joined him.

"You were saying, 'Come,'" said Mark.

"Is that all?" said Peter.

"That's all. That was enough."

"And here you are."

"Yes," said Mark. They walked another few steps. "Were you in prayer trying to call me? Or something?"

"Not that I remember," said Peter, chuckling. "Maybe I did it in a dream of my own. Who knows?!"

"I have to trust that I read the signs and circumstances right," said Mark. "Like you said once, the Spirit doesn't always speak in dreams."

"But sometimes he does," said Peter. "Sometimes he does."

They walked another block as Peter's home came into view.

"I suppose I'll dive back into the work of the church," said Mark. "I'll have to count on you to bring me back up to speed on what's going on."

"I'm leaving soon," said Peter.

"Well, can we get together tomorrow?" said Mark.

"I don't mean leaving here in a minute," said Peter. He gestured vaguely with a wave of his hand north and west. "I mean I'm going."

"Going? Where?" said Mark.

"Out there. Somewhere," said Peter. "It's time for me to go to the uttermost. Well, some of it, anyway," he added with a smile.

"How far?" said Mark.

"Probably as far as Galatia, at least. And somebody needs to get over into Greece."

"Wow! That's pretty far."

"You're looking at me like you think I'm too old to make the trip," said Peter. "I'm a half century young."

"I wasn't—" Mark began. "Well, maybe I was."

"That's okay, son." Peter grinned and continued his thought. "When Paul and I told the elders that he would go to the Gentiles and I would go to the Jews, it wasn't long before he left. Now, it's my turn."

"But there are Jews here," said Mark.

"And in every major city in Asia, Greece, and Italy. We're all over the world, son," Peter said. "Looks like I have my work cut out for me."

Mark had a wondrous look about him, that darkened slightly like the clouds blowing in. Peter stared out toward the horizon.

"I guess I just assumed you would be around when I got back," said Mark. "When are you planning on leaving? How long do you think you'll be gone?"

"Oh, I'll probably be here another month," Peter said. "Things to do. Things to prepare. I'll sell the house, I suppose. If I don't just give it to the church."

"Wait, what? Sell your house? Why?" said Mark.

"It's unlikely I'll be back," said Peter. "Even if I did return after a time, there's no one to keep up the house for me, and I could stay with somebody in the church if I showed up one day. But I've prayed about this for a while. I don't think I'll be back."

While Mark contemplated this abrupt revelation, Peter tried to discern his thoughts. He let Mark meditate on the news for a spell.

"I'm going to want a companion along with me," said Peter. "Somebody who can teach. Talk. Tell the gospel. Write. Plan. Somebody who's looking for his future and has the gumption to get up and go when he sees an opportunity."

Mark looked up from his reverie, unblinking, and saw the twinkle in Peter's eyes.

"Maybe somebody who had a dream. You know anybody like that?" said Peter.

"I think I do," said Mark.

It was a cyclonic month of activity for the elder and younger team members who were about to embark on a journey of unknown proportions and extent, to preach the gospel, start churches if possible, and reach as far as the Spirit would let them. They gathered compact provisions, enough to get them from place to place, stowed funds here and there in discreet pockets in their clothing, and mapped out travel routes for the first several hundred miles ahead.

Mark and Barnabas spent a day together, the latter having been unapologetically overjoyed at his cousin's return to Antioch, after having left with no plans to return. That Mark's appearance was to be brief was disappointing, but Barnabas had come to realize that Mark's course was being charted and piloted by someone higher than them both, whose purposes were not for the cousins' convenience.

Eventually, Peter decided to deed his house to the church, which would either use it for its original purpose or sell it, or even use it for expanded church activities. Mark had to dispose of his paltry property as well, since he had immediately accepted Peter's concept of the mission—it was to go out there, somewhere, and not come back. Or at least, not to stay.

Two days before they planned to leave Antioch probably for the last time, Mark and Peter met with the elders at the church, who had been joined by their wives and a few deacons. Shimon prayed for them lengthily and passionately. There was much indecipherable utterance in the room as the spirits of men and women gave the 'amen' and vocalized their deeply shared pleas for safety, grace, and boldness. Ultimately, the room fell silent as a gentle peace descended upon them.

"Brother Peter, brother Mark," said Shimon, "I have a word from the Lord for you."

"Say it—"

—"Say it," said Peter and Mark.

Shimon said, "The prophet Isaiah wrote, 'Tell the Daughter of Zion, See, your Savior is coming.' God sent the Messiah first to us. As he sends you to our people far away, he goes with you in power. And the gospel will be established through your words."

Mark didn't know about Peter, but a shiver went up his spine, and back down again, too.

Early one morning in the middle of the week Peter and Mark were ready to go. As they prepared to board a cart going to Seleucia, they went around embracing people in the substantial crowd that had gathered to see them off. Barnabas was there. He clasped Peter's arms. He hugged Mark, wiping away a tear or two as inconspicuously as possible, which wasn't much. Mark choked back his own tears. Then he and Peter got into the cart and waved to everyone as they rumbled down the road and away.

Barnabas turned and walked back up the street and into the hilly neighborhood where his house was. It was really a lonely place. He had no wife. His parents were across part of the Great Sea. There was the church, of course, but it wasn't the same. His best friend was his cousin, Mark.

And despite the technical possibility that both of them allowed to hang in the air, Barnabas knew they were playing a game. He would never see Mark again.

29
Asia and Parts West, c. A.D. 55-

Three hours after they navigated the Antioch streets and got onto the highway to the coast, the newly formed team of two was in the port city and hunted for a ship making its first stop in Tarsus. They found one leaving the next morning and then found an inn for the night. Just after dawn they went back down to the wharfs and paid their passage for the little jaunt of a day over to Tarsus. Bounding through the unusually hearty waves near shore at Seleucia, they made good time in crosswinds as they traveled half the distance to Tarsus by sea that they would have walked or ridden if they had gone by land.

There were plenty of Jews in Tarsus, Paul's home turf, and Peter and Mark made several visits to the synagogue there, finding a number of believers already thriving in the relatively calm city of pagan, Jewish and now Christian faiths. Within the month they traversed the mountains of Cilicia and went into lower Cappadocia, arriving in Caesarea. Their investigation of the climate for the gospel in Caesarea led to the belief that brief, previous work there was growing slowly among Gentiles but that the Jews were still not entirely decided against Christ. They won a few converts in the synagogue, most of whom decided to remain among their own people until and unless it became impossible to pursue discipleship to Jesus as part of the Jewish fellowship.

After months of witness it was on to parts west and north, into Galatia. They headed for Ancyra, trusting that if they could reach substantial numbers of Jews there, believers would then take over and radiate throughout their own country. They learned that Paul's previous preaching in the lower districts of Galatia had resulted in fairly strong work, but Galatia spread northeast for hundreds of miles, into the foothills and mountains where Peter knew there were little synagogues with Jews whose hearts held the ancient hope of a chosen-one. Patiently, they won Jews in Ancyra, one by one, and taught the slowly growing church to see beyond themselves, to encompass their whole country for Jesus, the Christ.

In his fourteenth year as emperor of Rome, Claudius died, and the news came of the name of his successor: Nero. Nobody knew for certain just what kind of ruler Nero would be, but some people said he was a hardliner about everything.

News was good about everything Roman but not very informative about what was going on in Peter's and Mark's home country. Certainly they had heard nothing about the church in Antioch. They could have hired messengers to send a letter back home, but that was relatively expensive, and they had to think about the responsible use of their funds. Even if they had done so, they couldn't be certain where they would be; they couldn't tell a messenger to bring back word from Antioch if they didn't know where they'd be when he got back. After the first two years in Asia, the realization had sunk in to Mark that his home was now wherever they traveled, and that he would likely never see Antioch or Jerusalem again.

"Do you ever wonder what's going on back in Antioch?" said Mark one day after they had spent hours visiting homes in Ancyra.

"All the time," said Peter. "Obviously, you do, too."

"I miss Barnabas," said Mark. "Everybody else, too, of course, but Barnabas is family. We were always close."

"Of course," said Peter. "I don't have family left, but it was still home. Silas was like family, I suppose."

"Where do you think he is, now? Where *they* are," said Mark.

"Who knows," said Peter. "Paul and Silas could have been back to Antioch by now and gone out again. No idea."

"You think there's any possibility we'll run into them somewhere? While we're out here?"

"Anything's possible," said Peter. "I imagine we'll cross their path even if they've been and gone by the time we get there."

"How long do you want to stay here in Ancyra?"

"We'll know when the time comes."

And that was the way they decided things. And so it was that one day, a year or more after they had begun work in Ancyra, they looked at each other and read their common thought, that it was time to move on.

It was hard travel going over the mountains to the north, but there were well-used passes and other people who knew the roads, and they eventually came into Bithynia and Pontus. At the first sizable towns they began preaching in little synagogues in the southern region of the country. But they pressed on and finally came to Nicaea, on the eastern end of Lake Ascanius, not far from the northern sea, which the locals called Axeinos, due to its being inhospitable to sailors. There were Jews in Nicaea. A modestly sized synagogue stood on the western side of the city, and Peter and Mark worshiped with their fellow Jews the first Sabbath they were in town.

For several weeks, they kept a low profile so as to take the spiritual temperature of the people. The Nicaean Jews were decidedly not Pharisaical, as far as they were here from Judea and as surrounded and culturally influenced as they were by Greeks. They had not been not lured into the worship of Greek deities, however, or the Roman gods and goddesses whose images festooned public buildings. Overall, Peter adjudged the climate as reasonably friendly to the gospel, and before long he and Mark began making inroads with the message that the long-awaited Messiah had come and was being proclaimed in an ever expanding circle from the spiritual epicenter of Jerusalem.

Mark and Peter spent months in Nicaea, watching with humbling gratitude the growth of a small fellowship into a larger one, and finally into a self-sustaining church. They taught them how to teach the gospel simply and persuasively. Peter modeled powerful preaching and witness. Mark concentrated on expounding the ancient scriptures.

The Nicaean believers were lovingly possessive of Peter and Mark. And they developed a strong sense of their own missionary calling. Members began to talk about reaching fellow Jews in surrounding towns and throughout Bithynia. That was the kind of thinking that encouraged Peter and Mark to believe that at some point, they could confidently move on to someplace else with the gospel.

Late in the second year of Emperor Nero, as the winds of coming winter whipped the froth of Axeinos into nightly frenzy and fishing on Ascanius dwindled in the chill of fall, Peter and Mark sat one evening talking by a fire pot outside a little house they had rented during the summer. It was time to go again, they agreed.

"I'd like to be in Mysia within the week," said Peter.

"Headed toward Thyatira?" said Mark.

"I don't think so," said Peter, "unless the Spirit says to. I say we go to Troas."

"To the port?" said Mark.

"Yes," said Peter. "I've had Greece on my mind. Perhaps Corinth. After that, either come up through the country or maybe go farther around."

"You're thinking of going to Rome," said Mark, believing he had become suddenly aware of it.

"What makes you say that?" said Peter.

"Because it's sort of like the heart of the beast."

"Ah," said Peter. "So, don't just nip at the limbs, but go to the heart, eh?"

"Paul will get there eventually, if he hasn't already. But if he's mostly trying to reach Gentiles, don't we need a two-pronged attack? You reach the Jews?"

"That's your soldier-father's blood in you talking," said Peter amiably.

They rubbed their hands in the fire's heat and soon decided to go in for the night. In the morning they went around to the leaders of the young church and informed them of their decision. By day's end the fellowship's grapevine had informed everyone in the group and decided on meeting in the evening to tell Peter and Mark goodbye and send them on their way.

The church shared provisions and money with the two missionaries and with great emotion saw them off. It took Mark and Peter five days to get to Troas. They didn't stop to try to preach in the synagogue there. Somebody already had. Instead, they found a ship going south through the Aegean to Athens and then Cenchrea. From Cenchrea they would travel on foot to Corinth.

Ebullient commerce greeted every visitor to Corinth. Mark and Barnabas found its Lechaeum harbor a beehive of activity, its ships alternately rising in the water and then sitting low again as they took on ever-changing cargoes. In town the wide main street was a scene of endless varieties of mobile trading. Columns stood like stalks in a granite and alabaster field, and citizens, sailors and transients scurried like insects in and around their bases.

Peter and Mark took a little while to orient themselves to this brilliant, white place, and they picked up some fruit and freshly baked bread from roadside sellers before inquiring about the location of the Jewish synagogue.

They were surprised to learn that Claudius had ordered the expulsion of all Jews from the city some time back. While this order had resulted in Jewish residents' having to move, they could still come into the city to visit markets and do business. Mark hunted for a face that looked like home, presently finding a woman he believed might be a fellow Israelite, and she was. She told Mark and Peter that a converted home outside the city served as the Jewish contingent's new, possibly temporary synagogue. She gave them directions.

It wasn't a short walk to the synagogue and the duo were winded when they got there. They rested in some shade near the house of worship and then tried to find anyone who might be able to direct them to an elder. By chance the third person they approached happened himself to be one of those elders, a rabbi by the very scriptural name of Samuel.

"All the way from Antioch?" said Samuel.

"By way of much of Asia," said Mark. "Most recently Nicaea."

"Well, you've had quite a trip so far," said Samuel. "What is your ultimate destination?"

"We don't know," said Peter. "That's up to the Lord."

"Holy is his name, yes," said Samuel. "Where are you staying?"

"We don't know that, either," said Peter, trying not to make it sound as if he were fishing for an invitation. "But long enough to need a place for perhaps a few weeks, or longer."

"Well, there are places to be had," said Samuel—if he thought Peter were hoping for an offer, he didn't make one— "a widow or two who rent rooms. And, of course, the inns here are excellent."

"You can point us to one of those," said Peter.

"Straight down this road. The city begins where the columns begin. An inn is on the right. You'll see it."

"Thank you," said Peter. "Let me ask you, do you have many worshipers on the Sabbath?"

"About fifty, now," said Samuel. "Used to be twice that."

"Until you had to leave the city?" said Mark, making an assumption.

"Until Paul came to town," said Samuel, startling both Mark and Peter. Mark studied the elder's face. He couldn't detect measurable disgust, but he assumed Samuel was not elated by the diminution of his congregation.

"Paul?" said Peter. He thought further identification was probably not necessary, but he played dumb.

"Yes. Jew. Preacher. Says a man by the name of Jesus, from Nazareth, was the Messiah. Says he was crucified and then came back to life."

"We know of Paul," said Mark, cautiously noncommittal at the moment.

"He started a group in the city, not far from here. Began with Gentiles, which surprised me."

"So none of your congregation, then?" asked Peter.

"Not at first. But later, yes, some of our people listened to him."

Mark still couldn't tell how Samuel felt about things. Perhaps the rabbi was being deliberately coy. Perhaps he was actually neutral. Maybe he had seriously considered the gospel himself.

"One of the city's leading families was the first to join him, so I've learned," said Samuel. "Fellow by the name of Stephanas. Very influential. Very helpful to the Jewish community, too. Which is probably why some of our people paid attention to what Paul was preaching."

"How many have left the synagogue over it?" said Peter.

"Maybe ten," said Samuel. "Another dozen are still here every Sabbath, but they meet with the Christians—I think that's what they call them."

"Christians, yes," said Mark. He was getting closer and closer to revealing his and Peter's loyalty.

Peter said, "Have you found that those who still come here but go there, too, are any different?"

The rabbi twisted his gray beard at his chin and thought a few seconds. "I'll tell you, I thought they would be. I thought they would make trouble. But they don't. It's almost like they're happier." The elder stared at the ground, as if contemplating his own words.

"Well, that's good," said Mark. "That's the way it should be." He felt Peter looking at him, and he turned his head. Peter's face said, 'We may not want to tell him everything just yet.' But it was too late.

"Should be?" said the rabbi.

"Yes," said Peter, taking control of their side of the conversation, "when we Jews have differences of opinion. Be at peace to differ, and be happy that we worship the only true God."

"Yes, of course," said Samuel, detecting the misdirection. "Men, tell me: Are you Christians?"

For a fraction of a second, Peter thought of looking at Mark, and Mark was thinking the same thing: should they stall? But both of them realized at the same time that now was the time to be instantly forthcoming. The gospel required boldness in the moment.

"We are," said Peter calmly, with the winning smile he had always had as long as Mark had known him.

"We are," said Mark, overlapping Peter.

"Ah," said Samuel. "I thought so."

"Rabbi," said Peter, "Do you mind if I ask whether you have considered carefully the news about Jesus?"

Rabbi Samuel studied first Peter's face and then Mark's. "That will have to be a conversation for another time," said Samuel. "I have people I must see today."

So he *had* considered it, thought Mark instantly. If he hadn't, he would have said no immediately, if not angrily.

"Of course," said Peter. "We'll worship with you on the Sabbath.

Can we speak with you there, perhaps afterward?"

Rabbi Samuel smiled gently. "If you like, yes," he said. "Peace be with you." He gestured a blessing and turned, walking up the street away from the synagogue.

"A promising start?" said Mark.

"Perhaps so," said Peter. "Perhaps so."

They started down the road toward the edge of the city. The official city limits began, as the rabbi had said, where the columns began. The view of Corinth from this side was impressive.

"We didn't ask him where the Christians meet," said Mark.

"I was aware we hadn't," said Peter. "I thought to myself that he might not know. Even if he did, we don't really need to know until the Sabbath. That's just two days. We can ask one of the happier people."

Mark grinned.

Their visit to the synagogue on the Sabbath was the usual sort of experience. As Rabbi Samuel had said, the Christians in the group were happier—Mark and Peter had no trouble identifying almost all of them, as confirmed by conversations with two of them after the meeting broke up. A young couple happily engaged in conversation with the two travelers outside the house-synagogue, excited to meet the Apostle Peter in person.

Mark memorized their directions to the meeting place of the church that Paul had begun, but before they could close out conversation and be on their way, the couple changed whatever previous plans they had and invited them to eat with them at their home. They did so, which resulted in a further invitation to stay with them as long as they were in Corinth. The couple had inherited their house from the husband's parents and had plenty of room.

The next day being the Lord's Day, Mark and Peter went with their hosts and found themselves in an even larger house that now served as the church meeting place in Corinth. By the time they arrived, it was packed with more than a hundred Christians. When the elders found out that the Apostle Peter was in their midst, whatever plans they had made for the day were scrapped. Peter eventually wound up preaching, off the top of his fisherman's, sun-weathered head, and he invited Mark to contribute as well, which privately complimented Mark and gave him the opportunity to share thoughts from his most recent scripture study.

Stephanas's family, whom Rabbi Samuel had mentioned, was present, but Stephanas himself was not, as the congregation learned in an update given by the elders, who had received a communication from him. Stephanas was accompanied by Fortunatus, another leading member. The two had been in touch with Paul and expected to be again. The message from Stephanus did not say where Paul was at the time, so Peter and Mark were still in the dark about Paul's whereabouts, and whether Silas were still with him.

After the worship time, which was about two hours in length, Mark and Peter sat around with several members who were eager to hear all about their travels and about churches far and wide. The members talked enthusiastically about Paul, the amazing power that everyone felt when he talked, though in some ways he hadn't looked imposing. Some of their people had experienced healing during the days of the beginning of the church. Some people who had been converted were so radically changed that practically the whole city knew of it. The Holy Spirit had obviously been active in their midst. Numerous people had displayed the gift of languages, as the first disciples at the Great Pentecost Event had. Presumably, Mark thought, they made use of this divine enablement to reach sailors in the port, who came from all over the Great Sea. He hoped that was the case.

Mark and Peter learned that a regional preacher named Apollos had also visited Corinth, staying a month or more. He had been especially popular with the congregation. He was not only an impressive orator but a passionate preacher, and if Paul knew more about scripture, Apollos certainly ran a close second.

Paul had written to the church twice already, addressing situations he had previously encountered or had learned needed attention. The elders showed Peter the letters. Mark looked over them and then asked if he could read them at greater length in a few days. With no reason to deny the companion of the Apostle Peter this privilege, they consented. Mark fully intended to make copies of the pages.

The conversation could have gone on and on, but it was almost mid afternoon and everyone went home to eat and then get on with the day.

What started out as perhaps a few weeks' stay turned into several months, during which time Peter was asked to preach or teach regularly, which he humbly did.

Mark found Peter's preaching to be lofty in a down-to-earth kind of way. It was either that or it was casual in a sublime sort of way. He had a gift for saying things as if he were a friend making conversation and a father giving wise counsel, all at the same time. At first, Mark just sat riveted on Peter's messages. Then he found himself analyzing them, understanding Peter's thought process as he moved from truth to truth. They were plain messages, but deceptively profound. They were deep messages, but strikingly simple.

Every time Peter preached, back at their accommodations for the day Mark would go to his bedroom—each had his own—and use the supply of paper and ink he had brought to recall some of what Peter had said. Peter's memories of his years with Jesus was good, though he rambled a bit when he got to telling a story. Over time, Peter himself had whittled some of his accounts to the memorable basics, and Mark pared down some of those further in his notes on Peter's teaching. There was an art to crafting even lengthy accounts into what could be memorized for transmission to others. Every Hebrew child had been taught his genealogy and his family's history through easily remembered prose and verse, and every dutiful child grew up to teach his own children the same things. Mark had learned from his mother. He had no one to pass on his family history to, but he employed the same art in writing down the stories Peter told, the teachings of Jesus he remembered.

Just now, they were scattered notes, occupying a leather satchel. What those notes would ever be, he wasn't sure. He had talked about the need for an account of Jesus' life, a gospel story. But probably someone else had already begun one. For all he knew, someone had completed one and he just didn't know about it yet. But then, for all he knew, nobody had written anything.

He remembered Peter's having said that most days he just went places and did things until or unless the Spirit said No. Mark wondered if that was what he should do now: write about Jesus' life and get the story out there, where churches could use it. Unless the Spirit said No.

The messenger arrived from Jerusalem and parts west during the early fall of Nero's third year as Emperor. Paul had been arrested in Jerusalem.

The church in Jerusalem, beleaguered as it was, had thought it vital to get news of Paul's imprisonment out to the churches. They paid for a messenger to sail to Tarsus, Attalia, Miletus and Corinth, spreading word of Paul's crisis to churches in these representative points and asking those churches to try to get word to surrounding regions. The Jerusalem church was calling the church abroad to prayer for the Apostle Paul. Obviously, the Jerusalem Christians assumed Paul's was not to be a short stay in jail. The Jewish authorities wanted Paul gone for good and they were mounting a serious case against him.

The message contained little else of import to Peter and Mark. They met with the church, of course, and everyone prayed for Paul. What was on Peter's and Mark's minds was their agreement that the time was upon them to go to Rome. They had their hosts' house to themselves one day and sat on a marble bench in the shade of several fir trees. They could see the aging and partly broken down temple to Aphrodite on the Acrocorinth. No doubt hundreds of temple prostitutes were working the streets around it and down the hill into the city, as they did every day, every week, every month of the year.

"We could stay for the rest of our lives and the city would still be filled with immorality and vice," said Peter.

"So, next week, then?" said Mark.

"Next week."

"Do you want me to try to find a ship scheduled for the second day, the third—what?"

"Let's sail the Lord's Day," said Peter. "The church will already be gathered. We'll want to say goodbye to each other. Might as well do it when we're all together anyway."

"What if we can't book passage that day?"

"Go the next."

"The bigger the ship, the better?" said Mark.

"Never know what the weather will be."

"There have been merchant galleys coming and going every day. One of those?"

"The big ones?" said Peter.

"Biremes, it looks to me. Moving crated cargo. There would still be passenger space."

"Faster than a corbita," said Peter, "but more expensive to

bargain with the captain for. He has to pay all those oarsmen."

"There are twice as many corbitas in and out every week. One of them would probably take nine days to two weeks," said Mark.

"That's acceptable, I suppose. We'll see if we can book one of them."

The day before the Sabbath Mark learned at the wharves that a corbita carrying a full load of amphorae was expected—one could never guarantee arrivals by sea—the next day. It would dock overnight while unloading and then reload on the morning of *die Solis*, the Lord's Day. If loading were done by noon or not more than an hour thereafter, the ship might get underway for five or six hours of active sailing before nightfall.

Mark and Peter met with the church on the Lord's Day and bid them goodbye. Everyone had a sober concern for them as they were going into the belly of the beast of Babylon, as Christians were privately calling their Empire's capital. And the news out of Rome made it an even more sobering matter, since Nero was making non-approved worship more and more difficult, certainly close to home.

The duo accepted some generous gifts for their journey and sustenance—they would be expected to have their own food on board—and they made their way to the Lechaeum harbor and found a likely corbita that didn't show any signs of life. They learned that it was docked for at least two days, and even when it left it was going to ports east, not Rome. The ship Mark had been told about had not arrived. Mark and Peter found a spot up the hill where they could keep watch. In an hour, while Peter was napping, Mark saw a ship approaching.

It turned out to be the vessel they had hoped for. It unloaded in less than three hours. But it would stay in port overnight. Mark bargained with the captain for a price for passage plus the privilege of staying below decks overnight. It wasn't standard practice, but the ship was empty, the sailors had mostly gone ashore, and it wouldn't hurt anything, so the captain 'reluctantly' accepted the proffered payment and Mark and Peter spent the night in the cargo hold.

Early in the morning they woke to the sounds of sailors beginning to come aboard, and as the crew loaded the ship Mark and Peter retreated to dockside and found a seller hawking baked goods. They stowed away some last minute provisions and ate some still-warm loaves. The loading of crates and amphorae continued for four hours, commencing just after sunup and ending well before midday. By noon, they were underway.

Sailing the Great Sea was unpredictable in any of the three seasons it was regularly navigated, but best in the early summer, which was when Mark and Peter set out for Rome. As Mark had estimated, it took the better part of two weeks to arrive at the mouth of the Tiber River, where they hired a cart into Rome proper.

What glimmered in the afternoon sun as gilded mountaintop decorations five miles distant, steadily came into sharp focus, becoming the parapets and pinnacles and then the granite and marble edifices of one of the grandest cities on earth. Rome!

30
Rome, c. A.D. 59

Jerusalem was an impressive city, especially in a historic sort of way. Antioch was a bustling center of business. Some of the other cities Mark and Peter had visited were fairly large, usually old except for the newer, Roman temples, and sometimes quaint. But Rome! Rome was an awesome sight.

It was tempting for Mark to stop every hundred paces or so and gaze spellbound at the magnificent buildings, the lifelike sculpture, the phantasmagorical columnar decorations, the colorful banners, the decorative gardens, the astonishing exactitude of the architecture, and the cleanness of the heavily populated city. Peter probably felt the same distraction but he prodded his protégé along so they could find lodging and then see if they could locate a synagogue.

Predictably, inns in Rome were superior to those in many places they had stayed, and they cost more, accordingly. But Mark hoped they would be in one no more than a single night. They agreed they would have to make discreet inquiries in the streets about Jewish communities, which they did, finally obtaining information from people passing by about an enclave in a certain sector. Then, from still other persons, they got directions. The next morning they set out and found the general neighborhood and a quasi synagogue, which functioned and was otherwise identified for all intents and purposes as a home. It was outside the city proper, on the eastern side of the Tiber, due to Claudius's sentiments but ineffective orders and more recently Nero's enforcement of them.

Jews in the streets of this indistinct neighborhood were understandably reluctant to identify themselves forthrightly, but once recognized as an ethnic Jew, and especially once he had been verified to be the Apostle Peter, of whom many Jews had heard by now, he and Mark were able to make inroads into the community and learn who and where their Jewish brethren were to be found gathering.

The first Sabbath they were on the outskirts of Rome, Mark and Peter gathered with their dispersed countrymen and worshiped. By the second week there, they had located a few Jewish Christians and congregated with them on the Lord's Day. In the weeks following, they felt they were secure in staying in the area for a while, as they attempted to lend strength to the contingent of Christians. Believing, in the belly of the beast, had become a challenge befitting the Apostle's understanding of Christ's world-changing commission.

Strategically moving about between small congregations of Christians week by week, Peter and Mark met numerous strong disciples while developing a network of friendships among them all. After staying in an inn for days, they were offered a guest room in the home of a modestly successful Jewish businessman, himself a believer, accommodations that they accepted for a small price with tremendous relief and welcome.

One brilliant Lord's Day they were in a rare, outdoor meeting of worshipers on the banks of the river, led by two elders of a small congregation calling itself privately the Tiber River Believers. Calev and Edan were about Mark's age. Between them, according to the Christians in this diminutive enclave, they had brought probably fifty Jews to faith in Christ—people who had dispersed into various surrounding church houses rather than create a large congregation that would have been more easily identified and persecuted by Roman authorities.

"I can't tell you how blessed we are," said Calev, "to have you here with us."

"Amen," said Edan.

"No more blessed than we are to be here with you," said Peter.

"There have been times when we were ready to give up," said Calev. "But this has been our home for several generations, long before we heard of our Messiah."

"This is why you were here," said Peter.

"That's why we *didn't* give up," said Edan. "Like Esther, we came to this place just for such a time."

Peter grew a knowing smile, remembering Jesus' words to him what seemed like a lifetime ago: 'Flesh and blood didn't reveal this to you, Peter, but my Father.'

"You must go on believing it," he said. "Much work to be done."

"We hope you will stay with us, at least a while," said Calev. "There's so much we want to know about Jesus. We know too little."

"We have what the prophets wrote," said Edan. "We have all the scriptures—well, at least we have them between us all. Some are in our synagogues, of course. A few copies of the scrolls are shared between our congregations."

"Nothing in writing yet about Jesus," said Calev. "If our Messiah returns soon, of course, we can hold out with what we have."

"But if he doesn't—" said Edan. He didn't complete his sentence. He just left the implication of uncertainty.

"We don't know where we'll go from here, Mark and I, or if we will," said Peter. "We've come this far because the Spirit has led us. We won't leave until he speaks to our hearts."

"Will you teach next week?" said Calev.

"It will be my privilege," said Peter.

The four men joined Calev's and Edan's wives and families for a meal and a restful afternoon. Later, Mark and Peter returned to their lodging near nightfall.

"Time has come for you to write, son," said Peter, as they sat in their shared room. "I can't do it."

"Well, you could—" said Mark.

"In my native language, perhaps," said Peter, "But like I've told you, a fisherman's Greek isn't good enough for this."

"I have a stack of notes," said Mark.

"I know," said Peter. "Can you make anything out of all that rambling preaching?" Peter laughed.

"If you'll help me," said Mark. "I need more."

"Get it while my memory holds out," said Peter. "Sometimes it seems like yesterday. Sometimes, not so much."

"No time like the present," said Mark.

"No, there isn't," said Peter.

And so, Mark took out some of his supply of papyrus sheets, trimmed a pen, and uncorked a tiny flagon of ink. As the night wore on for the next hour, then two, Peter reminisced and Mark wrote, drafting notes, filling in the gaps of the story of the Messiah who had come to Israel and to the world.

Several months into their indeterminate stay in Rome Peter had become an established figure in the Christian community, though still somewhat undercover in nature. Mark had determined to stay as much in the shadows as possible, both because in the company of Peter he was the decidedly lesser figure of importance and because he didn't want to increase the visibility of the team there in the heart of the Roman government.

For his part, Peter avoided being thought of as the de facto leader of the church in Rome. He was a late arrival, after all. Twenty or more years of believers in the Empire's capital had preceded him. He had come there not so much to lead as to witness to the life and saving acts of Jesus. Nevertheless, in twenty years no one in the community of believers in Rome had emerged as a singular Christian leader; it was arguable that no one needed to. But as the best known of the disciples of Jesus, Peter was beginning to be accorded the honorary position as the eminent believer among Roman Christians.

Because Peter and Mark had begun the habit of going around to the various groups of Christians worshiping week by week on the Lord's Day, Peter's visit to any particular church group was greatly anticipated, which predictably resulted in special dinners nearly every week, at least for the first year or so that Mark and Peter were in the city. Because they were functioning as a roving evangelistic team, the two were also often given monetary sustenance, which enabled them to afford their housing and upkeep.

When there was news, the congregation they were with was the first to impart it. And so it happened that when they arrived for worship with the Tiber River Believers one Lord's Day morning, the latest report from the homeland of the Jewish believers in Rome was breathlessly given to Mark and Peter. The Apostle Paul, who had been arrested nearly two years ago in Jerusalem and kept in prison since that time, had arrived in Rome, still a prisoner.

Details were sketchy at this point, but he had been brought in under guard only days ago and was being held in a facility in the central part of the city. What the Tiber River Christians had been told was that while in Caesarea Paul had actually appealed his case to the Emperor, resulting in his transport by sea to Rome for eventual trial.

Peter asked the Tiber River Believers to find out anything else they could within a few days. He intended to try to see Paul, or to have Mark try to do so, before the next Lord's Day. By midweek Mark had learned of the location of Paul's imprisonment, which was not in the dungeons of the Tullianum but rather in a low-security building where he could receive visitors fairly freely. Visitors would be searched, but Paul was not being heavily guarded or monitored.

The day before the Sabbath Mark and Peter hiked into the city, crossing the Tiber on the Pons Aemilius. They navigated the main forum and wound up at an unimposing building probably like several others throughout the city, perhaps bought from previous residents for the purpose of holding prisoners awaiting trial for low-level crimes or even for civil proceedings.

After being checked for contraband, Mark and Peter were escorted into the interior of the spacious house, past several other rooms with heavily barred doors, finally coming to Paul's quarters. The guard leading them took the bar from the door and stepped aside. Realizing one of them was to open the door, Mark pushed it inward and let Peter go in first. Sitting on the opposite side of the room under a small window with bars installed in it was Paul. He was just sitting there, relaxing or praying. He looked up as the door opened.

No one had told Paul to expect visitors. The look on his face was one of controlled delight. He looked first at Peter and then at Mark, displaying no difference between the two in the deep joy that was evident on his face. He stood up, embracing Peter.

"Brother!" said Paul softly. "I never imagined I would find *you* here."

"I think *we* found *you,*" said Peter. The guard behind him closed the door, remaining outside it.

Paul looked at Mark. "Brother Mark," he said. He reached for Mark and the two clasped arms. "You're in good company, I see."

"We've been here nearly a year," said Peter. "We spent quite a while in Bithynia and Pontus before sailing to Corinth. Then came here."

"Corinth!" said Paul. "One of my favorite places. A city of vile corruption and some of the most wonderful believers anywhere!"

Mark and Peter laughed knowingly at the description.

"They spoke highly of you, too," said Mark.

"They told us you had come there most recently from Athens," said Peter. "Where else did you go?"

"As you know, Silas and I headed to Troas first. Then through lower Galatia, up to Mysia. Went across to Macedonia, down through Greece. Corinth was one of our last stops, as it turned out. Almost three years. After we left Ephesus, we sailed to Caesarea and worked our way back up to Antioch." Paul sounded a little melancholic.

Peter stepped a little closer to Paul. "What exactly brought you here," he said, quietly but with great intensity.

"False charges," said Paul. "Which will no doubt be padded with half truths and exaggerations between now and whenever I get a hearing. No mind. Just think: if I'm tried before Nero himself!"

"I *have* thought it," said Peter. "What we know of Nero—"

"But the chance to speak the Name in front of him—*that's* the prize!" said Paul.

"Perhaps you won't be the only one," said Peter.

"Tell me about you," said Paul. Peter described for Paul his and Mark's coming to Rome, the state of the churches here, and what they were doing in and among them.

"Mark has been my right hand man," said Peter. Mark glanced at the floor. "He's like a son to me. And he does the yeoman's work wherever we go."

Paul looked from Peter to Mark, and Mark observed that the Apostle had not lost the inexplicable sense of warmth he first showed to Mark when the cell door was opened.

"I'm sure he does," said Paul.

"Brother," Peter said to Paul, "we're going to come back. As long as you're here. We're told we can bring you what you need. What *do* you need?"

Paul looked around the sparing room. He had a bed, a chamber pot, a little table, and a chair, a water pitcher and bowl, and virtually nothing else. He told Peter he could use some paper and ink, perhaps another covering for sleeping or just keeping warm as the fall progressed. Prisoners were fed in a rudimentary way but they could have food brought in. Peter and Mark promised to bring, or send someone with, the needed items. After spending about a half hour with Paul, Peter and Mark left, returning through the city and crossing the river to their lodging.

"The last time I saw Paul," said Mark, "he was still distant and cool toward me. I suppose I became used to that."

"Didn't seem that way today," said Peter.

"No," said Mark. "You didn't exactly have to brag on me, you know."

"Didn't have to. Wanted to," said Peter. "Every man deserves a fair description."

"It doesn't have to be so glowing, though," said Mark, in playful self-deprecation.

"Do you think Paul thinks better of you because of what I said?"

"Maybe."

"But I saw the way he looked at you before I ever said a word," said Peter. "When you opened that door, he already felt that way."

Mark realized Peter was right.

"Age and experience have a way of softening a man, sometimes," said Peter. "If he's disposed that way. I think Paul has aimed to be a person who loves loving people, ever since he went blind going to Damascus. Even though, before that, he loved hating people. You grow into what you long to be." Mark mused on this uncommon, common sense.

"You copied the two letters he wrote to the Corinthian church," said Peter. Mark nodded. "In that first one, he wrote about love."

"I remember," said Mark.

"That wasn't just a lot of pretty words. All he'd been through? He'd grown into that kind of man. Persecution breaks you or makes you. Depends on your anchor."

"So, you think he's softened because of that?"

"And of course, there's being in jail."

"Jail?"

"Jail will make you appreciate just about anybody," said Peter. The two chuckled.

"And then," said Peter, "sometimes you're just wrong." He looked at Mark knowingly.

"Okay, so there are three possibilities," said Mark: "he has just grown more loving over time; or persecution and jail made him appreciate people more; or he was wrong about me to begin with. Is that about it?"

"Maybe a combination," said Peter. "If I were you, I wouldn't analyze it too much. Just go with it."

Mark studied on that answer for a little while. They ate supper and went to different parts of the house and yard to be alone for a time of meditation and prayer. Mark found himself praying earnestly for Paul, his needs, his spirit, his outlook, his health, and of course, his upcoming trial, whenever that might be. In the current state of things, it might not be anytime soon.

Over the next few months Mark personally made the schedule for visitors to Paul. He made every third visit himself and kept a little inventory of provisions Paul was running short of, and anything new he might like to have. Mark kept him supplied with his needs, especially better food than was given him at the expense of the Empire, which was little more than bread and water. Paul had skins of grape paste from which he could reconstitute wine. He had pocket bread, dried fruits, sometimes fresh fruits, and plenty of nuts. Visitors brought him salted meats and dried fish, and kept him supplied with olive oil. The slightly gaunt impression he had left on

Mark when they first saw him in the prison facility disappeared within two months.

Sometime during Nero's sixth year as Emperor, when Mark and Peter had been living on the western outskirts of Rome for a little more than a year, Mark brought a bundle of things for Paul one day, finding that he already had a visitor. After asking if Paul wanted another visitor that moment, the guard let Mark into Paul's room.

"Mark!" Paul said, from his seat on his bed. "Good to see you. This is Luke." The man sitting in the little chair at the table was somewhere near Mark's age, dressed well but not richly, and was smartly groomed. He got up and offered his hand to Mark.

"Luke," said Mark, as they grasped each other at the elbow.

"Luke is my doctor," said Paul.

"I'm not sure about that," said Luke. "I'm a doctor, it's true, but I'm not certain I'll claim Paul as a patient." He grinned and Paul laughed.

"I eat too well," said Paul. "I think that's against doctor's orders."

"I'll have to take some of the blame for that, doctor," said Mark. He opened the bundle and showed Paul some of what the women in the churches had sent him this week. Paul motioned for him to put it on the table.

"I might have starved if they hadn't found me when I first got here, Luke. I got a little of my flesh back," he said, pinching his waist.

"Keep it up, Mark," said the doctor. "I don't want him getting too thin. Seriously."

"We will," said Mark. "How long are you here? In Rome? —Or are you from here?"

"No. I studied medicine in Antioch—the Syrian one. But Troas most recently. That's where I joined up with Paul—what?" he said, looking at Paul, "nearly eight years ago, now?"

"That's about right," Paul replied.

"I've moved here temporarily. It's the least I can do for Paul. And I can practice anywhere, of course."

"I'm sure he appreciates it," said Mark. Looking at Paul, he said, "We all do."

"Paul, I'm going to go," said Luke. "Looks like Mark has things covered here."

"Like the son I never had," said Paul.

Luke tapped on the door. The guard opened it, and Luke left. Mark indicated he would be staying a few minutes, and the door was closed and barred again.

Mark sat in the chair Luke had warmed for him. He and Paul remained wordless for a minute.

"I don't suppose you've heard anything new about your hearing?" said Mark.

"No," said Paul. "And I may not, until the day it takes place. The way I hear it, they just come for you one day and you go, and what happens happens."

"Who told you that?"

"The guard."

"Seems unfair."

"The only one who is fair in this world is the Lord, son," said Paul.

There was that word, 'son,' again, thought Mark. He didn't suppose he had thought, years ago, that Paul would ever feel disposed toward him in that way. The surprise of it had worn off, however, and Mark felt the warmth of acceptance. He made a mental note—indeed, a spiritual note—to be ever deserving of Paul's fatherly sentiment.

It also occurred to Mark that he had lost his father before he really knew him. Now, he had two.

During the winter of that year Mark worked not furiously but steadily and carefully on his account of Jesus' life, ministry, death and resurrection. When he listened to Peter preach and teach, he took especial note of the pattern of it, the things he repeated and stressed, the core of the message he returned to, sometimes in different ways, again and again. Mark didn't want his account to sound like Peter's sermons, but he did want it to be as convincing, as multi-layered, yet as simple as the way Peter explained the gospel.

He tried to organize the dozens and dozens of notes he had made over the past few years. Uncertain how they all fit together, he switched around their order, compiling some and separating others. Peter hadn't always remembered which teaching came first or which event came last—not during most of the ministry, anyway. They went to so many little towns! There were so many people healed, so many parables and so much teaching!

It was important to keep the major events in order, of course—and doing that was easy: baptism, calling disciples, public ministry, private ministry, arrest and crucifixion, and resurrection. For the rest, Mark relied on Peter's memory as far as it went, and then placed words and deeds where they seemed to fit or must have taken place. Sometimes he pared things down even after spending a lot of time writing them. Better not to be too lengthy, he reasoned, and the thought seemed right.

As he worked, Mark fell under what he could only describe as the impress of the Holy Spirit. He didn't always know why he ordered things the way he did, or why he chose to say what he said, but he was increasingly filled with the awe of the task he was undertaking, occasionally being touched with a feeling of the consequence it might have. And yet, the more he was convinced of the contribution of his work to whatever was left of God's time of grace on earth, the less he felt worthy to be the one doing it. He found the bridge between those feelings to be the perfect and consummate grace of God.

Somewhere in the seventh year of Nero, Mark was finished with his account of the good news of Jesus Christ.

Toward the end of his work he had been tempted to second guess himself about whether to include one of the stories known to some of the other disciples, and to his own mother, about Jesus' birth. In the end, he just didn't think it was what the Lord wanted him to write. And he had also struggled with precisely how to end the entire account—whether to describe some of the forty days Jesus had actually spent with Peter and the other disciples before disappearing into heaven in front of their eyes. Finally he had picked up a fresh sheet of papyrus and wrote a brief conclusion. If there were anything he thought of changing at the last minute, it would have been that.

Before calling the book complete, he read it over carefully, taking about an hour to go through the thirty-seven pages. The lettering was as neat as he could make it and as compact as possible and still be easily readable. It began:

ΑΡΧΗ ΤΟΥ ΕΥΑΓΓΕΛΙΟΥ ΙΗΣΟΥ ΧΡΙΣΤΟΥ ΥΙΟΥ ΘΕΟΥ
—THE BEGINNING OF THE GOOD NEWS OF JESUS CHRIST THE SON OF GOD...

The next step would be securing the services of competent copyists, who would not only accurately copy every word in Mark's text, but also do so in scroll form, so that the resulting book could be widely read in the form most used by both synagogues and churches.

Meanwhile, Paul was at work on a piece of writing himself. Tychicus, a Christian originally from the Lycus Valley cities, had come to Rome to see Paul. A competent scribe and willing helper, Tychicus had agreed gladly to help Paul write some letters to Asian churches.

One of the believers in the churches west of the Tiber told Mark of a new visitor to Paul's place of confinement, and Mark went quickly into the city hoping to meet the newcomer. Paul's having gotten permission to have Tychicus stay with him for extended periods of time, he was still there when Mark arrived.

"Mark!" said Paul. "I hadn't expected you today."

"I was told you had a new visitor," said Mark. He turned to the slightly younger man seated at the table, pen in hand. "I'm John Mark," he said.

"Tychicus," said the other, getting up. "Glad to meet you."

"Tychicus came to the Lord when I was in Ephesus," said Paul. "After that he came along with me several other places until I headed back east."

"I see you're writing," said Mark.

"Letters, yes," said Paul, interrupting. "I could have asked you to do it, but Tychicus here is something of a scribe by trade. Among other things."

"I run a messenger business," said Tychicus. "Began with my father, years ago. He died. I've been running routes from as far as Spain to Syrian Antioch."

"Sounds exciting," said Mark. "And maybe a bit dangerous?"

"Now and then, yes. You never know about travel by sea, and of course, there are always highwaymen."

"He was opening a location of his business in Ephesus when I preached there," said Paul.

"I just happened to be passing by the synagogue when he was there," said Tychicus. "Heard the gospel and became a believer."

"It doesn't sound like there was any happenstance to it," said Mark. "It sounds to me like the Holy Spirit."

"Did you come just to meet Tychicus?" asked Paul.

"Yes," said Mark. "While I knew he was here. I didn't know what his schedule might be."

"I'll stay until we get finished with these letters," said Tychicus.

"Then it's off to Ephesus."

"I'm writing to the church there and the one in Colossae," said Paul. "And one personal letter."

"Do you have a place to stay?" said Mark to Tychicus.

"I'm in an inn across the Tiber."

"Not anymore," said Mark. "I'll find you a place with some friends."

"Thank you," said Tychicus. "I never know if what few things I have will be at the inn when I get back."

"Always a problem," said Mark. "I can wait for you if you're almost finished for the day."

"We can stop now," said Paul to Tychicus. "Thank you, Mark."

Presently the two left. Mark inquired of someone in the Tiber River Believers and by the end of the afternoon Tychicus was being housed by one of their group.

During the week Tychicus stayed with Paul several hours per day, finally finishing three letters, which he stowed in three identical goatskin pouches for delivery back in Asia. At week's end he left Paul's detainment facility, went to his accommodations across the river, said goodbye to Mark, and set out for Asia. While he had often traveled by land, he had not come to Rome on his horse on this occasion, and he booked passage by raeda to Brundisium, where he would find a merchant ship headed to the port at Ephesus. From there he would go inland to Colossae. Mark thought it would easily be at least two months before he would return.

But Tychicus made speedy work of his deliveries and had returned to Rome in seven weeks. He had gone through Ephesus both going and coming back, and the members there asked him to return to Paul with a request.

They wanted additional teaching material.

Tychicus returned to Rome and went to his lodging, deposited his traveling pack, and then went immediately across the river into the city and to Paul's prison-house.

The Ephesian elders hadn't put anything in writing but had simply entrusted to Tychicus the communication of a feeling and conviction they had about their needs. The letter Paul sent to them was full of doctrinal statements and explanations, of course: a bird's-eye view of God's saving plan in Christ; principles of spiritual growth; the nature of the church; a description of a practical Christian lifestyle; and directions as to how to live victoriously through the Holy Spirit. The Ephesian Christians told Tychicus to express their deep appreciation to Paul for his letter filled with challenge and encouragement.

What the Ephesian church—to be sure, all the churches in Asia and everywhere else—had begun to want at this juncture was an account of Jesus' life and ministry. This was the specific need they asked Tychicus to transmit to Paul. Were there such accounts available, the elders wanted to know?

Mark came to Paul's prison-house on his regular day to bring supplies and sit with the Apostle for a while.

"Tychicus returned today," said Paul.

"So soon?!" said Mark.

"He said he came into the city about noon. He came here right away."

"Something important?" said Mark.

"I think so, yes," said Paul. He didn't finish the thought.

"What is it?"

"First, I have an admission to make, son," said Paul.

"Sir, you don't have to—"

"Now, you don't even know what it is, yet," said Paul. "Let me say it."

"I'm sorry. Of course."

"I've told my life story five hundred times over the past twenty-five years—maybe more. You know it almost as well as I do. The most sublime part of that story is about the commission I got directly from the glorified Jesus. It still scares me and awes me and thrills me all at the same time, every time I think about it."

"Me, too," said Mark. "And I wasn't even there."

"And you know my teaching about Jesus. It's centered around who he is today. The exalted Christ."

"Yes, sir."

"But over the years I've realized that Peter—all the disciples—and even you, know more about the things Jesus did and taught during his lifetime than I do."

"I don't know that *I* do; I—"

"Now, don't contradict me." Mark closed his mouth and Paul continued. "I was aware of Jesus at the time. I was only two or three years younger than he was, and I was in Jerusalem by the time his ministry started. But I never met him. I didn't know his disciples until after he was crucified and rose. I had no firsthand knowledge until I saw him in my vision.

"That's a different kind of knowledge," Paul continued. "And it was what I needed to do the job he sent me to do. But it isn't everything. Not everything that the churches are beginning to need."

Mark believed he knew what Paul was going to say, but he had been shushed twice and he was going to wait for Paul to complete his thought.

"They want the story of Jesus' life, Mark. They want to know what he did, where he went, what he said, what happened—more than just the basics. They want the story that Peter knows firsthand. Doctor Luke and I have talked about this very thing, and I think he thinks that sometime—he doesn't know when—he'll probably do some thorough research and then write something. But he hasn't done it yet. But people need the story now. The story the *rest* of the

Apostles know—though they're off to the wind, now. I don't know if any of them is out there writing something. Peter is still around. But I think he feels he's not schooled enough to write it all down."

Paul stopped, reached for a cup of water, took a sip, and set it down. He looked back at Mark.

"But you are." Mark watched Paul as the Apostle studied his face a few moments. Mark was respectful and silent. He didn't think Paul was finished quite yet. And he wasn't.

"You've talked about writing just such an account," said Paul. "I think the churches need it now."

"Sir," said Mark, "I assume Peter told you about my writing. I haven't said anything about it recently. I haven't even told him. But I've finished it."

Paul's eyes gleamed, and a smile grew out of his thinning lips. He nodded slowly.

"Somehow, I knew," he said. "Tychicus hurried back here with a message from the Ephesian elders. They want the story of Jesus. In writing."

"I finished it the day before Tychicus *first* came here," said Mark.

"That was three months ago," said Paul, a bit surprised.

"Yes. I've been waiting and praying about the next step."

"Do you think this might, just *possibly*, be your answer?" said Paul wryly.

"I hope so," said Mark. "What do you have in mind?"

"Well, son, you're a great help to me here," said Paul, "and we were once teammates in mission, but I'm not the one to direct you. Not any more. Even if you needed someone to give you direction, you were with Peter for several years, a lot longer than you were with me and Barnabas. But really, you know, you're your own man. What do *you* want to do?"

The *mare clausum* would begin soon. The Empire restricted ships on the Great Sea from the eleventh month to the third, and if Mark was to go to Ephesus with his gospel account it would have to be within a few weeks. Tychicus readily agreed to make the first copy of the account Mark had written of Jesus' life. Mark would take this copy with him to Ephesus and leave the original in Rome with Tychicus. Tychicus would work on yet another copy. After that, Mark would need to find another scribe.

If he were going to go to Ephesus, Mark wanted, and felt he needed, to get the blessing of Peter. Since they had been in Rome, Peter had depended on his help less than Paul had; Paul was in continual custody and Peter wasn't. But in some ways Mark had become part of Peter's life since they had left Antioch some ten years ago—could that be right? If he went to Ephesus now, he wasn't certain when or if he'd be back. He wasn't certain that *if* he came back, Peter would still be here, or alive. That went doubly for Paul.

So Mark took a day trip to the northwest side of the city, where Peter had located himself among homes of Christians spread out, *incognito,* along the west side of the Tiber. Many of them might be forced to move soon due to Nero's impulsive building of a new Naumachia to hold his pretend naval war games in. For the moment, a sprawling community of lower class homes held on to what they had. Peter had nursed a struggling congregation into a vigorous Christian community there, some three miles from the neighborhoods supporting the Tiber River Believers.

Mark found Peter teaching some children at his little house, their mothers waiting and talking outside in the shade. He stood at the back of the room where Peter was telling stories about his time with Jesus. In a few minutes he brought the teaching time to an end and told the children to go out to their mothers. They were finished for the day.

"That brings back memories," Peter said, when the last of the children had scampered outside. "Only it was Jesus with the children and the rest of us sort of marveling at it."

"Mother told me he had a special way with them."

"I wasn't much good with children when I was younger," said Peter. "I don't know why. After all, I *was* one, once."

"I think we just forget how it was to be a child," said Mark. "We just wanted to grow up. But eventually we want to get it back. I think when that happens we remember childhood, and we enjoy being with children again, like when we *were* one."

"Makes sense to me," said Peter. "Probably what happens to grandparents." He pondered that thought a moment. "I never had children. So, no grandchildren. These are my grandchildren. But you didn't come to talk about grandchildren. Do you need something?"

"Nothing tangible, no," said Mark.

"Help?"

"No," said Mark. "I need your blessing."

"Whatever for?" said Peter.

"To go to Ephesus," said Mark.

"Ephesus? To help Timothy?"

"In a way, yes. I went to see Paul two days ago. I heard from our member who had taken him supplies that day that he had a new visitor. I wanted to see who it was."

"And?"

"Do you know a fellow by the name of Tychicus?" said Mark.

"No. Who is he?"

"A scribe and courier from Ephesus. He came to help Paul with some writing."

"I thought you would have done that," said Peter, curious.

"I would have done anything he asked," said Mark, "but he just opted to ask for Tychicus' help. I took it as something of a compliment, as a matter of fact."

"Why is that?"

"Because I think it implied that he thinks of me now as much more than a secretary."

"As you are," said Peter. "You're a teacher in your own right."

"Which brings up the subject. I've finished it, Peter."

"Finished? —What, your book?!"

"Yes."

"Great!" said Peter. He looked to see if Mark had the book with him. "Well, where is it?"

"I didn't bring it. I will, or I'll have someone bring a copy to you."

"Who's copying it?" said Peter. "Tychicus?"

"Yes. The first copy anyway. Others should be made, but I need one to take to Ephesus. They want the story of Jesus' life. To use in teaching."

"That's what you've wanted to do for a long time." said Peter. "The Spirit put the longing in your heart."

"And Paul wants me to take the book to Ephesus personally."

Peter looked happy and concerned at the same time. "Are you coming back?" he said.

"I think so. I don't know. Surely at some point."

"But this is what the Lord wants of you right now."

"I'm certain of it," said Mark. "And I want your blessing."

"My bless—" said Peter, "well, of course you have my blessing! What a thing to say!"

"I didn't want to leave you in a lurch," said Mark.

"Well, it's not that I wouldn't love to have you around. But this is a great opportunity, son. You have to take it."

"Promise to pray for me," said Mark.

"Right now, and every day," said Peter. And they stopped to pray about Mark's upcoming venture.

Mark found Tychicus hard at work on not just the first copy but a second copy of the gospel story. Tychicus was nothing if not prolific, and he told Mark that his writing was well phrased and altogether legible and therefore easy to copy quickly. He was happy to do it.

"In that case," said Mark, "I believe I'll take both the original and one of the copies with me. I may be able to have another copy or two made while I'm in Ephesus. I'd like to get the story into the hands of some of the churches down toward Colossae."

"If you don't mind," said Tychicus, "I can have another one made here."

"Feel free," said Mark. "In fact, ask Paul where he'd like to send copies. I'll gladly pay for them to be made. I'm sure you'll have to get back to your business."

"I'm selling my business to the men who've been my partners for years," said Tychicus. "I think I'm going to have my hands full with Christian business for a while."

"Well, may God bless you in it," said Mark. "Is that it?" he said, pointing at a scroll.

"Yes, that's the first one. You said you wanted a scroll to take. I'm doing the second one as a scroll, too. How about the others?"

"The same, I think. They can be stored and protected better that way." Mark picked up the scroll and inspected it. The work was immaculate, and the paper was of good quality. Mark reached into his purse-bag and pulled out several silver coins, giving them to Tychicus.

"This is for more copies," said Mark.

"When are you leaving?" said Tychicus.

"Day after tomorrow, I think," said Mark. "I think I'll go the way you go: Brundisium by land first. I would hope to be in Ephesus in about two weeks or so."

"Will I see you before you leave?" said Tychicus.

"Probably not."

Tychicus reached out and clasped Mark's arms and they clapped each other's shoulders. Their goodbyes and blessings shown from their faces. Mark took the scroll and left. As far as he knew, this was the first account of Jesus' life anyone had written. If Jesus didn't return soon, perhaps for a generation or two, maybe Mark's gospel account would be used from Spain to Antioch. Who knew?

31
Ephesus, c. A.D. 62

The iron-clad wheels on the relatively large carriage Mark took through the country for four long days were hard on everyone's spines. They were all glad to get to their destinations, a few of them to places along the way but most of them, like Mark, to Brundisium to board ships in the remaining days available to them before cooler weather and fickle seas shut down travel.

In the already choppy waters around the southern extent of Italy, there were afternoons and early evenings when Mark wondered if God were going to interrupt his own providential plans with disaster, but the sailors were especially seasoned and brought them through in good time to the western coast of Asia, sailing up the coastline to the port at Ephesus.

This was new territory to Mark, and he availed himself of the helpful directions of people here and there at the docks and in businesses catering to travelers and merchants. Finding the church meeting place was easier than he expected, but there was no one there at present. It was little more than a house with a few walls knocked out—he could see through the crack between shutters on a front window. He stood outside and looked one way and the other wondering if anyone who was a Christian and came to worship here lived nearby.

He started on a canvass of the neighborhood and didn't have to go to but three houses before he found someone who gladly welcomed him in and volunteered to take him to Timothy's house. The volunteer was sure Timothy would be at home at this hour since it was late in the afternoon.

He was, and he welcomed Mark heartily. The two spent an hour talking about Paul, his health, his last letter, the helpfulness of Tychicus, and anything else on which they shared common ground.

When Mark told Timothy that not only had he come with the latest news from Paul, but also that he had also come with a written gospel account, Timothy was overwhelmed.

"We had no idea anyone was at work on such a thing," said Timothy. "I knew of some little collections of Jesus' sayings. Nothing really long or significant."

Mark held out the first copy of his work, a scroll of some thirty feet in length. Timothy took it gingerly, as if it were fragile, perishable, and unrolled a foot or so.

"It's beautifully done," he said.

"That's Tychicus's work," said Mark. "Even the original isn't as neat as his writing is."

"I'll want to read this in the morning," said Timothy, "when we can sit in the sun out back. How long did it actually take you?"

"I started thinking of writing about Jesus' life fifteen years or more ago," said Mark. "Then Peter and I teamed up for a while, and it just sort of came together. Once I started writing from my notes, it took several days. But it just poured out like water."

"You could hardly have been with a better eyewitness than Peter," said Timothy.

"True," said Mark.

"How is he, by the way?"

"Well. Very well. He's trying to keep a low profile in Rome. I don't think they know he's there, yet. The Empire, that is."

"Are you hungry?" said Timothy.

"Very."

"Let's go," said Timothy, getting up and going for the door. Mark followed without a word. They went down the block to the home of a family in the church.

"I eat here several nights a week," said Timothy. "The members of the church take pity on me. I don't have a wife, so they assume I can't cook for myself."

"Can you?" said Mark, amused.

"Enough," said Timothy, "but I don't let on. If I can walk a quarter mile and get the best cooking in Ephesus, it's worth it."

Back at Timothy's house later, night deepened and Timothy showed Mark to a guest room. After aching bones from land travel in Italy and restive sleep on board a tossing ship, he slept soundly and lengthily on multiple cushions that night. By the time he opened his eyes naturally it was mid morning.

Timothy was already mostly finished reading the gospel account by the time Mark wandered out into the yard in back of the house. Timothy told Mark he was reading about Pilate at the moment. Mark retreated inside the house and peeped out the window now and then to see if he could tell when Timothy had finished the book. When he saw him rolling the scroll back to its beginning, he knew he was done.

Timothy set the scroll down on the bench beside him and leaned back on the seat back. He appeared to be meditating. He was praying. Eyes still closed, he wiped away a tear.

Momentarily, he came in.

"I've learned so much," he said to Mark. "You don't know how much this is going to help us. Well, maybe you *do*."

Mark insisted he didn't want to intrude upon Timothy's privacy by staying in his house further, and when Timothy couldn't persuade him it wasn't any imposition at all, he finally arranged lodging with an older couple in the church who had lost a son to shipwreck some years ago and were eager to have someone about his age to help fill the hollow spaces in their house. Mark stayed there as long as he was in Ephesus.

The church devoured Mark's writing. Mark himself tried to stay in the background but it was increasingly hard to do it. People wanted to ask him questions about accounts or teachings, as if he had witnessed these things personally. Repeatedly he reminded them that these were mostly Peter's memories of Jesus' life, not his own. Still, he had come to know these stories as if he had witnessed their unfolding himself. He didn't tell them about his personally witnessing the crucifixion from a distance. He also didn't reveal the identity of the young man whose clothes had been torn off in the Garden of Gethsemane.

Mark continued responding to people's questions by referring to Peter's authoritative remembrance, and then going on to comment on the truths that Peter—and therefore anyone reading the account—could derive from the stories.

The novelty of having the gospel's author in their own church wore off some over time, but it still helped Mark to get away from Ephesus now and then, which he did. He went into Macedonia for an extended trip, delivering a copy of his account of Jesus' life to the Philippian church and asking them if they would share it with the churches at Thessalonica and Berea, or even have it copied twice more so those congregations could have their own scrolls.

He went the other way, returning to the church in Nicaea, finding it stable and growing. They were thrilled to have his book, and promised to try to have it copied.

Over the next two years or more, Ephesus was his base of operations as Mark made forays into the interior of Asia, visiting churches, telling what he had last heard from the Apostles in Rome, and teaching from the recollections of Peter.

Eventually, Mark began to wonder intensely what was going on with Peter, and Paul, and with the Christians on the other side of the Tiber where he had felt he was an integral part of the work of the church. After returning from a little trip to congregations in the

Lycus River valley, it came as something of a shock to Mark, though a delightful one, to learn, from a messenger that Paul had been released from prison, and not just recently. Apparently he had been set free not too long after Mark had set out for Ephesus, and he had subsequently traveled into Macedonia and who knew where else, continuing his mission activity. Why Mark hadn't heard about Paul's freedom before, he didn't know, unless a previous messenger had gotten waylaid.

Mark and Timothy had intense conversations about what they might do. Could they find Paul? If they did, could they persuade him to come to Ephesus? Would it be even remotely possible to get Paul to try to disappear into the interior of Asia, maybe somewhere where there were no authorities eager to have him sent back to Rome with fresh charges? Was such a goal even slightly in the Holy Spirit's plan for Paul?

Not having any idea how to locate Paul, for the moment Mark stayed in place. And within another six months the questions he and Timothy had debated were rendered irrelevant. A messenger sent out of Rome from Peter to dozens of points east by land had worked his way to Ephesus with the message that Paul was once again in prison, this time not in minimum security but more or less in a dungeon. He was still allowed to see visitors, but he was more heavily guarded.

The hope that had briefly encouraged Mark, Timothy and the Ephesian church to think that Paul would be around for a long time to come was dashed by this news. The sobering likelihood of Paul's coming experience was more firmly hammered home by a second letter from the Apostle's hand, or more likely, a helper.

Timothy shook his head as he read the letter. "He's low, Mark."

"Does he say what's happening?" said Mark.

"In a way. He says his departure is near. I think he must have gotten wind of a trial date."

"I should go back," said Mark. "I've been feeling uneasy for a while."

"Well, that's probably the Spirit speaking," said Timothy. "Because that's what he asked for."

"Me to come back?" said Mark.

"And me, too," said Timothy.

"I can be ready anytime, brother."

"I'll need to meet with the other elders. Make sure things are covered here."

"Of course," said Mark. "Anything else in the letter you want to pass along?"

"You can read it for yourself."

"I'd like that," said Mark. "It's not too personal?"

"It's personal, but it's not private," said Timothy. "Or ought not to be." He put the letter into the leather packet it had been delivered in, and he handed it to Mark.

"He says Luke is with him," said Timothy.

"He was there when I left Paul in the other place. Luke is a good man. I like him."

"I do, too," said Timothy.

"Fortunately, we're in a good sailing season just now," said Mark. "I hope we can find passage quickly."

"Me, too," said Timothy. "Oh, and I need to take a few things he wanted. He mentioned scrolls and parchments in particular. I suppose I'll take them all."

"Let's pray he has time to make use of them," said Mark.

In two days, the pair carried packs of food and other provisions with them to the port and booked passage with a clumsy looking ship that turned out to be quite efficient and well manned. Three weeks later, after stops and delays and then land travel, they finally dragged into Rome through its southern access along Via Latina, entering the Porta Latina gate.

There were games in the Circus Maximus that day, making progress through the city slow for the pair, but they finally arrived at the prison-house where Paul had previously been held. There they inquired about Paul, and the guards were well aware of where their by-now famous 'detainee' was being kept. Mark and Timothy worked their way through the busy city to the other prison and requested to see Paul. The guards searched through everything in their traveling packs and then let them see the Apostle. Luke was with him, and the four men had a deeply joyful, but quiet and somber reunion.

"Peter was here yesterday," said Paul. "The local officials are beginning to be aware of his presence in Rome. It may be dangerous from here on out."

"I'm surprised he has managed to avoid notice this long," said Mark.

"I think the local government simply has more on its plate than suppressing Christians right now," said Luke.

"That, and probably they've been holding some of their meetings underground," said Mark.

"What do you mean?" said Timothy.

"There are some underground chambers various places outside the city walls. Must go back centuries. Some of them have been found up there near where Peter's congregation lives."

"I understand mostly Jews are using them," said Luke.

"It's going to get much worse before it gets any better," said Paul. All eyes went to him in the silence. "I didn't mean to bring you two here," he said, nodding toward Mark and Timothy, "with the idea that I'm going to trial next week. It'll be more like two or three months, I think."

"How do you know this?"

"I don't know it for certain. But the guards here aren't just empty suits of armor. They have a lot of experience in and around the courts, and they rotate a lot. I've had some good conversations with many of them."

"One of them became a believer," said Luke quietly, so the guard outside the door wouldn't hear it. "Secretly, for now."

"Anyway," said Paul, "Nero has been away recently. Went to Corinth for one thing. They're planning to build a canal down there and he went to turn a spade of dirt. But he's probably going to be back in a month. And he'll be urged to thin the prison population a bit. That's what he did before."

Nobody spoke for a minute.

"You mean when you were released?" said Mark.

"You found out about that."

"Eventually, yes," said Mark. "What in the world happened?"

"The case evidently became stale," said Paul. "Nobody around to prosecute it. Meanwhile, Nero was going mad. Released prisoners willy nilly. Including me."

"On any conditions?" asked Mark.

"Not to preach in Rome," said Paul.

"So you—"

"Went to Macedonia first," said Paul.

"Then how did you—why are you back here. And in *here?*" said Mark, gesturing around at the dank cell.

Paul smiled faintly. He got up, a little creakily and went to pour a cup of water.

"He came back," said Luke. "Preached in public, right near the Forum."

"To test the waters," said Paul.

"To test—" said Mark.

"This is Rome," said Paul. "They tell me Jesus once said a prophet could not die outside Jerusalem."

"This isn't Jerusalem," said Mark.

"I'm the Apostle to the Gentiles," said Paul. "This is their Jerusalem."

"You're saying you *wanted* to—" said Mark.

"I didn't *want* to. I don't *want* to die," said Paul. "This is just where I have to make my final mark for the gospel."

The little group sat silent in the echoing wake of Paul's words. Timothy peered distractedly out the little barred window. Luke stared at his patient and friend. Mark studied the stone floor.

"So here we are," said Paul, breaking the silence. Then he changed the subject. "How are things in Ephesus?"

"I can't tell you what it meant to us to have Mark's account of Jesus' life," said Timothy.

"I didn't have anything to do with it, of course," said Paul. "All his doing. And Peter's of course."

Mark was fussing with some of the papers he and Timothy had brought.

"We brought the scrolls you asked for," said Mark. "And we presumed you wanted blank parchments as well as the others."

"Yes, oh yes," said Paul, reaching for the stack. "Thank you."

"Brothers," said Luke, "I have to go. I actually have a patient to see. Turns out there are actually too few doctors in Rome. I can pretty much write my own ticket."

"Thank you for everything you do for Paul," said Timothy.

"Oh, Mark," said Luke, "do you think you could—would you let me read a copy of your book?"

"I'd be honored," said Mark. "If you want, you can go by to see Tychicus and get one of the copies he has. Tell him I said so."

"I will," said Luke. "I can make use of it."

"And Luke," said Mark.

"Yes?"

"Why don't you just keep it for now?"

"Are you sure?"

"If I give you some money will you hire a scribe to copy it another two or three times?"

"Mark, my brother, I'll do it myself for free."

32
Mission, c. A.D. 67

Peter had, indeed, been underground now and then during the past two years or so. Christians on the west side of the Tiber were multiplying and so was the viciousness of their critics and the threatening rhetoric of the Empire. But the work of the church couldn't be done in secret. The witness of Christians to the gospel of Jesus Christ was in the streets, the homes, and the highways and byways. If Nero got nasty there was little believers could do about it. What would happen would happen.

Mark divided his time between Peter and Paul to some extent. But Paul was not without other visitors who could help with his needs. Neither was Peter, for that matter. The church on the entire west side of the Tiber was growing strong even though it was relatively covert. Its devotion to the Lord whom Peter preached was only enhanced by its now having the written life of Christ in its hands.

Peter and Mark met for lunch one day out by the banks of the river, not far from where the Pons Aemilius traversed the water. They sat watching the river flow steadily and powerfully out to sea.

"Nothing can stop it," said Peter.

Mark looked at Peter as the Apostle pondered the rushing rivulets, the current carrying boats swiftly down river toward the Tyrrhenian Sea.

"Are we talking about the river?" said Mark.

Peter smiled. "The messenger I sent? To tell everybody about Paul?"

"Yes?"

"One of many. Men come and go from here regularly," said Peter. "By land, by ship. I know more about churches around the Empire than you could imagine."

"And how did all this happen?"

"Just sort of came together while you were away," said Peter. "This ragtag bunch has become the beehive."

"You're right; I didn't know."

"No reason you should've. If it became known, it would be shut down. I should say *when* it becomes known. Can't keep it secret forever."

"Speaking of which," said Mark, "the word on the street about you—"

"I'm a marked man," said Peter. "Just a matter of time."

"What will you do?"

"Question is, what will *you* do, Mark?"

"Me?"

"You're not going back to Ephesus, I suppose," said Peter.

"I don't know."

"You could go back to Jerusalem. Antioch. Nicaea."

"I would have to feel something, someone, drawing me," said Mark. "And I haven't felt anything like that since I left any of those places."

"Cyprus, then?" said Peter.

"There, either," said Mark.

"I didn't think so," said Peter.

They sat a few minutes without speaking.

"A messenger came a few months back, while you were still in Ephesus. He had been from Jerusalem around the coast, through Egypt. Brought word about your church in Alexandria."

"What did he say?" said Mark.

"The church has about a thousand, now."

"That's wonderful!"

"But their pastor is beleaguered, and sick as well. He may recover, may not. And there's growing persecution. The church is having a hard go of it."

"It could be a rough place when I left there," said Mark. "Unpredictable."

"Moses told us the Lord defeated the Egyptian gods more than a thousand years ago," said Peter, "but they never went away."

"No," said Mark, "the bundled all the gods into one. Sirapis—the great idol."

"My messenger said the church is feeling the heat from his worshipers," said Peter. "Worse than when you left it."

"I hope they can hold on," said Mark.

"They need help."

Mark watched a boat coming up river, a large bireme, powered by its many oarsmen forcing the craft ahead against the current. At the prow stood a soldier calling out to the teams manning the oars that were digging into the water and thrusting backward in unison. His voice could be heard even at this distance: "*Porro! Porro!*" With every pull of the oars the ship ground its watery way forward toward its destination.

"I was hoping you would go lead them," said Peter, "—again."

Mark looked away toward the river, seeing the bireme round a curve just south of the city. He looked back at Peter. He nodded slowly, his face fixed with resolve.

"Have your messenger tell Anianus I'm coming in two weeks," said Mark.

At that hour, just south of the Jewish quarter in Alexandria, in a room at the back of the Temple of Serapis, a group of men had met to finalize their plan. A few dozen people in all of Alexandria meeting here and there to worship a new god was no more trouble than women gathering to swap recipes for onion stew. But a thousand or more people, their numbers growing steadily, convincing household after household to stop buying idol images and stop making offerings at the Great Serapis's temple was making a dangerous impact on the historic worship of the city.

Ptolemy Soter himself had envisioned the deity Serapis and had issued the order for the people to revere him. Egyptians had done so dutifully for three hundred years. If this new religion, The Way, became more influential, not only would their heresy bring conflict with other worshipers, but it might also bring down the further wrath of Rome. This was no time for timid souls. The faithful followers of Serapis had to act and do it now.

"We can't eliminate all of them," said Mikabh.

"No, but we need only cut off the head of the snake," Kaphiri said.

"Still, few will want to be so brazen," said Minkabh.

"If only a few of us are bold enough to take the appropriate action," said Jabari, "then so be it."

"We will need larger numbers to hold back the Christians," said Minkabh.

Jabari sneered. "A handful will do. They won't stand up to us."

"No," said Kaphiri, "their Christ preached love. They will be the same. Cowardly."

"We'll enter their worship house in one month," said Jabari, "on *die Solis.* Three of us will march to the front. Whoever else is with us will keep the weaklings at bay. Nuru will have the horses outside, ready for us."

"How will we know which one to seize?" said Minkabh.

"Thabit, our man on the inside, will give us a signal," said Jabari. "We take the man who is leading them. When he is dead, they will die out."

33
Departure, c. A.D. 67

The day after the Lord's Day the following week was bedecked with stunningly sunny skies and cheerful, innocent clouds, the kind that pose no threat to sailors whose interpretation of the previous evening's pink horizon portended delight at sea. Mark, Peter, Tychicus and a few believers who without any noticeable fanfare had gathered to see Mark off, promised their fervent prayer on his venture across the Great Sea.

Mark and Paul had spent an hour together the day before, as Luke, Tychicus, and Timothy had brought church to the prison, singing softly in the daylight gloom of his stony cell. The men had shared prayerful goodbyes and optimistic wishes before going their separate ways, except for Paul, whose ministry to Mark would be conducted from this confined space, but one with an open pathway to heaven.

Tychicus handed Mark the original sheets of the gospel account, from which he had made two more copies. Mark tucked the leather packet containing the papyrus sheets into his pack along with his supplies. He had paid for his passage. All that remained was to embrace those who had come to the docks, and to board ship and find a place to settle in for the voyage. He went around to each friend, clasping the arms of Peter last, who breathed a prayer, eyes open, for the power and grace of the Lord Jesus to come by the Spirit upon Mark.

Then the evangelist turned and walked up the gangplank onto the ship and made his way forward. In minutes the planks were drawn up, the heavy ropes securing the ship to the dock were heaved to, and the vessel slowly left the slip.

The ship's bow made froth of incoming swells as the crew trimmed sails in the coastal winds, and the shape of the vessel grew gradually smaller against the blue-green waters. Mark's friends retreated up the hill where they could see the craft gently rock to and fro in the undulating tide, making its way out to sea, the oft navigated, diligently studied, earnestly plotted sea, and they watched the evangelist head out into the distance, his future known only to God.

www.ingramcontent.com/pod-product-compliance
Lightning Source LLC
Chambersburg PA
CBHW060553310726
48982CB00008B/1113/J

* 9 7 8 0 9 9 9 5 9 2 9 9 1 *